ROBERT LLEWELLYN WROTE HIS FIRST NOVEL at the age of twelve. By the time he'd published *The Man on Platform 5* (his first published work of fiction), thirty years had passed. In the intervening period he'd worked as an artist's model, a bespoke shoemaker, a tree surgeon, a screen-writer, a comedian, actor and TV presenter.

He has appeared regularly on British television since 1987 in various guises including under quite absurd amounts of rubber in *Red Dwarf*; covered in grease and dust in *Scrapheap Challenge*; in terrifying machines on *How Do They Do It?* and sitting in a car chatting in *Carpool*.

Robert Llewellyn writes under a rack of solar panels in Gloucestershire; *News from the Squares* is the sequel to *News from Gardenia*.

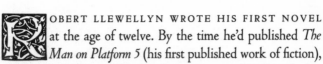

Also by Robert Llewellyn

FICTION

News from Gardenia

The Man on Platform 5

Punchbag

Sudden Wealth

Brother Nature

NON-FICTION

The Man in the Rubber Mask

Thin He Was and Filthy-haired: Memoirs of a Bad Boy

Therapy and How to Avoid It *(with Nigel Planer)*

The Reconstructed Heart: How to Spot the Difference Between a Normal Man and One Who Does the Housework, is Great in Bed and Doesn't Get All Iffy When You Mention Words Like Love and Commitment

Behind the Scenes at Scrapheap Challenge

Sold Out! How I Survived a Year of Not Shopping

News from the Squares

Robert Llewellyn

unbound

This edition published in 2013

Unbound
4–7 Manchester Street Marylebone London W1U 2AE
www.unbound.co.uk

Typeset by Bracketpress
Art direction by Mecob
Cover design by Kid-ethic.com

A CIP record for this book is available from the British Library

ISBN 978-1-78352-007-7 (trade hb)
ISBN 978-1-78352-006-0 (ebook)
ISBN 978-1-78352-008-4 (limited edition)

Printed in England by Clays Ltd, Bungay, Suffolk

For my children Louis and Holly

and maybe one day their children

and then possibly, their great grandchildren,
just so they can have a laugh.

Preface

Utopia, Dystopia and Men

I READ ANTHONY BURGESS'S 'A CLOCKWORK Orange' when I was 15 years old. The pages gripped me with terrifying intensity, I thought it was an ingenious, original and exciting book that created a grim future world at once stimulating and nauseating. I quickly followed that by reading *Brave New World* by Aldous Huxley, an equally influential book with an utterly convincing and cruel vision of the direction the human race might be heading.

Of course, during the 1970s, in the middle of the Cold War it was mandatory to read *Nineteen Eighty-Four* by George Orwell because we needed to understand how bad communism was. *Nineteen Eighty-Four* was part of the English syllabus; we HAD to read it, which immediately made me suspect the motives of the teachers who forced it on us.

Three books by three white men, three books about the future that became enormously influential for many years. Reading them made me suspicious of technology, of the lies of politicians, of the lies of corporations telling us everything would be fine. They taught me to be dismissive and cynical of technological and social development, nuclear power, better guns, bigger banks. In some ways, looking back, and with a better grasp of the history of the period, this was not altogether a bad thing.

It was around the same time that I somehow ended up reading two other books that would have an equally powerful, and in some ways balancing, effect on me. One was *Approaching the Benign Environment* by, among others, R. Buckminster Fuller. The second was *The Limits to Growth* by Donella and Dennis

 Meadows, Jorgen Randers and William W. Behrens III. What inspired me to read these books or how I heard about them now totally eludes me; they're not exactly the sort of thing you'd expect a 16-year-old boy to gravitate towards, but I read them avidly.

Much of the content and meaning escaped me altogether and some of Buckminster Fuller's ideas struck me as barking mad. (We don't need to worry about nuclear waste, we can just shoot it out into space.) However, I believe both these books made a huge impression on the youthful culture of the era.

It was around this time that the first pictures of the earth taken from space were seen by the human race. We could suddenly see that we really did live on a little blue-green planet floating in a vast and inhospitable void. The image was used on the front cover of another publication I devoured with nothing short of obsessive fascination, *The Whole Earth Catalog*, created by the incredible Stewart Brand.

These publications challenged many of the perceived notions of the period; that constant and never-ending expansion, consumerism and 'growth' were all good things; that the only financial and political system that worked was based on such notions, and everything else was doomed to fail.

I was still in my mid-teens when I went to see Stanley Kubrick's film, *2001: A Space Odyssey*. Although originally released in 1968 when I was 12, it became such a cult classic that art house cinemas ran the film for years, which must have been where I saw it, sitting in the back row sharing a spliff with my teenage hippie pals and saying 'oh wow, man' every now and then.

I was entranced by the vision, the extraordinary scope and imagination of this film. Human evolution, technology, artificial intelligence and really cool space ships pointed to a far more hopeful way to think about the future and what it could hold.

It stimulated my interest in computers, in ingenious hardware and body-hugging space underwear. Even now, the vision of this film – the understanding of space, the art direction, the set design and the proposed technology – is nothing short of breathtaking. However, more importantly than any of this, it had an inherent optimism, not that the world would be perfect, but that the human race would continue to evolve and explore.

There are many theories that works of dystopian or utopian fiction are inspired by the era they emerge from. *Nineteen Eighty-Four*, *Brave New World*, *A Clockwork Orange*, all written in the early- to mid-twentieth century, tell us a lot about the struggles and challenges those generations were facing: totalitarianism, communism and the expansion of state control. But there was also a feeling of optimism in the rapidly emerging 'subculture'; there was the NASA space program, breakthroughs in technology, achievements in medicine and our understanding of the planet we live on and the universe that surrounds us.

While *A Clockwork Orange* is a small masterpiece of 'literary' fiction, much admired by the well-educated elite, it is still dystopian fiction.

For me then, it sits in the same misery pit as *The Road*, *World War Z*, *Mad Max*, *The Terminator*, or any number of recent sci-fi films and stories utterly obsessed with doom, the inherent violence and short-sighted aggression of the human condition, the end of days, pseudo-religious nonsense and Armageddon.

All these stories depict a world gone mad, bad and dangerous to live in. So, is the dystopian novel or story essentially a white male fantasy? I suggested this on the social networking site Google+ and was impressed with the breadth and depth of knowledge that flooded in through the comments.

I was pointed to multiple examples of science fiction books, mainly about zombies, doom, death and destruction that were written by women. I was also reminded of *The Handmaid's Tale* by the wonderful Margaret Atwood, which, although about as dystopian as you can get, is written from the perspective of an even-further-into-the-future world where, she implies, things have improved.

However, I'm going to stand by my claim that dystopian

visions are, in the main, created by white males and I wish to put this claim in context; it is in part influenced by the work of the German sociologist Klaus Theweleit and his extraordinary work first published in English in 1987 as two books, titled *Male Fantasies, Volume 1: Women, Floods, Bodies, History* and *Male Fantasies, Volume 2, Male Bodies: Psychoanalyzing the White Terror* – I love those titles. *Male Fantasies* are not what they might sound like, i.e. books exploring what men think about when they are busy self-abusing. Theweleit's works are detailed studies of the thought processes and fears of the men who helped inspire the Third Reich in Weimar Republic Germany.

However, his remit was wider than just a history of twentieth-century European fascism. For me, Theweleit really got to the nub of the European male dilemma. The books were more a study of a group in society who had enjoyed unparalleled power, privilege and cultural dominance for thousands of years. Obviously I'm talking about men. To be specific, white, European men who had created and controlled the monarchy, military, legal and religious systems and national governance without let or hindrance for as long as anyone was able to remember.

What started to emerge around the turn of the last century were philosophies and political movements that finally challenged these well-entrenched arrangements. The struggles of the first half of the twentieth century leading up to the Second World War have always been portrayed as being between 'left' and 'right' but, with the benefit of hindsight, I think it is possible to see them as being a clash between patriarchy and pluralism; between the rest of the world and white men. They saw themselves standing together against a torrent of what they perceived as unregulated licentiousness, chaos, powerful women and a blatant lack of respect for their male power.

The fascist male is, by definition, terrified of the world, terrified of change, but most of all terrified of 'the other'. Women, homosexuals or people of other races; yeah, terrifying. They feel themselves drowning under waves of chaos and disorder, mud, blood (always menstrual, they have a real problem with that), faeces, vomit and general human filth.

Theweleit uses writings, pamphlets and personal diaries of the men of the Freikorps, the fledgling fascist army roaming 1920s Germany. The musings of these tragically damaged men are incredibly revealing. Their deeply ingrained misogyny is the one unifying factor; if you think some drunk bloke shouting the 'c' word in the pub is a misogynist, he's got nothing on the Freikorps, baby. Their rampant hatred was conflicted and torturous for them; they all adored their mothers but feared and despised women and the power they possessed.

Obviously their hatred and fear of homosexuals and Jews was pretty full-on, but it was the twisted pain their fear of women created which made their lives so difficult. It was easy to hate Jews, they were different; homosexuals, scary because any man could be one, but just beat them to death and then you feel more manly. But women? You loved them and hated them, you wanted to dominate them but they were clever and would tie you up in emotional knots and you needed them to have babies. Nightmare.

Thankfully, the more violent mass male spasms represented by the Third Reich have largely dissipated in Europe, but the clue that not all is well with the supposedly beleaguered white male, I postulate, is in the preponderance of dystopian fantasy. Without question the unresolved fear men have of 'the other' is still very much in evidence. They spend endless years formulating ever more elaborate stories about how the world is about to collapse into the mire, to be engulfed in the filth of the other.

The endless drumbeat of right-wing Christians in America or disgruntled white men everywhere is that society is collapsing, that the rule of law is failing, that we are being drowned by needy immigrants getting everything for free and that the family

– as in the institution with a white male at the head of it – is disintegrating. *Gay marriage? That's it, it's all over, load your guns and start killing, it's the only answer*, seems to be their knee-jerk reaction.

These stories, be they books, movies, TV shows or, especially, video games, are based on fear and always driven by the perceived loss of power and control. Normally this can only be restored by resorting to extreme levels of violence, of being prepared to fight off the hordes. They've got around the simple accusations of racism or manic homophobia by painting 'the other' as zombies. The zombie is the virtual Jew, woman, Arab – take your pick; the zombie represents the horde.

Then there is the fear of technology. Again, a perceived loss of power and control is, I believe, at the root of this too. Films like *The Terminator* and *The Matrix* feed from this fear, that the machines we made will take over and shaft us, extracting power from our bottoms or just crushing us under their merciless tracks. The invasion of privacy is often cited as the first step in this descent into powerlessness.

Let's just look at this for a moment. A train driver in India, or a factory worker in China, they have been powerless for generations. They eventually manage to get access to the world through a smartphone and the global ubiquity of the internet. Are they suffering from a sudden loss of privacy? They wouldn't even know what you were talking about.

Now compare those two with a couple of old white guys who use computers in the 'developed world'. An invasion of their privacy has a whole different flavour. They are used to being powerful and in control and all this technology is taking away that power, it's redistributing it and of course that is frightening and seems unfair.

But if we look at the big picture in human history over the last thousand years, and here I agree with the linguist Steven Pinker, contrary to the dystopian male vision of oncoming hell, the world has generally got better, kinder and less violent. Sounds bonkers, but all the figures seem to bear out Pinker's theory that we are living in the least dangerous, most civilised era of the human story so far, and all the signs indicate this is set to continue. Contrary to all the endless drip, drip of dystopian fiction, the world has and is continuing to get better for most people most of the time.

Therefore I would like to suggest that *News from the Squares*, and indeed the first book in the trilogy, *News from Gardenia*, is not utopian fiction. The world depicted in these pages is not static, a vision of a perfect society where all problems have been solved. There will always be problems, there will always be differing opinion and that is as it should be. The human story is constantly evolving. The days of dystopian or utopian visions are numbered. We are finally reaching a point where we can have a better-informed and clearer vision of which way we might want the great eclectic society we live in and the planet we live on to develop.

1

Rough Landing

'WHAT DO YOU THINK YOU'RE DOING YOU silly little man?'

That was the first thing I heard as the darkness slowly dissolved. Something was keeping my head still but I looked about as best I could. I wasn't in any pain, if anything I felt surprisingly comfortable and relaxed. There was a woman's face to my left, sort of peering up at me. She looked quite annoyed. I then realised she was holding my head in position with one hand, not violently, more like she was just supporting my head.

'Hello,' I said eventually. I wanted to reassure her that everything was okay and she didn't need to get upset.

'Are you hurt? Are you in pain?' asked the woman, this time sounding a little more sympathetic.

'I'm fine thank you, Susan,' I said. I know that's what I said but I don't know why. Why did I call her Susan? I didn't know her name, where did the name Susan come from and why did I say it? No idea but for some peculiar reason it amused me and I started giggling.

I realised at that point that I was still in the Yuneec and as everything started to come into focus my slightly elated mood began to sink.

'Oh dear,' I said.

The Yuneec was clearly in a mess. The windscreen had cracked, there was dust everywhere, wires hung out of the control panel, or rather what was left of the control panel. I could make out what might be a very badly damaged propeller beyond the cracked windscreen and then some sort of tree branch.

'There will be assistance here any minute, just stay still for now. You can explain what on earth you were doing later on.'

'What was I doing?' I asked. 'I'm not exactly sure what's happened.'

I seemed to be half buried in bits of plastic and seat padding, the cockpit was a right mess. I couldn't remember anything. How did this happen? I felt something slightly salty in my mouth, warm and salty, I wiped my mouth on my bare forearm and saw at once it was blood.

I was beginning to feel alarmed. I couldn't sense any pain but I was starting to become mildly nauseous.

'You've landed in our square,' said the woman. 'Why you chose our square I have no idea, why you were droning through the air I have no idea.' She turned away from me and looked back. 'It's okay, assistance has arrived.'

The woman slowly removed her hand and disappeared from view, downwards which was rather confusing.

I moved my head slowly, nothing hurt, I glanced around as best I could and what I saw was very distressing. Where the wing should have been was just torn fabric and twisted aluminium struts, broken off at different angles.

I let my head rest back against the mess behind me but after a few moments – I have to say moments of great peace, there was no alarming noise or sudden movement – two other heads arrived at my side.

'Let's have a look at you then,' said a woman. She was young and seemed to be wearing some kind of uniform; her hair was tied tightly behind her head. She slipped something around my neck which immediately inflated and tightened in some way, it wasn't uncomfortable and even as my head rose a little I understood this to be some kind of sophisticated neck brace. The man was running his hands up and down my legs, I couldn't see what he was doing but I could feel him.

'Legs seem okay,' he said.

'I think I'm fine, I've got some blood in my mouth though.'

Before I could say any more the woman was wiping away at my face with some kind of cool spongy thing. She didn't say anything, but I was reassured by her confident manner and quick actions.

'Get on the other side if you can, we're going to have to manually extract him,' said the woman.

I could just see the man nodding obediently and he disappeared. The woman continued to wipe my face, she pulled my bottom lip down and I tried to open my mouth, it was difficult with the neck brace in position. She inserted a small tube and I heard quite loud sucking sounds as she presumably cleaned out the blood that had collected there.

The man appeared to my left and without further explanation I was lifted out of the shattered cockpit by two clearly very strong people.

'Don't do anything,' said the woman. 'I just want you to let us manage your body for now.'

''K,' I said through gritted teeth as the neck brace was now holding my head rigidly in position and things were just starting to get uncomfortable. I regretted letting them move me, I just wanted to stay in the cockpit, it was so warm and comfortable.

The man and woman eased me up onto some kind of stretcher seat thing that was right beside the cockpit, I remember it had a light blue cover. This was the first time I got a look at where I was. Basically about fifteen feet in the air, the Yuneec was completely wrecked, the main fuselage was essentially resting in the upper branches of an enormous tree.

The woman eased me back onto the stretcher and her powerful hand on my chest indicated with no confusion that she wanted me to lie down. I did so, staring at the cloudless sky.

I clearly remember seeing some house martins flitting about overhead, I could hear them chirruping to each other. I felt movement and suddenly broken tree branches and bits of tattered wreckage came into view. I was being lowered down at speed by some kind of mechanical device, the movement was very smooth and there was no noise associated with it.

The view then changed again as I was manoeuvred into some kind of enclosed space, a white roof above me, I couldn't see much to either side. The stretcher thing stopped moving and a moment later the man and woman appeared beside me.

'How are you feeling young man?' asked the woman.

'I'm okay,' I said as best I could. 'Did I crash?'

The woman glanced at the man and made a peculiar expression I didn't quite register. 'You crashed,' she said.

So that was how I landed in the square. My memory from before that moment is very dim, I can remember coming out of the cloud, the anomaly as William had called it. I came out and saw a grid pattern on the ground that seemed to go on forever. I can remember that, but not much else.

The grid pattern, I soon came to realise, was because the dwellings I saw in the distance as I was lowered down from the wrecked Yuneec were arranged in large squares. Essentially rows of terraced houses facing onto a large space dense with vegetation.

I can only assume that I was trying to find somewhere to land, had made a fairly catastrophic error and ended up colliding with a tree.

Whatever I was lying inside started to move, I could sense that it was a wheeled vehicle of some sort but it made very little sound as it progressed. I am guessing that it was making its way across grass or something, there were a couple of small bumps and then I felt it accelerate along a very smooth surface.

The journey was short, within minutes I was being removed from the vehicle, I was slightly surprised to see that the vehicle was inside a building.

I assumed it was some kind of hospital and again I started to feel anxious, if I was in a hospital I must be injured and yet I was not conscious of any pain, only the slight discomfort of the neck brace.

The bed I was lying on moved along so smoothly it felt as if I was stationary and the building was sliding along over me. I glided through a door and looked up at a more complex ceiling, this one fitted with numerous lightweight mechanical arms and equipment.

A woman appeared in my field of vision which was still quite limited; she was wearing goggles and an elaborate breathing mask over the lower half of her face. The mask was transparent, I could clearly see her mouth, she was smiling, it was a sort of pained smile a mother might make toward a fractious child.

'What have we here then?' she asked. Her voice sounded peculiar, the only explanation being that she was speaking through some kind of wireless communication system being fed into speakers I couldn't see. I was hearing perfect stereo.

'Hello,' I said. 'I'm afraid I've had a bit of a ding dong with a tree.'

'I should think you are afraid,' the woman snapped. 'Didn't you work that out before you got into that ridiculous thing?' I could hear her sigh and then witnessed the rather odd sight of her slowly shaking her head inside the bizarre face mask as she uttered, 'I don't know.'

She shook her head as she watched what I imagined was a screen below my field of vision. I then saw a white object move over my body at great speed, utterly silent, not a bleep, whoosh or any mechanical noise.

'What a silly little fellow you've been,' said the woman in the facemask. 'You are very lucky, no fractures, no internal distress, just a cut lip.'

She held up a small, pen like device, I noticed it had a silver tip, she ran it over my top lip. The feeling was peculiar to say the least, cold, with a slight tingling sensation.

'All done,' said the woman brightly, again in a tone of voice medical professionals would use having just administered an injection to a child.

She brushed her hand over the side of the mask and it came loose and was retracted off somewhere by the thin breathing tube it was attached to. She then gently removed the neck brace thing from around my neck and the bed contraption I was lying on slowly became a chair. I don't mean it materialised from one thing to another like a badly rendered CGI effect, it folded itself from a flat bed into a chair shape allowing me to adopt a sitting position with no effort.

It was clear that I was indeed sitting in a brightly lit room in a hospital. I didn't immediately recognise any of the equipment that was either hanging from the ceiling or neatly arranged along the walls. What ever it was, it was very modern-looking and clean.

'Can I ask something?' I said eventually as the woman started to make a move toward a doorway.

'Me?' she asked, turning to look at me.

'Well, yes, there isn't anyone else here,' I said.

'Why d'you want to ask me something?' she said, she looked mildly offended as if I'd made an unwanted proposition or told her that her bum looked fat. Which it didn't, by the way.

'Well, I'm a little confused. The last thing I remember I was flying through a dense cloud, I came out of it and saw…'

The woman put her hand up to stop me talking. It was a very effective physical signal. I stopped mid-sentence. She turned and walked through the doorway. I say doorway as there was no door fitted in the doorway, it was just a gap in the wall, beyond it was another wall, as she went through the gap, she turned to her left and disappeared.

So I was left, sitting on the folded-up bed that had become a chair, feeling quite stable, not in pain, but still utterly confused.

All I could remember was coming out of the cloud, realising I was much lower than I expected and clearly not back in 2011.

Wherever I was, it was very different to the world I had just left. I could remember seeing this peculiar grid, mile after mile of squares stretching to the horizon. The squares were buildings, I knew that now. Each side of the square was made up of long terraces of what I took to be houses. There was something vaguely Georgian about them, very regular and clearly all built at the same time. By that I mean it wasn't a higgledy-piggledy mash-up of buildings from different eras and different styles that just happened to be crammed up together. This was designed, built at the same time to the same specifications, and when I say Georgian I only mean that by styling, not size, these building were huge.

One thing I can clearly remember from my arrival over the Squares was the very severe lack of anything that looked like a landing strip or even a piece of open ground. There was certainly nothing like the oil seed field I'd spotted when I arrived in Gardenia.

I dropped my head as I tried to recall what had happened next. There was nothing, no re-call. I'd never experienced this before. If I had ever been on a journey or witnessed an event in the past, I could always run through it in my mind's eye and recall it in immense detail. Not so now, I was able to recall waking in Gardenia, getting dressed in front of a crowd of anxious looking people, running into the Bow field, seeing the anomaly, getting into the Yuneec, seeing Grace through the window, Grace. Suddenly the memory of Grace hit me like a sledgehammer in the guts.

Where was Grace?

What had happened to her, to my potential child, to the life I was slowly getting used to in Gardenia? Why wasn't I there and, more importantly, where was I now?

I heard a movement at the doorway, I turned and saw another woman standing looking at me.

'Would you like to talk?' she asked.

I smiled and nodded. The woman raised her eyebrows as if making a mental note. She turned to her side and said, 'I think it's all fine.'

She then walked into the room, put her hand on the wall opposite me and part of the wall folded down and made a chair. The woman sat down facing me. She seemed quite young, clear dark skin and black hair, she was wearing a kind of slightly weird looking one-piece body suit with no obvious seams or opening. It didn't look like a wet suit or flight suit, it was lighter material and slightly tailored. Just as I know little about architecture, I know even less about clothing. I'd certainly never seen anything like it before, either in the real world of 2011 or Gardenia. The people I'd seen in New York, Beijing and Mumbai certainly didn't wear anything like it.

'How do you feel about it?' asked the woman.

Again I smiled as what she said to me made no sense.

'D'you think it's funny?'

I sat in silence for a moment. I think everything I had gone through in Gardenia had made me a little more aware of myself and the difficulty I clearly had in communicating anything when my mind was bursting with complex questions which would require equally complex answers.

'You've scared people, upset them, destroyed a garden, risked your own life and put many people to great trouble to protect and repair you, and yet you seem to find this amusing. Is my analysis correct?'

I shook my head and took a big breath. This was going to be complicated.

2

New Reality

TWO WOMEN DRESSED IN WHITE OVERALLS guided me from the room in which I'd been medically examined. They didn't say anything to me, just gestured for me to walk with them. I didn't say anything in case they didn't speak English, I didn't feel like trying to work out how to communicate, the sign language they used to tell me what to do was perfectly understandable.

I walked along a short windowless but well-lit corridor and into a rather pleasant room that did have windows, big windows that looked out onto a garden. The two women stood by the door and watched me for a while. I say door, but again there was no actual door, no hole-closing device, just a gap in the wall.

This room was yet again very familiar, but with one or two details noticeably different from the world of my birth, as opposed to the world I had just come from.

For a start it was very quiet; I assumed I was in some sort of city but the only noise I could hear was birdsong from the garden. The weather was good, a clear sky with bright sunshine was visible through the large windows but the interior of the room was cool, the air smelled fresh. I glanced back at the doorway entrance and the two women had gone. I shrugged, who knew what was going on, all I could hope for was that someone did, because I didn't have a clue.

I stared out of the window, trying not to worry about where I was. I didn't want to find out I had jumped yet further into the future when I was hoping so much that I would return to 2011.

Whatever I'd seen from the Yuneec when I came out of the cloud, it wasn't 2011.

I looked around the room. It was sparsely furnished but comfortable, a large sofa-type of thing facing the window, a single armchair-type of thing to one side. I say 'type of thing' because I'm not sure how to describe them. Their function was clearly designed to be comfortable sitting devices but I don't have any capacity for describing furniture. I don't have any taste apparently, that was what Beth had always told me. I suppose if I was confronted with a sofa in bright orange with gold trim and moulded plastic feet that looked like snakes I probably wouldn't like it, but if it was comfortable I'd still sit in it.

The furniture in the room wasn't like that, the big sofa looked odd but quite old, it had a high back, much too high for any functional reason. It was covered in numerous pieces of colourful cloth and some big cushions.

There was a low wooden table between the two chairs containing an elaborate flower arrangement sitting in what looked like a handmade pottery vase.

I stood looking at the flowers for a while, I was feeling fairly sleepy and more than a little disoriented. My mind was slowly ploughing through a mass of memories, worries and deep confusion. What had happened to Grace? Was I now further into the future and would I be able to read about her in some kind of databank, about her and my child? Was I going to have to go through the same weird experience I had been through in the woods in Gardenia? Reading about her death, and my child's death, and my grandchild's death, and then travelling around the world to try and find my great grandchild who could be a hunchbacked woman living in Mongolia or something?

I understood by this time that I was capable of being a little disconnected with the world I lived in, with people I knew and possibly loved, but my recent experiences in Gardenia and now wherever I'd ended up were not helping me connect, in fact quite the opposite. I realised that although I'd gone through an absurd amount of trauma, I felt oddly calm. It didn't seem right. Surely I should be writhing about on the floor, screaming and soiling myself in profound madness?

I sat down on the sofa-thing and indeed it was very comfortable, I stared around the walls that were covered in paintings, maybe festooned with them is a better description. All framed, all without any obvious glass covering them, I don't know how many but in the hundreds. Some large, some tiny, they were hung very expertly from waist height to the ceiling and this room had a very high ceiling. The proportions reminded me of Georgian houses I had been inside in Bath and Brighton, and yet it clearly wasn't Georgian, it was recently built. I'm not sure why I felt confident of this fact. It must have been the cleanliness and smooth lines of the structure, it somehow smelt as if had just been built.

Some of the paintings looked very old, I mean pre-2011, some of them looked like the unfathomable splotchy etchings I'd seen in galleries in London but had no idea what they were for, let alone what they were meant to be.

I felt my eyelids getting heavier and heavier, and I must have dozed off. I have no idea for how long, but it could have been a while. When I eventually opened my eyes again the light was different, more like a late summer evening light, I could see sunlight was filtered through the trees outside the window, it looked very calm and peaceful.

I sighed deeply and stretched my legs out straight on the sofa, then a small movement caught my eye. I started a bit, a woman was sitting in the chair on the other side of the table and she was looking at me. I pulled myself up quickly and rubbed my eyes, blinked a bit and stared back at her.

'Sorry, must have dozed off,' I said through what felt like a mouthful of cotton wool.

The woman continued to stare at me. She had a kind face,

 Mediterranean dark skin, dark hair, brown eyes. I would guess she was in her late forties but after my experience in Gardenia, she could have been anything between forty and a hundred. I smiled at her, then remembered how this had been frowned on by the women who'd treated me in the hospital room, so I stopped.

I turned myself and sat upright on the sofa, I noticed the woman glance up behind me, I turned and looked over my shoulder. The middle-aged women who had led me to the room was standing in the doorway with her two quite substantial arms folded in front of her.

I felt the need to re-assure them I was no threat, but due to the silence in the room I also felt I had enough time to consider the possible consequences of saying anything. I turned back to the woman in the chair, put my hands on my thighs and relaxed. I waited. Nothing happened. It was almost annoying, what did they expect me to do? This little surge of anger eventually resulted in my mouth taking over.

'Okay, I'll start,' I said finally. 'My name is Gavin Meckler, I'm thirty-two years old, I was born in 1979.'

I paused; I was waiting for questions, for doubt, for some kind of query. Nothing.

'I have accidentally travelled through time to the future, a place called Gardenia. While I was attempting to return to my own era using the same method, an anomaly taking the shape of a large and unusually formed low-level cloud that gathered around the base of a power tether, I came out above your city. I have no idea where I am, what the date is or who you are. I mean no harm and only wish to get back to the period of history I belong in.'

I sat back, suddenly aware that in being completely honest and explaining things as best I could, I felt like I had come across like a complete madman. Not even a funny nutter who's a bit confused, but a dangerous psychotic loon, someone who thinks he's had an alien controlling device shoved up his nose by a three foot grey bloke with a big head.

'I realise this may sound just a bit mad,' I said after a while. 'I wish I could give you a simpler explanation but that's all I know.'

After a long pause, the woman opposite me nodded.

'Would you like to tell me how you came to be in the drone?'

'It's not a drone, it's a plane, an aeroplane. I was piloting an aeroplane, a drone is remotely controlled.'

'Very well, would you like to tell me how you came to be in the... plane?'

'I'd very happily tell you that,' I said trying my best to sound sane and rational. But I was forewarned now, I knew I had gone through some kind of wormhole time dilation bizarre weirdness I didn't understand but it was possible this woman did understand. So I added, after a thoughtful pause, 'In return I'd like you to tell me, if that's okay, who you are, where I am, what date this is and if anything like my sudden appearance has happened before?'

I felt really clever and ahead of the game with the request. I was looking at the woman as I spoke and noticed no particular reaction, but as I had learned on many previous occasions I am not terribly good at judging the mood of another person, more specifically the mood of a woman. For all my experience I didn't have a clue, she could have been entering a life-threatening panic and I probably wouldn't have noticed.

She gave a tiny nod at the woman at the door and as usual I had no idea what this implied. I turned around half expecting to see the overall lady approach me with the special jacket with the very long sleeves. However, I saw her nod curtly in response and leave the entrance without giving me a glance.

'This is very interesting,' said the woman. There was another long pause. 'You say you come from another time, is that correct?'

I might, as some have suggested – OK, Beth has suggested it

 on many occasions, jokingly I hope, although I've had my doubts, anyway, Beth has suggested I might have mild Asperger's. I've not been officially diagnosed or anything, but when Beth described the symptoms to me it did all sound a bit familiar. However, even from my alleged position on the autistic spectrum, I could surmise that this woman didn't believe what I'd just told her. She was just humouring me in an attempt to get more information. My ploy wasn't working, she thought I was bonkers.

'I was born in 1979, my name is Gavin Meckler, my mother's name was Jane Meckler, my father was David Meckler, I was born in a town called High Wycombe in a country called Great Britain, or the United Kingdom, or England. Probably where I am now. I'm sure you have some kind of database you can look this up on.'

'Nineteen seventy-nine,' said the woman slowly. I nodded.

'So you are two hundred and thirty-two years old,' she said.

'Ahh, so it is 2211 is it?' I asked. I felt huge relief at this fact. I'd clearly just flown through a cloud and come out somewhere else on the globe, just a spatial jump instead of a time jump. I could find my way back to Gardenia and Grace and Goldacre Hall and all the wonderful people there. I could see my child, maybe even be there when he or she was born.

The woman smiled at me, a gentle smile that implied she could see right through my game, that it was indeed 2211 and that I must be a bit stupid to assume this would fool her. I tried not to let her attitude get to me.

'I flew in my aeroplane and went into a rather unusual looking cloud over a town called Didcot, that was back in 2011.'

'Twenty eleven,' said the woman slowly.

'When I came out of the cloud I found myself on the same date, the same time of day, the same geographical location but in 2211, essentially two hundred years later. I am not suggesting I have any ideas on how that happened, and I would readily agree it sounds very unlikely, but all the evidence I gathered over the next few months implied that this really is what happened. So a few hours ago the same cloud formation appeared around the power tether, this is near Didcot in Gardenia, except Didcot isn't there any more. I was hoping that for whatever reason if I had once been propelled into the future, then flying through the cloud again in the opposite direction would return me to my own time, what for you is the past. However, what appears to have happened is that I have merely travelled through space, not time. I don't mean space as in outer space, my plane doesn't go that high.' I realised two things, I was speaking too fast and I was smiling.

Mad alert.

I returned my face to stern as fast as I could and tried to speak more slowly. 'I simply mean geographical space. So my request is very simple, I'd like to go back to where I came from. To do that it would help me if I knew where I was now. Geographically I mean.'

Another long silence followed, I think there would have been a time when I found such a long silence uncomfortable, but since I had spent time in Gardenia, where silence and time seemed to be in fruitful supply, it didn't bother me so much. Eventually the woman took a big breath, held it and then said.

'Okay, Gavin Meckler, you are in London.'

'London!'

'Yes, London.'

'You mean, like, the city of London. But hasn't it… hasn't it been flooded?'

At last I noticed a reaction, the woman registered this information, it meant something to her.

'You ask if London has been flooded,' she spoke very carefully, clearly thinking about it. 'Do you mean the old city?'

I nodded. 'Yes, of course, the old city,' I said, 'I flew over what I would expect to be London a few months ago, when I was in

 Gardenia. It's just a big tidal inlet, it's completely gone, well, the centre of it has.'

'Mmm.' That was it, a small sound, barely audible. Again we sat in silence for a long time.

'You'll forgive me if I find your situation quite challenging. I'm going to seek some help in trying to understand.'

Another long silence, it's possible my mouth was hanging open as I waited for her to finish.

'I have never, how shall I say this, never experienced such an unusual situation previously. Although I have worked in this Institute for many years your circumstances are a little beyond my skill level. I will make sure you are comfortable and well looked after but I request that you remain in the Institute for the time being. I will return shortly with some colleagues who may be in a better position to help us.'

I took a deep breath and shrugged. There wasn't much I could do. It was obvious I'd wrecked the Yuneec, I had no idea where I was and no idea how to get anywhere else. Once again I had the uncanny impression I was actually dead and this was my spirit's way of assimilating the sudden change of circumstance. That did of course require a belief in things like spirits and afterlife, a belief I sadly lack.

'Don't worry Gavin Meckler, you are not dead,' said the woman with a kind smile.

Hearing this I froze. Had I just said something out loud without being conscious of it? I'd just been thinking I might be dead but it was a fleeting moment of thought. I wasn't saying the words 'I might be dead' either out loud or silently to myself. I was just rushing through a series of images and memories, of being in Oak House when I was told about the date, of drinking the weird tea with honey in it on my first day in Gardenia and suddenly this clear-faced woman just answered my question.

She stood up, that was a shock because she was hugely taller than I expected, she suddenly reminded me of someone, an actress from my era, the communist one, Vanessa Redgrave. She really looked like a Mediterranean version of Vanessa Redgrave.

'My name is Doctor Markham,' she said. 'We will speak again soon.'

She walked out of the room without making a sound. I mean not even a tiny rustle of clothing or the merest suggestion of a footfall. Once she had gone I brushed the finger and thumb on my right hand together to see if I had gone deaf. I could hear the skin rub together very clearly, and yet this woman had just moved right across the room, right past me and I could hear nothing.

I think it was around that time that I started to get properly alarmed.

3

The Panel

BY THE TIME THE SILENT WOMAN IN WHITE overalls with the big arms had shown me to another much smaller room, I was feeling more than a little disturbed. Whatever this place was, 'the Institute' as Doctor Markham had called it, it wasn't the most reassuring and comforting environment. I was trying to stop myself jumping to conclusions about where I was, I was trying not to panic, but it was getting increasingly difficult.

The room had a bed-type thing along one side, a weird chair that looked like it came out of the floor. The table, which also seemed to come out of the wall, was in front of a window that looked out onto another garden. This one I assumed was on the other side of the building, it had fewer large trees and was planted with vegetables and fruit bushes. It was incredibly well-tended, almost clinically neat. I could tell by the solid shadows that the sun; although going down to my left, was still strong, the sky was clear, more like a Californian sky than a mid-summer British one.

Nothing inside the room was alarming, there was no door, I wasn't locked in, although there was a slight flavour of prison cell about it. There was a blank sort of screen thing set into the wall opposite the bed but it didn't appear to be operating. It could have been a television, it was a light grey matt panel, that's the best way to describe it but had no obvious controls, I looked about the room for some kind of remote like you'd expect to find in a hotel room. Nothing.

The rest of the room was completely empty, no wires, plug

sockets, no obvious lighting. The bed had some kind of dark blue cover on it, not a blanket, a sheet I suppose, but the whole place was rather spartan.

I stared out into the garden for a while, it was very all very quiet and had an almost deserted feel to it. Clearly someone or something worked in the garden, everything was immaculate, almost too perfect.

I was therefore slightly shocked when I saw a man walk into view from below me; I had estimated that I was two floors up so there must have been an entrance to the garden beneath me somewhere. The man was carrying a garden fork and behind him there was a container, I suppose like a wheelbarrow except it didn't appear to have handles and he wasn't pulling or pushing it it, it was just following him. As he moved further away up the fearsomely neat garden I could make out from my vantage point that this wheelbarrow contraption was just gliding along the ground behind him. He stopped by a row of what I'm pretty certain were carrots, the container moved in beside him, settle a couple of centimetres to the ground and he started working the soil with a fork.

I couldn't guess his age, his skin was dark and his hair was thick. He was tall and very slim, wearing blue clothing that again looked like some kind of overall.

That was it, nothing dramatic happened. I don't even know why I thought something dramatic might happen, did I need something dramatic to happen? I then realised that I didn't remember thinking things like this before. Maybe it's because I'd never really had time, I came from a very noisy world where time was always in short supply, plus I'd just spent a couple of months in a very quiet world which I thought I'd got used to.

Now I was in a sort of Sweden-world, it was very clean, quiet, peaceful, well organised and just a little bit frightening.

I pondered on this feeling. I was definitely having a feeling and I was able to think about it, wonder about it. I'd never thought about a feeling before, I suppose I'd just had them and only afterwards realised the feeling had affected my behaviour. I was feeling fear.

I realised I'd never found Gardenia frightening, maybe when I came out of the Pod station in Beijing, or felt momentarily lost in Mumbai, but never in Gardenia.

I eventually lay on the bed and listened to myself breathe; there wasn't a great deal else to do. No one came in to kill me, no one held me down on the bed and injected me with some weird psychotropic drug. Nothing happened at all.

I must have nodded off again which I rarely do during the day, in fact I don't think I'd ever done it other than after I'd been on a long-haul flight.

Once again I woke up suddenly as if someone had shaken me, I opened my eyes. Doctor Markham was standing in the doorway looking at me, I jumped up and I may have expressed my surprise with bad language.

Okay, I'll admit it. I said 'Fucking hell, what now!'

This woman was really starting to freak me out. She was just standing there motionless, staring at me with her big brown eyes, looking so like Vanessa Redgrave it was more than uncanny.

'Would you care to come with me,' she said, no mention of the bad language and no reaction to it either. I didn't reply, I just stood up and followed her out of the door. As I passed the threshold of the small room I'd been in for who knows how long, I couldn't help wondering why I hadn't left before. There was nothing stopping me but it had never occurred to me to leave. I may as well have been locked in a prison cell.

I followed the tall frame of Doctor Markham down the corridor and back into the room I'd originally met her in.

This time however, it was very different. The big sofa thing was still in the same position but arranged in front of the window was a long table behind which sat five women. They were dressed in a similar way to the Doctor, floor length sort of lightweight coats. Not exactly burkha-style garments, they were tailored and

I suppose flattering, not that I am any judge of such things but I thought they looked nice. The women represented a wide range of age and skin colour, their hair seemed a little regimented, short or pulled back and tied neatly. Their costumes were in a variety of colours, I can't describe the clothing in any detail but definitely not uniforms. The one thing that united them was their silence and the rather chilling fact that they all had their eyes locked onto me.

'Please sit down Gavin,' said Doctor Markham. I did so and watched as she sat down at one end of the table. I was then confronted with six women looking at me. I considered smiling at them and saying hello, but whatever this Institute was, it clearly didn't encourage smiling.

'I have informed my colleagues of your situation and they have requested to meet with you directly. They have seen our previous talk and we are all very intrigued.' At this point she turned to her right and looked at the women beside her. I followed and focused on the woman sitting next to her. I would guess that this woman was in her early thirties, of African descent and, I will admit, I found her rather attractive.

This woman suddenly smiled at me, a lovely big friendly smile. I tried to keep a straight face but it was such a relief I think I smiled back.

'Hello Gavin,' she said. 'I'm Doctor Nkoyo Oshineye and I'll be helping you assimilate. I'm happy to explain where you are and what is going on.'

'That would be very nice,' I said, now captivated by this woman. Her gaze was so intense I couldn't seem to look away.

'As you might be able to guess,' she continued, 'your arrival has caused something of a stir, it was all very public and there is already a lot of talk about the man who fell out of the sky. Some people are very upset about it, some are interested to meet you and we are just trying to control the situation for the good of everyone, including yourself.'

I scratched my head as I listened.

'Is there something wrong with his head?' asked an older-looking woman sitting at the centre of the table. I turned to her.

'Sorry,' I said, 'it's just a bad habit, there's nothing wrong with my head…'

I was going to explain that I was anxious and didn't want to cause any trouble, but the woman who'd spoken looked shocked. It was almost as if she didn't expect me to answer her, almost as if it was considered rude for me to answer her directly.

I then noticed she was wearing some kind of elaborate jewellery that was noticeably absent on the other women. I had no idea at that time what the ornate necklace might represent.

Nkoyo raised her hand slightly as if to calm the situation, although from where I was sitting everything was almost eerily calm. I think I may have grimaced at that moment even though I was trying very hard to remain neutral.

'So, you are correct about the date,' said Nkoyo. 'It is August 5th 2211 and you are in London. If you have actually come from past, from as you say the year 2011 then no doubt the London you knew back then was very different, much smaller and more compact. The area you would have known as London is indeed now mostly a large tidal inlet, a small inland sea might be a better description.'

I nodded, clearly wherever I had ended up, I was guessing maybe somewhere like Norfolk, was just an area of Gardenia I hadn't seen in my brief travels. I was surprised though that William or someone from Goldacre Hall hadn't mentioned the squares. Whatever I did see for those few panicky moments when I came out of the cloud was on a truly impressive scale, it seemed a bit odd no one had mentioned it.

'However, although we are clearly very intrigued by your story,' said Nkoyo, 'and all the evidence suggests that what you are telling us is a truth, we are very confused by your references to Gardenia. Would you like to explain to us what you meant when you said you came from a place called Gardenia and a place called Didcot which doesn't exist anymore.'

'Oh yeah, sure,' I said, again I noticed the older woman with the necklace react to this, almost as if she found my voice upsetting. It made me nervous, I didn't know what to do, I wasn't shouting or making threatening gestures, I was sitting as still as I could which I admit may have included some nervous twitching.

'So, I was originally flying to attend a meeting,' I said trying desperately to speak slowly and clearly. 'This was back in 2011, flying from Enstone, just outside Chipping Norton, the airfield where I keep my plane.'

It was fairly obvious the names of towns and airfields were making no impression on them; they didn't know what the hell I was talking about.

'Okay, so I was flying in the plane on my way to a meeting in Basingstoke when I was engulfed by a large cloud, a very unusual cloud which I now know to be some kind of anomaly, that's how it was described to me, an anomaly caused by enormous amounts of electricity passing down a very fine cable from a high level solar kite. Sorry, you probably know all about this kind of thing, but it was all news to me. When I came out of the cloud I was in the same place, just outside Didcot, but at another time.'

'Can you describe the cloud in a little more detail?' said Nkoyo. 'This may be very important.'

I shrugged. 'Well, it was a cloud, I mean, it looked like a low-level storm cloud from my viewpoint. There were no other storm clouds around on either occasion, just this very dense, dark cloud in an otherwise fairly clear sky. It was cloud-shaped, a kind of cumulonimbus formation, the top height, probably more than six thousand meters, which is far higher than I can fly in the Yuneec, the base more like one thousand.'

'I see, thank you, carry on,' said Nkoyo. I did notice that as I was explaining the cloud they seemed to converse with each other in a subtle way that women always seem good at and I never know what's going on.

I carried on: 'I soon learned that I was two hundred years in the future, the year was 2211 and the place was called Gardenia. I stayed there for two months, I got to know the people, I worked with them, I travelled around the world using the pod transportation system they had, I became very involved with them.'

I had considered telling them about Grace and my baby but something, for once, told me to hold this information back for the time being.

'Then, this morning I was woken by the people who had looked after me so kindly and they informed me that the anomalous cloud had reappeared in the same place, they didn't seem to know what it was and I certainly don't. But I thought, stupidly I can now see, that it might be the way back to my own time. I took off in the plane, climbed as high as I could and entered the cloud. That bit is hard to describe and if you're not a pilot it wouldn't make much sense, but it was very disorientating. I couldn't see two meters in front of me. When I came out of the cloud again I saw the squares below me, just squares for as far as I could see. It made no sense to me at all. After that I'm afraid I don't know exactly what happened, only that I must have crashed and caused some damage to a tree for which I am truly sorry. Also my plane is obviously wrecked and that is very upsetting for me. That's really the best explanation I can give you at the moment.'

The women sat in silence, all of them staring at me except Nkoyo who was looking down at something on the table in front of her. I sat as still as I could but I noticed my right leg was twitching.

'So what you are suggesting?' said Nkoyo eventually. 'Is that you have been in an alternative reality, another world?'

'Oh,' I said and the shock ran through me. 'You mean, you don't know about Gardenia?'

Nkoyo shook her head. 'No, we have never heard of it. We have checked all our records and there is no mention of anything like that in London. You see Gavin, we are all struggling with our scepticism here. It sounds outrageous and impossible, but you do appear to be telling a truth.'

'A truth?' I asked.

'It would appear to feel like a truth to you. Clearly, from where we are sitting now, it's very hard to understand.' Nkoyo sounded sympathetic, but it was as if she was talking to a deluded fool, which, I have to say, is what I was beginning to feel like.

'So what you're now telling me,' I said, feeling the panic starting to rise, 'is that where I am is in London in 2211 but it's a different 2211 from the one I've just left, meaning that Gardenia doesn't exist?'

I think I flopped back in the sofa thing at that moment. My head was now, to use the parlance of my era, completely buggered.

'We currently have no other explanation at our disposal,' said Nkoyo. 'You are in London. It is anyone's guess where Gardenia is, how real it is, how real your experiences have been. You are showing no obvious signs of head injury or dementia but clearly we have to be cautious. We can tell from the tests we have already run that there are certain telltale clues which confirm to us that you are indeed from an era long ago.'

'Telltale clues?' I asked.

'Certain substances were discovered in your tissues that no longer exist outside a laboratory, you have clearly been exposed to certain toxins which are no longer in circulation.'

'Oh blimey,' I said, feeling ever more anxious.

'This is a fascinating turn of events,' said Nkoyo. 'You are, I'm afraid, Gavin, a fascinating case and you will attract a great deal of attention. For a start, Professor Etheridge—' she gestured to a woman sitting beside her '—is a historian. She would obviously like to learn more of your original era.'

 The woman she was gesturing toward gave me a curt nod.

'At present though, we have a problem to deal with. As I mentioned there is great interest in your appearance, we need to manage that interest so as to cause the least disturbance. It would be advisable for both yourself and the general population that you stay here at the Institute for the time being, we will then orchestrate a meeting where you can be exposed to the wider public.'

'How do you feel about that?' asked Doctor Markham.

This time I let myself laugh. It was all so bonkers, it was either that or end up a screaming writhing heap of madness on the floor.

'I don't know how I feel about anything,' I said. This seemed to meet with general approval from the women. 'I don't even know where I want to go back to. I feel really thirsty, is that any help?'

Doctor Markham looked up, I laughed again as I turned and saw the big-armed lady standing in the doorway. She nodded and departed out of sight, I turned back to discover all the women had stood up. Without thinking I did the same, they all froze, looking mildly alarmed.

'Sorry, it's okay,' I said, palms forward in what I assume is the universal sign of non-aggression. 'In 2011 it was seen as polite for a man to stand when a woman did,' I tried to explain. I wasn't even sure if this was true, but it made sense at the time.

The woman with big arms came back into the room and handed me a small plastic grey pillow. It didn't feel like plastic, more like velvet but it really was just a little pillow thing obviously containing liquid. I couldn't see an opening.

Nkoyo stepped forward, she had to be two meters tall, she bent down, took the grey pillow from me and pinched a corner then handed it back.

'Drink,' she said. I looked at the group of women staring at me, I put the pillow towards my lips and my mouth filled with some kind of delicious herby, fruity, room-temperature watery stuff. I just swallowed until the pillow was empty.

'Better?' asked Nkoyo.

I nodded. 'Thanks.'

Nkoyo stepped back, then reached out her very long arms and held me gently by the shoulders and said, 'Welcome to London.'

4

Big Steps

I WAS USHERED FROM THE ROOM BY THE BIG-armed lady. I followed her down the corridor and thankfully past the cell-like room I'd spent the afternoon in. I felt my mood lighten; at least I wasn't going to spend the rest of my life in there. At the far end of the corridor was a flight of stairs in a very spacious stairwell that for some reason reminded me of government buildings in Germany. I always remember thinking that Germans had more space than we Brits and built things like stairwells much more generously than we did.

The stairwell I entered was seriously generous, in fact the whole building was very light and airy. The woman with big arms led the way down the stairs. There really wasn't anything I could do but follow. She was about my height, maybe a little taller, but there was something in her manner that made the prospect of a dash for freedom followed by a physical tussle very unattractive.

I almost stumbled as I went down the first step, the tread was deeper than I expected; at a glance they just looked like stairs, but they had clearly been made with slightly taller people in mind. I found it quite difficult to judge and really had to watch myself. The big-armed lady said nothing, she didn't react in any way to the fact that I stumbled down the first step so I didn't try and make light of it.

At the bottom of the stairs we entered another similar-looking corridor, I followed her into a large room with two long tables surrounded by many chairs. It was spotlessly clean and there was no one else in the room.

The woman gestured to a line of small white doors at about chest height along the far wall. I walked up to them very unsure about what I was meant to do. There were no handles apparent but one of the doors gently folded itself away in a most uncanny manner revealing a nice bowl of what looked like noodles, next to it a tall metal-looking container and a pair of white chopsticks.

I turned back toward the big-armed lady to ask her advice as to what I was supposed to do, but she was gone. They really did have a very different way of behaving in London than I'd experienced in Gardenia. Not exactly hostile, but no one I'd met up to that point seemed to be pleased to see me.

I assumed it was okay for me to take the bowl and eat, which was just as well as I was fairly ravenous by this stage. I'd lost all track of time and obviously my phone, iPad and wallet were now in Gardenia with Grace and all the amazing people who, I was starting to slowly realise, I was going to miss more and more.

I stopped myself thinking about it. I felt the need to damn up all thoughts about who I was, where I'd been, who I'd met and specifically who I'd maybe started to fall in love with. I could tell it wasn't going to be easy.

Thankfully, I had hunger on my side and I sat at the long table nearest me and started to tuck in. The noodles were hot and delicious, not really like the food I'd been eating in Gardenia. For a start I had no idea what was in among the noodles or where the ingredients had come from or who cooked it. It was all much more like the 2011 I had left so long ago.

The metal container was full of water which I gulped down in one go and carried on slurping noodles. Without warning an enormous man walked into the room, I could hear him coming, his shoes made a noise when he walked which I found to be a huge relief. The man smiled at me, walked over and held out his hand.

'Hi, I'm Pete,' he said. 'How are you doing matey?'

I stood up, wiped my mouth on my sleeve and shook his hand.

 He was huge, his hand was huge, he was well over two meters tall.

'Hi, I'm Gavin, nice to meet you.'

'Nice to meet you too. Mind if I join you?' asked Pete.

'Help yourself,' I said. Pete jerked his head back a little as if I'd challenged him. I shook my head furiously, suddenly seeing that what I said could be misunderstood, I should have learned this in Gardenia.

'I'm sorry, my fault, please do join me, I'd like that very much.'

'Good,' said Pete, he pulled out a chair and sat down opposite me. He stared at me for a bit with a big grin on his even bigger face, then stood up again and walked over to the weird little doors, one opened immediately. He retrieved a large pizza type thing and a tubular metal container of some sort.

'I've been clearing up the square, where you crashed your drone,' he said, taking a huge bite out of the pizza, although I noticed it wasn't really a pizza, not as I would have recognised it. It was a bread type thing with stuff on it, a kind of open sandwich.

'My drone? Why do you call it that? It's a plane.'

'A plane? What's a plane?' asked the full-mouthed Pete.

'The machine I crashed,' I explained, 'it's not a drone, a drone is an unmanned machine, a person has to fly a plane, they're very different.'

'Oh right, sorry, Gavin,' he said, smiling and revealing even more half chewed food, it wasn't a pleasant sight.

'Okay, so I've been clearing up your … plane.'

'What, the Yuneec?' I asked.

'Yes, that's it!' he said as he chewed. He pointed at me. 'I read that on the side. Yuneec, that's funny, sounds like unique but it's spelled in a nezvyklý sort of way. Amazing bit of kit though, how did you get it?'

'Well, it's mine. I bought it,' I said, feeling like I'd been here before. I noted he used the word nezvyklý, I wondered what it might mean, sounded sort of Eastern European.

Pete stopped mid-chew. 'So, I can tell by your clothes you are not from London, but you sound like a Londoner.' He stared at me, smiled and carried on eating.

I admit I did glance around the room at this point, I didn't want the big-armed lady to rush in and silence me with a strangle hold. I understood there was a lot of interest in me, this place was obviously very unlike Gardenia, it seemed to be a far more structured society although I couldn't judge at that moment quite how structured, or how the structure might regulate my behaviour or communication.

Suddenly there was a man talking to me who clearly knew about the crash and seemed fully informed about my arrival at the Institute.

'I don't want to cause any trouble,' I said, 'I'm not sure if I'm meant to be saying anything.'

'Have you had a talk with the big girls? Did they tell you to olla hilja?'

'Sorry?'

'Olla hilja. You know,' he put his finger to his lips, the instantly recognizable signal for silence.

'Oh, well, I suppose so,' I said. 'I'm not sure I understood everything they were saying but they seem very concerned, they don't want people to get upset.'

'That's funny,' said Pete with a big grin. 'They are so sweet aren't they? They get so worried about everything. It's fine, you flew around London in a drone. Okay, so you're not meant to fly drones here, but you didn't hurt anyone. It was very early in the morning, hardly anyone was about, well, Vajra saw you.'

Pete took a big bite of the pizza thing and chewed. He swallowed and said, 'Vajra was awake with his baby, he thought he was going mad. He is so funny, you'd love him and little Tommy is such a little mtoto. He said he saw you appear in the sky and bounce off the raspberry bushes and crash into the old Ash tree. I didn't believe him until I arrived on the scene and the parky asked me to clear up the mess.'

'I'm very sorry, I don't even remember what happened,' I said.

'So you don't remember Vajra? He was the one who found you, he told me all about it.'

'Oh right,' I said. 'Is Vajra like a medical person, I remember two people got me out of the wreck, a man and a woman.'

Pete took another huge bite and chewed for a bit. He was a big lively chap, he seemed very excited and full of energy but not in a dangerous way, there was no air of malice about him, he had huge gentle eyes bedecked with impressive dark eyebrows. His hair was slightly curly and a bit of a mess, but he took great care in his movements; he wasn't like a big sporty bloke or some drunk thug in a pub looking for trouble, he was clearly very strong but had no need to prove it.

He shook his big head, swallowed and tipped up the metal container which he consumed in one rather bullish session, burped and smiled.

'Vajra just raised the alarm, the medics got you out and brought you here, were you tajuton?'

'Sorry, tajuton?'

Pete smiled and let his head roll onto his chest. 'Totally tajuton.'

'Oh, unconscious,' I said with a grin.

'Un conscious,' said Pete carefully, 'I like that.'

I decided not to worry about the odd words Pete used, I'd got used to the fact that over 200 years language changes, particularly English which had such a long history of absorbing words from other tongues. However, these new words were confusing.

'I suppose I must have been knocked out when I crashed,' I said. 'I can't remember anything after I came out of the cloud.'

I had no idea what else to say. No one had seemed that bothered about my arrival in Gardenia, I was just an anomaly, they all seemed to know what that meant and it certainly didn't seem to upset them that much. I wondered how much it would really upset them here. Maybe it hadn't happened before, maybe

I was the first person to ever try going back through the cloud.

'So, where are you from?' asked Pete. 'You sound like us although you use shonky words.'

'If I tell you where I'm from, can you keep it to yourself for a bit? Like keep it secret.'

Pete sat up to his full and rather alarming height. 'Matey, if you want someone to keep a secret, I'm your brother.' He leant toward me, which again was a rather alarming sight. He whispered, 'I won't tell anyone.'

'Okay, well, my name is Gavin, Gavin Meckler. I come from 2011.'

'Where's that? Never heard of it.'

'No, it's not a place, it's a time. I come from two hundred years ago.'

'Two hundred years ago! Blimey. Like proper olden days.'

'Yes, proper olden days,' I said with a chuckle.

'But why are you still alive? You don't look two hundred years old.'

'I'm not,' I said. 'I'm thirty-two years old.'

Pete sat back and stared at me, his huge mouth hung open which made me look away, he still had a mouthful of twenty-third-century London pizza.

'I suppose I've travelled through time, when I crashed I was actually trying to get back home.'

'Oh, you poor thing,' said Pete, he swallowed and put his enormous hand on my forearm and patted it lightly. 'That's so sad. Of course you wanted to get back home and now you're here, in vervelig old London. D'you feel really sad?'

'Well, apart from being very confused I suppose I'm okay. I don't know if I feel sad.'

'Wait,' said Pete. 'How can you not know if you feel sad? Did people not know how they felt in the olden days?'

I rubbed my chin for a moment, I had to admit that was a fairly intelligent observation.

'Okay, well, I don't think I feel sad at the moment, I might feel really sad tomorrow. I obviously had a right old wallop when I crashed and it's really knocked the wind out of me.'

Pete laughed very loudly.

'I love the way you talk,' he said. 'Is that old-fashioned talking? Right old wallop and knocked the wind out of me, such good misemo, I like them.'

'Okay, so Pete, please tell me this,' I said, partly interrupting him and feeling a little guilty. 'When I came out of the cloud, when I saw…' I just didn't know how to describe it. 'When I was flying over the city, I saw this amazing grid pattern. As far as I could make out these squares, buildings around squares of open ground. It just seemed to go on forever. Is that right, am I remembering it or did I dream that?'

'The squares? I suppose that's what you would see from high up. I've seen pictures from high up and it looks like squares, because it is squares.' Pete stared through the large window behind me, he seemed lost in thought for a moment, then: 'But you saw squares, yeah, that's what you saw. Have you never seen squares before?'

'Well, yes, I mean we had buildings around squares in towns, but each town was sort of separate, we had towns with, well, with open country between then. Farms and things. All I could see were squares, no forests or fields.'

Pete held his head in his hands. 'I feel so stupid,' he said. 'I should have listened to my teachers. I never listened, I just made stuff. I don't know anything about the olden days. I've only ever lived in London, I've only ever known the squares. You are going to think I'm really stupid and lazy. I want to learn now. That's funny isn't it, when I was young I could not get things interesting in my head. Everything except making things or fixing things just made me feel bored and I hated feeling bored. I'm not bored now, I'd love to learn about your olden day world, about how you had towns and fields. I'm not sure I even know what a field is, is that like a square with no houses?'

I nodded. 'Yes, that's it, a square with no houses, have you got any of those?'

'No, I don't think so. Maybe on the edge of North London, there's some really big parks up there. I've been walking up there when I was a mtoto. But London's been like this for, well, for a really long time.'

I sighed very deeply, there was something about this whole experience which was immensely tiring. I didn't really want to find out about another world, I didn't want to go through the whole confusing learning process again, it was just too distressing. I felt a bit dizzy and sick, maybe this was as a result of me being knocked unconscious. I sat breathing deeply for a moment trying to regain my composure. I wanted to think about something else, anything else. I needed to hold back the urge to scream out.

'So tell me what you make, Pete,' I said. Better to listen to him than try and explain anything more about my predicament.

'I only make small things,' said Pete. 'Furniture, fences, gates, latches, coat hooks, doors, windows, data sensors, toilets, beds, panels, anything people want. I fix stuff too, if things get broken or they just wear out, I fix them. That's what I've been doing today, fixing the square you landed in. I cleared away your drone and took it over to the store.'

'The store?'

'I'll show you, don't worry, I didn't leave any of it behind. I couldn't, a kid might have found dangerous stuff and played with it so I made double sure I'd got every last sehemu.'

'What's a sehemu?'

'You know, all the little sehemu, the odd small ... sehemu.'

He was miming picking up things with one hand and placing them in the enormous palm of the other.

'Oh, parts,' I said. 'So the Yuneec is in the store, is that like a shop?'

'A shop! No it's my building, it's where I keep things I might need.'

'Do you work here? Will I see you here again?'

'I come here when they ask me. I came today to fix a chair that wasn't working. It's like new now,' he said proudly. 'Oh yes, I know how to fix chairs.'

He stood up and pointed to the row of doors where we'd received food. 'You see that door on the end, the top one. That was not working last week, now, it's as good as new.'

'Great,' I said with steadily waning enthusiasm.

'So you're staying here? Is that what the big girls told you was happening.'

'I think so,' I said, worrying again because I had no idea what I was going to be doing.

'When this has all settled, when you've talked to Doctor Markham for a bit and you know how you feel, I hope you can come and stay in my house. It's got a blue door with an eight painted on the front. Did you have things like that in the history?'

I nodded.

Again I got the hand on the forearm treatment. 'Don't worry, Gavin, you'll be fine, I'll look after you, we all will. Don't worry about what the big girls say, they're not Weavers so you'll be fine.'

'Weavers? Sorry, I don't understand.'

'You don't know about Weavers, didn't you have Weavers back in the olden days?' Pete looked genuinely puzzled.

'Well, we had people who did weaving but it was mostly done with machines I suppose.'

'No, I mean Weavers, the Weaver women, you didn't have them?'

'I don't think so, I'm guessing they don't weave, like, they don't make cloth.'

'Hell no, they make trouble, the Weaver women are scary for you and me, but you're here, you're fine, the big girls are great, they'll get really worried but before long they'll have something else to worry about. They love to worry, it's what they do.'

Pete stood up, picked up the metal container, drained what little remained in one gulp and walked toward the door in the wall where it had come from. The door folded open, he put the container inside and it gently closed like a sea anemone that's been touched.

He waited for me, I stood up with my empty bowl and glass.

'I don't remember which door it came out of,' I said as I walked towards the wall of door.

'You don't need to,' said Pete. 'The door remembers.'

And it did, a door along the wall folded open, I walked up to it and put my bowl and metal container inside. I then stood and watched as the mechanism closed up again. It made no sound, just unfolded itself into a smooth and seamless door. I started to wonder what materials were involved and how it was originally constructed, I would normally have asked, and I could tell Pete would be only to willing to give me an enormous amount of detailed information about it, but I let it go.

'Beautiful,' I said.

'Thanks,' said Pete proudly. 'I made those.'

5

Massive Wad

WAKING UP IN A SMALL WHITE ROOM IN London was a very different experience to waking up in my wonderful old room in the converted barn of Goldacre Hall, or indeed waking up in my small cluttered bedroom in my house that probably no longer existed in Kingham.

The windows slowly faded from almost black to completely transparent as I sat up on the side of my bed type thing. I could see a clear blue sky; the sun was already high.

I had slept with the lightest blue cover over me that somehow, despite its minimal weight, was very warm.

I sniffed my armpit, although there was still a trace of the lovely unguent stuff that I'd been using in my wood panelled bathroom in Gardenia, I was definitely in need of a rinse.

My body flooded with feelings and caught me off guard; remembering the bathroom reminded me of Grace, and remembering Grace reminded me of Beth. I knew Beth had been dead for donkey's years, I'd almost accepted that, but Grace. What on earth could have happened? Did she not really exist? Indeed, if I was in fact technically dead then why were the experiences I was having so very mundane? I don't mean going through the cloud or the extraordinary world I was living in, that aspect was anything but mundane. But the minute-by-minute experience, being hungry, needing to use the toilet, feeling sleepy. Surely that wasn't what being dead was about?

How, I pondered, was a man fully immersed in the mechanics of the rational, with little or no grasp of matters spiritual, meant to make any sense of what was happening?

I sat up and looked around the room, relieved to discover there was no silent woman looking at me from the doorway.

I remembered then that Pete, the gangly man with messy hair had shown me how the door worked. There actually was a door, a larger version of the food doors in the canteen room I'd eaten in the previous evening.

He'd also shown me the bathroom, I was grateful because it was not immediately apparent what purpose the totally white box would have. It was a mystery how the systems worked, everything kind of folded away when not in use, and everything was clinical and spotlessly clean.

I stood up, pulled on my slightly skanky Gardenian clothes and shuffled toward the door. As expected, the door folded itself away into the floor without so much as a whisper.

Then I shuffled along the broad corridor to the bathroom only to find the foldaway door was closed. It didn't open as I approached it and I had no idea what to do. I was rather in need of a piss. I looked up and down the corridor but there was no one around to help.

I tried tapping on the door to see if anyone was inside. I could barely hear the tap myself; whatever material this door was made of, it seemed to absorb sound in an uncanny way. I stood back, twitching slightly. I really needed my morning pee.

Suddenly the door opened, well, more like the door fell down instantly and I was confronted with a man about my height. He looked oddly familiar and I realised it was the guy I'd seen in the garden being followed by the floating wheelbarrow with no wheels.

I smiled at him and he looked at me blankly, he then gave me an almost imperceptible nod and walked off down the corridor.

I went into the bathroom and relieved myself. The toilet system looked oddly similar to the one I'd used in Gardenia, it used some kind of vacuum system like in an airliner – even the design was similar. I stood looking at it for a while trying to work it out. If Gardenia was, as had been suggested, an alternate reality, maybe even just a possible future, and this place could be another possible future. The same time, the same place, even the same plumbing, but in every other way utterly different.

I just wanted to lie down in a dark room with a physicist who might be able to explain it to me. The reality of standing in that bathroom was too real to allow such bonkers notions to emerge. If I really understood that, if I really believed that was the case, then I would just have to start screaming and try to tear my face off. I shuddered a little and went back into the corridor.

'There you are,' said Doctor Markham. She was standing outside my room and if I could read any emotion on her face, which, let me tell you was not easy, I would guess she was just the anxious side of worried, but only just.

'Needed a pee,' I said. 'Actually, while we're about it, I need to have a shower but I don't have any clean clothes to change into.'

Doctor Markham didn't react, she just stared at me blankly for a moment.

'I will arrange for you to buy new clothes. Have you had any breakfast?'

'No, I've just woken up,' I said. 'I quite fancy something to eat.'

Again there was no immediate reaction, but then Doctor Markham started to walk towards me. I'll admit now that I was a little concerned. She was very tall, she moved quite fast and with no noise at all. She walked very near me and I noticed, with some relief, a very faint sound of movement as she passed close by. I nearly flinched, I was half expecting to be thrown to the ground or stabbed with some weird space age mind probe.

'Please follow me in order to get some breakfast, Gavin.'

Okay, so no space age mind probes, no implants, no using my body as an energy source for a technology I had no hope of understanding. Just breakfast.

I followed her down the flight of big stairs half expecting to go into the room where I'd met Pete.

We passed by that room and continued down the long corridor, I did glance in as we passed and noticed quite a few people in there, men and women, most of them staring at me as I passed. I tried to smile but I kept it minimal, just a happy glance, that's what I was aiming at.

Doctor Markham stood by another entrance into a smaller room decorated in a much softer manner, all along one side large glass doors looked out onto a delightful patio area. The room smelled wonderful. It took me a moment to register the smell, bacon? Yes, it was bacon!

I hadn't experienced that heady aroma in months. A large table at one side of the room was covered in beautiful china plates, mostly laden freshly cut fruit. However, there was one plate on which there was bacon, a fried egg, grilled tomatoes, mushrooms and toasted bread.

'Oh wow,' I said when I saw it. 'Actual food.'

'This has been prepared especially for you, we are assuming this is a breakfast dish you would be familiar with.'

'You're not kidding, this is amazing!' I said.

I watched Doctor Markham commit her elegant face to something that could be described as a smile.

'Is this really bacon?' I asked. 'Like bacon, from a pig?'

Her smile broadened. She put a gentle hand on my shoulder. 'Just as well you asked me that, many people today would not know what you were saying and would find your question disturbing. It's fresh print.'

'Fresh print?'

'Yes, I think the way you might understand is that it's printed, I believe some technology like this existed in your era. It is printed with exactly the same chemical components as bacon but it doesn't come from a pig.'

I picked up a slice of what looked like a perfect smoked rasher, sniffed it, took a nibble and everything about the experience said bacon.

'Help yourself,' she said, 'we're sitting outside.'

I watched her walk toward the large glass door that slid open for her with an almost imperceptible hiss. Nice action. I really wanted to find out about these doors.

I picked up my first proper breakfast since leaving Kingham two hundred years before. Okay so it was printed, but it looked like a proper breakfast. There was a metal container at one end of the table with a few cups near it. I assumed this was some sort of hot beverage dispenser. It was a bit like being in a posh foreign hotel on the first morning you have breakfast, you don't quite know how everything works and sort of fumble through while trying to look casual.

I held the cup near the container. There was no tap, spout or obvious way of retrieving the beverage. I shook my head and gave up, put the coffee cup down and then watched in utter amazement as hot coffee poured into the cup from an unseen opening. It seemed a bit elaborate and unnecessary – it was just a coffee pot, couldn't they just pour it? I then realised that even in the brief few months I'd been in Gardenia I'd become a bit of a purist. It was very cool how the coffee came out. I decided I liked it.

I carried my breakfast plate and coffee toward the door, again it slid open without a fuss and I emerged into a very warm outside world.

Now it was even more like being in an Italian hotel garden in the summer. It wasn't just a bit warm outside, it was actually hot.

'Good morning, Gavin,' said Nkoyo, she was sitting at a large metal table under a wonderful dark shade cloth stretched between delicate poles.

'Good morning,' I said, and although ravenously hungry and desperate to dig into my breakfast, I stared around the beautiful walled garden that surrounded us.

'Wow, what an amazing place,' I said, putting my plate down on the table and taking a slurp of what thankfully turned out to be delicious coffee.

‘I’m afraid this side of the building is in the sun in the morning, but if you sit down you will be shaded by the cover,’ said Nkoyo pointing up to the shade cloth. I glanced up at the building behind me and I got another shock.

I don’t know what I was expecting, just a building of a couple of stories, but it was far bigger than I expected. Probably thirty floors, maybe more. It was huge and it towered above the small garden I was in. For some reason I had got it into my head that I’d seen pretty much the whole place already. I’d barely seen one corner.

‘Oh my God,’ I said. ‘Is this whole place the Institute?’

‘Yes,’ said Nkoyo.

‘It’s huge!’

Nkoyo and Doctor Markham did not react to my amazement. I’m sure if I’d been in their position, I’d have reacted when someone was amazed by something I was accustomed to; however, that was it. Forget it and move on, that’s what I thought. I sat down opposite them and started eating.

‘I take it you slept well,’ said Nkoyo. ‘Did you find the bed comfortable?’

I nodded, my mouth chock full of bacon and eggs.

‘Doctor Markham tells me you would like to buy some clothes, is that right?’ asked Nkoyo.

I continued nodding, swallowed and said. ‘Well, yes, I’ve only got the clothes I’m wearing now. They’re from Gardenia, I don’t have the clothes I was wearing when I left, well, my era, you know, like two hundred years ago. I left them at Goldacre Hall.’

‘I see.’

‘Which is where I was living in Gardenia, which doesn’t exist. Plus I left my money there, they don’t use money, I had some money in my wallet, my phone and iPad, that was about it. So I don’t have anything to pay for clothes.’

‘I understand,’ said Nkoyo. ‘It is possible we can arrange for you to do some work and earn enough money to buy some clothes. We are not in a position to donate clothes to you.’

'Oh, right,' I said. I took another mouthful, thinking about having to work in London and what that could possibly mean. I remembered Grace bringing me clothes; there was never any suggestion of payment, or working for money. The concept sounded very bizarre even considering I'd been born and raised in a social and political environment where money ruled.

'There is an alternative,' Doctor Markham spoke slowly and deliberately.

'An alternative?' asked Nkoyo.

'Professor Etheridge did some deep research last night.'

I must have looked nonplussed because I noticed a hint of annoyance on the normally static features of the Vanessa Redgrave lookalike. 'You met Professor Etheridge yesterday, she was a member of your review panel,' she said rather curtly.

'Yes, I remember,' I said, which I did, more or less, I knew she was one of the scary women sitting behind the table looking at me.

'She found your records,' said Doctor Markham. 'The reports of your disappearance, she managed to verify your story and has traced your, I believe the word was, pension.'

'My pension?'

'Do you know what that is?'

'You mean, my pension, from 2011! How the hell could that be? I mean I had a pension, wasn't that much in it, maybe two hundred and fifty K, but I assumed, well, I didn't even think about it but I suppose I assumed anything to do with the economy of 2011 had ceased to exist long ago.'

'That is not the case, Gavin, your pension still exists,' said Doctor Markham. 'It took some finding; apparently the bank had to decrypt files from ancient data storage systems they had tucked away in a deep vault. Very few people know how to operate such devices, but thankfully some students at University College are working on a project to excavate very old data. They found someone who could collate the information.'

'This is insane!' I said feeling ever more disoriented.

'Why do you feel it is insane?' asked Doctor Markham. 'It is just financial data stored in crude coded algorythms, I don't think sanity has anything to do with it.'

I sat in front of them, rubbing my eyes, trying to make sense of what they'd just told me.

'It's a figure of speech,' I said. 'I don't mean the data is insane, just the, well the turn of events.' I stopped rubbing my eyes and looked up at them, trying to judge their reaction. I didn't have a hope, they both stared at me blankly and, as usual, I didn't have a clue what they were thinking.

'So, I've got some money, is that what you're saying?'

Nkoyo smiled at me and nodded. 'Yes, it sounds like you have some money.'

'Your pension is currently valued at a little over thirteen million kwo,' said Doctor Markham calmly.

'Kwo?'

'Yes, Kwo, did you not have Kwo?' asked Doctor Markham, for some reason my question seemed to offend her slightly, although on reflection my very existence seemed to offend her.

'I've got no idea what you mean, is it currency?' Again, a blank stare from both women. 'Money,' I said. 'Is Kwo like money?'

'Yes, Kwo, bits, often the common term is bits. Kwo is money, rather a lot of money,' said Doctor Markham.

It then became clear that this information was also news to Nkoyo, she was staring at Doctor Markham and turned to me, raised her magnificent eyebrows and grinned.

'Not bad to wake up after two hundred years and discover you have thirteen million in the bank,' she said.

I sat in silence for a while, going through the now tiresome rigmarole of trying to understand what had happened in the last two hundred years, how my pension had survived the turmoil, the collapsing economies, the many revolutions, minor wars and upsets that are the norm for human life on earth. Then I considered the possibility that if where I was sitting was, as it appeared to be, another possible future completely unconnected to Gardenia, then the history of what had come before could also be completely different.

'Are you feeling okay, Gavin?' asked Doctor Markham.

'Yeah, I'm fine,' I responded without thought. 'I'm just trying to adjust to being a multimillionaire.'

6

Meet the Press

FINDING MYSELF SITTING BEHIND A BRIGHTLY-lit table in front of literally hundreds of people was fairly taxing. I had appeared on panels back in my own era, most commonly public meetings about various large engineering projects, but I was usually there as a representative of a mining company and not the focus of attention.

This was very different. I was very much the focus of enormous amounts of attention. How anyone could enjoy this experience was hard to grasp. I felt my whole body shaking as I entered the room. People who want to be famous have to be seriously weird.

The large room I was sitting in was at the opposite end of the Institute I had by that time become slightly familiar with. After my breakfast I followed Nkoyo down the seemingly endless corridor as she explained what was going to happen.

'There are many international worders gathered at the Institute, we can no longer contain the information about your arrival and wish to clarify the situation.'

'Worders?'

'Yes, worders, I think you might have called them journal makers.'

'Journalists?' I suggested.

'Yes, journal-ists, we don't have journals any more but I suppose worders do much the same thing, they interpret events and distribute the information.'

'So you want me to talk to them?' I asked, feeling more

 alarmed. 'I'm not very good at communicating, not like that, especially not with large groups of people.'

Nkoyo gave me sympathetic glance. 'Don't be anxious, Gavin, I'll be right beside you. I will guide you. You will be fine and it won't take long, it'll all be over before you realise.'

Nkoyo stopped by one of the bizarre foldy doors, she laid a hand gently on my forearm, 'The only thing we would request you avoid is an explanation of Gardenia, of a potential alternative reality running parallel to ours. There is research into this area, still in its very early stages, I think revelations of the kind you have implied to us may confuse people. Is that okay?'

I nodded. 'Yeah, that's fine. Don't worry, I'll avoid the topic,' I said.

At that point the weird door slid open and Nkoyo stood to one side and gestured for me to enter.

As I entered I felt a new wave of fear surge through my body. I wasn't used to surges of any kind; it was all very unsettling. It was very noisy, a huge room full of people talking. Before I made it into the glare of the spotlights on the raised stage, I stared at the crowd in abject terror. This room was full of women; I could not spot one man among them.

I was shown up two steps onto a stage on which was a long table and as soon as I appeared from the shadows, the noise from the crowd increased. I sat down behind the table as directed, Doctor Markham sat to my left and Nkoyo to my right.

There were two other people already sitting at the table when I entered, the big-armed lady at one end and a woman who I remembered was Professor Etheridge at the other. The Professor spoke first. I could see no microphone in front of her but her voice was clearly amplified.

'Thank you for attending today,' she said. 'I am Professor Wendy Etheridge from the Institute of Mental Health, and I have been studying the story we are about to reveal to you today.'

I fear the shock may have been visible on my almost out-of-control face when I learned that the institute I'd been housed in was a loony bin. Mental health, so they did think I was a nutbag.

'The news we have for you is, without doubt, fairly dramatic. The man you see before you, Gavin Meckler, is in effect two hundred and thirty-two years old. He was born in 1979.'

The crowd in the room erupted with what I assumed were questions, consternation and confusion, but it all happened at the same time so it was hard to make out any individual comment. I could see many women staring at me incredulously.

'He was born in an area he would have known as High Wycombe, although we would now know this area as Dawson Square. The London we are familiar with now did not exist back then. He appears to be capable of controlling a manually operated drone to a certain level, although his skills failed him and as you all know this machine crashed in Franklin Square very near a children's play area. This happened early in the morning of the fourth of August and no one, including Mister Meckler was injured.'

Another wave of concern rippled through the crowd.

'Obviously we were alarmed when this incident came to our attention. At present an anomaly of some sort, caused, we think, by high levels of electrical energy somewhere in the vicinity of the Singh power-field at the southern end of the square.'

I noticed the Professor nod her head upwards, this made me glance behind me, what I saw momentarily took my breath away. Above and behind me was a huge screen with an incredibly detailed aerial view of the squares, it was shocking because it was exactly as I'd seen it when I emerged from the cloud. It was also shocking because it wasn't like looking at a screen, it was like looking out of a window, a window with optically perfect glass. The image was not merely photographic, it was so real looking it had to be real, the room I was in simply had to be floating above the square, we were looking down on it. I gripped my seat instinctively, I was frightened I would fall to my death as the image spun and zoomed, I felt slightly sick and yet my body sensed no movement.

The image flew in with dizzying clarity, swinging around so the wide-open space of the Singh power-field was in the foreground. Above the field was something I immediately recognised, a very large threatening cloud, now I could see it again I realised that its formation was not natural, no naturally occurring clouds are the shape of a giant traffic cone, dark at the bottom and getting steadily brighter higher up.

Suddenly a very recognisable image of my plane appeared out of the cloud and flew in a slightly crazed manner, a little reminiscent of a fly around a naked bulb, slowly descending toward the middle of the square.

I felt I understood something then. They had the same clouds in London as they had in Gardenia and as I'd seen over Didcot. The cloud over London had to be formed by similar vast amounts of electrical energy causing the anomaly in Gardenia but there was no cable visible, no tether. This was evidently something very different.

'We have now completed our investigation as to how this happened, and while the exact cause is still unclear, we did record a massive power surge which registered in accumulators and ultra-capacitors in the vicinity of Mister Meckler's appearance.'

People in the crowd were now shouting questions, I still couldn't make out any individual voice but they were obviously upset. An image of some kind appeared on the screen, I could not understand any of it, I assumed it was a representation of data but in a form I was completely unfamiliar with.

'At present there is no need to assume a repeat performance is possible, but we are looking into safety measures. I don't need to explain that this kind of breach in the stability of space–time is clearly a major security issue.'

Again the room erupted into a cacophony of questions, shouts and general conversation.

'Mister Meckler has undergone a battery of tests and is of no immediate danger to anyone. He is disease-free and although his body carries an alarmingly high array of toxins, they are not of a communicable nature and only a danger to him. They were toxins he would have been exposed to due to the crudity of the technology he was surrounded by in his era.'

I was learning as much about myself as the crowd were; all of them were now listening in rapt silence. I never knew I was so full of toxins. All that organic food I'd spent so much money on with Beth? Bit of a waste of time by the sound of things.

The Professor continued.

'At first we had no way of verifying his claims. He was interviewed by Doctor Alice Markham who some of you may know is London's leading psychological reader. Doctor Markham registered that Mister Meckler is incapable of sophisticated psychic deception, his development in this area is, as one would expect of a person from two hundred years ago, rudimentary to say the least.'

I did a kind of smiley shrug as if to say, 'that's me, I'm a psychological thicko', which was partly true, as I had no idea what she was talking about. My reaction caused another wave of noise to erupt from the crowd.

Professor Etheridge glanced across at me as a teacher would glance at an unruly six-year-old, cleared her throat and carried on.

'We have now been able to check out his claims using deep data restoration, and indeed there was a man who exactly matches his description who was born in 1979 and who also disappeared in 2011 while flying a manually operated drone which matches the description of the one that crashed in Franklin Square. It appears the authorities at the time assumed he was missing due to crashing into the ocean. Even though it seems highly unlikely, everything Mister Meckler has told us appears to be true. I'll now hand you over to Nkoyo Oshineye.'

52 Professor Etheridge sat back at this point and exchanged words with Nkoyo who then turned to me and said, 'Are you ready?'

I was going to say 'ready for what?' but I didn't get the chance, she leaned forward and started addressing the audience.

'Good morning everyone, my name is Doctor Nkoyo Oshineye, I'm the director of the Institute and I'd just like to lay a few fears to rest. As you may know, we already deal with a number of extreme cases here at the Institute but this is something very out of the ordinary. Dealing with the sudden arrival of Mister Meckler has been a challenge. As you will soon discover, he is a gentle and sensitive man, not exactly what we might have expected to emerge from the dark times but it's just possible we have a lot to learn from him about our distant past.'

I know my eyebrows raised a little when I heard my era referred to as 'the dark times.' I also noticed many members of the audience took note of my reaction. I turned back to look at Nkoyo which, if I'm being honest, was not a chore.

'I would ask that you try and control your inquisitiveness and give him time to answer. He is highly intelligent and understands most of what we say, although he may not be familiar with some of the eastern European or African terms that have entered our language over the past one hundred years or so. I would suggest you phrase your questions carefully and in as traditional English as you can manage.'

At this point, Nkoyo pointed to a woman in about the third row. As soon as she spoke I could hear her voice coming through a very sophisticated public address system.

'Gavin, can you tell us if it is your intention to try and influence our menfolk and cause upset and discord?'

I looked over to Nkoyo, I needed help with the very first question. She nodded at me as if to say 'the floor is yours'.

I turned toward the woman who'd asked the question then looked down at the table for some kind of microphone, there wasn't one.

'Well,' I said and got a shock, my voice was amplified, crystal clear, in fact it sounded rather good. 'Wow, that's amazing, I'll need someone to explain to me how the amplification in here works.'

I could see this comment caused confusion, even mild alarm among the members of the audience. I smiled.

'Sorry, I don't know exactly what you mean, but I have no intention of causing upset, I am far more confused than any of you. I don't know why I'm here and I don't know how I got here. I'm an engineer not a politician, from what I have already witnessed, I can see that you live in a very civilised city and I only want to learn how everything works.'

I turned to Nkoyo and grimaced, I had no idea if I'd said the right thing.

Another question came from someone so far back in the auditorium I couldn't see them but again it was a woman's voice.

'We are meant to believe you came from the past, other than your hair and clothing there is nothing other than the information we've just received to give us any proof that this is the case. Can you convince us?'

I leant forward and thought about it for a moment. I resisted the temptation to scratch my head, I didn't want to attract any more attention to my hair. The only two men I had seen up to that point wore their hair much longer than mine.

'My hair is, well, it's just hair, I don't know how to explain that, my clothes are, um, borrowed, my twenty-first-century clothes have been, um, mislaid. I don't know how to prove my twenty-first-century credentials other than the huge amount of knowledge I have regarding that period of history. So far all the information I have given the, err, the Institute, has been verified as you heard from Professor Etheridge. My family, my education, official records and the like are all verifiable, along with a great deal of photographic evidence. I really am Gavin Meckler, I really was born in 1979. I really shouldn't be here, but I am.'

That caused a fresh stir, not an angry one but I got the impression people really liked my final quote. I quite liked my final quote and decided to make it my tag line.

'I really shouldn't be here, but I am.'

A woman in the front row waved at me. I looked at her. Okay, I found her rather attractive which may be why she got my attention.

'We understand,' she said, 'that you have many millions in your account, what do you intend to do with it?'

At that moment I had been aware of my newly found millions for about an hour, suddenly it appeared that everyone knew about it. How could that be, had Nkoyo announced it on some sort of television system, or web-based network, if that was the case I'd seen no sign of it and I'd been with her the entire time.

'Oh yes, I, err. Well, I've only just discovered this and I don't know,' I said. 'That is as big a surprise as my landing in your square. I hope to be able to buy some clothes as these are the only ones I have.'

I was very surprised then that it seemed most of the audience laughed when I said this. Clearly they thought the clothes I was wearing were fairly odd, or even humorous.

There was then a lot of shouting, I couldn't make out a distinct question but I saw Nkoyo stand up and point to a woman at the far side of the auditorium.

'Do you have children, Gavin?'

'Children?' I needed time on this one. I didn't know if I had children but I knew it wouldn't be wise to say that. The woman spoke again.

'If you had children back in your own time, you may have descendants living here today.'

'Oh, I see, no. I didn't have children; I suppose I may have relatives in some form, my brother's children's children. I might be a very many greats great uncle to someone.'

I turned to Nkoyo and whispered, 'Do you still have uncles?'

Although I was whispering, it was instantly clear that everyone heard me. Nkoyo smiled and nodded and the rest of the audience seemed to be enjoying this moment, I even got a round of applause.

The woman at the end of the row was still standing. 'Would you like to have children now? Here in London?'

I know my eyebrows did a bit of a dance, as this elicited a lot of laughing and excitement.

'I haven't really thought about it. I suppose I'd have to meet someone I'd like to have children with,' I said. Again the reaction to this statement was not quite what I would have expected. It was a little bit wild, a sort of high-pitched cheer with whistles and applause. I'm pretty sure I heard some fairly suggestive remarks coming from the crowd.

'Boy children?' someone shouted. 'Can you have boy children?'

I noticed Nkoyo react to this statement, she stood up and pointed to the women in the front row.

'What are you going to do and where are you going to live?'

I was smiling now; whatever trepidation I'd felt before the questions started had fled, I was starting to enjoy the attention.

'I truly have no idea,' I said, 'I'd like to find out how things work here, how you all live, how you grow food, how you move about, how this incredible public address system works.' I was silent for a moment, something was happening but I didn't know what it was. I was suddenly missing Beth, missing my mum, I wanted to walk through Kingham again on a Sunday morning and actually buy a newspaper, something I'd not done in years. I was having feelings, really intense, strong feelings that seemed to emerge from nowhere. My throat felt tight, I couldn't focus my eyes.

'I'd like to do all that,' I said, 'but really, more than anything, I'd like to go home.'

That's when it happened, that's when the dam burst and that's when I cursed my feelings for happening without warning. I was crying as I spoke the last few words, tears streaming down my face, sobs breaking up the words. Just as I was starting to have a good time, to bathe in my newfound fame, I started bloody crying like a baby.

7

Perfectly Benign

A YOUNG MAN WITH WHAT APPEARED TO ME to be Photoshop-perfect skin stood behind a large desk in the enormous reception area of the Institute.

Photoshop-face man was much taller than me, he leant forward a little and held out a small glass container.

'Here you are,' he said in a surprisingly deep voice, he only looked about twelve, but a twelve-year-old with some kind of growth hormone disease that had made him unfeasibly tall.

I took the container but couldn't help looking at this man's face. I don't think I'd ever seen skin like it, not on an actual human being. It didn't look like he had make-up on but his face was eerily perfect.

'Thank you,' I said, as I took the small container and inspected it.

It was the morning following my emotional event in front of what I had later discovered to be a sizeable proportion of the world's press. I'd spent the remainder of the day in a quiet room with occasional visits from Nkoyo, who had been very patient with me. I'm not trying to cover up, I was in a right old state but I don't want to be boring about it. I didn't come to any sudden realisation about life, time, history, love and death. I just felt very sorry for myself.

I had woken early and was asked by Nkoyo to go and see Doctor Markham. I didn't really have anything else to do, so I went to the beautiful room where I'd first met her, sat on the big couch thing and spent some time talking about my family, my childhood, my education and my adult life.

I suppose it was a therapy session, although having never attended a therapy session before it could just have been a conversation. It was a bit one-way though, I didn't learn about her childhood, her education, her night fears or any aspect of her life.

She was disarmingly good at getting me to talk. The one thing that kept coming to me as I explained my life before Gardenia was how little I seemed to connect to other people. Initially I shrugged these suggestions off, not that Doctor Markham suggested anything in a blatant way. It was more that she asked questions, I answered them, and as I answered them I realised I was saying something about myself I'd never thought about previously. It was as if she made it possible for me to tell myself about myself. It sounds stupid and I'm embarrassed to even attempt the describe it. This kind of pointless worrying about yourself had always been anathema to me, it seemed that way madness lay. I'd rather let it all be and get on with my work, except now I didn't have any work to do and I was very rich.

I realised through this process that I'd lived a rather remote life. I hadn't really thought about my mum and dad since I had left in 2011. I realised I hadn't been thinking about them much before I left, or indeed my elder brother. I was always so preoccupied by whatever task was at hand. I wondered as I spoke to the Doctor if the reason I had been thinking about Beth was because I left her just after we'd had quite a bad row. I needed something that intense to even be aware of the interaction. If I'd just visited my mum and dad and had Sunday lunch with them, it would have made so little impact on my inner life I would probably have forgotten all about it half an hour later.

I'm not going to claim that going through all this nonsense with Doctor Markham immediately made me feel better but it did make me aware that I had feelings and these feelings, while not always apparent to me on a conscious level did sometimes affect the way I behaved.

To be honest, it was all a bit annoying. Yes, I had some feelings, but they didn't actually help me get stuff done, they didn't allow me to function more effectively.

So I was full of all these thoughts when Nkoyo had taken me to the spacious reception area of the Institute.

'You came in through the emergency arrivals section so you won't have seen this area,' she said as one of the slidey silent doors folded into the floor.

I was confronted with a cavernous hall, on the opposite side from the doorway I stood in was a massive glass wall the height of the fully grown trees outside. The floor was some kind of polished material, not made up of tiles, just one seamless cream surface. At the far end was a large desk or counter behind which stood the man with the Photoshopped face, opposite that were a few comfortable-looking sofa type things with half a dozen or so people sitting talking. They were all women.

'I know you felt a little worried when you discovered this was a mental health institute, but it may not be exactly what you think. It's more a place of learning, I imagine a mental health institute in your era meant a place where people were sent when their lives collapsed in chaos, when they were a danger to themselves or others.'

I nodded, that sounded like a fairly good description.

'However, in the present day we are facing new challenges,' said Nkoyo. 'We have essentially perfected physical medicine, we still have injuries and eventually death, but all of the many diseases which once beset the human race have been eliminated. We no longer get physically ill but we still suffer from what has often been described as the human condition. Depression, anxiety, confusion, psychosis and schizophrenia are still problems we occasionally have to deal with. We are able to treat these ailments with far more success than in the past and we are learning how to develop good mental health from an early age. The Institute is at the forefront of this research, hence our interest in you, Gavin. You are a very interesting case, you have not grown up in our environment, you have none of the advantages we benefit from, so we can use you as a kind of base measure.'

'Oh, right,' I said. 'That's very reassuring.'

So I was seen as a knuckle-dragging 'base measure', essentially a cave man, crude and stupid, emotionally undeveloped and immature.

'Please don't be offended,' said Nkoyo. 'We all find you utterly charming.'

She looked at me with her big, beautiful eyes, I couldn't really muster up any offence, I just felt very young and innocent.

'I find you utterly charming too,' I said, and of course immediately regretted it. I didn't want to start flirting; I wasn't any good at flirting anyway and was sure to make a right mess of it.

'Do you?' she said, she sounded genuinely surprised. 'Oh, I thought you would automatically distrust me because of my skin colour.'

That stumped me. I really hadn't seen that one coming. I felt myself flush, had I inadvertently revealed some kind of deep-seated, subconscious racism that I wasn't aware of? Of all the human hatreds and fears, racism had always been a mystery to me. I know I'd had vaguely homophobic reactions in my time, I had felt uncomfortable in the company of gay men. I didn't mind lesbians, I don't mean I found lesbians kinky or perversely exciting, I knew an engineer quite well who often referred to her wife, I didn't mind that. But two blokes kissing? Awkward.

Beth had been very critical when I'd thoughtlessly used terms like poof or bender when describing a gay man we both knew, but racism? I didn't think I'd ever had a racist thought in my life.

'I don't think your skin colour has got anything to do with it,' I said. 'Anyway, your skin is beautiful.'

I cursed myself, was I flirting again?

'I may have misread my history but there seemed to be a lot of hatred and mistrust between people of different skin colour in your era. I know slavery was less common but didn't white people hate and fear black people?'

'We didn't have slavery in 2011!' I stated. 'Racism had sort of, well, it was, it was really uncool to be racist, only stupid, ignorant people were racist.'

'That's reassuring to know,' said Nkoyo, she smiled at me. She had let the subject drop, but once again my mouth took over.

'I'll admit you seem quite different to many of the black people I knew back then.'

'Different? Interesting, would you care to elaborate?' again the smile utterly undermined me. She was spine-tinglingly gorgeous.

'Well, I suppose, well, you're ...' I realised as I was speaking that I was digging a massive hole for myself. I'd never actually spoken to a black person before about my thoughts on such an issue. What were black people like in 2011, what was I like?

Every experience, every conversation I had in this London always felt like as if it revealed something about myself to me and I didn't particularly like the feeling.

'You seem very confident, very well educated, um, not that black people weren't well educated back then, but you seem, well, like you own the place, which, I suppose ...' I looked around the reception hall. 'I suppose you do.'

'Fascinating,' said Nkoyo, thankfully still smiling.

'Were you born in London?' I asked.

'No, I came here from Kinshasa,' she said.

'Oh, right, the Congo,' I said, feeling proud of my geographic knowledge.

'No, Africa,' said Nkoyo, but without rancour. 'I think you'll find that Africa is a little different from your era, it's now a collection of City States, what you would have known as Africa is now more commonly referred to as either Lagos, Nairobi or Maputo.'

'Wow,' I said quietly.

'I used to run a similar Institute in Nairobi, then in Moscow, and for the last three years I have been based here in London.'

'Amazing, but you only look, well, you seem too young to have had time to do all that.'

'I'm fifty-seven,' said Nkoyo. I should have been used to these moments, I'd had enough experience of age confusion in Gardenia but this was way more extreme. I had truly put Nkoyo in her early twenties, maybe twenty-five tops. Not in her late fifties.

'But we are not here to talk about my age and professional experience, Gavin, we're here to sort you out.'

That didn't sound good, I felt I'd just been through an hour of being sorted out by Doctor Markham and my brain was mush. I couldn't contain a clear thought for more than a second. My mum, my dad, my annoying brother, Beth, Grace, time, death, my possible baby in a possible world that currently did not exist. I don't want to make excuses for myself, but I'd say that twisted concoction would be a challenge for anyone's mental stability.

This had resulted in being trapped in a strange institution and bursting into tears in front of a thousand women. I grimaced at the prospect of going utterly insane.

'Don't worry, it's nothing to be concerned about,' said Nkoyo and I suddenly realised how mad I must already appear. Standing in a big public space like the enormous reception lobby and my face completely out of control, I knew I had to try and pull what remained of myself back together and make an effort to deal with the present.

I stared at the little container the perfect-skinned man had given me, then Nkoyo gently took my arm and led me across the reception area to the far corner, presumably out of earshot.

I tried to listen to Nkoyo, after all it was a pleasant prospect even though she was old enough to be my mum, but I was being hugely over-stimulated by my environment. There was something about the reception area that was oddly familiar, I knew I'd never been in the space before but it had a kind of twenty-first-century feel about it. A huge glass wall all along one side looking out onto a small garden and beyond that, people. Crowds of people walking on some kind of street, there was colour and spectacle as if a special event was taking place, some kind of carnival, like they have in Venice.

The crowds all seemed to be walking in the same direction, I stood by the window staring at them, most of them tall and noticeably slender. I then noticed many children walking and jumping up and down excitedly and every race I'd ever seen was represented in their ranks.

Nkoyo touched my upper arm.

'I realise you might not be familiar with this system,' she said under her breath, 'but all you need do is swallow that.' She pointed to the glass container I was holding. Finally I managed to concentrate, I looked down at the small container in my hand, I say small because in terms of things you hold in your hand it was small, about the size of a triple A battery; in terms of things you swallow it was bloody enormous. I held it up in front of my face to make the point.

'Swallow this!' I said.

Nkoyo giggled. Although I really wasn't trying to find her attractive, the giggle was utterly enchanting.

'No, not the bottle, the kidonge,' she said pointing to the container. I looked at it more closely, inside was something a bit bigger than a grain of sand, it looked like a tiny drop of water, transparent but with a slight blue tinge.

'A what?' I asked.

'A kidonge,' said Nkoyo, 'it's your bit grip.'

'I wish I understood even some of what you're saying.'

'Okay, so you swallow that tiny thing. That's a kidonge.'

'A kidonge,' I said, trying to pronounce it correctly, it sounded like 'kidon-gay'.

'It will gently work its way into your system, most likely

 embedding into your bone marrow.'

'That doesn't sound good,' I said as another wave of alarm spread through me.

'It's completely benign, it will remain within you your entire life.'

I imagine Nkoyo stopped talking at that moment because of the expression on my out-of-control face, an expression close to abject horror. After a beat she continued. 'It's just a bit grip, it allows you to grip your bits.'

'I beg your pardon?'

'Your bits, your money,' she said. 'We all have them, usually we feed a kidonge to a small baby as soon as they take milk from a bottle but obviously you didn't…'

'So if I swallow this, I can buy things with my newly found millions, and if I don't, then I…'

'Well, you can't pay for anything and you'll wander around in those rags and slowly starve to death.'

I could not tell if she was joking or just stating a glaringly obvious fact.

I tried to open the tiny bottle by twisting the slight bulge at one end of it; however, I was already aware that it probably didn't open with a simple screw pattern moulded into the lip and lid, as would be the case in 2011. There was no obvious lid, it was just a small piece of transparent tube with closed ends.

'How do you open it?' I asked.

'You don't need to open anything, just put the end on your tongue,' said Nkoyo.

I opened my mouth, placed the flat end on my tongue and looked at her. She giggled again.

'Not that end, look, the end that's blue.'

I held the container up and inspected it again, as I slowly turned it I could see that one end was indeed slightly tinted blue. If you didn't know that, if you hadn't grown up knowing that all your life, I don't believe you'd ever notice the difference between the two ends. I say this because I want to point out I am fairly adaptable when it comes to new devices and materials, it's a realm I am familiar with but as I was constantly discovering in the new worlds I was exploring there was always something completely baffling waiting in the wings.

I put the blue end on my tongue and immediately felt a small sort of cold wormy thing in my mouth, it felt a bit weird as it wiggled about.

I swallowed and it was gone.

'Is that it?' I asked.

'That is it. I promise you won't die. I've had one my entire life, as does everyone else on earth, you'll soon forget you've even got it.'

'So this little thing I've just swallowed, it's like an electronic tagging system that communicates with remote devices and enables transactions between parties?'

Nkoyo looked a bit flummoxed. 'It's your grip. It keeps a grip on your bits, did they not have them in the place you came from?'

'Gardenia? No, they didn't use money, or bits or anything.'

'And did you not have something like them in, well, back in 2011?'

'No, we had cards and cash.'

Nkoyo repeated what I'd just said as if the words were magical. 'Cards and cash,' she shrugged. 'I don't know what that means.'

'Well, cash was money, like pieces of paper with numbers on them that represented their value.'

'I have seen pictures of sheets of money, I didn't know the word cash,' said Nkoyo.

'We also had online transfers, electronic payments, contact payments using smartphones.'

'Well, we don't have any of that,' said Nkoyo. 'I think it's a bit simpler now. You'll soon get used to it.'

Then I met Ralph.

What I was about to learn about Ralph would obviously stay with me, but the thing that struck me about him first was that he was so ridiculously tall. I'd hazard a guess he was over two meters tall, that's seven feet in old money.

'Ralph is going to take you shopping,' said Nkoyo as this lanky monster approached us across the perfect floor of the Institute's reception area.

This beanstalk of a man was wearing a bright yellow, skin-tight sort of body stocking and a large floppy mauve hat. At first I thought he was barefoot, but I could see as he approached that he had walking shoe soles attached to the bottom of his feet.

'Ralph, meet Gavin,' said Nkoyo.

The man held out a gangly yellow-clad arm that ended in long, spindly fingers. I shook his hand, a peculiar experience as his fingers where so long they reached right around to my wrist. Now I'm not trying to give the impression he was some kind of alien or genetic mutant, he was very human, just longer boned than anyone I had encountered previously. The other odd experience I had as I shook his hand was a slight feeling of emptiness, not pain or anything particularly unpleasant, just a kind of deflating slump in my belly.

'Nice to meet you, Ralph,' I said after a moment of confusion.

The tall man turned to Nkoyo. 'Oh Mungu, I'm so nervous.' Then he turned back to me, held my arms with his long spindly fingers and said 'I cannot easily believe what I know to be true, but it is wonderful to meet you Great, Great, Great, Great, Great Uncle Gavin.'

The silence that followed was very long. I suppose there was some kind of recognition going on, something familiar in his facial features, something about his hairline that looked, well, looked a bit like mine when I looked in a mirror. I knew if no one had given me a clue I would never have known I was in some way related to this man, but his description and obvious excitement was dizzying in its emotional impact.

'I don't wish to overwhelm you, Gavin,' said Nkoyo gently, 'but Ralph is the great, great, great, great, great grandson of your brother.'

Eventually I managed to speak. 'How do you do, Ralph,' I said. 'I think this is probably a very unusual experience for both of us.'

Ralph nodded slowly which in turn made it clear that his neck was freakishly long.

'Nkoyo contacted me yesterday, we did some checking through the family archives and found a picture of you and Giles, your brother.' At this point Ralph held up his hand and started to count off on his enormously long fingers. 'Giles was my great, great, great, great, great grandfather. You knew him.'

'Yes, I knew him,' I said. I didn't want to elaborate too much that Giles and I did not have much in common. In fact the biggest mystery to me was how two such utterly disparate individuals could possibly come from the same gene pool. Giles embodied the very essence of the sporting male. He played rugby, he talked about rugby, he watched rugby on television, he sang rugby songs, he was a little shorter but a great deal stronger than me. He drank copious amounts of beer, drove much too fast and blamed everyone else for anything that ever went wrong in his life.

When I had left Kingham back in 2011 Giles was single, working for Barclays Bank in Harlesden and nursing a knee injury he'd acquired playing rugby. As you may be able to discern, I didn't spend a lot of time with him.

'Oh yes, I knew Giles very well,' I said. 'Of course he didn't have children when I left in 2011.'

Ralph nodded solemnly. 'Correct, my three times great grandmother was born in 2014, she was your niece, my two times great grandfather was born in 2044, my great grandfather was born in 2069, my grandmother was born in 2097, my mother was born in 2135 and I was born in 2170.'

'Wow, you know your dates,' I said feeling duly impressed. Ralph glanced at Nkoyo for some explanation.

'I will explain later,' Nkoyo told me, 'but truly, it's not difficult for us to access such basic data.'

'I cannot wait to find out more,' said the spindly Ralph. 'In many ways, genealogy has replaced the religious illness of your era. We all want to know who we are by studying where we came from. I know about your family in great detail going back hundreds of years before you were born. Maybe one day we can find time to go over it together, but we have an altogether different task ahead of us today.'

'What task is that?' I asked, by now completely bamboozled by what he'd just explained to me.

'We are going to do some serious shopping my 5-G Uncle.'

'Ah yes, right,' I replied flatly.

Ralph stood back from me and looked up and down in a slightly over dramatic way while Nkoyo watched him, she was clearly enjoying this.

Ralph held his chin with his freakish hands and said, 'Can I just ask, quickly, and I don't mean to cause offence, but where did you get your drapery?'

I looked down at my simple Gardenian tunic and flat sensible footwear then back up at Nkoyo for guidance.

'It's okay, Ralph knows the entire situation,' she said.

'I know you're from two hundred years ago my friend,' said Ralph, 'but that get-up is something I've never seen in history logs and believe me, I've looked. If you want to know the history of drapery, I'm your source.'

'Oh, these aren't really my clothes.' I explained. 'I left my real clothes in Gardenia, I was given these.'

'Clothes,' said Ralph carefully. He was mimicking my delivery but I couldn't tell if he was taking the piss or just intrigued by the word.

'If I was given "clothes" like that, well, it would challenge my normally peaceable demeanour.'

Ralph proceeded to laugh at his own joke. I tried to laugh along but I don't think I was very convincing. I glanced at Nkoyo and she gave me a little nod that reminded me of nothing more than my mother encouraging me to 'join in' at a party or sporting event, something I'd never been terribly good at.

I took a deep breath.

'So, we're going shopping,' I said, 'and what are we buying?'

Again Ralph burst out laughing. 'Excellent!' he said. 'What are we buying? That is so funny.'

'We thought you might like to buy some drapery,' said Nkoyo kindly. 'If you wear . . .' she looked down at my outfit. 'Well, let's just say you may not want the attention such drapery might attract.'

'I'm not that crazy about clothes shopping,' I said. 'I buy everything online.'

Both Nkoyo and Ralph looked at me with completely blank expressions. Surely they didn't still have ugly great department stores and clothes factories in 2211? Surely I wouldn't have to try something on?

'I hope I understand you,' said Ralph, 'but clearly you've never been shopping in London, you'll have an excellent time.'

'Okay, let's get this over with,' I said feeling ever more despondent. I wanted to talk to Nkoyo about Africa, and mineral excavation and materials developments and I was going shopping for clothes, the one thing I truly hate doing.

8

Not Born to Shop

THE HEAT OF THE STREETS OF LONDON HIT me as I followed Ralph out of the Institute and down a smooth path away from the building. My eyes were feeling overloaded with what I was seeing, the experience was at the same time mundane and utterly overwhelming.

London was so unlike Gardenia it's hard to know where to start. All the time I was in Gardenia I felt I had time to consider what had happened and digest what I was learning. The pace was slow, the atmosphere was peaceful and time seemed to go on forever.

The streets, or maybe a more accurate description would be paths of London were anything but peaceful; they were vibrant with colour and spectacle. I am describing them as paths as there was no mechanical traffic of any sort in evidence, not even bicycles, everyone appeared to be walking.

Everywhere I looked I saw people in spectacular outfits and as we made our way along the wide path I realised that most of the truly spectacular outfits were adorning men.

If the auditorium where I'd burst into tears was full of women, the streets appeared to be the opposite. I was staring at the bizarre sights that confronted me as we made our way along the path. I was also very noticeably the focus of just as much staring back. People did double takes when they saw me, children pulled their father's hands and pointed as we passed them.

Before long I realised we had quite a crowd behind us, they all laughed and pointed and seemed quite happy and I noticed the gangly Ralph was lapping it up.

'This is my two-hundred-year-old 5-G Uncle Gavin and we are going shopping for drapes,' he announced. This raised a cheer from the steadily growing collection of onlookers.

After a few more paces I noticed we had been joined by two young women in something resembling a uniform. Not exactly a uniform but a dark costume that made them stand out from the crowds walking with us.

'Hello,' I said to one of them, she was an impressive young woman, well over two meters tall with broad shoulders and a walk that gave the impression of her being capable of looking after herself.

'Don't worry, Mister Meckler, we're just here for support,' she said without actually looking at me.

I didn't know at the time if they were police or security officers, they had that sort of standoffish authority and clearly the milling group around us kept their distance from these two Amazonian operatives.

I didn't feel intimidated by them, if anything they made me feel slightly safer as by the time we'd walked half a mile there was a substantial mob of excited people around us.

As I stared at people and buildings we passed, one thing became immediately apparent. The squares I had seen from the plane before I crash-landed were big. Not some recreation of a cutesy Georgian Square you might find in Bath, Kensington or Cheltenham. These were large open spaces surrounded by very large buildings, more like Central Park in Manhattan.

The Institute I'd been cooped-up in was one of many huge buildings along one side of the square. Above a line of trees in the square I could just make out buildings on the opposite side.

'So, tell me twenty-first-century Uncle, what you think of London?' said Ralph as we strode along – I was almost having to jog to keep up with him.

'It's impressive,' I said. 'Certainly not the city I remember.'

'It is spooky weird that you come from the way back when,'

 he said. 'Did all the horses really smell?'

'The horses?'

'You'll have to forgive me, Uncle, I love history but I've never been good at dates. Wasn't old London full of horses pulling things and women not being allowed to vote?'

'That was a bit before my time,' I said; I couldn't help smiling. 'Like, my great grandparents' time. I'm from 2011, cars, taxis, buses, trucks, trains, planes, smartphones, space travel, women prime ministers, we had all that.'

I realised as I was saying this that I was in some ways defending my era, I wanted him to know I didn't come from the Victorian age and that my era was fairly technologically and socially advanced.

'Oh right, the Beatles,' said Ralph.

'No, even the Beatles were before my time. I was born in 1979, the Beatles split up ten years before I was born.'

'I'm sorry,' said Ralph with a wave of his spindly arms. 'I've got no idea of dates, now you're going to think I'm really stupid.'

'Not at all,' I reassured him. I was lying; I had already decided that who-knows-how-many-G nephew Ralph was a bit of an air-head. I felt bad about that notion and added, 'If I'd met someone from two hundred years before I was born, I wouldn't have a clue what their lives were really like.'

We turned a corner and once again I was chilled to my roots. There in front of me on a raised plinth was a statue I recognised. It was the Shaftesbury memorial; better known as Eros, the statue that used to be in Piccadilly Circus. I stopped and looked around for telltale geographic references, maybe this actually was Piccadilly Circus? The surrounding buildings were unfamiliar, no graceful curve of Regent Street, no ugly video wall promoting soft drinks, economy diesel cars and cameras. The path we were walking on was lined with neat trees that reminded me of Parisian parks but the small, instantly recognisable statue really jumped out at me.

'You okay Uncle?' asked Ralph, who had continued walking while I stood glued to the spot. The two possible policewomen had stopped with me and turned to gently control the now enormous gathering behind us. They just watched me in silence and obvious fascination. They all seemed to know who I was.

'I'm fine,' I said to Ralph who walked back to join me. 'It's just that I recognise that statue, it used to be in the middle of London.'

'Well it still is,' said Ralph, 'pretty much, this is the middle of London.'

'But I thought London had flooded, and anyway aren't we near Didcot?'

'Didcot Mews?' asked Ralph, clearly puzzled. 'That's over the other side of Berners Lee Place, where the Institute is. Is that what you mean?'

I shook my head. 'It doesn't matter.'

We carried on walking across the wide-open space of what I took to be the intersection of four squares. Clearly this area was very popular with the many thousands of Londoners all around me; either that or they had all gathered to see me, I wasn't sure which. As we neared the statue Ralph stopped and looked up at it.

'Is that statue really old then? I've never bothered to look at it. It's always been there.'

'It was really old when I was born, so it's really, really old now.'

'Amazing, I love old stuff,' said Ralph and without further thought carried on walking.

'There's a little shop over here you are absolutely going to love,' he said when I caught up with him. 'My friend will be thrilled to drape you up.'

We walked past some cafés with tables outside, the customers stood up as they noticed us approaching and stared and waved at me. I waved back feeling more and more embarrassed. I noticed there were no signs above the establishments, nothing on the building that would indicate it was a café, just tables on a flat area in front of the building and some smartly-dressed waitresses dashing about with trays laden with food and drink. They were human waitresses, all women, not bizarre wheeled robots as I'd seen in Mumbai.

Ralph turned into a large opening in a building next to the café. I followed him inside and entered a cool hallway which was a timely way of being reminded of just how hot it was outside. I also felt a very faint kind of tummy chill as we entered, not altogether unpleasant but a noticeable feeling.

The entrance hall to wherever we were going was very wide with a high ceiling, at the far end an impressive flight of stairs. I say impressive because they were the sort of stairs you might see in somewhere like Blenheim Palace. Ralph's long legs bounded up the stairs with little effort, I did my best to keep up with him. When I got to the top I noticed the enormous crowd who had been following us had remained outside with the two possible police women.

At the top of the stairs was yet another high ceilinged atrium. Around the sides of this aircraft hanger scale hexagonal space were small rooms festooned with colourful cloth, furniture items and beautiful ornaments. The air was thick with an invigorating spicy aroma; it felt posh, inviting and I was definitely feeling stimulated in some way.

'Here we go,' said Ralph, jumping up and down on the spot – a man who had to be well over two meters tall, bouncing up and down like a three-year-old who's been taken to a sweet shop.

Ralph walked into one of the rooms leading off the central space where he was immediately embraced by an equally tall African man.

The two enormous men turned to me.

Ralph said, 'This is my 5-G Uncle Gavin, will you look at what he's wearing! The poor little chappy needs serious assistance.'

The African man struck a pose, a comical, camp pose with one hand on his hip, a finger to his lips and his eyes goggling as he looked me up and down.

'Carnage,' he said.

'Agreed,' said Ralph with an over-the-top laugh. To describe myself as uncomfortable in this moment is a substantial understatement. I had two slightly absurdly dressed and overly tall men denigrating the clothes given to me by the truly wonderful people of Gardenia. More accurately given to me by Grace. I could feel myself getting angry, I wanted to berate them for being so shallow. The men of Gardenia had moved on from such bitchy generalised observations, if this was an alternate future, I decided I preferred the original.

'That is Akiki,' said Ralph as the shop owner disappeared behind a beautiful curtain hanging across the space. 'This is his shop, you are going to love shopping here, and Akiki is soooo funny.'

I smiled through my pain.

'You don't think he's funny?'

'I'm sorry, Ralph, I don't know what to think.'

Ralph sat down on what appeared to be a huge pile of fabric, alarmingly his head was now nearer my eye line.

'I can see you're not enjoying it and I feel bad about that. Please just relax, we'll get you some nice drapes and then go and have a coffee and talk it over.'

Akiki re-emerged with a small white object in his hands. He pointed it at me quite casually and I heard a familiar chime sound, the sort of sound a smartphone makes when it's received a text message.

Akiki looked at the white object, raised one eyebrow and glanced at me.

'Nice,' he said. He then sat down behind a low table and picked up a large book made up of samples of cloth.

'I think dark to contrast with the pallid don't you, Ralphy baby. Dark dark dark.'

'Dark sounds good to me. He'd look swell in dark.'

'Dark it is.' Akiki brushed his hand over the fabric and pushed the large sample book across the desk toward me.

'Just feel that,' he said. 'Feel the quality of the weave my friend, is it not truly wonderful?'

I did as he suggested and indeed, the cloth felt very smooth and warm to the touch. It looked to my untrained eye like a dark tweedy sort of stuff. I wanted to ask about how it was made, where the raw materials came from, who wove the cloth. It was completely different to anything I'd seen before, a much finer weave than anything I'd seen in Gardenia.

Akiki turned to Ralph, suddenly speaking much faster.

'I've been trying this stuff out, it's a totally new weave, a totally fabulous weave.' He glanced up at me. 'Very hardwearing, you'll probably never have to buy anything else, so, what do we say. Yes to dark?'

Both men looked at me.

'Yes to dark,' I said hoping this was the right thing to say. This received whoops of approval and Ralph gave me a powerful hug.

Using the same white object he'd pointed at me, Akiki pointed at the sample in the book. Another semi-familiar beep sound emerged.

'Oh let him see the printer,' said Ralph who then winked at me surprisingly discreetly. 'He's never seen one like yours before.'

Akiki leaned back in his low chair and pulled a curtain to one side with his quite ridiculously long arm. Behind the curtain was a fridge-sized white box and as Akiki turned toward it the front opened in a way I was becoming used to. Essentially the door, if you can call it that, folded away somehow revealing quite complex machinery inside which was moving around at such high speed the many components were a blur to the human eye.

'My printer,' said Akiki gesturing toward it in a theatrical fashion. 'This little chappie is the kipaji.'

'What's it doing?' I asked, intrigued by the fantastically fast mechanism working silently away in the white box.

'Making your drapes,' said Ralph quietly.

Sure enough, about ten seconds later the machinery stopped and a table slid out from beneath the box. On it, neatly folded was what I assumed was some kind of garment. It was dark just as they had suggested.

Akiki picked it up, shook it out and I could see at once it was like a kind of wetsuit or an all-in-one body stocking. I also knew after one glance that I couldn't wear it, it was the sort of thing a mime artist or a ballet dancer might wear on stage.

'Try it on,' said Ralph, he was clearly enjoying this, and I totally failed to see why.

'Really?'

'You don't like?' asked Akiki, he looked mildly offended.

'Well, it's not what I'm used to.'

'But this is the karibuni mtindo,' he said holding the weird-shaped garment in front of me. I looked to Ralph for help, a pointless move as he was just nodding and grinning.

'I don't know what that means,' I said. 'I just don't think I'd feel comfortable wearing it.'

This clearly upset Akiki, he pulled his head back and stared at me, he was tall and bald and rather angry.

'My weave is the finest, the smoothest, the best. You will feel completely naked wearing my drapery, that's how good it is.'

He pushed the garment at me and I felt obliged to take it.

'Try it on brother,' he commanded.

'Okay,' I sighed, 'where's the changing room?'

The two men looked at each other. Ralph looked at me.

'The changing room?' he said slowly, making the term sound completely different. 'I don't know, is it a café?'

'No,' I explained, 'I mean the small room where you try clothes on.' Their expressions remained blank.

'Where I come from all clothes shops have a room, a special small room where you can try things on. In private.'

'Where do you come from?' asked Akiki.

'He's from out of town,' said Ralph quickly. He looked at me with almost comical fury. 'Just take off the slack garbage you're wearing and try it on.'

'Okay!' I protested and then and there, in the small shop off a large and busy atrium full of people, I took off my Gardenian clothes while trying to ignore the fact that I was completely naked in a semi-public space.

As I started to try and clamber into the bizarre cloth construction I'd been handed I felt angrier and angrier. I had been duped into being naked, these two very tall and possibly homosexual men were humiliating me and having a laugh at my expense. This was all just so wrong.

'Out of town?' asked Akiki. 'Out of his tiny skull more like.'

He took the garment away from me and I stood with my hands covering my genitals. Neither man seemed in the least uncomfortable at my nakedness and I watched carefully as Akiki pinched part of the garment around the collar area and then threw it toward me.

At that moment my body registered some of the most peculiar feelings it has ever experienced. The cloth kind of wrapped itself around me; this feeling was most disconcerting in the nether regions. Not exactly unpleasant, just like nothing I'd ever experienced before.

'Oh my God,' I said. 'What's it doing?'

But by the time I said that it had done it, it had engulfed me, I was wrapped. The garment, I have no other word to describe it, fitted like a skin, a skin you couldn't feel. I looked down at myself, I could not believe I wasn't naked, I couldn't actually feel it on me and yet I could sense I was warmer than when I actually had been verifiably naked only seconds before.

'Wow, that is utterly amazing,' I said as I wriggled around in my new, dark-coloured, slightly tweedy skin.

Akiki's face lit up, a massive toothy grin replaced the rather terrifying scowl.

'I knew you'd appreciate my weave. It's the best you can get my brother.'

'It feels so weird,' I said. 'I can't tell I'm wearing anything, is that how it's meant to feel?'

'Yes, that's how it's meant to feel,' said Ralph, he grinned at Akiki. 'He'll take it.'

I was stroking my hands up and down my flanks, in other circumstances this action could be construed as a little bit pervy, but somehow this skin coat just needed to be stroked. It felt like cloth, very finely woven cloth the like of which I had never felt before. Then I registered what Ralph had just said. Of course, I had to pay for this weird body stocking.

'How much is it?' I asked.

'What is he saying now?' asked Akiki, looking confused and possibly a little angry again.

'How many bits is it? How many Kwo have I got to give you in order to own this?' I said slapping my thighs, hoping my explanation would clarify matters.

'Thirty,' said Akiki.

'Thirty!' said Ralph indignantly. 'That's daylight robbery my friend. I have bought this poor badly dressed little man here exclusively, just to see you Akiki. We have not even looked elsewhere have we, Uncle Gavin.'

I shook my head, of all the things I expected to do when I was shopping in London in 2211, I don't think bartering was on my list.

'We came straight to you, I told Uncle Gavin, we will go to see my good friend Akiki, he is a good man and will not try to take you for a fool.'

'Twenty-five,' said Akiki.

There was a short pause, I shrugged. 'Sounds good to me.'

Akiki held out his hand, I reached over his desk and shook it. I then felt a slight slump in my belly, I couldn't pin down the feeling, it was very subtle but I felt a bit sad and empty, just for a moment.

I stood back from Akiki's low desk and noticed Ralph slap his forehead. 'Oh, you have a lot to learn my friend,' he said, rubbing his face with both hands.

Akiki then handed me a rather nicely shaped bag made of a similar material to my body skin garment.

'For your old rags,' he said with a big grin. 'Please don't leave them here, if my customers see those lying about I could lose major business.'

I stuffed my much-besmirched Gardenian clothes into the bag and pulled on my now very crude-looking Gardenian shoes.

'Okay, so how do I pay you?' I asked, looking up from my struggles with Gardenian bootstraps. Again the two men looked at me quizzically.

'You already have,' said Akiki who quickly turned to Ralph. 'Where is this man from, Venus?'

Ralph laughed, bid a hasty farewell and quickly ushered me out of Akiki's small emporium.

'I think going for a coffee now would be a very good idea,' I said as I caught up with him, we walked across the huge atrium through crowds of people who, unlike when we arrived, didn't give me a second look.

'I have no idea what just happened,' I said, 'I thought you had to buy stuff in London, how do I pay him? I don't want to get into trouble.'

Ralph stopped at the top of the enormous flight of stairs and turned to face me. 'Listen, Uncle Gavin. My friend. Next time, please let me arrange the shopping, you have paid way over the odds for your drapes. You paid when you shook hands, do you really not know that?'

'When I shook hands!' I said incredulously. 'But I shook hands with you when we met, does that mean I've paid you too?'

'Only a small facility fee because you're family, what did you expect, that I look after you for free?'

We descended the stairs and I felt another small depression hit me, it seemed to be located in my belly, or my solar plexus, some kind of deflationary feeling I'd never had before. I put it down to the realisation that I had left the most benign, gentle and evolved world and somehow returned to one that seemed crueller, harder and based yet again on money, on transactions, profit, competition and greed.

I suddenly felt supremely stupid wearing the one-piece tweedy type super lightweight body stocking thing. I wanted to be wearing a thick pair of chinos and a polo shirt.

I looked down at my body, I had to keep doing so because it was informing me I was in a public place with nothing on.

Ralph walked quickly when we reached the street level. I followed him, chewing over my feelings in a way I knew I never did back in 2011. The crowds had dispersed, but after a while I noticed the two smartly dressed possible policewomen were walking a good distance behind us. I did register that people glanced at me as I walked along but there certainly wasn't the rather feverish crowd following us in the way they had on our initial outing to the shops. However, even without the entourage, I wasn't feeling comfortable and I didn't feel in control, it was like I was in the middle of an argument with Beth, but there wasn't anyone to argue with, and I still knew I was losing the battle.

We turned a corner and I was faced with another enormous square, the centre of which looked like a forest. However, what marked this one as different from anything I'd seen in London up to that point was the truly vast building at the far end from where I was standing. This was more like the buildings I'd seen in Beijing in 2211. I don't know how high this building was exactly, but it was easily twice the height of any structure existing back in 2011.

'What's that place?' I asked, pointing to the colossal structure.

'Marie Curie tower,' he said without much thought, 'I would have thought you'd already seen it, this is the square you crashed your drone.'

'Is it!' I said. 'Where's the power-field, where did the cloud appear? You know, the cloud I flew out of before I crashed.'

Ralph stopped and looked at me. 'I don't know,' he said with more than a hint of annoyance, then waved his long spindly fingers towards the trees in the square. 'Somewhere over there there's some kind of powery business.'

He turned and walked on towards an extensive outdoor café under a delightful collection of large manicured beech trees.

We entered the area and made our way between hundreds of people sitting at dozens of tables. The place looked packed, I assumed Ralph was looking for an available space.

'Let's sit here.'

Somehow Ralph had walked across the vast café seating area and found a table where a small party of people were leaving as we approached. It was busy and noisy, I couldn't have hoped to be able to tell who was leaving or who was arriving. Ralph clearly knew the ropes.

'So, what goes on in Marie Curie tower?' I asked.

Ralph shrugged and a waitress appeared at our table carrying two stainless steel cups.

'Hi, Ralph,' she said. 'Two flat whites?'

'Spot on, Annie, and I really need a sweet bake.'

'A plate of bakes coming right at you,' said the waitress. She left as quickly as he arrived.

'The bakes they do here,' said Ralph sitting back and sunning himself. 'They are utterly to live for.'

I put my bag of Gardenian clothes down beside me and leant on the table.

'Look, Ralph, I'm not keeping up. I've just spent four months living in the most peaceful place the human race has ever conceived, and now I'm suddenly in this mad house.'

'It's not a mad house – it's London,' said Ralph, he was clearly slightly offended.

I pressed on, 'I need some explanation, Ralph. I need to understand what's going on here? Why are we in a café and it's mostly men and kids, what do people do?'

Ralph looked around the surrounding tables. He shrugged again. 'A lot of men with little kids meet up here after they've taken older kids to school, or they drop in on their way shopping or to playgroups and stuff.'

'Wait,' I said holding up my palms. 'You mean men have kids? Men give birth?'

'What?' Now Ralph looked genuinely confused. 'Did men give birth in the olden days?'

'No!'

'How can men give birth? What are you talking about?'

'Well where are all the women?' I asked. While there certainly where some women in the busy café, they were mostly either very old or very young, and they were in the minority.

'Working,' stated Ralph, as though it were the most obvious thing in the world.

'Right, so women give birth, but...'

'Men bring up kids. Is that different to your time?'

'Um, yes, like massively,' I said.

'So who raised the children?'

'Women, mothers, they did mothering.'

'Ooh,' said Ralph as though I'd just said something vaguely rude. 'Was that healthy?'

'I don't know, it's just, well, it's different, I mean a lot of women worked as well, but it was always seen as a woman's job to raise and nurture the children.'

'What did the men do all day?'

'Work. Well, the ones who had jobs worked,' I said as I started to remember the complex realities of my own time. 'There was a lot of unemployment to.'

'What was that for?'

'Sorry,' I said, confused once again. 'What d'you mean "what was it for"?'

'The unployment thing you mentioned,' said Ralph, clearly having difficulty with the unfamiliar word.

'Unemployment, it meant there were a lot of people who

 couldn't get a job, it was all a bit of a mess I suppose.'

'So the men who were ployed worked and the women looked after kids, is that why women couldn't vote?'

'No! What? Well, yes, but that was long before, look, women could vote, work, have children and everything, but generally it was men who worked and women who looked after kids. Not always, but generally.'

'Okay,' said Ralph. 'Well now, in London, it's mostly women who work, men look after kids and run homes.'

'So wait, when I met the panel of women who interviewed me, Nkoyo and all those rather fierce-looking women, who were they?'

'I don't know,' said Ralph. 'I wasn't there was I. Probably just bureaucrats and officials.'

'But they were all women.'

'So?'

'You mean, like, do women sort of, well, do they run the place?'

Ralph sighed very deeply and continued to stare at me.

'You do ask the weirdest questions, Gavin.'

The waitress returned with a plate covered with bizarre looking baked things.

'Help yourself,' said Ralph. 'This is just about the best place for bakes in the whole of London.'

They were of uniform shape, like small purple padded envelopes, I watched Ralph demolish one in a mouthful, I bit the corner of another, worried it might be like a mouth burning fast food 'apple pie' type product, mass produced in some factory and full of additives and E-numbers.

It was surprisingly delicious and wholesome, I got flavours of strawberries, rhubarb, some kind of subtle herby thing and the pastry itself was divine.

'Pretty good,' I said. 'But of course this…' I held up the half eaten pastry thing in front of me, 'just raises loads more questions. Where does it come from? Who makes it? How are they paid? Where do the basic ingredients come from? How does the economic system work, do you still have banks, is there an investment infrastructure?'

Ralph looked at me as a man might look at a slightly annoying barking terrier.

'You'll have to ask a woman, all that stuff is so boring,' he said eventually.

'Okay, well surely you can tell me what you do, how do you earn money, I mean bits, Kwo?'

'You don't know?'

'How would I know?' I asked incredulously, noticing a particle of pastry fly out of my mouth as I spoke.

'You just know, we all know.'

'How do you know?'

'What, I don't even know what you're asking, I'm a worder, I write, everyone knows that.'

'How do they know? Are you famous or something?' I was trying to remember if people were actually looking at Ralph as he walked down the street, they all seemed to be looking at me when we first set out. He certainly didn't get the reaction you might have expected from someone like Tom Cruise or the Dalai Lama.

'Famous!' said Ralph, he laughed. 'No, I'm not famous, everyone knows because they just do. It's, well, it's in your grip, I suppose you don't know how to feel it.'

'My grip?'

'You'll have to ask someone else, I don't know how all that stuff works. It just does.'

'I should ask a woman,' I suggested. 'Is that what you're saying?'

Ralph grinned a bit like a thirteen-year-old and nodded, 'Best to.'

'Okay, the power-field, the big open area,' I said nodding my head in the direction of the field I had appeared above. 'What happens there?'

'It's just the power-field, there's loads of them, they do power. I don't know.'

'Ask a woman?'

Another nod, this one less interested.

'Okay, Ralph,' I said, feeling ever more flattened by my hopeless quest for information. 'What do you write about? You must be able to explain that.'

'Restaurants, clothes, shoes – which reminds me, we have to get you some proper shoes, those look like old sacks strapped to your feet, it's humiliating having you walk around in those.'

'Are you gay?' I asked, I thought it was about time and I wasn't in the mood to hang around and try and guess.

'I'm very happy most of the time,' he said.

'Oh, right, you don't use that term any more, well, are you a homosexual?'

This time Ralph's laugh was so explosive he spat coffee all over the pastries.

'You ask the best questions!' he squealed, mopping his mouth with a large handkerchief he produced from his absurdly tight clothing. From another area of his ridiculous body suit he produced a small squashed up ball of some kind of material, it was about the size of a marble. He put it on the table in front of me and it opened up to be a little bigger than a sheet of A4 paper. A crystal clear picture emerged as I looked at it, a picture of Ralph standing next to a rather severe-looking woman and a girl of about twelve years old. I glanced up at him, my mouth open.

'My wife and daughter,' he said. 'Let's go and buy shoes!'

The waitress who served us appeared as soon as we stood up. 'Enjoy your bakes?' she asked. I told her I did and she held out her hand, not palm up as if she were expecting a tip, straightforward as if she was expecting me to shake it. I shook hands, I didn't know what else to do. As I did so again I felt a tiny kind of slump in my belly. I felt myself breath out as if I'd just jumped off a low wall and landed heavily.

‘Thanks,’ I said as we moved away from the table.

‘Come again soon,’ she replied and immediately started clearing our table.

I tottered along behind the striding form of Ralph as we passed through another place surrounded by wonderful tall buildings and then into another square, this one was very different to the squares I’d seen previously. Instead of open space it was covered in a massive tiered structure in that I assumed was a multi-storey garden of some sort. The best description I can come up with is that it looked like a multi-storey car park overflowing with greenery.

‘That’s amazing,’ I said. ‘What’s going on there?’

‘Covent Garden,’ said Ralph with little interest, ‘where stuff comes from.’

‘What sort of stuff, food?’

‘Yeah, food, it’s a garden, you must have had gardens in the olden days.’

‘Yeah, we did, but they didn’t look like that.’

I stared up at the construction. I counted eight floors, each one high enough to house fairly large trees. Once again the scale of the endeavour was mind numbing; it wasn’t so much the height, it was the massive footprint of the place, one structure that had to cover many hundreds of acres. From where I was standing on the path, I couldn’t make out the far end, it disappeared into the heat haze. It must have been several kilometres long.

Ralph turned into an opening in a building facing the Covent Garden Square and I followed. This time we descended a flight of stairs and entered a room with many people working on a variety of mysterious machines, there were hundreds of boxes piled up on tables and intriguing hoppers suspended from the ceiling. The room was dark and incredibly full of equipment, it was also very warm.

Okay, it was uncomfortably hot and I noticed the people working in it, mostly women, were sweating profusely.

 'Take those rag bags off, Uncle G, and stand over there.'

I undid my Gardenian boots and stood up, Ralph held my shoulders and pushed me gently forward, I looked down to see I was standing on a black square thing set in the floor, it had a faint grid etched into the material.

'Just stand up straight and choose your shoes,' he said into my ear.

In front of me, not on a screen, just appearing in front of me floating in space, an image of my right foot appeared. It wasn't an image, that term does the system no justice; it was just the same as looking at my foot, only much bigger. The reason I knew it was my right foot was because of the quite pronounced mole I have on the arch, I wriggled my toes a little and there, right in front of my eyes the massive toes wriggled about at the same time. Somehow the light around me had been excluded as though a thick curtain had been pulled around me, but if I turned my head to the side the image disappeared and I was back in the cramped and noisy room.

A series of soles then appeared under my foot, each one staying for a few seconds before rendering into another design. One appeared that looked something like a moulded sole I recognised, like the sort of thing you'd get on a lightweight walking shoe, essentially what I'd been wearing when I landed in Gardenia.

I missed those shoes; they were still in my beautiful room at Goldacre Hall. Annoyingly I started thinking about my shoes, I ignored what was going on in front of my eyes. If Goldacre Hall no longer existed, if it was just a possible future I'd seen, what had happened to my shoes which were, after all, solid objects from a period of time that really had existed. What had happened to my phone and iPad, my wallet, credits cards, money? Had they just evaporated? Slipped through a gap in time? It was bonkers. I had to stop thinking about it.

I tried to look at the image of my foot again; it was now showing my foot as if I was standing on my toes, this time with a woman's high heel design underneath. As if I was going to wear them! Eventually it returned to something that looked like a shoe sole I might consider, a moulded, grippy looking affair.

'Oh, I like that one,' I said to Ralph, I assumed he was still standing behind me but when I turned around I saw him sitting on a low chair at the far end of the room. I turned back, expecting to see another sole under my massive right foot but the same one was still there, and now a series of straps were appearing around my foot. They all looked really useless, like dainty strappy things you'd see on a woman's evening shoe.

I said nothing. I didn't know how to interact with whatever it was I was looking at.

Slowly, the designs that appeared at regular intervals started to cover more of my foot until one appeared that was the nearest thing to a trainer I'd seen.

'I like that one,' I said quickly in case I missed it. 'That one, that's the one I like.'

'You are most welcome, sir,' said a voice behind me. I turned around to see a woman looking up at me, she was really short and for some reason I immediately took to her. She had a lovely, friendly Indian face and a big smile.

'Oh, hi, I'm Gavin,' I said. 'I've come to buy some shoes.'

'I know,' she said with a kind smile. 'You are the man from the cloud. It is an honour to meet you, sir.'

'Oh, thank you,' I said. She turned around and opened a door on another box, this one less like a fridge, it was a dark blue coffin-sized contraption with a series of large hoppers mounted along the top. It was making more noise too, very recognisable mechanical noises and it shook slightly as it did whatever it was doing.

It was only then I noticed the short woman had picked up a pair of shoes in exactly the style I'd just said I liked in the weird 3D thing I'd been looking at.

'You are most welcome, sir,' she said as she raised the shoes up almost like some kind of religious offering.

'Um, thanks,' I said and took the shoes from her as graciously as I could, they were much lighter than I'd imagined and I was about to inspect them when the short woman held out her hand, so I shook it and felt the now more familiar deflated tummy feeling.

The short woman gave me a big smile. 'Thank you most kindly, sir, and welcome to London.'

She then turned around and sat behind a box, surrounded by footwear components of all types, sheets of material and numerous small, bench mounted tools the purpose of which was completely beyond me.

I joined Ralph on the low seat.

'That's what you chose?' asked Ralph picking up my new shoes. 'Gardening boots?'

'They're not gardening boots,' I said. 'They're sort of trainers.'

I took the new shoes from Ralph but then realised I had no idea how to put them on. I tried to push my toes into the ankle opening, there were no laces, buckles, Velcro or any form of fastening that I could see.

'Put them down on the floor, Uncle G,' said Ralph with more than a hint of impatience in his tone. I did so, and the shoes suddenly looked like some kind of bizarre sea anemone, the material of the uppers went soft, it looked like it was melting, but it quickly wrapped itself around my feet and turned back into the original design.

'That is sick,' I said as I watched the process take place.

'What?' asked Ralph who was now clearly bored by my fascination. 'How else do you put shoes on?'

'Well, we used to have to pull them on and lace them up.'

'I don't know what you're talking about,' said Ralph. 'How much were they?'

'What?'

'The shoes. How much did she say?'

'She didn't,' I said.

Ralph sat back with his long spindly fingers covering his face.

'Oh no, you shook hands didn't you,' he said, his voice muffled by his fingers.

'Well, I didn't know what else to do.'

'I told you not to negotiate, I told you to leave it to me, oh brak. It's too late now. Hang on.'

Ralph stood up and went over to the tiny Indian woman who'd sold me the shoes, I saw him gesticulate a bit, the woman continued to smile and Ralph returned shaking his head.

'You are one lucky man,' he said. 'She says you are the man from the cloud, she saw you talking yesterday and thought you were a nice man, she's given you a discount. They're only 15 Kwo.'

'Oh, was she at the news conference?' I asked.

'No you dooz, no, she saw you.'

I shrugged, I didn't know what he meant, I guessed he meant some kind of television.

'Is 15 Kwo cheap for a pair of shoes?' I asked.

'It's close to free, even for big, galumphing ugly gardening boots.'

I stood up and walked in a small circle in the shoes, they fitted amazingly well. I could barely feel them, they were so light and yet still supportive. I knew pretty quickly that these were the very best shoes I had ever worn.

'It's like they were made for me,' I said.

'Well who else would they be made for?' asked Ralph, he waved at the small Indian woman and we left the dark space and returned to the glaring sunlight of the square.

'I don't know, but as soon as I'd said I liked them she held them up in front of me. I suppose I thought she had some on a shelf or something.'

'They make shoes, they made your shoes while you were umming and arring. Why did you think I took you there, for the good of my health? They are famous for being the fastest shoe shop in this part of London.'

We continued walking along the path beside the massive,

multi-storey garden, every now and then I noticed people working in the various floors. The people working seemed to be mainly women.

I knew then, as I trotted behind the enormous striding form of Ralph, this London was going to take some getting used to.

9

A Unique Yuneec

ON MY FOURTH DAY IN LONDON, PETE SHOWED up at my door early one morning. He told me he had permission to take me to see what was left of the Yuneec in his storeroom.

'You have permission?' I queried. 'Who needs to give you permission?'

Pete froze for a moment, we both stood looking at each other in silence, I think I was trying to work out if he needed permission because he was a bit of a nutter and was under some kind of twenty-third-century supervision order, or if I was considered to be a bit of a nutter and had to be managed in a similar way.

'I asked Nkoyo,' he said. 'Hasn't she told you?'

'Told me what? Am I under arrest or something?'

Again Pete froze, he stood looking at me with his enormous mouth open.

'What is "under arrest"?'

'Sorry?'

'What are you saying?' asked Pete. 'I don't get it.'

'Am I a prisoner?'

'No,' he said eventually. 'But I had to ask permission.'

That didn't leave me any the wiser on this particular issue but by now I was learning the ways of the Squares, so I checked if this was going to cost me anything.

'Do we have to shake hands?' I asked.

'Not unless you want to,' said Pete, he looked a little crestfallen which then made me worry if it was possible to shake hands without transferring vast amounts of Kwo.

'I mean, do I need to pay you for your time or anything?'

'Pay me? No, I just thought you might want to see your drone, I've been working on it.'

'Have you?' My interest was suddenly piqued and I ignored his incorrect description. 'Oh blimey, well, yes, I'd like to see what you've done.'

I followed Pete down the corridor and the two flights of stairs, along another long corridor and into the reception hall.

'We're just going to see Gavin's drone,' said Pete to the man with the unrealistic skin. The man nodded and the huge sliding doors opened.

Walking along with Pete in my new shoes was much easier than trying to keep up with Ralph. Pete was tall but on a scale I was more used to and he didn't walk quite as fast.

'How far is your store room?' I asked.

'Not far, about ten minutes,' said Pete who then turned into a building on the corner I had failed to notice when I walked past it with Ralph. I knew what it was. I didn't understand how I knew, I just knew.

As we descended a wide flight of stairs, many people were coming up the other way. This time it seemed to be mainly women, their faces as serious as their dress code. None of them gave me a second look. It wasn't as if I expected them to give me a second look, but clearly I didn't stand out as I had done the first time I ventured out of the Institute.

At the foot of the stairs was a glass barrier, the crowd of people coming the other way put their hands on the doors as the approached, the doors then slid open at great speed. I followed Pete who put his hand on the door and passed through, I did the same, the door opened at the same time as I felt the very slight, but now familiar slump sensation in the belly.

I'd worked it out, when I paid for something there was a very subtle physiological reaction, at that point I hadn't been paid so I didn't know what would happen if I ever received a payment.

Once past the doors we were in a very wide corridor, there were stalls selling food and drink either side, all very brightly lit and colourful.

At the far end of the corridor was an array of glass doors that went on as far as I could see. It literally disappeared into a haze, thousands of people coming and going, some waiting by doors, some chatting with each other.

Pete stood by one of the hundreds of glass doors and put his hand on a circular motif etched into the glass. A moment later something white appeared the other side of the glass. It wasn't like some kind of magic mirage, it was a solid object that moved so fast and stopped so suddenly that to my old world eyes it simply appeared out of nowhere.

The door we were standing by slid open silently and Pete moved inside the white object that had an adjacent door already open. It was full of seats, a semi-circle of seats around a central pole. I entered the space and sat down opposite Pete, as soon as I did a white, padded, curved bar emerged from the seat and moved around my waist as another bar appeared across my right shoulder and clicked itself securely into the lap bar. It was a very simple automatic seat belt, nicely padded and not in the least constricting.

At the same time the doors slid shut silently and immediately the thing we were in started to accelerate at sports car speed. There was no warning and very little noise associated with this rapid increase in momentum.

'What the hell is this?' I asked.

'We're just getting the car over to my store,' said Pete. 'We could have walked but Nkoyo suggested we take a car, she said you'd paid for it which is very nice, thank you. I don't use them much, bit expensive for me. Rich chap like you could use them all the time.'

'This is a car?' I asked, as I peered out of the windows. We were on some kind of underground motorway, many other vehicles like the one we were in were zipping this way and that beside us, we seemed to have joined a very fast moving convoy that was constantly adapting, taking in more vehicles and loosing others that seemed to zoom off down side tunnels.

These transportation systems didn't feel like tunnels, like long narrow tubes, this was a vast, wide network of roadways, it was well lit, I'm not sure if there was a ceiling but if there was it was above my field of view, it was just like travelling along an urban motorway at night, brightly lit with a dark sky above.

Just as suddenly as we'd joined this frantic chaos of movement we slowed, turned a corner at neck-aching speed and pulled to a stop with just bearable violence. The seat belts retracted and the doors immediately slid open and we were in another, equally busy space, many people walking about, some maybe waiting for one of these cars. As we left the roomy interior a family of three entered the same car, the doors closed and off it zoomed.

'Come on then,' said Pete who I then realised was waiting for me as I stared around.

'That is amazing, does the system cover the whole city?'

'Yep, although if you want to go to the far North, South, West or East you'd be better off on a train.'

'Oh, you have trains?'

'Yeah, what d'you think, we walk two hundred K?'

I followed Pete up another flight of stairs, no sign of anything resembling an escalator but then everyone I saw around me seemed very fit. People ran up the stairs and although I like to think of myself as in relatively good shape by the time I got to the top I was actively pretending not to be puffed out. I didn't want people thinking I was out of condition because no one else seemed in the least bit stressed by the effort. Even an old lady I noticed seemed to be bounding up the stairs like an old goat and she had some kind of bag on her back.

We emerged into another open space; this one had enormous buildings dotted around its leafy centre, some many hundreds of meters in height.

'Wow, London seems to be one very big city,' I said.

'Yeah, quite big,' said Pete.

'How many people live here?' I asked as we crossed the open space that formed a neat junction between the four enormous squares around us.

'In the whole city?' asked Pete, I nodded. 'I have no idea, around seventy million?'

'Really? Seventy million people in one city? No, surely it's not possible. How on earth can that work?'

'We all chip in,' was the only response I got to my question. I suddenly felt all the questions I'd thought about since I arrived in London were about to burst out. I had to use enormous self-control not to grab Pete's arm and scream a torrent of enquiries. How did this incredible, crowded, overpowering city work? I knew I had to pace myself, for a start, there was so much to learn I feared I may have a mental breakdown if I received too much information but I felt compelled to start somewhere.

'Pete, tell me about the power-field.'

'Which one?' said Pete without alarm.

'The Singh power-field, the one I appeared over.'

'It's just a power-field; there's loads of them.'

'Yeah, okay, so there's loads of them, but remember, I don't know what a power-field is, I've never seen one before.'

'Haven't you?' Pete slowed down for a moment, he seemed genuinely surprised. 'I thought you'd have had them, they're really old.'

'Not as old as me.'

'Okay, so solar satellites thousands of kilometres up microwave power down, it's laser locked so the grid buried in the power-field collects the power and distributes in through the network. It's very simple.'

'So there's no physical link between the ground and the satellite?'

'What?' This time Pete seemed almost annoyed at my stupidity. 'How can there be a physical link? Why would anyone want a physical link? It's just a satellite, d'you know what a satellite is?'

'Yes, we had them.'

'Right, so it's just a satellite that collects solar radiation and beams it to earth, they're really old.'

'And do they make clouds?'

Again, I received a curt 'What?'

'I don't mean do they make all the clouds, I know how clouds are formed, but do the power-fields, the satellites, the beams, the microwave beam things, do they produce unusual cloud formations.'

'Yeah, every now and then.'

'Right,' I said, gratified that I had finally understood.

'Okay, now one other thing, you mentioned Weavers to me, the day we met in the canteen.'

'Yes, I remember, what about them?' said Pete.

'Well, can you explain them to me?'

'How come you don't know all about this, are you a bit thick or something?'

I glanced at Pete as we walked along, there was something in the way he said this quite rude thing about me that didn't sound rude, it sounded like a question with no hidden subtext, he was just asking me if I was thick.

'Maybe I am,' I said. 'I don't know how I would know about the Weavers, you know, I mean I just arrived from two hundred years ago, obviously I should understand everything.'

My sarcasm fell on deaf ears. I waited a moment, then Pete said:

'The Weaver women don't like us. They are mostly from Nairobi, Durban, New York, Riyadh or Hanoi.'

'What, they don't like Londoners? Why not?'

'No, not Londoners, us, men, me and you, male people, boys, men.'

'Oh, they don't like men. I see, and why not?'

Pete stopped in his tracks and stared at me, he looked genuinely concerned. 'You've got to work this out, you should know this. Have you talked to Doctor Markham or Nkoyo about it? There's something wrong with you, maybe it's your history brain, maybe it doesn't work, you should get them to have a look at it, really.' He shook his head and gave me a pat on the back, getting a friendly pat on the back from Pete was a bit like being nudged by a train.

I followed Pete down a shaded passage between two impressively lofty structures. Unlike rubbish-strewn alleys between buildings in American cop movies, this was very tidy and clean.

I don't know why, but I ran my hands along the wall of the building near me; it looked so smooth I wanted to know what the material was. It felt warm to the touch, like wood, but it wasn't wood, it was some incredibly smooth substance. Maybe I was doing this to resist the urge to ask more and more questions, after seeing his face when I'd asked a stupid question I decided Pete was not the right person to relentlessly pester.

'This is my store, this is where I fix stuff,' said Pete as he stood by what appeared to be some kind of large door you'd find on a factory or aircraft hangar. A young man emerged from a narrow opening. He was about my height and looked to be about fourteen years old. He immediately shook my hand and I felt a warm wave of well-being flow through my stomach, nothing as violent as a shudder, just a vague feeling of fullness, of health and I suppose, wealth.

'Hey, welcome, Gavin, amazing to meet you. I'm Yuseff, are you ready?'

I stood motionless, I knew by this point that if someone I'd never met before asked me if I was ready, something very weird was about to happen.

'We've got your Yuneec in here, has Pete explained?'

'Gavin knows all about it,' said Pete rather quickly.

'I, um, I'm not sure…' I said, I didn't want to upset Pete, he was so bloody enormous no one in their right mind would want to upset him, but I was feeling increasingly confused.

The young man put his hand on my back and confidently guided me towards the door. It slid open a little more and I was greeted with a round of applause. Not from five or ten people, no, this was applause from a massive audience.

The door continued to open revealing the most extraordinary spectacle.

The Yuneec, well, many parts of the Yuneec were displayed on a kind of stage. Around three sides of this were steep seating banks in which sat hundreds of people. They were all clapping, hooting and waving as I was ushered forward.

The teenager who'd shown me in waved his hand at the audience and they slowly settled down.

'Okay guys, this is Gavin Meckler, the man who flew the Yuneec E430 into a tree.'

A roar went up from the auditorium, it was from the timbre of this roar that I realised that the vast majority if not every member of this audience was male. The sound was very different to my press conference. It sounded like a crowd at a football match, deep and very loud.

To describe myself as a rabbit in headlights is to gloss over the whole experience. I was struck dumb and felt myself rapidly closing down. I didn't want to be there, I didn't want to be a spectacle for all these cheering people.

A number of other young men were standing around the Yuneec. They all looked very charming, like models in a Benetton advert, every race and body shape represented. They were surrounded by machinery, what could have been tool racks although I didn't recognise any of the tools. I saw a kind of large trolley loaded with materials, long metallic struts, neatly mounted rolls of sheet material and several containers of small parts.

'So, Gavin, what do you think?' said the young man who'd

guided me in. 'We are all going to witness the re-build of your fabulous manually operated drone.'

This announcement was greeted with another cheer from the audience. I didn't say anything as I was led toward the pile of bits that was once my beloved Yuneec.

Pete appeared beside me. 'Sorry about this,' he said slightly under his breath. 'Normally it's just me fixing stuff in here, but some friends asked if they could bring people along to watch.'

'Guys,' said the young man, he addressed the packed seats in the room while confidently standing in front of the wreckage. 'I think we should all be a bit quieter, I don't think Gavin was expecting this kind of event.'

He turned to me and gestured to one side. 'Gavin, take a seat and we'll let Pete and the lads continue.'

I saw two large sofa things placed to one side of the stage area, the confident young man led me over. I sat down but kept looking over my shoulder at the Yuneec behind me. I wanted to know what they were doing to it, not that they could bust it up much more. It was totally written off. I turned back to the young man when he spoke.

'This has got to be fairly intense for you,' he said, only then did I register that his voice was amplified.

'It's all a bit much,' I said. My voice was also amplified but I suppose I was expecting it this time.

The response from the crowd was oddly re-assuring. It was the sound a father makes when he holds a young child who's fallen over. It was a gentle sound, not the sarcastic 'aww diddums' I'd regularly heard from TV chat show audiences back in my day. This was a genuine expression of care, the men in the room felt genuinely sorry for me. They were actually expressing empathy, something Beth had constantly told me I was not very good at.

I glanced behind me again, the young men who'd been standing around the Yuneec started to get busy. Pete was clearly the lead figure in the procedure. He was using an unidentified small tool in the battered nose cone assembly. Even from this distance I could see that many changes had already taken place in the engine compartment.

'Let me explain, Gavin,' said the young man. I turned back to listen to him. 'I run a number of maker schemes in London, we like to learn about engineering and making things, fixing things, stuff like that. These guys here,' he gestured toward the audience, 'are students and individuals who're interested in machines and systems. Obviously when you crash-landed this little baby we were all fascinated. We don't do winged flight any more, so we are not familiar with the systems used to achieve it. That's why we're here, we want to learn. Oh, I should also explain that there's a couple of hundred mill watching this at home right now.'

'It's now seven hundred mill,' said a voice from behind us.

'Okay, seven hundred mill, there you go, Gavin, I think you can see there's a lot of interest in what you've brought to us, and not just in London, I mean all over the world.'

I could feel my head shaking; I took a deep breath and tried to contain the feelings rattling around inside me. This was a ridiculous experience. What on earth was I meant to do? In all the time I'd been in Gardenia I'd never experienced anything like this. Of course Gardenia was disturbing, confusing and bizarre when I first arrived, but it was gentle and things happened slowly enough that I felt I had time to take things in.

Here in London it was just over the top, things happened before I could mentally prepare for them, people kept asking me if I was ready. How could I ever be ready for this? Around five hundred men had gathered in a large dark room to watch some kids and an overgrown weirdo rebuild a two-hundred-year-old aircraft while the man who'd flown it in through a tear in the fabric of space time was being interviewed by a teenager. How was I supposed to grok that?

I suddenly remembered my catch phrase, I hesitated, I worried it might sound a little cheesy but went ahead anyway. 'I really am Gavin Meckler,' I said. 'I really was born in 1979. I really shouldn't be here, but I am.'

Again the unusual sound of five hundred men expressing very gentle concern reached me across the large space.

'I understand you want to know about me, or you want to know about my plane, I know you call it a drone but I call it a plane, an aeroplane. Anyway, I also know you can look that up. I'm sure, judging by the technology you have at your disposal, you have the ability to study history. Particularly from my period as this was the flowering of what we then called, "the digital revolution".'

'The digital revolution,' repeated Yuseff. 'That is spectacular.'

'The thing is,' I said, slowly feeling my confidence building. 'I want to learn about your world, your public address systems, how you generate power and dispose of waste, how your doors work, I want to know about your financial and political systems. I want to know what you all do.'

At that point I noticed four women sitting together in the front row of the audience seating. They didn't look threatening, they were just sitting looking at me, but then so were all the men around them. They did stand out though, they were more formally dressed, the men were in the same colourful garb I'd started to grow used to. I nodded towards the women but they didn't respond in any way I could read.

I continued when I saw Yuseff's enthusiastic head nodding at me to carry on.

'I want to know how on earth you have built this incredible city, two hundred years ago this was all fields, small villages, towns surrounded by open country. Our cities were cramped places with houses and streets very close to each other. I want to know why you chose squares instead of streets. I mean, well, streets and cities all squashed up together. It had been like that for thousands of years, people built cities all over the world in the same way, squash everything together, narrow streets between buildings but now, here in London, it's all spread out.'

'Fascinating,' said Yuseff. 'Well, we want to know how you built this drone, sorry, aeroplane and how you fly it, how did you learn?'

I was happy to explain and I did, I told them everything. The whole story, I explained about the cloud while carefully missing out any reference to Gardenia. Something about the presence of the four women in the front row reminded me to steer clear of that topic.

After some time I realised the entire room was hanging on my every word. I was speaking to a huge group of people clearly and with confidence. I only noticed after some time that I had my hand on my chest. It was, I suppose, a slightly camp mannerism but I remember thinking it was a way I had of checking my feelings. I really didn't want a repeat performance of sudden tears as I'd experienced at the press event. I was, I suppose, checking myself for a sudden and untoward explosion of sadness. I seemed to be coping, I felt safe in this large group of men; I didn't feel judged or looked down upon. Maybe it's because they were all engineer types, the sort of men I was used to working with, the sort of men who understand machines better than women. Could that be it?

Eventually I ran out of things to say, and young Yuseff spoke up.

'So, Gavin, what will you do now your machine is repaired?'

I turned around to look at the wreck that was behind me and froze. The Yuneec was shrouded in a complex array of machinery, the young men were controlling arms of machines that looked like they were either gluing or fabricating material on various parts of the wings and fuselage. I couldn't really see the plane but what was immediately apparent was the fact that it was no longer a pile of damaged parts scattered around a stage, it was essentially getting back to its original shape.

Pete gestured to the young men, they stood back and as they
did so, so did the mechanical arms surrounding the Yuneec. The arms silently folded away into small containers spread around the stage.

'What? How?' was all I could say.

The crowd cheered and clapped, and Pete stood looking at me with a big grin on his enormous face.

The Yuneec, well, what had been the Yuneec, was now in one pristine, shiny piece. It looked like it did the day I bought it, no, better. The nose section was slightly bigger, the area under the cockpit was subtly different and the wings looked like second-gen, like a product that had undergone a subtle re-launch. They just looked better.

'Let's join Pete and let him explain what's been going on,' said Yuseff. The crowd clapped and cheered, Pete gave a shy wave and we walked over toward him.

'What d'you think?' asked Pete, his low voice suddenly amplified.

'I don't understand, is it real?' I asked, staring past him at the beautifully lit aircraft.

'Yeah, it's your drone,' said Pete.

'Yes, but is it like a hologram or something, can I go and touch it? Is it really there?'

For some reason this made the audience laugh, I noticed two of the women in the front row were also laughing; the other two remained fairly stony faced.

'Yeah, go and touch it, Gavin, it's a hundred per cent real,' said Pete with a big grin.

I walked toward the Yuneec; my head was involuntarily shaking all the time. What I saw was just too much to take in. They had the technology to rebuild a very badly damaged machine that they'd never seen before, had no experience of and didn't really understand.

'It's got a new motor, the original had a tree branch rammed into it,' said Pete from way behind me although I could hear him perfectly. 'I got the motor from a car, it's a B850, lightweight, little bit more powerful than the unit you had in there. Actually it's a lot more powerful, you'll see we also replaced the propeller.'

I was standing by the nose and had noticed the propeller was a new design. It was easy to spot as it hung limply from the nose cone and was made of a material I'd never seen before.

'The original was a low speed rigid design,' said Pete. 'I think you'll find this one is a bit more effective.'

I ran my hand along one of the three propeller blades, if that's what you could describe them as. It had a very smooth fabric feel although I could sense they had weight to them.

'We've strengthened the wings a bit,' said Pete. 'But don't worry, the whole machine is now a hundred and twenty kilos lighter, we used some modern material to rebuild the structure but tried to keep to the original design.'

I lifted my hand and tapped the wing above my head, it felt completely different, the original wing on the Yuneec was built of aluminium struts and covered in a tough plastic and fibreglass skin. This was something far more solid feeling, I pushed upward on the wing and immediately the whole plane started to move. This caused a gasp to come from the crowd.

'See, much lighter,' said Pete. 'And check the slight bulge under the centre of the fuselage, that's your new power pack. We'd like to put your old batteries in the science museum if that's okay. This is a H3P power pack, the sort of thing we use all over the place.'

'And d'you think we should tell Gavin what an H3P pack is Pete?' said Yuseff, helpfully.

'Oh yeah, sorry, helium 3 polymer, ultra dense solid state energy, you'd probably call it a battery but it's not really a battery, you don't need to charge it from an external source. We just couldn't fit the unit into the original battery bay so we extended it a bit and modelling suggests it won't alter the flight capabilities of the Yuneec.'

'So, Gavin, what d'you think?' Yuseff asked. 'It is very impressive isn't it?'

'Utterly amazing,' I said. I leaned over and looked into the cockpit, this too had been changed beyond recognition. There were still two seats but they were white and made up of some kind of quilted material, the controls were essentially the same, just better and the dashboard was now one solid sheet of what I supposed was glass. No dials or obvious control systems.

'We didn't know what to do with the interior so we've kind of used existing systems we use on specialist machines with human operatives. They might take a bit of getting used to, but we can go over the control systems later.'

'So, Gavin, come back and tell us what you think,' said Yuseff. I turned and saw that they were all waiting for me. I wandered back over to the seating area feeling very frail.

'I don't know what to think,' I said as I sat down. 'I don't know why you've done it, I don't know if I've paid for you to do it, I don't understand anything that's happened to me since I arrived.'

I didn't say this to gain sympathy from the audience but that is what happened. I looked up at the crowd and noticed one man with a handkerchief wiping his eye, the man sitting next to him had his arm around him, comforting him. If this was what men had turned into in the past two hundred years, it was becoming slightly easier to see why the women of 2211 had felt the need to take over.

10

The Weaver Women

'I'VE GOT A LOT OF QUESTIONS,' I SAID AS I met Professor Etheridge the following day.

'I imagined you might,' she said holding out her hand as I approached her. We shook hands, it was automatic for me and it was only when I experienced a little rush of pleasure as our hands touched that I understood she was paying me for my time and company. Maybe not a lot, it was the merest stomach flutter, but from what I could comprehend, I'd definitely received some kind of payment.

The Professor had informed me when I returned from seeing the Yuneec rebuild that she would like to take me to the history museum, apparently a group of her students wanted to meet me.

The following morning, after I'd had a lonely breakfast in the strangely deserted canteen room, I met the Professor in the reception of the Institute.

She was wearing a lightweight floor length coat topped off by a very bizarre hat. It wasn't really a hat, more a moulded helmet made of incredibly fine filigree. It looked a bit like coral, or the skeleton of some bizarre sea creature.

'Wow, cool hat,' I said.

'I'm assuming that is positive terminology and I'm glad you like it,' she touched the side of the hat gently with the palm of her hand and I noticed a shimmer of gentle movement run through it. 'You may not be familiar with such devices. It is as you describe, a hat, but it also performs the function of being a memory enhancement system.'

'Wow, amazing. So you can, like, get information from it?'

The Professor explained slowly and patiently, 'When I wear this, I have increased and focused recall into a vast database of historical facts, dates, names and key events from roughly the last three thousand years. It is very history specific unlike my kidonge.'

'With you,' I said. I was lying of course, I didn't understand how the hell the wobbly hat of glowing marine creature type thing could possibly work.

The Professor seemed to ignore my interjection. 'Obviously merely having access to such data is only useful if you know how to interpret it, to put it in a context that has relevance to the present day. It also designates my position.'

I felt my annoying eyebrows start their dance of confusion.

'A visual key informing people that I am a Professor of History,' she explained. 'Although most people would know anyway, it's really just an old tradition and I only wear it if I am creating a particular dissertation or on formal occasions.'

'Oh, right, is today a formal occasion?' I asked.

'It is, it is a formal visit to the London Museum of Human History where the authorities are expecting us.'

'Blimey,' I said. 'I don't have to give speeches or anything do I?'

The Professor smiled gently. 'No, but I'd appreciate it if you would be generous enough to converse with some of my students.'

'No probs,' I said.

We walked a kilometre or so from the Institute to the entrance of the roadway system Pete had escorted me on previously. The only difference on this day was the weather, a hot wind was blowing. The clouds were low and dull grey.

'It was never this warm in London back in my day,' I said, almost having to trot to keep up. Already I felt my weird clothes sticking to me.

'We are approaching the rainy season,' said the Professor as she strode along.

'The rainy season, you have a rainy season?'

'You will find the weather patterns have changed considerably since your time, we have had to adapt to a very different climate. We now have very brutally cold winters and very hot and humid summers, I believe our climate is more like that of New York in your era.'

We descended the flight of stairs that once again seemed very busy and although I was still intrigued by the system, it was already becoming mundane.

We waited about a minute as the crowds surged around us, then got into a car and off we zoomed.

'The museum is about eighty kilometres away so it won't take long, about fifteen minutes,' she said as I felt the surge of acceleration push me into my seat. I automatically did some mental calculations using the information she had just given me that gave me a result of an average speed of over 400 kilometres an hour. As I glanced out of the tinted windows at the overhead lights flashing past us, I felt confident my calculations weren't far off the mark.

'Okay,' I said. 'I'm in London, you call it London but clearly it covers an area far bigger than London used to be back in 2011.'

'Indeed, London is the term most people use to describe the entire land mass you would have known as England,' said the Professor. 'The city has developed over the last one hundred and fifty years and particularly in the last fifty. The old concentrated cities you would have known have all gone, there are a few historic relics remaining but essentially there is little for you to recognise from your period.'

I was becoming quite adept at taking in earth shattering revelations like this, but of course I wanted to know more.

'And men raise children?' I asked. Professor Etheridge looked a little confused at this.

'Are you telling me they raise children or are you asking me?'

'I suppose I'm asking if that is correct, from what I have seen over the past few days and from what my relative Ralph told me it seems that men raise children, but how, well, what do women do?'

Professor Etheridge stared at me for a long time. I smiled, I wanted to show her that I didn't mean to be rude, but her expression remained fairly neutral. I couldn't tell if I'd offended her.

'I'm not sure I know what you mean. We work.' Another pause. She clearly had to really think about this. 'We administrate, educate, medicate and defend. Not all women are in positions of responsibility, there is no coercion for us to do what we do. It's a matter of individual choice. Is that what you mean?'

'So women run the place?'

'Well, I don't quite understand what you mean by "the place", but it's true most of the serious administrative positions are held by women, the Mayor was on your review panel, she's taken a great interest in your case.'

'The Mayor?'

'Yes, Mayor Hilda Mickleton of London, she was at your review panel, did you not know who she was?'

'No. How would I know that?'

The Professor nodded and smiled. 'Of course, you didn't have your kidonge then did you.'

'My kidonge, oh, the thing Nkoyo gave me, but I thought that was the thing that helps me grip my bits.'

'It is, but it's also what tells you who you are with. Do you not sense it?'

I sat motionless; I think my eyes might have been doing rapid side-to-side movements as I tried to understand what she was saying.

'No,' I said.

'Look at me, Gavin,' said the Professor, she was sitting opposite me in the car, her back to the direction we were blatting along in. I looked at her for a moment, something I always find a bit disconcerting.

Nothing.

'Try and focus,' she said. 'Look at me and let yourself to relax.'

I did as she asked. I found it very uncomfortable. I don't like staring at people when they're looking at me. Maybe I'm insecure, maybe I fear intimacy, maybe it was all to do with the way I'd been brought up, but I didn't enjoy it. Until…

'David,' I said. 'Your husband's name is David and you have one child, a daughter. Her name is Helen and she's thirty-four years old, you live on Dunning Square but I don't know which number, oh my God, how did I do that?'

My hand was over my mouth for the last part of the list. The information just formed somehow, it just appeared and it was simple. There's no other way to describe it, I just knew this stuff. If you sit down and describe the basic facts about someone you've known all your life, say your brother or sister, the information would just form and you can tell someone about them. Just the basic facts, age, partner, children, job, that sort of thing. It was exactly like that. It felt as if I'd known these facts all my life.

'How, how do I know that?'

'It's just a simple kidonge pairing, there's nothing to be alarmed about.'

'Derren Brown, eat your heart out baby,' I said.

'Was this Derren a friend of yours?' asked the Professor.

I shook my head. She closed her eyes for a moment and then nodded. 'He was a magician,' she said. 'Now I understand.'

'So can you learn to sense things like that all the time?' I asked, I was feeling slightly panicky because I had no idea what I'd done, I'd just looked at this woman who appeared to be in her late thirties, discovered she was married and had a thirty-four-year-old daughter.

'Yes, now you've done it once, you'll find you can do it without effort. I can't really imagine how a complex society could run without it.'

'No, I s'pose not,' I conceded.

'I understand you had many problems with your personal security, the possibility of fraud, identity theft. I understand you often didn't truly know who you were with back in the early twenty-first century, we imagine this must have made life stressful and full of anxiety,' said the Professor.

'Yes, we did have a bit of a mess on our hands,' I said. I felt the car going around a corner and then accelerate even more violently. I gripped the sides of the comfortable seat I was on, the car wasn't rocking about or dealing with unmade roads, it was all very smooth and quiet, just a faint background hiss.

'Don't be alarmed,' said the Professor. 'We've just turned onto main one, it's the busiest North–South arterial roadway. We had to speed up to blend in with other users.'

I shaded the interior light with my hands and peered out of the window, we were jammed in with many other vehicles only a centimetre away from us, also moving at this breakneck pace. I could see people in the other cars chatting away and obviously relaxed and oblivious to the incredible speed at which they were travelling. The lights in the roof above the road were just a vague blur; we must have been approaching 480 kph.

I sat back and tried to relax, the Professor was sitting very calmly opposite me which, I suppose, made me feel safe enough to ask a difficult question.

'Professor, it seems to me that there are more women than men in London, is that because most of the men remain in their homes with their families, or is there an imbalance in the population?'

'That is a very perceptive observation,' said the Professor after a moment's thought. 'You are correct, there are many more women than men in the general population. The ratio is about five to one, this has been a deliberate policy for the past 100 years or so.'

'Blimey, it's all a bit Malthusian isn't it, what do you do with the male babies, leave them on a mountain ledge to be devoured by eagles?'

This time the pause was longer. The Professor gently touched the side of her illuminated headgear.

'I now understand the reference,' she said with a nice smile. 'That's very amusing but the answer is no. We perfected what you might know as family planning many years ago so male babies are simply not born in any significant numbers. It was generally considered beneficial to the whole population to keep the numbers of men to a minimum. This was an agreement worked out with the support of the vast majority of the male population too.'

'I see, but can I ask why? I mean, I can't help wondering why men are so awful, why we need to be bred out of existence?'

'There's certainly nothing of the sort happening, not at the moment.'

'Not at the moment?' I suddenly remembered the thing Pete had mentioned, the women who hated men. 'You mean you might change your mind! Is this the Weaving thing, the Weaving women?'

'Oh, the Weavers. Yes, they very much wish to eliminate men from the earth, I admit they are a powerful lobby but at present in London anyway, they don't have any real standing.'

'Can you explain about them though?'

'Just relax, Gavin, you can find out everything you need to know about such topics if you relax.'

That really didn't answer my question, my mind was full of suspicion, what did she mean relax? Why couldn't she just tell me, why did everything have to be so damned mysterious? I sat back and tried to relax.

Immediately the information flooded in, it was like revision, I could distinctly remember being on the bus going to school when I was in the sixth form, heading for an exam and running through information in my mind, like strings of facts emerging from somewhere in among my neural networks. Weaver women were named as such because of their adherence to the teachings of a group of women who came to prominence in 2073. They belonged to a scientific research group based in Africa, India,

Asia and Australia. Five Myrmecologists came up with Weaver theory, I thought about Myrmecologists as I didn't know what they did, then I knew they studied ants. These women studied Weaver ants in particular. Weaver ants are so called because they make hanging nests out of carefully woven leaves, they live in colonies of many hundreds of thousands and are the most socially advanced living creatures on the earth besides *Homo sapiens*. They are also entirely female except for the rare occasions when they need to breed in which case the slightly smaller 'minor' ants allow a few of the babies to become male. The nursing ants can define the gender of infant ants with chemicals.

Although I was receiving this knowledge in a torrent I couldn't take it all in and interpret it. I knew there were more Weaver ants on the planet than human beings and they had survived for millions of years, dominating the area they inhabit and using some other insects as cattle. The Weaver women started a movement which rapidly gained popularity, encouraged women to start working together, outside the political, social and cultural structures imposed upon them by men. They wanted to move towards a more just and gentle society that didn't rely on men for its continuation. They were clearly very successful.

Within two generations the number of men in Africa, Asia, India and Australia had dropped to an all-time low, ratios of fifteen to one in favour of women were not uncommon by the turn of the twenty-third century.

I finally managed to utter something to the Professor. 'That's kind of terrifying,' I said.

'Indeed, it has been a major challenge,' she replied. 'I would suggest that in London most women revere the men they know. What the Weaver women have proven beyond doubt though is that men as they were, as you were, had a very negative effect on the world and women in general. We have seen a massive drop in crime and violence in the last one hundred and fifty years. We don't have wars, we don't have violent behaviour on our streets, we don't have domestic violence, child abuse and we don't have rape.'

I sat in silence. What she had just told me was such a damning indictment of my gender that I could come up with no response. I wanted a reason to contradict this ridiculous notion, that everything wrong with the world I had come from was men's fault, however, what I had seen in London indicated that I was dwelling in a very large, very sophisticated, complex and vibrant, but very peaceful city. I'd knocked about a bit before I left my own time, I'd been in strange cities where people had warned me about certain 'no go areas.' In all my conversations with Pete, Nkoyo and Ralph no one had mentioned areas that were 'a bit unsafe at night' or anything of the sort.

'So, out of all the men who live in London now, there are no murderers or rapists? Surely you have the odd nutter who goes crazy and commits a crime?'

'I would guess there are two reasons why this doesn't happen, and you are staying in one of them. There certainly are very severely mentally ill people who, without due care and understanding could be a danger to themselves or others, there is also another very important reason however.'

'Which is?'

'That the vast majority of boys are raised by their fathers, when a boy has a solid, reliable and loving father in his early life we have observed that he grows up to be a solid, reliable adult who is far less likely to resort to violence to resolve problems. Can you excuse me for one moment?'

I shrugged, that was not merely food for thought; that was a bulk food delivery truck for thought. I stared out of the window for a moment watching the lights flash past at epilepsy-inducing intensity. I heard the Professor mutter something and turned to face her. She had her eyes shut and was saying something under her breath, I couldn't make it out, I was wondering if she was praying. Maybe these cars were not quite as safe as I'd assumed.

She opened her eyes and looked at me. 'I beg your pardon, I was just talking to Nkoyo, she was asking about you.'

'Oh, right,' I said. 'Can you talk to people through your kidonge too?'

The Professor smiled. I liked her, she had a far gentler demeanour than many of the other women I'd met.

'No, I was using the phone,' she said pointing to a small pad on the side of her seat. I glanced down at my seat, there was a pad there but it was blank.

'Think of someone you've met,' said the Professor.

I thought of Pete, his picture immediately appeared on the little pad, I sat upright, startled by the response speed.

'If you want to talk to him you can, unless he's busy. Is there a little blue square beneath his picture?'

'Yes,' I said.

'Then he's busy, and we are at our destination.'

As soon as she'd said that I felt the car slow down, veer off to the left and rise up a slight incline. I really had to push my head back as we slowed. I couldn't describe the deceleration as actually violent, but it was close enough to violent to be alarming. The car stopped and the doors opened immediately. The Professor stood up, adjusted her rather bizarre headgear and left the vehicle.

I followed her out and of course there was another surprise. I should have started to get used to them but it still made me stop and stare. A crowd of maybe thirty people stood in a large semicircle in front of me. They all looked like teenagers, they were all smiling and they were all looking at me.

'Welcome to the London Museum of Human History, Gavin,' said a young woman. 'We are very excited to meet you.'

11

Museum of our Past

THE STORY OF THE PREVIOUS TWO HUNDRED years as seen from the perspective of the Squares of London in 2211 was completely at odds with the story I'd learned in Gardenia, or what led up to Gardenia.

The tales I read of the brutal regimes that had come and gone, the economic and social collapse that had taken place in the Gardenian past seemed to be completely lacking in London.

Now, instead of reading a beautifully made book in a beautiful quiet room in a barn conversion, I was casually strolling through two hundred years of human history in the company of a load of students and a professor with a weird hat.

'Do you recognise that?' asked one of the young people as we entered the massive building. It was hard not to. Harrods department store was directly in front of me. I don't mean a picture of Harrods; I mean the actual building.

Harrods department store was dwarfed by the colossal structure surrounding it; the whole Harrods building resembled nothing more than a dolls house in a playroom. The London Museum of Human History was, as I was about to learn, a very large place. Not only was the structure beyond the scale of anything I'd seen back in my day or even in the Gardenian world, it was incredibly busy. The teeming crowds who were wandering around the massive halls reminded me of exhibitions I'd unwillingly visited with Beth; events like Grand Designs Live and the Ideal Home show at the NEC. But this museum was on a scale that made Grand Designs Live look like a Tuesday afternoon amateur watercolour exhibition in Chipping Norton library.

'Is that the actual original Harrods?' I asked the attentive little crowd around me.

'Yes, it was reconstructed about a hundred years ago,' said another of the students, a young woman. 'It was retrieved from the seabed and rebuilt here, does it look anything like the original?'

'Abso-fucking-lutely,' I said. I noticed this term meant nothing to them so I tried another response. 'It looks exactly the same as it did in my day.'

The little gaggle of faces nodded at me and smiled. They all looked South East Asian to me; no blonde, or even light brown, hair on display.

We wandered along a slightly raised walkway to the side of the Harrods building and another rather iconic building came into view.

'That is St Paul's Cathedral,' said the young woman beside me. The way she enunciated the words made it clear that none of them was familiar to her.

'Oh God help me,' I gasped as my eyes fell on the vision of St Paul's Cathedral looking pristine and spectacular but somehow rather small.

I stood holding the handrail on the walkway as I scanned the incredible vision before me, St Paul's Cathedral next to Tower Bridge. Behind it, the Houses of Parliament, to one side, bizarrely, the MI6 building made iconic by the later James Bond movies and behind that, 30 St Mary Axe, better known as the Gherkin. All these buildings were now exhibits in a museum, all of them dwarfed by the fabulous structure that housed them.

'It must be an odd experience for you, seeing all these buildings, do you recognise them?' asked the Professor who was now standing beside me.

'Yes, I do, I know all of them. How did this happen?'

'It happened a long time ago, as the sea levels rose and the city expanded and spread out, about a hundred and fifty years back, some of the more enterprising women of the time managed to arrange to have the buildings dismantled and reconstructed here.'

'But, why? It's insane! Such a colossal undertaking, it must have taken years and cost a fortune.'

'It certainly took many months, of course most of the process was automated,' explained the Professor. 'We now grow buildings rather than construct them from parts as many of these old structures were made, but we think it's important that present and future generations understand the ingenuity and inventiveness of previous times. I know you had museums back in 2011.'

'Yeah, but blimey…' was really all I could say. I noticed that much animated discussion was taking place among the students behind me. I turned to them to try and work out if I was the cause of the slightly hushed conflict.

The young woman at the front, physically diminutive but clearly a leader among the group smiled at me with a slightly pained expression.

'We have no wish to upset you but we noticed when you saw the old buildings you made a cry for help from a deity.'

It took me a moment to untangle what she was saying, then I realised.

'Did I?' I asked.

The massed ranks of students staring at me with serious expressions nodded in affirmation.

'Oh, wait, you mean when I said "God help me"?' I know I was smiling as I spoke, somehow I knew what they were thinking and I found it amusing.

'You think I was actually saying it because I believe in a God or something?'

More nods.

'Well, it was a very common expression back when some of those buildings were standing in their original position. People who didn't believe in God or go to church or think of themselves in any way religious would say things like "Oh my God" or "For

God's Sake" or "Jesus Christ!" as expressions, I often say them to stop myself using swear words.'

There was a general sigh of relief from the crowd, I'd noticed a couple of them had started to move away before I spoke, they had turned back to hear what I had to say on the topic.

'There were still loads of people who believed in religion, God and all that stuff back in the twenty-first century, but not all of us. I never did.'

I noticed many of the students look to the Professor for confirmation. She adjusted her bizarre headgear and explained. 'Gavin has been thoroughly tested, he does not appear to be damaged by his exposure to religious illness,' she said. 'It's a great lesson for all of us to understand that even as far back as 2011 the illness was in decline.'

'You see it as an illness?' I asked. 'That's a bit harsh isn't it?'

'It is now classified as a treatable mental condition, it's not fatal but it's clearly not a good state for any individual,' said the Professor, explaining it as if it was bloody obvious.

Surrounded as I was by the incredible visions of my old home world in a museum, I didn't want to get into a discussion on religion and philosophy. 'Let's move on,' I pleaded. 'Without the help of any God.'

We moved along the walkway, behind me I could sense a lot of restrained chatter was going on as the students discussed the topics just aired.

I, on the other hand, was fascinated by the exhibits in the museum; as we moved along, I saw that Harrods was only a façade, the interior of the building was missing, what was behind it was a series of exhibition spaces filled with things from the early part of the twentieth century.

Over in one corner of the space was a massive steel construction, an oil rig. Not a model of an oilrig, I'm talking the real thing, hundreds of meters high just sitting in the corner like a discarded lawn mower.

 'Holy shit, look at that,' I said. I think I may have said this many times during my visit.

'Did you engineer things like that?' asked one of the students.

'What, oil rigs? No, not me, I knew people who did, the fossil fuel industries employed loads of engineers like me but I was more involved with mineral extraction. Quarries, mines, stuff like that.'

'Like that,' said one of the students who pointed behind me. I turned and saw a Hitachi EX8000 hydraulic shovel; when I left 2011 these big eight-hundred-tonne babies were still on the drawing board. This massive caterpillar tracked earthmover was clearly well used and a bit knackered looking.

'Bloody hell,' I said. 'Yes, I recognise that.'

'You might see some other things you're familiar with,' said one of the male students I was standing near. 'Do you recognise the Ford Angular mechanical vehicle?'

I looked in the direction the young chap was pointing, there on a plinth was a light blue car. I had indeed seen it before, funny looking little thing.

'I think it was actually called the Ford Anglia,' I said, correcting his description. 'I had an Auntie who drove one of those but they were already old-fashioned when I was born.'

'It looks so cute,' said the young man. 'Is it really true you had to make it go yourself, it didn't know how to move.'

I nodded. 'Yep, that's right, you had to learn to drive, you had to pass a test, an exam to make sure you were a good driver.'

'It all sounds so dangerous,' said the small young woman. 'Surely people made mistakes and the machines caused injury and damage.'

'All the time,' I said. 'It was really dangerous, many thousands of people were killed and injured every year, if you were sensible or even just vaguely intelligent, you knew you were taking a big risk when you got behind the wheel.'

'What do you mean, got behind the wheel?' asked the young man.

'I mean,' I had to think for a moment. 'I mean you sat in the seat behind the wheel inside the machine, then you took control of the machine using the pedals with your feet and a wheel with your hands.'

I mimed the position you took when controlling the steering wheel and for some reason this made them laugh.

'You also had to change gear with one hand, you had to time the change with the position of your feet, you had to use the clutch to disengage the . . .' I could tell two things at this point. The first and most obvious was that they didn't have a clue what I was trying to explain, the second was a slightly chilling realisation that the technology I had once thought of as sophisticated and complex was monstrously crude and basic.

By now, the remainder of the crowd had joined us, they were all gathered close by listening to every word I said. I repeated my description of cars of the twentieth and twenty-first centuries, explaining the rudiments of road travel as I'd known it, the expense of owning a car and how it depreciated and how much effort was put into making them safer and how people loved them despite all the risks and damage they caused.

They seemed to be lapping it up as Professor Etheridge moved in beside me. 'Thank you Gavin, they are clearly enjoying everything you say.'

'Pleased to help,' I said.

'He must see the next installation, Professor,' said the young male student who was standing near me, 'we really want to hear his explanation.'

So saying, the young man gently touched my arm and guided me to the opposite side of the walkway. Directly in front of me was a large amorphous yellow shape tucked in beside the oil rig. I don't know why I hadn't noticed it previously, as it was fairly enormous but also bizarrely nondescript. It wasn't a tent, more like a thick cloud of gas or mist. Hanging above what I took to be the entrance was what looked a bit like a film prop, a hazard sign in some kind of alien-looking sign language. I recognised one of the symbols instantly, radiation, a fairly well known symbol. Then I registered some of the other symbols, a skull icon, a burn icon and a particularly graphic animated icon of a human being vomiting and collapsing in a constantly repeating loop.

I walked through the entrance followed by the students and was frightened by what I saw. Endless rows of steel barrels all covered with similar symbols. This was Tardis time, although the exterior of this installation was fairly big, say about the size of a large warehouse unit on an out-of-town industrial estate, the interior appeared to be a hundred times bigger. It was decked out like a cave and, I suddenly noticed, it was as quiet as a cave. The general noise level in the museum was fairly high, thousands of people walking about talking to each other, the sounds of some of the displays all built up to a verifiable cacophony, however, inside this installation all that sound was removed.

The Professor moved up beside me. 'This is real,' she said, 'I don't mean this actual image you are seeing now, but the feed is live, it is coming from the deep caverns outside Trondheim where we have had to store this dangerous material from your era.'

'You mean this is nuclear waste?'

'Yes,' said the Professor, 'many thousands of tons of it. It has been a huge problem for us and will continue to be for many thousands of years. It is strange to think that the nuclear age, or the end of the dark times as we often refer to it, has left us with such a monstrous legacy.'

'But you could have used this fuel, why didn't you develop technology to use it?'

The Professor turned to her students. 'Did you hear that question, does anyone have an answer?'

A very tall Japanese student smiled at me. 'We didn't need to use it, when the cost analysis was done it was clearly ridiculous, we admire the ingenuity and bravery of the people who tried to make this technology work.' She looked around for reassurance on this statement, she got it from many of her fellow students who nodded and looked at me as if to reassure me. 'However, other much safer and much, much cheaper systems of energy harvesting had been developed and the notion of burning very dangerous material became nothing other than ridiculous.' I noticed the student glance at the Professor who discreetly nodded back. The student continued; 'It was seen as traditionally male technology, it was seen as being from the dark times and we only have to stand in this exhibit to see the very negative consequences of such actions. If you stand quietly you can hear one of the problems we still have.'

Everyone went quiet, I could hear nothing at first except the ringing in my ears. As the peace descended I picked up a faint repetitive sound, dripping water. The classic echoing drip, drip, drip of water in a cave. I glanced around at the students.

'The dripping sound?'

'Yes, the dripping sound,' said the Professor. 'This is a problem. The nuclear waste as you call it is buried thousands of meters beneath the earth's surface sealed off with millions of tons of reinforced concrete. It is meant to be completely sealed-off from everything and yet water has found its way into the containment area. We know for certain that if water can find its way in, it can find its way out. We know this material has to be stored for many thousands of years, we know the contamination could still spread. The surrounding thousand square kilometres is now completely sealed off and is cause for inter-city concern. The very concept of waste is such a symbolic representation of the dark times for us. We have to educate our children on what the term "waste" meant to the people of your era. We only understand waste now in terms of time, we know people can waste time and we strongly discourage it, but to waste material wealth, to waste finite resources appears to us like a form of madness.'

'Did you really think this technology was admirable?' asked

 another female student, her question wasn't exactly accusatory, it seemed genuine but coming from such a different mindset I found it hard not to be a little offended.

'Well, there were certainly great hopes for it when I left,' I said. 'I mean we understood that there were long-term problems with the, um, the waste, but we thought technology could overcome that and we could produce electricity using all the weapons' grade materials we had left over from previous generations. It wasn't my specialised area although I did work in related industries. Uranium extraction in Australia, I mean that was a huge business, a huge task, you know, to dig up the uranium ore to feed the, to feed the power stations around the world.'

As I was trying to explain, I became increasingly aware of the blank stares of utter disbelief my explanation was resulting in. They really thought I was mad to say such things. 'Um, but I'm learning now,' I said, feeling that back tracking was probably the best option, 'that this technology probably didn't work out and we left behind a bit of a mess.'

The Professor gave me a forgiving smile. It didn't really make me feel any better but at least I felt she didn't hate me. I spent some time looking down the long lines of dimly lit corridors of deadly material. I couldn't see the far end, it literally disappeared. On a small table to one side was a screen, really the first screen I had seen in the museum, indeed in the whole time I'd been in London. As I looked down at it I could hear the easily recognisable clicking of a Geiger counter, I knew then that this was also a live feed coming from the radioactive tomb buried under Trondheim. Above the meter reading on the screen which showed dangerously high levels of radiation in the space, there was a countdown figure. It was at 49,782 years; that was how long it would be before the material in the storage vault would be safe. I couldn't help it, I laughed sardonically. Yes, it was utterly insane. I stood looking at this installation for a long time, I had always put my faith in nuclear technology, I firmly believed it was the answer to many of the problems I knew we were facing in the twenty-first century and I was not alone. Pretty much all the scientists and engineers I knew would have agreed with me. Using this massive stockpile of plutonium was surely far preferable to relentlessly burning hydrocarbons. This train of thought sent me down a long road into a deep sense of misery and possibly some guilt. I was very much part of the problem on this one. I wanted to argue with the students, I wanted to point out that they had in fact 'wasted' an opportunity, if they had continued to develop the technology they could have used this toxic nightmare as fuel, it seemed such a waste to me.

When I turned I was surprised to see I was alone, I glanced about, I was alone in a silent cave with millions of tons of highly radioactive waste, it wasn't a nice place to be.

I left the installation and rejoined the students and Professor Etheridge in the noisy museum. 'Wow, that is fairly sobering,' I said.

'Yes, it is the one exhibition in this section which is a little chilling,' agreed the Professor. We started to move along the crowded walkway.

'But what I want to know,' I said, 'is what happened after I left?'

The Professor gestured toward a large doorway. 'We arrived in the nineteenth- and twentieth-century entrance, the next room is the start of the twenty-first century, about the time you left your world.'

We headed toward the door.

12

Museum of our future

'DOES IT MAKE YOU FEEL SAD?' ASKED A young man who walked beside me as we passed through the enormous door between the twentieth and twenty-first centuries.

'What, seeing the whole world I knew as museum relics? No, I don't think so,' I said. 'But then I've never had the verbal capacity to explain my feelings.'

'You must be able to feel things though,' said the young lad.

'Yes, I probably can feel things but they don't make much sense.'

Behind the unusually diminutive figure of the young man, I recognised an image on the wall. It was a giant, blown-up picture of the Queen and Tony Blair awkwardly holding hands in the 'Millennium Dome', as it was then known, in Greenwich on New Year's Eve, 2000. My body flooded with feelings, more than I knew what to do with. A longing for Beth, for home, for familiarity and a world I had confidence in.

'Okay, that picture makes me have feelings,' I said.

'Who are those people? Did you know them?' asked the young student.

'I didn't know them personally, the old lady, she was the Queen, sort of like a Mayor but of the whole country, and the man beside her, he was the Prime Minister, sort of like a Mayor too.'

The young man didn't ask any more questions, he clearly wasn't interested in who these people were and moved on with the rest of the crowd of students. I stared at the iconic image for a while, studying the faces of the Queen and Tony Blair, so familiar but now just a dusty footnote in the human story. They seemed, and probably indeed felt, as if they were important at the time, and yet a mere two hundred years later, even a highly educated student had little idea who they really were and even less interest in finding out. Of course, what this really brought home to me is that I should have been an even lesser footnote in history, just in some list at the back. Long gone and forgotten and yet here I was, standing alive and looking back through time at them.

We continued along the raised walkway, along the wall to one side were posters and photographic images I recognised; adverts for SKY television, the 2012 Olympics that the country was preparing for when I left, tube station signs, road signs, village name plates, countless examples of ephemera from my world neatly displayed behind glass.

'Personally I prefer the Tudor period,' said the small male student walking beside me. 'That was a fascinating period and I love the architecture, the food they had to eat, the way they made cloth and the clothes they wore.'

'Judd likes dressing up as a Tudor page boy,' whispered one of his fellow students, an alarmingly tall Japanese girl standing behind him.

'Right,' I said, 'Yeah, people back in my day liked dressing up too. Mostly as characters from science fiction movies and TV shows.'

This meant nothing judging by their blank stares. I let the subject drop, but I stared at Judd as he wandered along looking at the objects in the glass cases. It wasn't hard to believe. Judd as a Tudor pageboy, I could just picture him in doublet and hose.

The crowd in front of us thinned out and I glanced up into an even bigger space, the sheer scale of it took my breath away. I had entered a structure so vast the opposite end was far enough away to be slightly obscured by the internal atmosphere. It was big enough to cover a small town. The roof was so high up I couldn't quite make out the design, certainly elements of a geodesic structure, many thousands of triangles a little like the enclosed courtyard on the British Museum of old, just ten thousand times bigger.

'Heaven above!' I said. I smiled as I looked at the students. 'I just said that so I could avoid saying something rude.'

'What is something rude?' asked the petite female leader of the students.

'Well, I said "heavens above" to stop myself saying "fuck my old boots", which would be a more vulgar expression from my era.'

'Did men have sex with shoes?' asked Judd, the doublet and hose boy.

'I'm sure some did,' I said with a grin, 'but I don't think it's meant to be taken literally, it was just an odd expression. You could also say "fuck me" and not want to have sex with anyone, or "Jesus fucking Christ" and not mean to be offensive to a religious figure.' I stood there grinning. I wasn't getting a lot of grins back. 'I admit now, standing here with you lot it, all does sound a bit weird.'

I turned back and looked into the space we had entered. To call it a room, or even a hall, is ridiculous, it actually had clouds floating about in the upper reaches. To give some idea of scale, I would guess a couple of kilometres long, at least five hundred metres high and maybe a kilometre wide with no supporting pillars. How anyone could build a roof with the span of a suspension bridge was beyond me.

This vast arena was teeming with people, thousands milled around its spacious, multi-layered exhibits. The walkway we were on had a kind of ramp gently sloping down to the ground floor. I was guided that way by the flow of people we were among.

Something caught my eye, a logo I was familiar with, the Android logo was on a dusty illuminated sign to my right, I then saw that behind that was a Google logo.

'Is that still going?' I asked.

'What?' asked the bright young woman student.

'Google, is it still going, is it still a company?'

She shook her head as if I was mad. 'Do you remember it?' she asked.

'Yes, it was one of the largest, wealthiest companies the world had ever known.'

'I've read about Google,' said a young woman I hadn't spoken too before. 'They were a kind of library weren't they?'

I felt my eyebrows rise automatically. 'Yes, I suppose you could call them that, I suppose we called them a digital information search company.'

'A digital information search company,' she repeated, making it obvious she was hearing about something so obscure and distant that the only equivalence to me would be a manual printing press used by Caxton.

'Was it a good digital information search company?'

'Well, it was very useful,' I said, 'very popular.'

We reached the ground floor and I turned to look at the Google display. Glass boxes that appeared to float above the floor displayed a laptop, a chrome book I think, a few variants of Android phones and an iPhone 5.

'Ahh, that one shouldn't be in there,' I said, pointing to the iPhone. 'That was made by a rival manufacturer called Apple.'

'Apple? Like the fruit?' asked the young woman.

'You've not heard of Apple? Apple Mac. MacBooks, iPods, iPhones, iPads?'

She shook her head.

'Wow,' I said. 'Never mind, they made a few computers and phones back in my day. They were sort of fairly successful, like, unbelievably successful.'

My comments drew no discernible interest, so I stared at the collection of electronics in the case; all of them looked insignificant, grey and very, very old. The glass on the iPhone had clearly gone a bit manky, it was a kind of matt green colour. All that innovation and excitement, the feeling that these things were world-changing tech, now so dated and useless other than as museum exhibits.

I followed the small group who were in turn following the Professor. I glanced up for yet another heart-stopping moment. Directly in front of us was the Shard, it did look fairly massive as we were standing on ground level looking up at it, however, the roof of the building was just above its highest point.

'That is uncanny,' I said, 'I remember seeing that being built.' This comment caused a bit of amazement among the little troupe, they stood looking at me and then at the Shard, then shaking their heads in amazement.

Around the base of the Shard were a large number of exhibits, a civilian HumVee next to a Chevrolet Volt, a Range Rover Sport and a Nissan Leaf. Exhibited next to this odd collection were many different styles of motorbikes and bicycles and hanging above them all a Robinson R22 helicopter and an Airbus A380.

No, I'm not getting it wrong, I know my planes, a full sized Airbus A380 was somehow suspended above our heads, no thick wires were visible, it just seemed to float there.

Further along the wide walkway were a series of funny looking little pod cars.

'Wow, when are these from?' I said slowly moving toward the exhibit.

'Those are early Urbee units,' said Judd, the young man who liked the Tudor period.

'I've never heard of them,' I said. 'After my time obviously.'

I got to the railing in front of the plinth displaying the machines. They suddenly looked a little wonky and archaic, even I could understand the construction methods used to produce them, the pressed panels, the crude mechanics of the doors, they looked dusty and worn out and yet they dated from a period of history long after my departure.

A series of diagrams and a description appeared in front of me making me momentarily close my eyes and rub them with the back of my hands. Alarmingly the words were still there even though my eyes were shut.

'Oh that is sick, how does that work? The words, the words are in my eyes,' I said turning my head away. 'I don't like that.'

I felt a hand on my shoulder; it was the Professor standing beside me.

'Don't be alarmed, Gavin, it's just the museum connecting to your kidonge. There's no harm done, if you don't like it move away from the exhibit.'

I shook my head and read the very clear text I could see as if it were floating ten feet in front of me.

'Early autonomous vehicles produced in 2048 by Musk Autonomy Dynamics of Abu Dhabi. Powered by 4 micro asynchronous in-wheel electric motors and lithium-air battery pack with induction charging. The vehicles were used in many cities for over thirty years.'

Some ridiculously high definition video footage then explained how the vehicles charged from induction coils in the roadways and parking areas.

It all seemed somehow dated and slightly redundant, the machine that had brought me to the museum with the Professor was a completely different beast and didn't look like this battered old thing. It was like comparing a Ford Focus with a Model T, no, not even that, it was like comparing a Vauxhall Ampera with a steam car from 1895, yes, they were both cars, but that's about it.

We moved on, past an old church, probably just a village church from somewhere. Next to it what looked like a temple, possibly a Sikh temple, I couldn't quite place it, certainly an Indian style building. I walked a little closer and the words appeared before my eyes. I was looking at the Guru Nanak Gurdwara from Smethwick, a Sikh temple built in Birmingham.

The text read: 'During the multi-thousand year period of

 religious illness, these buildings called "temples" were considered vitally important to the well-being of many people. Structures like this were built all over the globe. People gathered in huge numbers to engage in what they described as "praying" or "worship" which was believed to be a private conversation with an unknowable higher being.'

I couldn't help feeling slightly defensive for all the millions of people from history who were given solace and security by their religious beliefs. I know I didn't share in such things but I had never thought of religious belief as an illness. It made me uneasy, it made me think the people of London cruel, insensitive and soulless.

We moved along a few hundred meters and there was a building I recognised, the Regent's Park Mosque. I read the description that streamed before my eyes. It was fairly damning of the Muslim faith going on to describe how different religions, even when they came from a geographically similar root as in Christianity, Islam and Judaism, often caused conflict and misunderstanding throughout the world. It described how through history such belief systems held back scientific progress and as the text suggested, most importantly, kept women oppressed and powerless. I felt myself begrudgingly agreeing with this rather generalised statement.

'If you come over here you can see a timeline,' said the Professor.

On the opposite side of the wide walkway between all the buildings and installations, some kind of play was being performed. It was only after watching for a moment or two that I realised I wasn't looking at actual living people, I was watching some kind of hologram thing, except it wasn't like a hologram of Princess Leia in Star Wars, these creations looked one hundred per cent solid, they cast shadows, they had weight and seemed anchored on the ground.

'This is overwhelming,' I said. 'What am I looking at?'

The Professor watched the procession passing before us, I assumed these people were key figures who had wielded power and influence over the past couple of hundred years.

'That is the first female Mayor of New York,' she said pointing to a woman who walked past us and smiled, just as if she were a model on a catwalk.

'That is the first female Mayor of Beijing,' she said as a Chinese woman approached us, smiled and walked on by.

A procession of smartly dressed mostly middle-aged women continued to approach where we stood, all races represented. Suddenly a woman approached that made my heart skip a beat.

'Bloody hell! Maggie! What's she doing here?'

Margaret Thatcher walked past us. Not a waxwork that looked vaguely like Margaret Thatcher, it was as if I was outside 10 Downing Street in about 1981 and there she was. Utterly and chillingly lifelike.

'I believe she was the first female Prime Minister of England, is that not correct?' stated the Professor.

'Yes, well she was the first female Prime Minister of the United Kingdom.'

'Indeed,' said the Professor and she looked around the young people standing nearby. 'That's often a hard concept to grasp. Would anyone like to expand on the concept?'

'The United Kingdom was a political construct designed to bind all the city states together,' said the very bright young women at the front of the group.

'Well, I suppose you could call it that,' I said. 'Although we didn't have the concept of city states, we had countries.'

'Countries?' asked Tudor dresser Judd.

'Yes, the world was divided into separate countries, often with their own language and culture that was quite distinct from other countries. We didn't have city states.'

'It was a rather inefficient system which often led to unnecessary wars and strife,' said the Professor flatly. She was addressing the students, not me. 'Endless competition which was seen as progressive and an encouragement to scientific and technological development, but as we can see all around us, it often held back progress.'

I looked around me at the spectacular human achievements on display, I wondered if she was right. The Professor was in full flow by now, 'The development of the city state removed many of those conflicts allowing smaller groupings to work together more effectively. We'll be going into more detail of this change in the next semester.'

Seeing Margaret Thatcher had a similar effect on me to seeing the picture of Tony Blair and the Queen. It brought my old life rushing back, it released waves of strong feelings, of the dizzying new reality I was living in, the nauseating truth of what I was experiencing. I started to miss Beth again, even though we disagreed on this particular topic, I missed those disagreements. Of course, Beth was a very keen supporter of Margaret Thatcher even though, as with me, she'd only been a toddler and child during the period of her stewardship. My family had loathed Thatcher so it was always a little awkward when we visited my parents and Beth praised her and expressed her admiration.

I also remembered Beth talking to me about the role women played in society and I'd just lose interest, I simply couldn't engage with such conversations. I didn't have anything to say. I'd like to explain that I didn't think women should be oppressed or sent back to the kitchen to breed and cook. Far from it, I enjoyed working with the few female engineers I came across on various projects, but now, suddenly as I stood in this incredible museum, I started to question everything.

Six women walking arm in arm then approached us and stopped as a group. They represented a range of races, African, Indian, Asian and Caucasian. They hung on to each other and laughed, other than their clothes which all looked a bit unusual to my eyes, they could have been in a clothing store advert from

2011, they were laughing and talking and just having a 'really good time' like models in a magazine.

'Those are the original Weaver women,' said the Professor. I stared at their faces, these creations were so incredibly real, solid looking and yet I knew enough about them to know they had all died many years earlier.

'So let me get this straight,' I said, as many better-dressed women passed us by as part of the historical pageant before me. 'Women took over running things about a hundred and fifty years ago?'

Professor Etheridge seemed to wait for her students to ask, when none of them did she said,

'I don't think the term "took over" quite describes it. It was a slow process that had, I believe, started long before your era. If you look back through history, indeed, pre-historic research shows quite clearly the dominance of the woman. In pre-patrilineal cultures women were always more dominant as mothers of course. In most ancient belief systems a woman existed first, her son was a secondary being, her offspring. Women created life, this is of course before the connection between sex and childbirth was understood. The human race then went through a ten thousand year period of patriarchal dominance. The power of the father, that was until the Weaver women, and Das Mutterrecht, the mother right.'

'The mother right,' I repeated, I'd never heard this term before, not even from Beth when she was on one of her rants.

'When women had control over their reproductive systems and became better educated,' said the Professor. 'Two very important things happened, population growth started to diminish and more and more women emerged who not only gave birth to children but also managed the world around them.'

'So is that when you took over?' I asked.

The Professor continued: 'Women started making strides toward power long before even you were born. Women's suffrage was when, just after World War I? The first woman Prime Minister in the United Kingdom in 1979, the first woman to be President of the United States of America in 2016, the first woman president of China in 2022. It was partly that, but also due to the emergence of city states in the mid-twenty-first century. These were generally already run by women Mayors and as the old national institutions became more and more unwieldy, more and more men started to give up and resign.'

'So the men just gave up? I've got to say that doesn't sound very plausible, there were so many power crazed men in my era, men who would do anything to seize or maintain their grip on power, these blokes would rather die than give up power. In fact they often did die.'

'Indeed,' said the Professor. 'But the change was seen as more psychological than political, so many men seemed unable to maintain their power-base; their lives seemed dogged by scandal and revelations of hypocrisy. This has to be seen in context of the emerging and far more successful and popular city states, localised and more manageable democracies with longer governing periods. Once a Mayor was elected with a twenty-year electoral cycle, planning became far more long-term and less likely to be damaging to the environment or electorate. Many cities began co-operating with each other far more successfully than nation states seemed able to do. What you knew as nation states slowly broke up and hence city states mostly run by women expanded and this filled the power vacuum.'

While the Professor explained this to me, I had moved back from the display so words and descriptions of the women before me didn't leak into my eyeballs. Out of all the technologies I'd come across in my travels that one was the most unpleasantly intrusive.

Even though I was now getting a potted history of how the current situation in the Squares of London had evolved, as usual it raised far more questions than it answered.

I was aware even back in 2011 that women were rapidly becoming far more successful in their education than men. I knew that an increasing number of women were in key positions in some companies but it was still unusual, the world I grew up in had always felt utterly dominated by men. What I was being told seemed to indicate that men had kind of given up. It wasn't so much that there was a power struggle that women had finally won. It was more that the blokes shrugged and wandered off and the women just took control because someone had to.

We started to move past the Shard and arrived in an area filled with dull looking boxes in various shapes and sizes. As I walked near one of the nondescript objects the annoying text appeared in my vision.

'Hyglops P13, first mass-produced cuisine printer.'

'A cuisine printer?' I said, turning toward the gaggle of students.

'Didn't you have these in the old days?' said the tall Japanese girl.

'Um, no. I mean I know what cuisine is and I know what a printer is, is it like, a 3D food printer?'

I looked behind the box device and saw a picture of cows in a field, the sort of image a supermarket would use to show how natural their produce was.

'These were early model food printers,' said the Professor, 'very crude by today's standards, but essential and lifesaving.'

'Why were they lifesaving?'

'Quite simply,' said the Professor, 'once we'd passed the eight billion mark in global population, there was no way we could feed everyone using the forms of agriculture you would have known. We had to develop new methods of producing food, especially meat.'

'So you can print meat with one of these!'

'Well, these old printers could produce something that looked like meat, it had many of the benefits of meat in terms of vitamins and protein but it tasted a bit like old cloth. If you follow me…'

The Professor walked along the display of dull looking boxes until she was standing in front of a smaller unit.

'This model, the P96 was the game changer. There are still many of these in use today even though they are often more than seventy years old. This machine can produce meat that is in every way better than any animal could possibly produce. More protein-dense, lower fat, more nutritious and of course, utterly delicious.'

'But what do you put in it, what does it use to print meat?'

The Professor pointed to a display next to the box, a shelf supporting a series of small plastic containers filled with liquids of different colours.

'Okay, but where does the stuff inside the containers come from?'

One of the students pointed to a display further along the wall, it looked like the interior of a large warehouse, the sort of thing Ocado, the grocery distribution service, once used to store and sort products. However, instead of plastic bottles and tins of refined food, each bay contained some kind of growing vegetation.

'We use a wide array of non-edible plants as raw material,' said the student. 'These have all been modified to produce the maximum amount of ingredient they are best at producing. In many ways, just like an animal that converts plant food into meat products, we do the same, only bypassing the animal.'

I stood looking at the small, innocuous box in front of me. 'Yep, that's pretty amazing,' I finally agreed.

'Wait 'till you see the next display,' said Judd the Tudor dresser.

We went around a corner and into an area that had been created to resemble a blasted desert. It was like a studio set for a movie, a kind of sandy fake desert setting and a fairly realistic looking backdrop of sun bleached clouds slowly moving across the giant screen. In the foreground lying among rocks and sand were hundreds of spent brass cartridges. To one side, a small mountain of weapons, some I recognised as assault rifles, even an ancient-looking Kalashnikov were piled up in a useless heap. Behind them were the remnants of military vehicles riddled with holes.

'Do you know what those are?' asked the tall Japanese looking girl.

'What, the guns?' I said.

'Yes, guns. Did you have one back in 2011?'

'What, a gun? No, of course not, I wasn't a soldier.'

'Did anyone shoot at you with a gun?' asked Tudor Judd.

I shook my head. 'What's all this about?'

As we got closer to this large display area a word appeared before my eyes. 'Crystalliser Field.'

I couldn't help rubbing my eyes again and I stood back so the wretched words didn't appear in my field of vision.

'What's a crystalliser field?'

The Professor nodded toward the display. A figure appeared from behind a blasted vehicle and walked toward the front of the display. Again this looked utterly real, like a real woman in a real military fatigue outfit, she was carrying an assault rifle in one hand and a small spherical device in the other.

'The inventor of the crystalliser field,' said the Professor. 'Rene Marion, she was a biochemist who worked in North Africa and the Middle East around 2083, she was working on crystallisation systems for water and energy storage when she discovered that she could also use the method to disable explosives. The chemical components of the explosive charges were made inert by being separated into their constituent ingredients in inert crystal form. It's essentially a very simple process, but once she developed the ability to transmit this field over short distances, she demonstrated how effective it could be in violent disputes where these crude weapons systems were still used. With the backing of many of the world's Mayors, she was able to develop and improve the system until by about 2095 there were no more functioning guns in the world.'

'No guns, I suppose you mean no more guns that go bang and fire bullets using explosive charges as their propellants?'

'Exactly correct, Gavin.'

'But you presumably have other weapons systems?'

'No. None. No one has weapons, the desire to own or use a weapon is now seen, like religion—'

'—to be a form of mental illness,' I said, finishing the now familiar motif. The Professor smiled at me kindly, she was impressed.

I did have a thought at that moment, along the lines of 'everything is a bloody mental illness to these weird freaks', but I kept that thought to myself. At least I hoped I kept it to myself, it was becoming more apparent that the very notion of thoughts, privacy and secrecy was extremely porous in 2211. Anyway, no one reacted, I took a last glance at the piles of useless guns dropped in the fake desert setting and we moved on.

Around the next corner the intensity of the whiteness almost hurt my eyes.

At first I found it hard to judge scale or even sense where the floor actually was. It was a white space, with, I could just make out, hundreds of small white boxes standing in serried ranks.

'I don't imagine you know what these are,' said Judd the Tudor lover.

'I don't know, freezers?' I suggested.

'It's what you might think of as a hospital,' said the Professor. I admit I was surprised, other than the fact that the whole area was a massive expanse of some sort of smooth white material there was no clue that this was a hospital.

'Okay,' I said, still baffled.

'This is a technology first developed about eighty years ago,' explained the Professor. 'These machines are Ndoc printers, they produce the essential elements we now use in medicine. We no longer use chemical drugs to try and battle disease and infection, we use nanoscopic doctors although we generally refer to them as Ndocs. These small machines produce even smaller machines, the individual units are all under one hundred nanometres in size and invisible to the naked eye. I believe you may have known the theory for such devices two hundred years ago?'

'Yes, well, I'd read about the theory, I know IBM had done some work in this area but they didn't really exist out in the wild.'

'Well, they do now, in their hundreds of billions. These machines produce about ten million of them every hour, we use them for many different purposes, not only medicine although clearly that's where they have been of enormous benefit. The ones made here are programmed to carry out specific tasks in the body. The kidonge you took has a small selection of Ndocs within it that will already have scanned your tissues for any potential problem, they will report back to a central system which can alert you for any possible future complaint.'

'So you really don't have diseases any more?'

The Professor shook her head.

'No one has cancer?' I asked.

'People still occasionally develop cancer but they probably never know about it, the Ndocs eradicate the damaged cells before any danger occurs.'

It was impossible not to stand in this wonderful white space without being overpowered with the wonder of the achievement. This technology must have changed the human experience more than anything else I'd seen. No more disease, the human race had done it, we had finally conquered our own biology.

'So what Nkoyo was telling me, no more physical ailments but you still have people who are a bit, well, crackers.'

'I'm sorry?'

'Bonkers,' I said, but still the same look of confusion rested on the Professor's face. 'Doo-lally, barking, mad as a cut snake, insane, lunatic, psychotic, crazy.'

By now the Professor was nodding and she gave me one of her rare smiles. 'They are not terms we tend to use,' she said. 'But yes, we still have to deal with the human condition. Some people find life in the city very stressful, hence the continued development of the talking cure.'

'The talking cure, what's that?'

'Oh, I assumed you would know about that. It's certainly not new, the talking cure, the process of personal understanding, therapy, psycho-analysis.'

'Oh blimey, Freud, Jung, all that nonsense,' I said. 'No matter what you're doing or thinking, really it's about sex or the fact that your mum didn't breastfeed you properly.'

I laughed as I spoke but the Professor didn't join me in mirth, she just looked at me blankly.

'It's what you've been doing with Doctor Markham,' she said.

'Have I?'

I couldn't help it, I felt a bit sick. I was being assessed, I was being head-shrunk and the realisation made me feel mildly aggressive. I didn't need to be treated, I was fine and whatever problem they saw in me, well, as far as I was concerned that was their own problem. I was busy having an inner rant but this came to an abrupt halt as it dawned on me I was doing just that.

I was like a screaming kid throwing themselves about in a temper, I slowly felt my spirits sink as I started to see myself very clearly. Essentially what I saw was probably one of those special Freudian moments, a sudden vision of yourself from outside, a horrible, spirit crushing realisation that I had a man's body with a sulking, moody child inside. It was annoying, I didn't want them to be right about me but I couldn't deny it.

'So you think I'm a bit of a nutcase then,' I said, I was grinning, not to show that I was a nutcase but to indicate that I was partly teasing, although it was a perfectly serious question. The thing I was rapidly coming to understand is that if, after all I'd been through, I had gone bonkers, I'd probably be the last person to know.

'Doctor Markham is one of the leading figures in mental health in the city, you are very privileged.'

That wasn't really an answer; in fact it seemed to me to be tacit agreement. They thought I was a nutter, they were keeping tabs on me and it didn't feel comfortable.

As we walked through the long rows of white printers, the next thing I saw made me spin me into near despair.

'Now that is a great honour,' said Tudor boy.

By far the densest crowd I'd seen all day was about two hundred meters in front of us, all of them looking up. It took my eyes a moment to fully comprehend what I was looking at, when I did comprehend I experienced many intense and unsettling feelings.

Hanging from a long cable in a setting made entirely from giant clocks was something I knew intimately.

The Yuneec.

13

Anger Mismanagement

'WHY IS MY PLANE HANGING IN THE BLOODY museum?'

That's what I shouted at Pete when I eventually found my way back to his store the following day.

'It's a bloody exhibit in the bloody London Museum of bloody Human History! How does this bloody city work? Why does no one tell me anything?'

Pete stood with his hands clasped in front of him like a gigantic naughty schoolboy. He said nothing.

I paced around the large empty space; there was nothing in the room that day except a complex array of plumbing made of transparent pipework which presumably Pete was working on.

'What am I supposed to do?' I shouted. I really was angry, this wasn't an act, I could sense my heart rate being way up, I felt my fists clench and unclench. I knew I wasn't about to start punching Pete, I probably couldn't have reached his head unless I was standing on a chair. It would have been a bit like a kitten taking a swipe at a full-grown lion.

That said, my anger and volume clearly upset Pete, he was cowering now, he really did look frightened, and I suddenly felt like a school bully picking on a little kid.

I sat down on a toolbox in the middle of the space and held my head in my hands.

'I thought,' I said quietly, 'that the reason you were all busy fixing up my plane, you know, my drone, was so I could fly it out of here, try and get back through whatever it was that brought me here.'

I glanced up at Pete, at first I couldn't quite take in what I was seeing. I couldn't tell if he was doing some jokey, big bloke bad acting. After a few moments I realised he wasn't acting, he was actually crying. A man of probably a hundred and fifteen kilos and at least six foot seven was sobbing. His shoulders rocking up and down as he stood looking a little bit pathetic at the other end of the huge space we were in.

'Oh blimey,' I said. 'I'm sorry, I'm sure it wasn't your fault. I just didn't know what to do when I saw it. It was such a bloody shock.'

Pete was nodding and wiping away the tears with the back of his enormous hands.

'I didn't want them to take it,' he said.

'Who?' I asked.

'The security officers, the ones who sat in the front row the other night,' Pete pointed to the approximate position their seats would have been in.

'The four women?' I asked.

'Yes. They met with me after you'd left. The advised me that it would be sensible to get the illegal drone out of my store.'

'Illegal! I didn't know it was illegal,' I said.

'Strictly speaking it is, heavier than air machines aren't allowed to be used over the city. Well, it's a bit silly because there aren't any heavier than air machines around, it's an old law I think.'

'No one ever said anything to me about it being illegal. Why didn't someone explain?' Again I noticed I was holding my head in my hands. This really was desperate, seeing the plane come back together had really lifted my spirits and made me hope that I wasn't completely trapped in this endless city.

'So they just took it?' I asked.

Pete nodded, his face wet with tears. 'They said they'd look after it. Not long after that a transport arrived and they took the Yuneec away.' He paused for a sob and then said in a rather weedy high-pitched voice, 'I was really upset, Gavin.'

'So the women just told you what to do?' I asked after a moment or two. Pete nodded. 'And you didn't tell them to piss off?'

Pete looked genuinely shocked and concerned. 'No, why would I do that?'

He had a point; it wasn't a very mature response. I pondered for a moment then asked, 'Why didn't you tell them to come and talk to me, after all, it's my bloody plane.'

'I did ask about that,' said Pete. 'They assured me you'd be informed.'

'This is brilliant isn't it. What am I supposed to do?'

'I don't know,' said Pete who started blubbing again.

'Look, it's okay,' I said, I got up and moved over to him. I didn't really know what to do so I reached up and patted his enormous forearm. 'It's not your fault, Pete,' I said, 'I know you were under a lot of pressure and the whole thing seemed to get a little out of your control. You know, having a bloody TV crew turn up and transform your store into a TV studio, it was all a bit much.'

'It was fine, it wasn't a problem, we do that all the time, usually it's with toilet systems or heat pumps, you know, strip them down and re-fit them. But your drone was special which is why so many folks turned up.'

'But there was an audience here!' I said.

'Those are all my friends,' Pete explained 'I was happy that they all came along to watch and we did a good job didn't we? We fixed the Yuneec up really good.'

'You did, it looked amazing,' I said trying to reassure him.

'I didn't want to upset you, I'm feeling so sad that I upset you, I wanted to be your friend, not someone who made you angry.'

More blubbing, I couldn't believe it, there really was no call for it, why was he crying? Why had I started crying when I'd been in front of all the press women, the worder women? What was all this? Men crying at the drop of a hat, it just didn't seem right. I started to wonder if the kidonge caused it but then I remembered I hadn't swallowed the little light blue worm thing when I started blubbing in front of the press. This was something else, maybe it was in the water, maybe the women were pumping oestrogen into the water to make the men less aggressive and assertive. I was really starting to dislike the women of London.

14

An Unusual Proposition

'WE NEED TO TALK,' I SAID TO NKOYO AS I travelled back to the Institute. I sat in the car on my own as it rocketed through the tunnel. At that point it didn't even occur to me that this incredible machine knew where I wanted to go. I can't think of a time I have been less interested in how a complex transportation system worked and how the tiny, microscopic wormy thing residing in my bone marrow had communicated with it.

All I knew was I was in a right old stew. I looked down at the small screen at the side of the seat, Nkoyo's face appeared and she smiled. I hadn't dialled a number, I hadn't pressed a button, I thought about Nkoyo and I was sitting next to a phone.

'What do you want to talk about, Gavin?' she asked, but I could tell she already knew.

'You already know,' I said, and of course, I was right.

'The drone,' she said, a very serious look on her face.

I'd never been right about this sort of thing in the past, how come I knew so much about what other people were thinking, even when I wasn't with them. Derren Brown, you've already eaten your heart, time to start on your liver.

'Yes, the bloody drone, I don't know why everyone calls it a drone. It's not a bloody drone it's an aeroplane.'

'You're coming back to the Institute?' she said, it was a question but clearly she knew the answer and this annoyed me further.

'I might, or I might not,' I said, recognising a familiar feeling rushing up from my stomach. I think it could be expressed as immature, maybe even childish. I wanted to hurt her. I wanted to make her feel my pain and disquiet. It was pointless, she wasn't in the least bit upset.

'When you get here, I'll make sure I can put some time aside to discuss it with you. I can see you are upset by the turn of events and I will do my best to explain the situation.'

It was all so sensible; it was what I should have requested in the first place. More than anything else, I think it was being kept in the dark that had been the most upsetting thing. No one had said anything, I suppose I was meant to know why they'd done this but I still didn't know how to access such information.

'Okay,' I said, feeling more than a little crestfallen. 'I'll talk it over in a calm and sensible way.'

'Thank you, I will see you shortly,' said Nkoyo.

The screen went blank just like that, no shash or signal failure, no little text message informing me that the connection was terminated, in an instant it went from a beautifully lit image of Nkoyo's face to a flat grey panel. Just as I was about to sit back and relax the screen pinged very gently, a woman's face appeared on it, not a still image, it was someone looking into a camera and waiting.

'Hello,' I said eventually, there was no one else in the car with me so it wasn't that embarrassing to say something only to discover the face on the screen was nothing more than an advert – not that I'd seen anything resembling an advert anywhere.

'Hello, Gavin, my name's Anne.'

'Hello, Anne,' I said, only now trying to work out where a camera might be that could be sending my image to this woman.

'I was at your worder conference the other day, I just saw you were around and dived in, you don't mind?'

'Um, no,' I said. 'I don't mind.'

I had no idea who this woman was or how she managed to contact me.

'You're not an easy man to get hold of,' she said.

'Am I not?' I asked, I wasn't being flirtatious, I really didn't know how easy or hard it might be to get hold of me.

'The Institute has a block on your coms.'

'A block on my coms?' This was getting increasingly weird.

'People like me aren't supposed to be able to contact you,' she said quickly. 'So I'm on proxies.'

'Okay, well, just for the record, I probably understand ten per cent of what you're telling me,' I said.

She spoke quickly. 'I was hoping we could meet. I really need to ask you some questions.'

'Oh, okay. Um, well, I'm staying at the Institute, it seems everyone knows where that is.'

'I can't come there, would you meet neutral?'

'Who's neutral?' I asked.

She explained slowly. 'I mean, would you meet me in a location that is neutral.'

'Oh, right, I see, like a café or restaurant or something.'

'How about the Erotic Museum?'

'The what?'

'You'll love it, it's in Carson Square.'

The screen went blank. Just like that. I didn't know what to do, there wasn't a re-dial button, in fact there were no buttons anywhere, this place was like the heaven Steve Jobs and the Amish must have hoped for. Utterly button free.

'Hello,' I said pathetically. 'Hello, Anne?'

Nothing. I felt the car lurch and change direction. I cupped my hand at the window to allow me to see out. Other vehicles where pulling back slightly to allow the machine I was in to safely change lanes. We took a fairly sharp turn to the right and accelerated, joining another stream of incredibly fast moving machines. After another minute or so we moved off that flow and went up a small incline, slowing all the time until violently coming to a halt. The doors slid open and I could see a small crowd of young people waiting politely for me to exit.

I stood up and left the car. 'Sorry,' I said as I passed the young people.

'Wow, it's the flying man,' said a young lad. 'You are awesome, sir.'

This lad had an American accent, the first one I'd heard since arriving in London, I stared at him but the doors slid shut and the car was gone in an instant.

15

The Erotic Museum

IMAGINE IF YOU WILL FOR A MOMENT, YOU were a visitor to Copenhagen in say, 1998 and someone said to you 'Let's meet at the Erotic Museum'. I'm choosing Copenhagen because I believe they really did have an erotic museum at one time, and no, I never visited.

Well, for a start you might think the person who invited you was a little odd, or had a slightly dodgy agenda, so you'd be on your guard. Then you'd have to find out where the Erotic Museum was, you'd have to ask someone, a passer-by on the street. Embarrassing. Maybe the receptionist at your hotel. Awkward. And even if they told you, you'd still need a street map to find your way in an unfamiliar city.

If you'd visited in 2011 you could at least have Googled it and used the street map app on your smartphone. In London in 2211 you just go there, you already know where it is. You don't know how you know where it is but you do, not only do you know where it is but the machine you have been travelling in adjusts its route without any signal or conscious interaction and when you get out of it, you are on Carson Square.

I must admit I didn't know I was on Carson Square until I emerged from the subterranean transport system. I saw a sign on the wall next to the exit. It said in nice big clear Gill Sans font 'Carson Square' and underneath a small plaque explaining that the Square had been named thus to commemorate Rachel Carson in 2164, two hundred years after her death.

I'd heard of 'Silent Spring', her famous book criticising the overuse of pesticides and weird chemicals used in agriculture. I also suddenly knew it was originally published in the early 1960s, but of course I'd never read it. Now she had a square named after her in what was possibly the biggest city ever created by the human race.

I turned left out of the exit and walked about a mile down the side of the square. This place was very different, the buildings were smaller, the square itself was a mass of colour and trees making up an expansive and very well tended garden busy with people working. I noticed that quite a few of them were men, digging, planting and I assumed harvesting various crops. It was urban gardening on a truly impressive scale. I could see in the distance that there was another multi-storey agricultural complex, the structure of which was only intermittently visible such was the density of foliage tumbling down its flanks.

I stopped outside a fairly nondescript building. It didn't look enormously different from the rest of the structures facing the square, a delightful five storey building with large windows, its paintwork seeming to glow in the sun.

I entered through a large pair of glass doors that slid open silently as I approached. Inside was a spacious lobby or gallery decorated with fairly explicit images of very fit young men in various states of undress and amorous arousal. In the centre of the space was a kind of circular desk behind which sat an equally well-built and seemingly naked man. I can't confirm that he was totally naked but his torso was very much on display and it was nothing short of magnificent. He smiled at me, I smiled back and gave a little nod. That was all, nothing was said.

I wasn't alone in the hall but a glance around the space confirmed that nearly all the other people were women and already quite a few of them were staring at me. There were a few men in evidence, small groups of men hanging around together. I noticed two of them holding hands. I tried to wander around as if I was at the National Gallery in Trafalgar Square. I was attempting to look interested and nonchalant. It wasn't easy.

This space was, to say the very least, fairly challenging for an average, run-of-the-mill heterosexual man from any century. It wasn't as if I hadn't seen images of naked men before but the particular images on display on the wall were very confronting to the averagely endowed male.

'Gavin, I'm Anne,' said a very hushed voice behind me. 'Don't turn around, just give a few beats then follow me from a good distance.'

I knew at once her name was Anne Hempstead and she was thirty-eight years old, she lived on Curie Square and had no children. She was a well-known worder with a very high reader count and was a leading writer on the Weaver supporters log. I knew all this instantly she spoke to me although I admit I didn't really know what half of it meant.

I can't explain how I knew, where the information was coming from or if the source was reliable but I was getting used to suddenly knowing stuff. I moved forward casually as if I was studying the anatomy of a young man who was nursing a reproductive organ that resembled nothing short of a well-polished Jacobean Chair leg. Eye watering.

After a few moments staring at his enormous and frighteningly high definition image I turned and saw a women in a floor length grey gown walking away from me toward a doorway into what I assumed was another gallery. I followed at a distance, aware of the many women who turned to stare at me as I passed. Some of them smiled, some looked slightly shocked.

I entered the next room which had a very different theme, many more paintings some of which even I recognised as an old Rembrandt and possibly a couple of Renoir-type things. I'm not very good at remembering painters but I recognised some of them. Some highly explicit paintings of men and women making love, women and women making love, men and men making love, basically a room full of massive sex paintings.

I almost lost sight of the woman who was now going through

yet another doorway, she turned to her right as soon as she'd gone through the door, I wandered around for a short while pretending to look at the plethora of naked bodies on the wall then entered the same doorway.

She was standing by the wall as if hiding, a staircase led up to another floor and it seemed there was no one else around.

'Follow me, quickly,' she said. She bounded up the stairs at such a rate there was no way I could keep up with her, the speed of her ascent was inhuman and I sensed that she was wearing some kind of mechanical enhancement on her legs.

Two flights later I caught up with her, I was panting like a long distance runner after a particularly hilly section of a marathon, she was totally calm.

'In here,' she said.

We entered a large brightly lit library room, she pulled something out of her bag and put it on the reading table we were standing beside. A small black container that looked a bit like a trendy glasses case.

'Blocker,' she said nodding to the small box. 'We have about five minutes so please listen.'

She was speaking in very hushed tones, constantly looking toward the door. 'Sit down over there, I'll find you something to read in case anyone comes in. If they do, you don't know me.'

She scanned the bookshelves beside her and pulled out a large illustrated volume of erotic drawings from 2130 according to the cover. I opened it with the full intention of going along with her deception but the images inside this beautifully printed tome were a little distracting.

'I just want to know what's going on,' said Anne Hempstead. She spoke incredibly quickly, faster than I'd ever heard any human being speak and yet I could follow what she was saying. 'I'm writing a story about you and I've been getting a lot of intervention. This is unusual, we have free speech, we can say anything we like, we can criticise the current administration and not fear reprisals but clearly you are seen as a special case. Who sent you here?'

'Sorry?'

'Who sent you?'

'Who sent me? Nobody sent me, I came here by some completely weird set of ridiculous circumstances,' I said.

'So you're claiming you've not been sent here by any organisation, public body or military unit?'

'No, what? A military unit, no! What are you talking about?'

'I want to know how you really got here, and where did you really come from? Is it your plan to reinstate the patriarchy, to teach men how to rape, defile and oppress womankind, to help return the world to the dark times?'

This woman was clearly mad, maybe she'd escaped from the Institute. On the other hand my arrival in this place was so utterly implausible, the circumstances so unfathomable and the technology so advanced, maybe she knew much more about my circumstances than she was letting on. Maybe she knew that the authorities in London did bring me through the cloud without my knowing it, brought me through for some bizarre purpose I didn't at that point understand.

Then I looked at her again, decided she was mad and I wanted to leave.

'I don't know what you're on about. All I know is that I came here from 2011, there's no way I could have planned it. You've got no idea what I've been through, it's a nightmare.'

'I think you know exactly what's going on, Gavin Meckler. I think you knew why you came here, you knew what an impact your arrival would make; the timing is too perfect for it to be chance. You knew you could travel back in time and change history.'

It was at that point I decided she really was crackers, I got up to leave but she put her hand on my shoulder to stop me.

'I have the right to know, we all have the right to know

who you are and who sent you,' she said incredibly quickly. I shrugged her hand off and stood up. I felt angry and tired and very confused.

'Look, Anne Hempstead, whoever you are. I've no idea what you're talking about. I know nothing, as far as I'm concerned time travel is impossible, well, as far as I knew before I arrived here. I'm just a man who arrived here due to some kind of freak, meta-physics, I'm an ordinary man, I don't believe in patriarchy, I don't even really know what patriarchy is. I certainly don't believe it's my right to rape women, I don't want to crush women back to the dark times, I don't want to be the dominant master race, I don't think women are second class citizens who should live their lives barefoot and pregnant at the kitchen sink or any other nonsense. I'm just a bloke from two hundred years ago who wants to go home.'

Anne stared at me and possibly smiled, I couldn't tell, she had a weird mouth, one of those people with a mouth that looks a bit like a cat's bum. Not attractive.

'Quite simply, Gavin Meckler, I don't buy it,' she said eventually. 'You are clearly here for a reason. It's possible you genuinely don't know that, but believe me your arrival is anything but accidental. You are here at a crucial time in history. Your sudden arrival could not possibly be accidental. You know about the Assembly vote, I take it.'

'The Assembly vote?'

The look this rather fierce woman gave me can only be described as an unpleasant mix of hatred and disbelief.

'The Assembly vote next month, that must be why you are here.'

'I wish I knew what you're on about,' I said.

She wiped her mouth with her hand. It was a rather ugly gesture.

'You know exactly why you are here, no one else does yet, but they soon will understand.'

She picked up the black box and secreted it into her gown.

'Bloody hell,' I said. 'You should try and get some help.'

'Why would I need help? Are you threatening me?'

'Threatening you! For goodness sake, you're the one being threatening and aggressive. I don't know what your problem is lady, but clearly it's nothing to do with me.'

'I'm afraid it's very much to do with you. The established authorities know if they don't do something soon,' said Anne Hempstead much more slowly. 'Then the world will become a hundred per cent female within a generation.'

'And that's a good thing?' I asked. Her face gave her away; although she didn't say anything, I could tell there and then that I'd just met a fully kosher Weaver woman.

16

I Want Him!

I RETURNED TO THE INSTITUTE IMMEDIATELY after leaving the Erotic Museum. I kept my eyes resolutely on the floor as I left, I didn't want to see or remember the multitude of stimulating images on display.

So I was in London in 2211 and the world wasn't in chaos due to running out of fossil fuels, food or building materials, it was running out of men.

I became increasingly aware of the imbalance of genders as I walked back to the transport entrance, I only saw women, hundreds of women and I have to say most of them didn't look all that happy.

But the men I had met, they all seemed like decent blokes, they didn't come across as bullies, rapists or violent murderers. They were proper men, big tall hairy blokes who seemed if anything unusually gentle. Okay so 5-G nephew Ralph presented as rather camp and Akiki had to be on the extreme gay end of the human sexuality spectrum, but the rest, Pete, Yuseff and all the men who watched the Yuneec being rebuilt, they were just regular blokes. They dressed differently, they were a bit over emotional for my liking but they were men and there seemed to be enough of them to make a respectable crowd.

What was even stranger about the world I had landed in was the intrigue. It wasn't even clear there was any intrigue or subversion or gun-toting revolutionary elements buried deep and unseen. Not that the guns would have been much good, they couldn't shoot guns with bullets any more, that was obvious.

I then considered not only what Anne had told me, but what

 she could have done to me. I was alone with her for a short while, if she was as mad as she seemed and saw me as a direct threat to the Weaver women's aim of eradicating men from the planet, then why didn't she kill me?

Maybe she didn't need to, maybe the blocker thing she had used in the quiet library was really a knacker adaptor, a testosterone terminator, maybe she had used some subtle technology to ensure I could only ever create female babies.

It just didn't make sense, I'd seen no sign of dissent and everything I'd seen pointed to stability, sustainability in both technology and politics. London struck me as an incredibly stable and safe place. I hadn't been mugged or set upon by gangs of dangerous-looking youths, in fact, I hadn't seen any gangs of youths. I pondered this for a moment, soon realising that by definition gangs of youths who might attack and rob you tended to be men and there weren't that many men or boys in evidence.

There were no obvious uniformed police, though there had been the women who walked along with Ralph and I on my first outing and the four women watching me when I was in Pete's store witnessing the Yuneec rebuild. They looked like they could be some kind of security detail and there probably was surveillance of some kind but it was so universal, so embedded that everyone seemed to know everything anyway. It wasn't surveillance as I would have understood it, secret agents listening into conversations or reading e-mails, it didn't feel like there was a GCHQ somewhere keeping tabs because everyone was able, so it seemed, to keep tabs on everyone else.

Yet the unpleasant Anne had used the blocker thing. I'd been a fool, I'd assumed at the moment she revealed it to me it somehow blocked the signal from the kidonge. I have no idea how I knew that and as I lay on my bed that night I started to doubt my initial assumption. What on earth could a blocker do? I remembered she said she couldn't read me so maybe the blocker meant she couldn't sense what I was really thinking as Nkoyo and Doctor Markham seemed very adept at doing. The very idea of something like a blocker existing suggested that indeed someone could keep very close tabs on me. Anne's secret agent behaviour in the Erotic Museum also suggested that she knew how to work around the systems that I had to assume were in place.

I had already accepted that my kidonge meant it was possible to discover where I was located at any time but it hadn't really worried me. My old twenty-first-century phone did that, so it was nothing new. I had nowhere to go anyway, I didn't want to do anything subversive or dangerous, the whole experience of landing in their rather mysterious city was danger enough.

These thoughts clanging around in my head must have eventually worn me down because I slept for a long time.

As the tint changed on my window when I woke up, it was already bright outside.

After my morning ablutions I made my way downstairs with the intention of getting some breakfast. As I approached the bottom of the extra big stairs I heard shouting. A woman was making a lot of noise somewhere down the long corridor, I couldn't make out anything that was being said but it sounded a bit dramatic. My normal reaction to such events in the past has always been to close down, to try and ignore, to keep moving and get away from the emotional turmoil. I'd never felt the need some people have, to grab any chance to witness anything upsetting. If I passed by people having a row on the street back in the old days I'd always keep moving, keep my eyes on the ground and hope they ignored me. I'd never wanted to watch disaster clips on YouTube, I didn't want to see people making stupid mistakes and either injuring themselves or dying as a result of their actions.

Now, however, I found myself approaching the ruckus like a pin being drawn towards a magnet, I wanted to know what was going on. Instead of being desperate to get away, I wanted to see if I could help, it was as if I felt an emotional pull from hearing the cries of despair.

I glanced into the big room where I'd done my first interview with Doctor Markham and the panel of powerful ladies. One of the silent big-armed women appeared to be hugging a struggling dark haired woman who was standing in the middle of the room. Beyond them I could see Nkoyo and Doctor Markham looking very concerned. As soon as Nkoyo saw me she moved across the room at speed. The struggling woman turned her head and I could see the anguish on her face. She reached out an arm towards me as if begging for help. I felt hugely torn, should I intervene? Should I rush to try and rescue her from her beefy captor?

The woman's face was twisted with anguish, she screamed 'I want him! That one! I want him!'

Before I could react Nkoyo was beside me, she grabbed my arm and ushered me along the corridor. I don't want to imply that I am physically weak or that Nkoyo was unladylike in her strength but clearly she was no wilting wallflower when it came to imposing her physical dominance on a dramatic situation. She gripped my arm hard and pulled me along with some quite distressing force.

'Hey, easy!' I complained, as she ushered me into the canteen room. As soon as we were inside the door slid up silently behind us.

'I didn't want you to see that, Gavin,' she said as she looked directly into my eyes. Awkward. She was standing very close and there was nowhere for me to look without making a point, I just had to hold her gaze, stare directly into her large dark eyes. Okay, it wasn't that bad.

'What's wrong with that poor woman?' I asked, rubbing my upper arm, I was definitely going to get bruises.

Nkoyo relaxed a little, sighed and composed herself, she sat on the edge of one of the canteen tables, reached over and a box in the wall opened, inside was a tall metallic liquid container, she extracted it and passed it to me.

'Your morning tea,' she said. 'I didn't want you to see her, or more importantly for her to see you at that moment. It was very unfortunate because the woman is in treatment and at a very critical stage of her cure.'

'Oh dear, what's wrong with her?' I asked, I was just about to take a slurp of tea and held the container in front of my face.

'It is sadly becoming very common. There are so many women who have no hope of ever finding a male partner to share their lives with. Many of us are happy about that; myself for instance. I have never felt a burning need for male company. The poor woman you saw is having a kind of nervous breakdown, if she ever sees a man on the street she cannot stop herself from approaching him. Her life lies in ruins, she has a daughter who she cannot look after any longer. It's a very sad and all too common occurrence.'

I lowered my tea. 'Oh, I see, but she seemed like a fairly good looking young woman, surely she can find a bloke in the end.'

Nkoyo looked at me for a while without speaking. 'No, Gavin,' she said eventually. 'She has virtually no chance of finding a male partner, even a mere male friend is very hard to find.'

'But I've seen loads of men, there was a big crowd at Pete's store when they mended my plane that's now hanging in the museum.'

'Yes, there are men in London, but they are far outnumbered by women. We have also found that many of the men you will have met are not interested in devoting their lives to one woman, your nephew Ralph is an unusual exception. While it's true you will have seen plenty of men who are in one relationship and who look after their offspring, this is becoming increasingly rare.'

'So, there's just not enough men to go around?'

'Precisely. It's a very difficult balance, I know you spoke with Professor Etheridge about the current imbalance and the influence of the Weaver women.'

'Yes, I did,' I said carefully, fully expecting to be questioned about my visit to the Erotic Museum. No question came.

'Anyway,' said Nkoyo after a deep sigh, 'I wanted to talk to you about your drone.'

'Aeroplane.'

'Yes, as you wish, I know you are anxious and upset about it.'

'Well, it was a bit of a shock,' I said feeling my blood rise. I was still angry but it was focused and clear. 'No one said anything to me. I know I just landed here, I understand I have no rights, but blimey, common courtesy, openness, you know, like honesty, transparency, you've given me the impression those were all things you valued.'

For the first time Nkoyo bowed her head, I could see what I had said actually affected her, I could sense that she found the moment unpleasant and awkward and of course I immediately felt guilty.

'I'm sorry,' I said, I couldn't help it.

'I am very sorry too, Gavin,' she replied eventually. 'I have had a word with the Mayor's office and it was their decision. You need to understand we have very strict rules about airborne devices. We no longer allow them in the sky, this is an old law dating back over one hundred years and no one could be sure you wouldn't try and fly in the machine again. It is deemed too dangerous to have such machines in the air, we had a great deal of trouble with drones many years ago, I'm sure Professor Etheridge would explain the details and point you in the right direction to learn more of the reasons behind the global ban. We no longer need drones for transportation or any other reason, they are a redundant technology. Obviously your machine is of great historical interest, there was no desire to destroy it and it was seen as the best option to put it on display. That way the many people who are intrigued by your story can see the machine for themselves. It's currently the most popular display in the museum.'

'I could see that,' I said. 'But what am I supposed to do, stay here?'

'Well, I can't think of what other options you have,' said Nkoyo rather flatly.

I shook my head in frustration, what she was telling me was eminently sensible, I completely understood it but it did mean I had no chance of leaving, of making any sort of attempt at getting back to my own time. I knew of course this was never going to happen, what ever had taken place to bring me here was way beyond me, and it seemed way beyond the people who inhabited London even with their kidonges, self-driving cars, huge garden squares and print-on-demand meat.

'I want to go home,' I said rather pathetically.

'I understand,' she replied. 'It's very difficult; the adjustment could take a long time. However, I want you to know you are welcome here, you are a valued individual and you do have rights. They are rights that are held in a framework of responsibilities to others of course, and one of those responsibilities is not to put people in danger by flying around in a heavier than air drone machine.'

17

Back to School

RALPH CAME TO COLLECT ME EARLY THE following morning and I assumed, although I tried to hide my dread out of politeness, he was taking me on another nightmarish shopping trip.

However, he wasn't alone, he was accompanied by a young girl who I immediately knew to be his daughter.

I remembered the picture he showed me at the cafe and to my confusion a fairly clear image of the photograph appeared before me, kind of overlaid on the real image of Ralph and Natasha, I also suddenly knew her name.

Ralph was grinning and looking if anything even taller and thinner than last time I'd seen him.

'I'm just walking Natasha to school and we wondered if you'd like to come along, some of the teachers have asked if you would be happy to visit and maybe give a short talk to the children this morning.'

So it was worse than shopping, at least if I went shopping I wouldn't have to give 'a short talk' to anyone. I remembered the last time I had been asked to talk to a load of kids, in the learning hall at Goldacre Hall in Gardenia. That didn't end well. I was just rubbish at talking to people, especially kids.

'Oh, right.'

'You don't have anything else to do,' said Ralph as if it was obvious, which it was. I suppose it was pointless making rubbish excuses, he'd known in some spooky, kidonge-based way that I was doing absolutely nothing other than eating breakfast and sitting with Doctor Markham for an hour in the afternoon talking about my mum, my childhood and my sexual fantasies. They are rather dull by the way. They involve what I now understand to be fully consensual sexual intercourse between a man and a woman in private, in the dark, under the covers.

'Yes, sure, I'd enjoy going for a walk,' I said. I don't think it sounded like I thought it would be fun, but then Natasha smiled at me and held out her hand.

I glanced at Ralph. 'It's okay,' he said. 'She's only seven, she's not allowed DT yet.'

'DT?'

'Sorry, of course,' he turned to Natasha. '5-G Uncle Gavin doesn't understand a lot of things yet darling, but he's learning fast,' he turned back to me. 'Dual Transaction, she is not able to charge you, you can give her pocket money if you want, but she's already had her allowance this week.'

'Oooh, dad, you shouldn't have told him!' said Natasha, sounding just like a seven-year-old. She was so tall that I had assumed she was much older.

I held Natasha's hand and we walked out of the Institute and turned left, not something I'd done before.

'How far away is your school, Natasha?' I asked as the heat of the day engulfed me.

'If I run all the way I can get there in exactly thirty eight minutes.'

'Wow, that's still quite a long way,' I said, 'can't you get a bus or something? Do you have to walk or run there every day?'

Natasha turned and looked up at me with a peculiar expression on her perfect face. 'Yes,' she said, as if my question was utterly absurd.

It took us almost an hour to get to the school but the walk was pleasant if at a pace that was just short of a jog for me. I'll say one thing for the inhabitants of London in 2211, they are no slouches.

Of course walking through a city without being surrounded

 by mechanical traffic is a very different experience from the cities I'd grown up in. The only sound was the breeze in the trees, bird song, the chatter of passing people and occasionally music coming out of open windows. I soon worked out that this wasn't some sophisticated sound system; this was people playing actual instruments. Through a window just above street level I saw a woman playing a cello.

The school was a building like most of the others in London, part of a terrace maybe three storeys high and facing a large area of woodland which seemed to cover the square.

'What an amazing place to go to school,' I said, looking around. 'You're very lucky, Natasha.' I was saying this in my 'this is how you talk to children' voice, it didn't seem to impress Natasha, she shrugged and jumped up the three wide steps that lead to the ubiquitous sliding glass door at the entrance.

She turned back towards Ralph and I as she stood in front of the door, other children passed her as she looked back at us.

'Bye bye sweetest child,' shouted Ralph. 'I'll see you this afternoon.'

Natasha smiled, waved and ran inside. It was such a normal vision, a child entering school and yet as I was about to discover, this was very unlike any school I had ever seen or heard of.

'Listen, Ralph,' I said as I stepped back to allow a gaggle of children to pass. 'I really don't want to talk to all the kids, I've got nothing to say and I tend to get upset. It just reminds me of what I've left behind; it's too hard to deal with. I never had children and I left my wife all alone and she thinks I died in a plane crash. It's all a bit difficult.'

'That's fine 5-G Uncle,' he replied. 'Don't do the stress thing. The headmistress asked me if you'd be happy to talk and I said you were very chatty but if you get upset, she'll understand. I thought you'd like to see how a school in London works though. You might learn something yourself, you never know.'

Large numbers of children were now arriving at the wide

school entrance, two enormous trees stood sentry either side of the entranceway giving blessed shade to people entering and leaving. London was so hot, I really appreciated a bit of shade.

We joined the slow procession up the wide steps toward the entrance, many of the kids around us were walking with their fathers. There were one or two women were walking with children, most of whom were girls from what I could make out. I started to check to see if I could see any boys.

'Is this an all-girls' school?' I asked Ralph. Again I got that look, the look that told me I was some kind of moron or possibly a pervert.

'No, it's a school, just an ordinary school,' came the slightly offended reply.

'Oh, right,' I said. 'It's just that I can't see any boys.'

Ralph turned and pointed to two boys coming up the steps behind us. 'What are those then, goats?'

'Good morning, Mister Meckler, what a great privilege to have you visit the Greer Academy.' I turned to see a grey-haired woman standing in the large entrance lobby. She was tall and wearing a long grey tunic of some kind and she had similar coloured gloves on. In fact she looked almost ghostly because her skin was so pale and her eyes were a weird grey colour. It was as if she had tinted contact lenses.

'Um, thanks,' I stuttered. 'It's, um, well, it's a lovely surprise to be here.'

'We would like to welcome you in the staffroom before this morning's assembly. I know many of the children are excited to meet you.'

I walked along a corridor with this woman who I somehow knew to be Candice Jago, the headmistress of the Greer Academy. 'Um, the thing is, I'm not very good at speaking in public,' I said as I trotted to keep up with her. Even old ladies walked fast in London. 'Especially to children. I did a talk in a school once, years ago.' I wanted to cover up the fact that it was merely months ago and in a learning hall that might very well never have existed. 'I found it very challenging. I have no idea what to say.'

A door slid open on our left and I entered a room full of men. They all started clapping as I walked in, I looked around for Ralph but he was nowhere to be seen. I wanted to understand why these men were clapping, I was completely in the dark. Somehow I knew things like the headmistress's name, but I could not understand this admittedly cheerful response to my appearance. I nodded a greeting and waved rather pathetically at the group of men in the room.

'This is my wonderful teaching staff,' she said with a sweep of her very long arm. 'Good morning chaps.'

'Morning, Miss Jago,' said the men, almost in unison and almost in a jokey sort of way. Almost, but not quite. The headmistress passed me a cup of coffee, again in the ubiquitous utilitarian steel mug.

'They all know who you are, Gavin. You understand that, don't you?'

'Um, well, yes, I'm learning, it's very confusing.'

She put a gloved hand on my shoulder. 'It's fascinating, I have never met an adult who hasn't had a kidonge since they were a baby, you are a very unique case. So allow me to explain. As you know we all have a kidonge, it's a simple communication enhancement and with practice it is, as you may have discovered, very useful.'

'It's amazing, baffling even.'

'Well, imagine you are say, five years old and suddenly you have all the information that has ever existed in all human experience immediately available, can you imagine what that might do?'

I was desperate to say 'cause a bit of a head fuck?' but I didn't, although just thinking that made the headmistress's weird grey eyebrows jump a little.

'I imagine it would cause a few problems.'

'Instant insanity,' said the headmistress without humour. 'So here at school we teach the children how to access the information in a controlled manner. Unlike in your era where certain facts and figures needed to be learned, where the rather frail human memory system was the often the primary arbiter of intelligence, all our children, indeed everyone, has the potential to know everything. The human mind cannot deal with such abundance, I understand you have experienced overload at times.'

I nodded.

'It's not pleasant. Knowing how to filter, access and interpret such abundance is what we teach here. We do it by talking, by communicating without the use of the kidonge, we then slowly allow the children to access certain levels of information as they become more adept.'

The 'wow' was on my lips but I suppressed it. I wanted to appear knowledgeable and intelligent, I didn't want this woman thinking I was a Stone Age thicko.

'I completely understand,' I said. The headmistress smiled revealing her teeth, even they were grey. The woman was a freak.

'I'm quite sure you don't fully understand, Gavin, and that is nothing to be ashamed of. We are all learning as we go along, that is the way it should be and there is no shame in ignorance. Ignorance is the fuel of knowledge and understanding.'

'Okay, fair enough,' I said. She was quite something this Miss Jago. She turned to the men standing around us. I had been unaware that they were all listening to our conversation.

'Chaps, if you could escort Gavin into morning assembly, I think we should get started,' said the headmistress.

'Yes, Miss Jago,' they said, and again I couldn't quite fathom out the emotion behind their response. It was absolutely automatic, it wasn't like some recently imposed ruling, they were all used to it. It must have been me; I found it a bit disturbing that a group of grown men took an order from an elderly woman, regardless of how commanding she was.

I followed the group of men out into the corridor and down a wide flight of steps.

'This must be so weird for you, dude,' said a blonde man about my height. 'I cannot begin to imagine what it must be like. Do we seem kind of unusual to you?'

I stared at him for a moment, he looked fairly human and normal really. True, he was wearing a kind of one peace almost yellow suit thing, but then I was wearing a similar outfit so I couldn't judge. 'It's utterly confusing most of the time. I never quite know what's going on, are you all teachers?'

The men nodded. An Indian man said, 'We're mostly part-time. I have a young daughter so I only do mornings.'

'Most of us have kids to look after,' said the blonde man, he had a fairly strong American accent. 'I do two days a week but I came in special today. My dad's looking after my daughter.'

We turned left and entered another huge auditorium. The headmistress was already stepping onto the slightly raised platform at one end of the space but as soon as I entered there was a deafening round of applause and much cheering. I don't know how many kids were in that room, a couple of thousand at the very least. They all looked very happy and healthy, many races were represented and they were mostly female.

Again I waved rather pathetically as I followed the other men onto the stage.

'Good morning everyone,' boomed Miss Jago above the din, the schoolchildren soon settled down. The blonde man, who I suddenly knew was called Porlock, showed me a seat just behind the lectern at one side of the stage.

'As you know, we have a very special visitor today, his name is Gavin Meckler and he comes from a long, long time ago. I expect you've heard your mothers and fathers talk about how he arrived here, through an anomaly in space-time. You may not know that the Physics Institute on Lovelace Square is investigating this phenomenon at the moment.'

Against all my expectations of children, this lot looked thoroughly interested in the work of the Physics Institute on Lovelace Square. Somehow, I could not imagine a group of kids at a comprehensive school reacting in such a way back in 2011.

'Now, as I'm sure you can imagine, Mister Meckler is finding our world not only very different to the one he grew up in, but also very difficult to understand. He would like to join us today to try and understand how we learn at school, so I would ask you to be kind and tolerant of Mister Meckler if he joins your talk group.'

I really did feel exposed and embarrassed sitting in front of all those kids, they all seemed to be looking at me, I didn't sense any hostility, only sympathy for the poor fool. It wasn't pleasant.

One of the male teachers addressed the school informing them of a sporting event that was taking place that afternoon and that the maker room was open to grade 7 from lunchtime.

There was then some very energetic singing, I'd say an African influence was fairly strong in this short session but clearly the whole school took part. Some of the bigger kids played instruments, and by bigger I mean the girls were way taller than me. There was a lot of drumming, some bagpipes and a few guitar type instruments but mainly it was a couple of thousand kids singing at the top of their lungs. It was very uplifting and energising. I couldn't understand the words as they weren't singing in English as far as I could make out but it was all very jolly.

When the assembly was over the children filed out, there was plenty of noise although they seemed very disciplined and orderly. I followed the blonde man called Porlock and ended up in a large room with raised seating around the walls. There were huge windows high above us giving the place the most extraordinary light feeling. Most of the school children in this class looked to me to be in their early teens, there were three boys among the forty or so kids in the room, it was easy to notice and count them as they were so rare.

'Okay, I'm going to explain to Gavin what we do in here guys. It might be good if we ran through some of the exercises we did yesterday. Jum and Ned, would you take the floor.'

A young girl and a very tall gangly boy stood in the centre of the room, I found a seat next to Porlock and watched with interest.

The boy called Ned started running around in circles as the girl called Jum was shouting at him to be careful. The class started laughing, which was understandable, Ned's gangly great legs and hopelessly waving arms reminded me of a baby giraffe, very unstable. Before long he did a quite badly acted fall and followed this up with some equally unconvincing pain acting.

'I've grazed my knee,' he said. 'My skin is broken, aaarrrggh. I've got a hole in my skin, will it stay like that for ever? Oh no, my blood juice will all escape and I'll turn into a zombie.'

For some reason this made the class roar with laughter which slowly calmed down as Jum waved her arms around.

'Don't panic, your adult stem cells will repair the hole.'

The room went very quiet, I looked around realising that I had clearly missed the point.

'What's going on?' I asked Porlock. He leant over and whispered in my ear.

'They're accessing stem call data, they don't know anything about stem cells, each improvisation brings up a new topic, only Jum and Ned had a clue, I suggested stem cells to them this morning.'

'I don't know anything about stem cells,' I whispered back. Porlock pulled his head back in genuine shock. 'Wow, did you go to school?'

I smiled and sat back in my seat and tried to do the relaxing thing. I knew at once that stem cells are biological cells found in all multicellular organisms, through a process called mitosis they can divide and also differentiate into diverse specialised cell types and can self-renew to produce more stem cells.

I just knew that all at once. Again it was as if I'd always known it.

'That is amazing,' I said as Ned started running around again.

'Okee diddle de dokee!' he shouted as he ran his gangly circuit once more. 'My stem cells are renewing the tissue on my knee, the hole will heal over, my blood juice will stay in my body sack!'

Another gale of laughter from the rest of the class.

'Thanks guys,' said Porlock. 'Top stuff Ned and Jum.' The two beamed at each other as they received a warm round of applause. 'And, I think Mister Meckler learned something too. Back in his day students had to learn by reading paper books and memorising quite stupendous amounts of facts. They would, however, also learn to interpret information as they grew familiar with a subject, they would be able to analyse information and reject what was not relevant. Is that correct?'

He was looking at me as he asked the last question. I nodded. 'Yes, I suppose so.' I said. I really didn't want to talk, I wanted to observe and not be noticed.

'Okay, that's okay,' said Porlock, he patted my forearm reassuringly.

'Can I ask a question?' said one of the other boys in the room. His name was David, I just looked at him and I knew his name was David, he was fourteen.

Porlock looked at me. 'Is that okay?'

'Yes, sorry, go ahead.' I said, I didn't want to be surly and sit in total silence.

'What was fighting like?'

That came out of the blue and of course the fact that he could ask me that revealed so much about these children's lives.

'Fighting? You mean like wars and stuff?'

'No, fighting with someone, another person you knew but didn't agree with. Would you hit them?'

 'Well, no, I never did, certainly some people did, boys and girls but mostly boys. There were boys in my school, which as Porlock has explained were very, very different to this. Some of the boys in my school would get into fights. I would avoid them if I could, and I got quite good at running fast.'

I laughed as I said this, but no one joined me; the looks on the faces in the room made it clear they didn't think running away from someone who wants to hurt you would be funny. They were right of course, but I wanted to explain that such events could be funny in the re-telling.

'So not all boys had to fight,' asked David.

'No. Not in my time. I can tell you it was horrible, I certainly got hit by other boys once or twice but I never hit back. It seemed stupid and pointless to me. My brother liked to fight, he was one of the boys who would get angry and hit people, he hit me loads when we were kids. It's not nice and if you really don't fight any more, well, I think that's great. But I suppose it's important to explain about the dates and the time I come from. I left my home time in 2011, we weren't at war.'

'What about the invasion of Afghanistan and Iraq and the problems in Somalia and the Sudan,' said a girl who I would swear was under ten years old.

'Ah, so you do know your history, okay, yes, there were wars going on, but not huge ones that involved everybody. My grandfather fought in World War II, he was a sailor and although he survived many of his friends were killed or injured. I never fought in a war, I wasn't a soldier, I didn't know how to fire a gun or fight people, not every man back then was violent, I want you to know that.'

Some of the kids nodded to show me they understood.

At that point Porlock stood up and clapped his hands.

'Great stuff, okay, let's start another exercise,' said Porlock, then turning to me he said. 'Mister Meckler, you are welcome to stay and join in.'

I did so. I learned about autologous embryonic stem cells

generated through therapeutic cloning and stored in vast databases for use in physical repairs after severe accidents.

I watched as the children expanded their knowledge of the world of biology at an incredible rate, my feeble twenty-first-century brain had no chance keeping up with them.

By the time we broke for lunch I was exhausted. The kids ran outside into what was, I suppose, the garden behind the house although it resembled woodland more than a garden. I watched through the windows of the staffroom as they climbed trees, ran about after each other and sat about talking.

Porlock joined me by the window and handed me a container of delicious juice.

'Thanks,' I said. 'This is an amazing place. I was dreading coming today.'

'Oh really, why was that?'

'I'm just not cut out to speak to kids, I can still remember how weird I thought adults were when I was their age, it makes me uncomfortable and self-conscious to talk to big groups of kids.'

'You don't need to worry about it, Gavin, I think they were really intrigued by you, they would have asked you questions all day if I'd let them.'

'They're really bright though, is this a special school for super bright kids?'

Porlock laughed. 'Not at all, it's just a standard school, they're all the same, we don't have schools for special kids, they all muck in together as that's a far more effective method.'

'But I can't help wondering if they really know and understand anything if they have instant access to all knowledge. I mean like mathematics, can they really understand how numbers work together if they just sort of, well, have . . .'

I ran out, I didn't even know how to ask the question but Porlock was nodding. 'Okay, so they may not be able to write, you know, like I suspect you can, write with a hand-held writing tool.'

'A pen.'

 'I guess that's what I mean, they may not be able to use a pen to make marks on a piece of paper say, a column of numbers and add them up, but they can look at a column of numbers and the answer will appear to them; however, they also understand how those numbers add up, why they do and how any adjustments within the column of numbers would affect the end result. We can all do that, you could do that.'

'Amazing. I have to accept it works but it is so alien to anything I could understand,' I said. 'But tell me this, the data base, the source of the information. That, surely, is reliant on a complex communication system, a series of networked artificial intelligence systems, computers. Surely that's reliant on a constant energy supply, if that failed wouldn't everyone suddenly be back in the dark times. No one would know anything, you'd all be in a right mess.'

Porlock had to think about this for a moment. 'That's a very intelligent question, Gavin, I'm impressed. Okay, so the system is not centralised, it is, as you suggest, networked over a vast area, powered by so many millions of separate, independent power sources that, well, if the sun went out, we would be in serious trouble, but then we'd all be dead anyway. So it really isn't something we worry about. The data isn't stored in one central place, or even in many large places. The data is woven into the fabric of the structures that surround us.'

He rested his hand on the broad windowsill in front of us. 'In here, in the paint, the structure of the building.' He pointed up to the high ceiling above us. 'Up there, the entire building is a data storage system. Every part of the city built in the last one hundred years or so is part of the network. Not only that, every part of every building exposed to direct sun light is in effect an energy harvesting system, this is backed up by geostationary solar stations which deliver massive back-up power regardless of time of day. I believe this power transfer, down to the power-fields which I believe you are aware of, this is what appears to cause the anomaly physics you became a victim of.'

I brushed my hand along the visually perfect surface of the windowsill, it was incredibly smooth and regular, clearly whatever technology was embedded wasn't some kind of printed circuit or any kind of microelectronics that I would recognise.

I thanked Porlock and then ate lunch with some of the men who taught in the school. Many of these men, including Porlock, had to leave immediately afterwards to return to their own children. They were replaced with a few other men and a small handful of women teachers who I learned were coaching the older children in more advanced classes.

In the afternoon I sat in on a music class which was mind-blowing; children playing all manner of instruments and playing all manner of music. Most of it was unknown to me but they did at one point play some 'classics'. One of those was LA Woman by the Doors played brilliantly by a group of ten-year-olds. Breathtaking.

I met Ralph outside the school at the end of the day and walked with him and Natasha back to the Institute. As we walked I reflected on how I suddenly understood so much more about how my body worked, how the chemicals needed to allow my muscles to function were carried through my circulation, I didn't read a book or watch a film, I didn't listen to a teacher try and impart this knowledge, I just knew it.

Nkoyo was in the reception of the Institute when I arrived back there.

'You look very happy,' she said as I walked in.

'I've had a fairly amazing day, I went to school,' I said with a big grin on my face.

'I know,' she said. We walked together along the now very familiar corridor back to the lovely room where I had my first breakfast. 'Now, Gavin, I know you don't enjoy appearing in public but I'm receiving a lot of requests for your presence at various gatherings. Would you be prepared to attend maybe one or two?'

I felt a weight descend on me. I didn't want to be a celebrity with loads of people looking at me thinking I was a freak.

'What sort of gatherings?' I asked.

'I would only suggest the most prestigious, I don't want to burden you but there are some really influential, and I want to add, very sympathetic and kind people who would love to meet you.'

I sighed, it was a kind of fake big sigh, the sort of thing a school kid would do when they realise they have to do something for the grown-ups. I had to remind myself that I was thirty-two years old.

'Yes, okay,' I said finally. 'But not too many.'

18

Skimming the Waves

IT'S STATING THE OBVIOUS THAT I'D SEEN ships before, who hasn't? Even if you know nothing about them, everyone who's been to the seaside has probably seen a ship. I've even had the opportunity to sail on a few massive tankers in South America and the Middle East through my work back before 2011. I never fail to be intrigued by the fact that a massive metal object can float on a vast quantity of unstable fluid.

My first experience of large ships was as a ten-year-old, when we caught the ferry from Dover to Calais for a family holiday. My mum didn't want to go through the Eurotunnel because she thought it might leak. She didn't say this outright, she just said she 'had her reasons'.

I assumed it was because she was afraid of it leaking.

Being a fairly precocious young fellow, okay, a really annoying know-all according to my brother Giles, I managed to get hold of some safety statistics regarding cross channel shipping and some engineering data on the tunnel.

We made the crossing to France during very high winds resulting in a great many holidaymakers heaving up their fried egg and chips in the crowded toilets.

My brother and I thought it was a great adventure and spent much of the time on deck hanging on to the railings looking at the grey, angry churning sea.

As the ferry rocked and lurched its way toward the Northern coast of France I went inside and kept mum amused with statistics of ferry disasters and the very high safety record for rail travel. Eventually dad told me to shut up and I went back outside to join my brother.

As a ten-year-old I remember thinking that ferry was enormous, when I saw the Yin Qui as a thirty-two-year-old, I realised I could have had no notion as to what enormous really was. The Yin Qui was a seven million ton passenger and freight ship.

Yes, I've got those figures right, seven million tons.

The trip from the Institute to the docks took a full fifteen minutes by car. I say car, I mean the round white thing you sit in that goes underground very fast that everyone in London referred to as a car.

I was travelling with Nkoyo, although very little of why I was going anywhere was explained to me verbally before I departed the Institute. Nkoyo had given me a small package and an even smaller explanation.

It was basically another case of 'would you care to come with me Gavin'. However, thanks to my kidonge I had allowed myself to understand that we were travelling to South London to board a surface ship to attend something called the General Assembly that was located in a massive building in Lagos.

I just knew that, don't ask me how I knew, it felt as if someone had told me the day before and I was remembering what they told me. That's the best explanation I can give.

I was also suddenly aware that the General Assembly was not always located in Lagos, it had only been there for four years. Before that it was in Tokyo, before that in Beijing. I knew that in about a year's time it would be in Paris but the same representatives would be in power for another twelve years. I knew that each political administration was in power for twenty years, that's how often they had elections. Once every twenty years.

'Why have elections only every twenty years?' I asked Nkoyo as we surged along the hidden motorway.

'It was decided a long time ago, politicians with short terms in office always made short-term decisions. Politicians who know they are going to be in power for a long time tend to make longer-term decisions more carefully, knowing they are very likely to still be in a position of responsibility when whatever decision they make comes to fruition.'

I sat staring at Nkoyo in silence; there really wasn't anything to say to that. I couldn't argue with it, it sounded rather sensible but I worried about the source of the information I had just become aware of, was it really that straightforward or were there dissenting voices that would come up with equally sensible arguments as to why it was a terrible idea to allow politicians to be in power so long. I couldn't seem to find a way to know that.

'How do I know what you're telling me is generally accepted by most people, I mean I understand the theory, it sounds eminently sensible but . . .'

'You need to learn how to access more data,' said Nkoyo. 'It's all available, there are plenty of articulate voices that would give a very different opinion to mine.'

We sat in silence for a little longer, well, I say silence, there was a faint hissing noise as the machine we were in barrelled along the subterranean motorway.

'So how do I access such information, through my kidonge?'

'You might find it easier to use a screen,' said Nkoyo. 'You'll have time when we are on-board the Yin Qui.'

When we came out of the terminal building in South London I was completely unaware that I was staring at a ship. As far as I understood things I was walking along yet another street in this endless city. A street that had recognisable buildings on one side and a large flat, white wall on the other. I couldn't see the far end of the wall, it disappeared into the haze of the morning sunshine.

'Where's the boat?' I asked as we walked briskly down the street in South London.

Nkoyo gestured to her right, at the high white wall.

'There,' she said with a smile.

 I looked up as my slow old brain started to work out what I was looking at.

'Is that a boat?'

'Yes, the Yin Qui is one of the big fourteen,' she said.

'The big fourteen?'

'The Yin Qui is one of only fourteen passenger and cargo ships of this size. Relax, you'll soon learn all about it. I think it will interest you.'

I managed to mentally relax as we walked along and could quickly understand that what I was walking alongside was essentially a floating city.

The Yin Qui was just short of four kilometres long, a little over one wide and yet only fifty meters high at the bridge. Although I had never worked in shipping, I knew enough about basic nautical science to understand that a seven million ton ship would exhibit fairly massive displacement, if my calculations were correct it would have to displace, let me see, seven million tons of water.

This marine behemoth should, if my calculations were correct, ride rather low in the water. In the case of the Yin Qui I discovered that this wasn't the case, only a meter of the massive vessel was beneath the surface due to the many square miles of flat bottom, this bizarre monster literally rested on top of the waves.

The first thing that utterly baffled my 'constructed from parts' engineering understanding was that the hull of this ship was made from glass. Not like a sheet of glass joined at the corners with crude extruded aluminium fittings. No, this was one massive lump of glass, effectively printed on an enormous industrial sized 3D solar compressed beam printer in the Gobi dessert. It was a ship made from sand. Even though I knew this, I was sceptical, how could that possibly be achieved and on such an overwhelming scale?

The area of this vast construction that came into contact with water was covered in a superomniphobic surface that could be activated by electrical charge. I'd heard of this kind of material

being developed for the American military but as a woven cloth.
Essentially an update on waterproof material, this stuff could, theoretically at least, be resistant to toxic chemicals, acids and blood as well as water.

From what I could understand, the material on the hull of the Yin Qui was a charged sheet of this stuff covering the literal square kilometres of its base. When the charge was applied it essentially repelled water, but it did so in one direction, and that in turn propelled the ship.

'No propellers then,' I said.

Nkoyo didn't respond and I didn't pursue the matter, she probably didn't know what a propeller was and it suddenly sounded as archaic as hollowed out logs and paddles.

As we walked along by the side of this ship I tapped the side with my knuckles. It hurt. I felt a bit stupid, it was so solid and inflexible, of course it was going to hurt. I banged against it with the palm of my hand, it didn't make a sound, I was a mere fly tapping one tiny leg against a mountain.

About a kilometre down the road was a large entranceway at street level. A very smartly dressed African man greeted us both by name as we approached.

'Doctor Oshineye and Mister Meckler, delightful to meet you both, welcome aboard the Yin Qui,' he said. He held out his hand in greeting, Nkoyo stood back, so I shook his hand and as I did so it was as if I'd been punched in the belly. I literally felt the wind knocked out of me. I leant forward a little and felt the gentle hand of this man on my shoulder.

'Are you feeling unwell, Sir? Would you like a session with one of our doctors?' he said kindly.

'I think he's fine,' said Nkoyo. 'It's very nice to meet you too Hamisi, what time to we depart?'

'We will cast off very soon, just a few stragglers left; however, I am here to guide you to your area, I am here most especially to greet you.'

His smile was full of joy and optimism. Okay, it probably cost me a fortune, but it really cheered me up and I started to recover from my fiscal belly blow.

He gestured for us to go on-board although you could be forgiven for thinking, especially if you came from 2011, how hard it was to believe you were getting on a ship. The experience was similar to entering a large building.

We walked down a wide and seemingly deserted corridor until we came to a corner, the vista that opened up to me at that moment was truly spectacular.

Another seemingly endless hall or maybe mall would be more appropriate, it was many storeys high and literally teeming with people.

'Fucking hell,' I muttered to myself, I could sense that Nkoyo heard me but hopefully our delightful guide didn't.

I stuck as close to Nkoyo as I could as we made our way through the noisy crowds; it was like walking through a busy cosmopolitan city.

'You have an interconnector on starboard floor 14,' said Hamisi. It was at that point I realised I hadn't forgotten his name. I know I'd heard Nkoyo say his name but previous experience had shown me I was able to forget a name in seconds, this time it was different. If I merely glanced at this impressive African, I knew he was Hamisi.

As we made our way through the crowds I could let myself relax and know the names of all the people I was passing. Helen, Marissa, Gene, Jean Claude, Sonia, Anne. The names just appeared in my head as if I'd known these complete strangers for years. I had to shake my head and take a deep breath and kind of tighten up in order for this flow of pointless information to cease.

Suddenly Anne's name popped up in my mind again, this time the full name, Anne Hempstead, the woman I'd met in the Erotic Museum on Carson Square. I hadn't seen her here, and I started to glance around anxiously. I was following Nkoyo so I don't think she noticed, but I couldn't be sure. I also wasn't sure if it was a problem. The name evaporated as quickly as it appeared and I shrugged it off. So what if she was on-board, it really wasn't my problem.

I followed Nkoyo and Hamisi through an entranceway to one side of the giant hall and into a long corridor. This time I knew where we were heading, I could sense the space above me and to the left. There was no obvious visual clue but the smoothness and impenetrable integration of this information input had already become normal for me. It dawned on me that the feeling of being lost was something you could barely imagine if you had a kidonge, you'd have to read a book about it to understand what it meant.

We reached a broad flight of stairs leading off one side of the corridor and climbed two flights, turned onto another corridor without hesitation and then through an entrance into a wonderfully sunlit room.

Either side of the modestly furnished room was a kind of bunk bed set into the wall. Possibly a better description would be an inset sleeping module as it was clear the bed was a self-contained unit capable of floatation. No one explained this to me, I just glanced at it and understood that the bed unit was placed next to the exterior of the ship. The foot of the bed was attached to an ejector hatch system facing out to sea. There would have been a time when I'd have wanted to study such an installation to try and understand the engineering that had gone into it. Now I could have explained it in quite comprehensive detail to anyone who didn't have a benign kidonge nestling in their bone marrow. The thing is, everyone did, so there was no need for me to say anything.

The spacious windows between the two bed pods looked out onto a narrow body of water with dense woodland covering the land beyond.

I was suddenly less certain of my surroundings, I was guessing that I was looking at what once would have been Southampton harbour, I knew we were on the far side of the ship from the entrance on the dock, it had taken long enough to walk across the ship's width so that made sense but there was nothing recognisable that side either. South London was how Nkoyo had described it. Again I relaxed and understood the geography, it was completely at odds with the Hampshire Coast I was vaguely familiar with. Due to the dramatic sea rise we were effectively five kilometres inland from any coast I would have known.

'Don't worry, Gavin, we are not sharing a room,' said Nkoyo after conversing with Hamisi in a language I wasn't familiar with. 'That would be inappropriate.'

She smiled as she said this, and I admit I nurtured a very mild hope that it might not be inappropriate forever. I know it's wrong and I know I was married and I know I had cheated on my wife with Grace, but now I wanted to cheat on both Beth and Grace and I felt guilty about that. Nkoyo gave me a look that simply underlined how inappropriate such activity would be. Of course, she knew what I was thinking; I turned away from her in embarrassment.

I undid the wide belt/bum-bag that Ralph had given to Nkoyo, who in turn had handed it to me in the Institute canteen that morning. It contained another body suit thing like the one I had bought from Akiki, identical except a shade lighter. The cloth was so fine and thin that the entire garment would fold and reduce to the size of a book of matches. The belt also contained some of the amazing not-paper stuff like the stuff Ralph had used to show me his family pictures. The sheet contained a vast collection of photographs and easy to understand floating data explaining the clear genealogy of my extended family from my great grandparents in the 1900s up to the present day. It also contained a vast amount of information about the great cities of the world, the first one being Lagos.

'Are we going to Lagos?' I asked as I slid the information up the smooth sheet.

'Yes, that is our first stop,' said Nkoyo. 'We will be travelling for two weeks.'

I didn't react. This wasn't like the tethers of Gardenia, slide up, slip off, grab on, slide down. This was quite literally the slow boat to Lagos.

My next glance out of our window caused a mild shock, no longer trees in the background, now merely the wide-open sea.

'Oh, we've set off,' I noted.

'Just this minute,' said Nkoyo from the other side of the room. She was shaking out items of clothing from her belt, it seemed no one had bags, just a belt that carried everything you needed.

Toothpaste, make-up, toiletries, nail scissors, all the little bits and bobs you'd have with you on your twenty-first-century travels had seemingly been dispensed with. This was travelling light to an extreme I could only have dreamed of. Yes, it's a cliché but when Beth and I had travelled to a holiday destination together – Crete being the place I recall most fondly – I left home with a small black shoulder bag containing a few changes of clothes, lap top, sunglasses, tiny flight-acceptable toilet bag and numerous re-chargers.

Beth, realising that we had a two-bag allowance managed to fill two huge wheelie bags, in fact they were more like chests. They were both just under the maximum allowance of twenty kilos, so she managed to transport close to forty kilos of clothes and support products for a ten-day sojourn in a luxury hotel that supplied everything anyway.

Travelling in the twenty-third century was less stressful. I was travelling with a woman with no bags. As far as I was concerned, if nothing else, that simple fact alone represented a genuine leap in human progress.

19

Selective Breeding

THE JOURNEY FROM THE SOUTH OF ENGLAND, okay, South London to the West African coast by ship would take about seven days in 2011. I'd imagined as we were on a ship, and Nkoyo had said we'd be away for weeks, this trip was going to be at twenty-first-century marine speeds, maybe a little faster. But this trip was a great deal quicker; we made it in under thirty hours.

The Yin Qui started moving so gently I really didn't notice, I learned that it accelerated one kilometre an hour per minute, meaning that after an hour it's doing 60kph, after two hours it's reached 120 and after three hours 180.

Yes, a seven million ton vessel travelling at 180 kilometres per hour across the tops of waves, absolutely no discernible motion on-board the ship. As so little of the ship was in contact with the water there was no cavitation at the rear of the vessel and hence minimal drag.

Nkoyo and I ate in a vast restaurant at the front end of the ship, watching the wild sea slide rapidly beneath us almost as if it was a back projection. The ship wasn't completely silent, I could occasionally register some low level vibration but the Yin Qui's propulsion system had no moving parts. Breathtaking technology and something I would normally have had to discuss with someone, but being on board meant I seemed to know how the system worked, there was really nothing to discuss.

The one thing I really missed while I was on-board was going out for a breather on the decks. I always loved standing outside on a ship, holding a handrail and feeling the wind in my hair, the bracing ozone rich air and salty taste on your lips from the spray.

None of that on the Yin Qui, the very idea of 'going outside' was as absurd as opening a door on a passenger jet at 40,000 feet to get a bit of fresh air. A 180kph wind would make a relaxed game of deck quoits a bit of a struggle.

My dinner with Nkoyo on the evening of our maiden voyage reminded me a little more of Gardenia. We ate in a large space where the kitchen staff and the dining area were in the same room. I could sense that quite a few passengers were helping out, maybe that was a way of paying for your passage. Nkoyo explained the various foods on offer as the choices were strongly African influenced. We served ourselves from a long heavy table that ran along one side of the vast interior cabin.

I had Fufu, not something I'd ever eaten before. A kind of curd made from cassava, it tasted a little plain but there were amazing sauces you could dip it in. I also selected a beautiful plate of vegetables and some beef cubes. They looked like cubes of beef and that's how a very attentive man at the serving area described them to me. I could just about tell that whatever it was I was eating was probably not beef from some kind of animal.

'It's fresh print beef,' said Nkoyo discreetly. 'They make it on-board.'

I didn't complain. It was delicious.

'The reason we have been invited to Lagos is because you are a very special case,' said Nkoyo when we had found somewhere to sit down. 'Your arrival in London has intrigued the scientific community, many of whose leading members are attending a conference in Lagos.'

'Okay,' I said as I dipped another lump of fufu into a tasty dish of sauce.

'I didn't want to explain anything before we departed for the simple reason that what your presence represents could cause distress and confusion among the general population.'

I listened carefully, at this point I still had no idea if Nkoyo knew I had met Anne the worder, she possibly knew more than she was letting on. I relaxed and tried to sense if she did know anything, clearly I wasn't very good at perceiving the more subtle kidonge signals and I got nothing. I tried not to think about what Anne had told me, but even the effort of trying to order my thoughts in such a way meant I was thinking about it and surely Nkoyo would sense that. I was still confused as to how anybody did anything or made any sort of decision when everyone seemed to know everything already.

'I understand you now know we are having some problems with healthy male births,' said Nkoyo after a short silence.

'Yes,' I said, it was pointless lying about it. 'A woman called Anne…'

'Anne Hempstead, yes, she is on-board the Yin Qui,' said Nkoyo, interrupting me without hesitation. 'I know Anne. She is a good woman with a pure heart. I understand what she's doing and I approve, however, this is really a matter of timing. There is nothing underhand or covert taking place and I wish to be completely open with you. As Anne will no doubt have explained, we are facing a crisis in male population.'

'She did mention it and I have noticed,' I said. Nkoyo nodded and wiped her mouth with a beautiful linen napkin.

'This has not been publicly acknowledged by the authorities in London, in fact most Northern Hemisphere city states have been concerned by the constant decline in male births for a long time. The world's population is currently about 70/30, that is seventy women to thirty men.'

'Yes, I understand that,' I said impatiently, 'But why? You must know why this has happened?'

'There are many theories, currently the most popular is that through selective breeding by women over the last one hundred years or so, there is a preponderance of men who produce female children. It's not that men today are any more or less fertile than men from your era, only that for a long time women chose to have daughters. When they have had sons, their fathers are generally men who produce more girls than boys. The longer this goes on, the more girls are born. We have had the ability to understand which men are most likely to provide female babies and they have been at a premium. This has now turned around. The woman you witnessed at the Institute yesterday, the woman who was very distressed?'

'Yes.'

'Her husband has produced two male children, the pressure on the family has been intolerable, a man like that is now much sought after.'

I continued to eat as I was being told all this. As I dipped the last of my fufu into a particularly delicious sauce bowl, I asked, 'And you can't artificially recreate sperm, can't you just print some?'

Nkoyo stopped eating and sat with her hands clasped on the table in front of her. 'Yes, we can, we have done and we have paid the price. Although we can create male babies very successfully using cellular printing techniques and the resulting males are handsome, healthy and perfectly charming, they are all infertile.'

'Surely with all this technology you must be able to solve something so basic.'

Nkoyo was silent for a moment. Then she looked up at me. 'Well, indeed there may be a way to, as you say, solve something so basic. This is where you come in Gavin, it is unfortunate for you in some ways, your testicular health is of great interest to us.'

'My testicular health?'

'Yes, you see, Gavin, for the last hundred years or so, due to the cultural choices many women have made, the number of men able to produce male babies through natural insemination has been on a steady decline. Not only that, due to the numbers of women who don't have children, I myself am an example of such women, the entire population of the world is now dropping very rapidly, both men and women, but the male population is reaching critically low levels. You will notice that in Africa in particular there are very, very few men. The ratio over the whole continent is more like three hundred to one.'

'Wow, I can't imagine what that's like.'

'You won't need to imagine, you will see. The conference has been called to address this problem. It is one of many we have had over the last few years. In some ways there are resonances akin to the international conferences from your own era that Professor Etheridge has told me about, the big meetings between nations that took place when the first signs of climate change became apparent. We are currently going through a similar period of reaction to the news. Have you heard of the five stages?'

'The five stages, um, no, is that to do with addiction, like alcohol?'

'It is something we all learned at school, every schoolgirl, sorry, child learned about the historic struggle to remove the need for fossil fuel. We learned about the five stages in the process, denial, anger, depression, bargaining and acceptance. Starting with denial, the long-held belief that there was no real problem, then anger as people blamed either the governing bodies or the big fossil fuel corporations for lying to them, then depression as the true and devastating impact started to affect more and more people, that was around the time the centre of the old London was under constant deluge from the rising sea and many coastal cities were lost. This was followed by bargaining as people tried to mitigate the effects of burning fuel by trying to capture and store the resulting toxicity but continued to use the fuel. And finally acceptance, which was about a hundred and twenty years ago when we finally stopped burning fuel to do what we needed to do.'

'Blimey, that's quite a litany,' I said, trying to take all this in. I had noticed that list of words floating above some of the exhibits in the twenty-first-century section of the London Museum of Human History but they didn't mean anything to me.

'So, just like then, there is now much dissent about the demise of the man, some people, it has to be said the more conservative elements of the female population, claim this catastrophic imbalance is not a problem. There are many women who think the world would benefit from an exclusively female population, there is still much anger at men for what took place in the dark times. The advances we have made in the last one hundred years are, so it is claimed, entirely due to the demise of male dominance on the world stage. Not everyone agrees with this notion.'

'I take it you do not agree.'

'You would be right in that assumption; however, you will meet some women at the conference who will see you as a direct threat. A man from the past, from the dark times when, particularly in what was once Africa, the Middle East and parts of Asia, women were cruelly oppressed by the male population. On the surface this is all in the past, but not far beneath there is still long-held resentment.'

'Righty ho then,' was all I could say in response. This trip sounded like it was going to be a right old romp.

20

Jungle Tracks

AFRICA, WELL, OF COURSE IT WASN'T CALLED Africa anymore, the part I landed in was called Lagos, but as with London, it wasn't the Lagos I could have visited back in 2011.

This Lagos covered an area about the size of France, a vast, sprawling but clearly incredibly prosperous mega city. Poverty in Africa? In the twenty-third century? Don't make me laugh.

Lagos made London look positively scruffy and run down. It was so much more advanced, that much was obvious with even the most cursory of glances out of the large windows at the front of the Yin Qui as we approached the vast docking area. If the huge crowds standing along the quayside were anything to go by, Lagos had an enormous population.

Along the coast as far as I could see were vessels of a similar size and design as the Yin Qui, they went on for miles and miles. The buildings behind were gleaming white, massive in footprint but not high, maybe five or six storeys at the most. The style of these buildings was very different to the structures I had grown used to in London. They almost looked like giant loaves of white bread, their edges were not uniform, their windows were randomly spaced and deeply set back from the outer walls. I could make out deep balconies and large pointed structures on the otherwise flat roofs.

As the Yin Qui slowly manoeuvred into position alongside the enormous pier I could see down one of the gaps between the buildings facing the docks, I couldn't describe it as a street, more like a long strip of dense woodland, maybe jungle would be more appropriate. The same style of buildings stretched as far as the horizon, slowly working their way up a distant hill. The gaps between the buildings were completely obscured by dense deep green foliage so any surface transport was impossible to make out. The endless procession of similar white buildings was broken in the distance by a truly colossal structure that must have been many thousands of meters high. To call it a tower is a little misleading, it looked more like an oddly shaped mountain with many bizarre exterior projections coming out of each side. Even as I was staring at this distant man-made monster I couldn't understand what my eyes were taking in.

'It's the main power station for Western Lagos,' said Nkoyo. I was slowly getting used to her insightful explanations, she always answered any question I might have asked just before I knew I was going to ask them.

Nkoyo and I spent an hour making our slow way back to our cabin through throngs of excited passengers who milled around the central mall.

Once we arrived back in our sleeping quarters I found a piece of clothing neatly folded on my bed, it hadn't been there when I left. I picked it up and understood it to be a kind of floor length garment called a Kanzu I'd seen Arabian men wear back in the old days. It was a bright lime green with delicate embroidery around the collar. There was a tapping sound on the partition that separated my half of the sleeping quarters from Nkoyo's, I said 'come in' and the partition folded away silently revealing Nkoyo looking utterly stunning, wearing a similar garment in bright orange.

'You will feel more comfortable wearing the Kanzu,' she said. 'The temperature outside is a little warmer than in London.'

The partition rose again and I quickly changed, packed everything easily in the small belt arrangement and was ready to explore. I had spent a very comfortable night on-board the Yin Qui and had barely thought about the beautiful African woman sleeping the other side of the partition.

Okay, I had thought about her a bit, but not enough to cause concern. There was something about the containment of a ships bunk I found very reassuring, especially one that can fire you out of the side of the ship in the event of a mishap. There was no mishap so I don't know what that experience would have been like, but I kept imagining it, which helped me stop imagining anything in the realm of intimacy with Nkoyo.

After a wait in the crush of people leaving the ship, we finally experienced the incredible heat of a tropical mega city. Just before we left the spacious confines of the ship, Nkoyo handed me a small plastic item.

'You might find it very bright outside, these will help.'

I watched as she put her beautiful hand across her forehead, when she removed her hand her eyes were covered with a face-fitting pair of dark glasses. I put the device in my palm and pressed it gently over my eyes. It immediately fitted itself to me, no supporting bars over my ears, they just stayed where I'd put them and other than the fact that they shaded my eyes very effectively, I was unaware of their presence.

Then it hit me, as soon as we left the shade of the exit corridor and stepped onto the crowded dock, the unspeakable heat and almost choking humidity engulfed me. I had experienced similar temperatures in the deserts of the Middle East back in the twenty-first century, but then I was cushioned by endless air-conditioned cars and buildings, all cooled by burning fuel. As I almost struggled for breath under the sudden onslaught of a hundred per cent humidity and a temperature around 53°C I was a little hesitant at the prospect of surviving such an experience for any length of time.

I then understood that I been well-protected from the heat by whatever system of ventilation the Yin Qui used, but walking along the enormous pier I found some shade under a gently arcing structure that covered the central walkway. The direct sun felt as if it was cooking me in an oven but I noticed many people walking happily in the bright light. Even with the gentle warnings Nkoyo had given me I had no notion of just how hot Lagos would be, my Kanzu was the best thing to wear, that much was obvious, this was a very harsh environment.

As we moved slowly forward with the many thousands of people around us, all busy chattering and laughing, full of excitement, I was prepared to be inspected by some kind of authoritarian figure in some kind of customs building.

As we continued to move towards what appeared to be the edge of this city nothing happened, there was no border, no checkpoint, customs office or goods inspection.

'So you don't have passports or customs any more?' I asked.

'I don't know what you mean,' said Nkoyo.

'Like, security, a border, you know, like police checking to see who's arriving.'

'Everybody knows who's arriving,' said Nkoyo, as we eventually made it to the blessed shade of the nearest tree. Standing in direct sun was nothing short of brutal. 'The local authorities know you are here,' she continued, 'and the authorities in London know you are here, in fact anyone in the world who wants to know, knows you are here.'

She gestured toward the even bigger gathering of people standing in the shade of the trees that fringed the quayside. I don't know how to judge the size of such a multitude, it had to be many thousands.

'They certainly know you are here, it might be polite to wave,' said Nkoyo, she had a strange look on her face. I might almost suggest it was pride.

I waved in the direction of the crowd and the cheer that went up was staggering, like a crowd at a stadium rock concert when the scrawny lead singer makes an appearance.

 'Is that for me?' I asked Nkoyo.

'Yes, they all want to see the man who fell from the cloud.'

'Amazing, do I have to do anything?' I asked, half dreading that I would be expected to make a speech.

'No, they just wanted to see if you are real, there has been much speculation about your arrival.'

I waved again, saw the many thousands of people waving back at me and had no idea what to do. Then suddenly above the din I heard a high-pitched cry, a kind of musical wail quickly followed by the explosive sound of mass drumming. It was so loud and had such impact it made me jump.

A group of people emerged from the crowd with massive long drums balanced on their heads, they were beating the skins above their heads with long drum sticks but the intensity of the sound I was hearing was clearly not coming from the drums alone. As they moved forward two things became clear: one, they were all women, and two, they were incredibly tall. I don't mean very tall by the standards I'd grown used to, maybe two meters tall. No, these women were like another species. I didn't get that close to them, but they made everyone else around them look like little squibs. Their drumming was spectacular and extremely energetic, they all appeared to be grinning wildly and even though they had enormous drums balanced on their heads they danced around, performing impressive leg kicks, even more impressive because their legs were giraffe-scale long.

'Oh my God,' I said to Nkoyo, 'they are so bloody tall!'

'The average height of the Burundi drummers is two meters forty,' Nkoyo shouted above the din. 'They are usually the tallest people in Africa, they have come to drum just for you, the man from the cloud.'

We watched the entire performance and I was happily mesmerised by the spectacle and noise. When they finally stopped I clapped wildly and cheered, it was totally uplifting, I'd never seen anything like it and I wanted them to know I appreciated it.

There was a load more cheering and waving before Nkoyo

leant near to me and said 'We need to move on now, Gavin, there are people waiting to see us.'

I nodded, waved one last time at the vast crowd and followed Nkoyo into the darkness of the jungle path.

We carried on walking a bit and some of the crowd fell in behind us but it seemed the majority had got what they wanted. They saw the man from the cloud get off the big ship and that was enough for them.

The mass communication system used in 2211 was still utterly beyond me, but clearly this lot all knew I was coming. I hadn't seen any sign of television, newspapers or any kind of printed material other than kinky drawing books in the Erotic Museum. I supposed they just knew in the same way that I was discovering I just knew things. The Yin Qui's propulsion system, the sleeping pods being lifeboats, the fact that the streets of Lagos were in truth carefully managed jungle paths.

I shrugged, if everyone knew where everyone was at all times, there really wasn't anything anyone could do to upset the system, as long as everyone played along and there weren't elements knocking around who didn't join in. But then I realised they'd stick out like a sore thumb. If I met someone and relaxed and their name didn't pop into my head instantly, I'd be very alarmed which in some way explained why people reacted to me as they did when I first arrived in this utterly transparent society. They wouldn't have known who I was, it must have been disconcerting.

As we progressed up the wide, tree-covered path between the massive white buildings the crowds pouring out of the Yin Qui started to thin out, many entered a building to my right which I somehow knew was a subterranean transport system, not cars like they have in London, but high speed trains called Nyumbu.

'Firstly we will call upon someone who has specifically asked to meet you,' said Nkoyo. 'I would ask that you make yourself as calm and quiet as possible before meeting this person.'

'Wow, is he some sort of religious figure?' I asked.

'No, he is very old and frail; however, he is much loved and revered for his wisdom and experience. I think you will learn a great deal from him.'

'Sounds very intriguing,' I said. I let myself relax a bit to see if I could garner from Nkoyo who this mysterious person might be, but as I did so I became aware that my whole body was so hot I was sweating like a stuck pig over a roaring blaze.

I glanced down at my Kanzu but could see no sighs of sweat patches. I'd always been embarrassed about sweating through my clothes, I was just a sweaty type of guy in this sort of humidity. I'd sweated bucketloads when I'd been in hot countries in the past, and left massive stains on my polo shirts. Whatever material my Kanzu was made from, it didn't seem to stain, but believe me, it was sweat monsoon season underneath.

Nkoyo turned a corner and I followed, we were walking along a path surrounded by thick African jungle but either side of us I could catch glimpses of the ubiquitous white buildings through the dense and dripping foliage. I had to remind myself I was in a huge city, I could hear no traffic, aircraft or air conditioning humming away, just the sounds of the jungle. Above us the trees were alive with birds, their unusual song was enchanting and loud, I walked along looking up into the branches and saw movement. It was a monkey of some sort darting along a high branch. The trees were so dense and enormous there was clearly a lot of wildlife hanging around up there, right in the middle of a massive city. I saw a few people walking about as we made our way along this sun dappled path, but not that many. True, they were mostly African women but I noticed a few were European and Asian looking. However, all of them were wearing beautiful floor length robes covered in intense coloured patterns.

'Here we are,' said Nkoyo. 'We will bathe before we enter the inner courtyard.'

I followed Nkoyo through a wide entrance into one of the buildings; the air was instantly cooler, not a massive air conditioning fan blowing down from above us, just the shade and a cool breeze coming from within. I removed my dark glasses and tucked them easily inside my belt and then followed Nkoyo further into the building. We were met by an enormously tall woman sporting a huge headdress. Her ancestry could not be doubted, she was very African. She gently embraced Nkoyo and they spoke momentarily in a language I couldn't begin to understand at first. I let myself relax and started to comprehend what they were saying.

'This is Gavin Meckler, the man I have been telling you about,' said Nkoyo.

'The man from the dark times,' said the African woman whose name I knew to be Nantale. Nkoyo nodded. The woman looked at me with what felt to me to be unadulterated hatred, her nostrils flared, she stared down at me as if I was a threatening dog, a mixture of fear and disgust. I smiled.

'How do you do?' I said in English. There was no change in her demeanour.

'He is not as we imagined,' said Nkoyo. 'And you know Olumide wishes to meet with him.'

The woman seemed to relax a little and showed us into a small courtyard, it was shaded from direct sunlight although open to the sky. In the centre was a deep pool surrounded by a wonderfully decorated canopy. A curtain was drawn across the centre of the pool, Nkoyo nodded toward one side.

'You must bathe yourself carefully,' she said and pointed to one side of the pool. 'You will find oils in the bottles over there, use those to cleanse your skin.'

I went to one side of the pool where I was shielded from the rest of the courtyard. I removed my Kanzu, picked up one of the bottles of oil and stepped into the beautifully cool water of the pool. There were gentle steps leading to the centre, I plunged in gratefully and stayed under water for a moment allowing myself to cool down. It was then I made a little mistake for although the curtain separated the two sides of the pool above the surface, there was nothing to separate them under water. I saw Nkoyo's naked body through the aqua-haze, an image that would haunt me for the rest of my life. Just the most beautiful, long-limbed black woman's body I have ever seen, lit with flecks of sunlight refracting through the green water. Damn, if only I hadn't looked.

I emerged as quietly as I could and stood on one of the steps. I wiped the water from my face and tried to forget the image still fresh in my mind. I didn't want Nkoyo to know I'd seen her.

I used the contents of the bottle to wash myself with, what ever it was it foamed up luxuriously and I washed myself vigorously for a while, rinsing off by plunging back into the deeper water only this time keeping my eyes firmly shut. I stood on the side of the pool for a few seconds and felt the water dry off me. I dressed myself again, this time in a fresh robe that was neatly folded beside the one I'd discarded. I didn't remember seeing it when I'd arrived and still have no idea where it came from. I then joined Nkoyo and Nantale by the entrance to the courtyard.

'This way,' said Nantale in English. Nkoyo and I walked barefoot along a corridor and into what seemed to be a tented courtyard further into the complex of buildings. Three women were standing in the centre, one was of Chinese origin although much taller than I would have expected, the other two were African. Seated on a low chair before them was the small, white-haired figure of a very old African man. I had never seen such an elderly-looking human being, even in Gardenia. This ancient fellow looked a little like the dried-up mummy that once rested in a glass case in the British Museum. He looked like he'd been dried in the sun. The top of his head was shiny black, thin wisps of white hair hung around his huge old ears and a long, straggly beard hung down from his chin.

This was old man Olumide Smith and his gaze took my breath away.

'Welcome Gavin Meckler, come, sit beside me,' he said in perfect English. 'It is wonderful to meet the man who fell from the sky.'

21

Olumide Smith

I SAT WITH OLUMIDE FOR MOST OF THAT day, we were either side of what I can only describe as a day bed, a very large and comfortable padded structure shielded from the harsh sun by a billowing dark awning strung up above our heads. A cool breeze occasionally wafted over us, it felt natural but it was rather rhythmic so could have been artificial; whatever was causing the movement of air it always came as a huge relief.

I don't know how long I was there, many hours, but in Olumide's presence I became unaware of time. I was to learn that his take on the previous two hundred years was somewhat at odds with the rather clinical version I'd seen in the London Museum of Human History.

'Gavin, they tell me you are an even older man than me!' said Olumide, his toothless mouth formed into a big, gummy grin. He had what I would recognise as a strong sub-Saharan African accent but his grasp of English was impeccable, his voice was deep, soft and utterly enchanting.

'In some ways, yes, I suppose my memory goes back in history even further than yours, Sir.' I replied. I have no idea why I addressed him as sir. I knew this was common in North America but somehow, when someone was obviously as old as Olumide, a respectful term seemed appropriate.

'Would you like me to tell you a story?' he asked. I nodded. 'Are you comfortable, not too hot?'

'I feel very comfortable,' I said, another strong breeze wafted past us, cooling the sheen of sweat that I knew covered my entire body. Olumide leaned back against the cushions behind him, closed his eyes and started speaking.

'Let me tell you, Gavin Meckler, what happened to the men. When I was born in the year 2070, it was a very pivotal year, before 2070 this world was a very different place.'

If what he said about his birth date was true, I quickly calculated that he was one hundred and forty-one years old. I didn't have any reason to doubt it, after all why would he lie? And surely if he was lying then the women surrounding us would know. I was also aware that they would know I was possibly doubting what Olumide claimed so I tried to stop, but a hundred and forty-one years old! It was preposterous.

'I don't use that term lightly, it is a year most historians now agree as being pivotal. In 2070 things really started to change and my whole life has been spent reflecting on those changes and teaching others to be aware of those changes. What is important beyond all else is that I just happened to be born then. I am not, as some have suggested over the years, a second coming, a divine presence or most amusingly the son of a God. Are you understanding me so far?'

'Yes Sir,' I said without hesitation.

'Due to the changes taking place in the world and due to the women I knew I grew to understand myself from a very early age. A man, Gavin Meckler, who understands himself is very different from one who does not. But I am not speaking about just one man, one man who could see the error of the past, the strictures of the God grip, the restrictive Judaeo-Christian mindset or the Islamic yoke that crushed the lives of millions and stopped the world from changing. That had all started to fade long before I was born. It was only kept alive in places where men were still insane with anger; men who didn't know what to do with their anger. The question facing men was very simple. What do we do if we no longer fight or rape. Have you ever asked yourself that?'

This caught me off guard, it almost made me jump. I was momentarily confused, I couldn't tell if he was accusing me of killing and raping, or if his question was meant to make me think about such things and realise there was an underlying passion for such activity. I decided there wasn't.

'No sir. Quite the opposite, I never fought anyone and I never raped anyone so the question never arose.'

'That is very commendable, although I wasn't asking if you, the man I see before me, you had fought and raped, but many men had done one or both. It was a driving force for so many men and what would they do to replace that activity? Team sports maybe?'

He sat looking at me as he said this. 'I know that in your day team sports were seen as the perfect distraction. If men support a team, their city team or their country team, it was seen as a way to dissipate their desire to fight and rape. However, it didn't remove that desire, it never tried to understand that desire and grow beyond it. Merely replaced it with something else, and of course if the men who controlled things in the dark times deemed it necessary, that desire could easily be channelled into war and rape again. The desire was ready and waiting, the anger was kept alive by the sport. But as fewer men were born and fewer men fought and raped, the desire also waned. Slowly, slowly we have changed. We have changed from what you are into what I am. This is why I wanted to meet you. You are the beginning, I am the end and now we meet. I would never have dreamed this is possible. Many years I have waited.'

He held his hand up with far greater speed than I would have expected of a man of his vintage, he stared at me with incredible intensity and corrected himself. 'I don't mean I was waiting for you Gavin, I was not waiting for the man I see before me. I do not believe that you are divine or that you are a man God. I'm not sure what you believe, that is for your conscience alone and not my business. I do not judge. But I can sense that you and I are so distant and yet so alike. So we meet, the beginning and the end, it is like a snake, you know that notion? A snake with its tail in its mouth.'

I nodded my recognition. 'Ouroboros, the circle, the beginning and the end,' I said softly.

Olumide looked around at his companions, pointing at me with his long bony finger. 'He is a clever one, this man who fell from the clouds, a clever one.'

I don't ever remember feeling calmer than I did when sitting under the awning in the sweltering heat, a light sense of incredible serenity; the women gathered around us seemed somehow to be above our talking. I didn't feel they were listening to what was said and they were certainly not intervening, they merely sat calmly and stared into the distance in silence.

'When I was born, Gavin Meckler, things were very different. Oh yes, there were many angry men in the world and things were not pleasant. In Africa there was fighting, in Asia there was fighting, in the Middle East there was fighting. Everywhere men were fighting and killing and raping. In Africa from the coast of the Mediterranean to the tip of the Cape, from the violent waters of the Atlantic to the serenity of the Arabian Sea, men were fighting, always fighting each other. But here was the question no one asked. Over what were they fighting?'

'I don't know, probably not much.'

This caused Olumide to burst out laughing, nodding and resting his wizened old hand on my arm.

'Probably not much,' he said, coughing rather violently, he did a passable impression of a posh white chap with a plum in his mouth.

'Probably not much is right, he is a clever one this one,' said Olumide to the women around him, again they barely acknowledged his observation. 'The men were fighting over probably not much, they said it was because one man did not respect the God of the other man, or one man believed he owned the land or the woman of the other man and blamed the God of the other man. They said they were fighting over a God they could not see, could not measure, could not record or verify. That's what their men leaders told them and they believed this idea. They thought they were fighting for their God, their father, the father within them but really they were fighting over their mothers.'

This observation caught me off guard again and Olumide, through his almost opaque dark eyes didn't miss it.

'You did not know that, did you Gavin Meckler? I am not surprised, I hope you don't mind me saying that I am not surprised. No man from the dark times understood that, they kept themselves busy fighting while all around them the women were growing the food, teaching the children and taking care of things. Against all the odds, against terrible hardship and suffering the world started to improve. Yes Gavin, when I was a little boy, Lagos was just a town like London, all squashed up and busy, cars and trucks and buses and noise and smell. I can remember. A big, smelly old city it was.'

For some reason this also made Olumide laugh, I nodded but I didn't quite know why.

'And I talked to the men, they were angry, always angry, always wanting to fight, but angry about what, eh Gavin Meckler, why were they so angry?'

I stared at my hands for a moment, I didn't really know why they were angry, I felt a bit guilty about it because I was white and white people had done terrible things to black people in Africa for hundreds of years. You didn't need to be a history graduate to know that. Okay, so it was a long time ago and it wasn't me personally doing the bad things, but I have always believed you have to accept your heritage, good and bad.

'I'll tell you why they were angry. It was because of their mothers and their sisters. It's the same all over the world, the mothers, the sisters, they suffered but they got on, they suffered but they persevered. They suffered but they became stronger, they supported each other, they became these strong women.'

He gestured to the women sitting around us, I glanced at Nkoyo who didn't return my gaze, but it was true, she looked beyond strong, she looked nothing other than regal. I cannot describe her in any other way. Regal and incredibly beautiful, unattainably beautiful and I felt the weight in my chest. A longing, I don't know, some emotion that was strong and needy and didn't help me relax.

'Oh yes, Gavin Meckler, women are so strong, any man who does not understand that will suffer in his own pain. These women made the world better which of course only made the angry men even more angry!' Again the old man laughed. 'They were always angry, they were angry at their children, angry at their wives, angry at each other so they fought each other more. They were not able to understand that the anger they felt, they didn't understand its source. The source of this pain was the mother. It was not because their mothers were bad to them, quite the opposite; you cannot lay blame at the foot of your real mother, the woman who nurtured you. No, they were angry because all men lived under the phallus.'

Olumide stared at me, waiting for a reaction to what he'd just said.

'The phallus,' I eventually repeated.

'You know what it is?'

'What, the phallus? Yes, I know what it is. The penis, you're telling me the men were living under the penis?'

My question caused a gale of laughter and coughing from the ancient man. He waved the incredibly pale palm of his hand at me as he tried to regain his composure.

'Not the penis, Gavin Meckler, the phallus.' He pointed to the thin white hair on his head. 'The phallus in here, the phallus of the man's soul.'

Now he nodded like a proper old sage, his eyes closed, his absurdly ancient face serene and fascinating. 'When the man is trapped by the sexual phallus, he is trapped by the woman, he is in awe of the women, he worships and hates the woman at the same time. Do you know this feeling Gavin Meckler? When you love and hate a woman at the same time?'

I shrugged, I wasn't sure I knew that feeling but after a moments contemplation I started to understand that part of my problem not understanding women was that I didn't want to. I saw that in many cases I was scared of them and kept them at a distance. I would describe it as being attracted to them and annoyed by them at the same time, the same basic notion as love and hate but with a bit less passion.

I nodded slowly. 'I think maybe I do.'

Olumide smiled very gently, he stared at me and I didn't feel threatened or patronised by him, I felt understood by him. He closed his eyes for a while and then said, 'So finally, after five thousand years of this pain, men began to accept that they were trapped by the sexual phallus and could only be freed from this burden by the spiritual phallus.' Another pause, Olumide moved his head a little and stared at me. 'When I say a spiritual phallus I do not mean a God, Gavin Meckler, not something they could never see, never touch. This was solid, hard, familiar, personal and physical but also of the soul. They began to understand that all men had the same burden. It didn't matter about the God they had fought and killed for, and thus the Gods disappeared like a mist in the morning. Gone, forever, leaving only the man with himself, alone in the universe, responsible for his own actions. The man finally accepting himself for who he really is. The man who comes from woman, the acceptance of that simple fact set men free. The mother is first, the son only follows.'

I thought about that for a moment, it made sense but I couldn't see how this would stop men fighting. Could it really be that simple?

'You have questions,' said Olumide. It was true, I had questions but it was mildly annoying that he knew before I realised I had them.

'I don't understand about the whole spiritual phallus thing, have I got one?' I asked. I was beginning to doubt the old man's sanity. How could a phallus be spiritual, it all sounded bonkers, it sounded like something my hippy Uncle Nigel would have said when I was a kid. He was really annoying and we always dreaded his occasional visits.

Olumide stared at me as a gentle smile emerged from the dark folds of ancient skin.

'Listen to what I tell you, Gavin Meckler, and then listen to the truth inside you. A man like you, a man living only in his own sexuality, the use of his body, his phallus, the physical agency of his masculinity is by definition dominated by the mother.'

He emphasised the word 'definition' in a slightly annoying way. I knew he was just emphasising the word but I also knew it was an annoying thing to do.

'Since everything connected to the body including the phallus is her instrument, yes, the phallus is her instrument,' he said, staring at me, willing me to understand. 'The sexual phallus is servitude to the mother, the darkness, the dark times. The spiritual phallus is freedom from the feminine, it is light, like here, the light is clear, the man's spirit is free from anger.'

I think my eyes widened at this point.

'For thousands of years, this state of mind kept men in the constant distress they always experienced, the need to fight, compete with each other, feel stronger and better than each other, start wars and dominate the earth, struggle to dominate the mother. That way failure and pain lies, that way we are trapped in eternal damnation. Now we don't need to do that, we men can find our spiritual fulfilment without the need to struggle against the mother. We don't need the mother. You know what I refer to when I say the mother.'

'I suppose so, you don't mean my mother, like, my mum, you mean the kind of inner mother, the sort of psychic mother thing, the inner parent, the earth mother and all that Freudian stuff.'

The big gummy smile returned to Olumide's face. 'That is indeed what I mean Gavin Meckler, all that Freudian stuff if you like to think of it that way.'

He laughed and had a little coughing fit. Then he continued, 'The men like you stopped fighting. They just stopped fighting and were finally able to help the women make the world better. No more praying to an angry God, no more beliefs in revenge, no more allegiance to family, to clan, tribe, race, colour of skin. Men had no more need to struggle for domination. There was nothing to dominate other than the sexual phallus.' Again Olumide pronounced the word 'dominate' very slowly, making it sound like a swear word of profound offensiveness.

'That is when men could really become the father. They could love their children without anger; the boy child grew to be a better man because he had the clear love of his father, the girl child grew up to be a less needy woman because she had the clear love of her father. The father is external. The father does not really exist at a primordial level, so contact with the father is essential because for thousands of years people had replaced the hole left by the father with the insanity of a God belief. As there is a mother inside us, we don't need a mother to care for us when we are not children, but there is no father inside us, having a father care for us makes us whole. My father cared for me, my mother loved me but my father cared for me. That is how I became the man you see now, one hundred and forty one years later. A long, long time, and that is why you have been brought to see me Gavin Meckler, I want you to see what has happened since your time. Oh yes, we have the ships, the cities and technology, yes we have boundless energy to make our day-to-day lives more comfortable, we have the abundance of our technology. I know you admire that, but I want you to know and admire our men.

They know how to live with each other, with women, not by shouting and fighting and raping, but by doing much harder things like raising their children, like growing and preparing food but most importantly by being truly loving, and truly able to receive love.'

22

Riding the Nyumbu

I MUST HAVE SAT ALONE UNDER THAT softly billowing canopy in the mysterious courtyard for a few hours after Olumide been helped away by the women we'd been sitting with. I watched him walk slowly across the courtyard and through a distant door; that movement alone must have taken twenty minutes, he was very frail on his scrawny old legs.

I felt exhausted just sitting still but without question I felt different after speaking with him. I felt older and calmer, but of course I was still full of questions. I could completely see how men had been trapped by their anger. I could understand how they could be trapped by their need for release through a woman and how that release would never truly be achieved. However, I couldn't see all women as being benign, patient, caring and in some way superior to the male. I kept thinking about Beth and how aggravating she could be, and how short-sighted and belligerent, and how many of her opinions I found to be a bit cruel and judgemental. After all, in my old home that no longer existed either in London or Gardenia, I was the lazy atheist who tried not to judge people. Beth was the rigid Christian who went to church and judged everyone she met. She was a woman who believed in a ridiculous God, I was a man who didn't. So much of what Olumide had said to me didn't add up, most of the men I knew were atheist and many of the women were infected with religious madness.

I was the one trying to change the world and she was the one who wanted the world to stay as she imagined it might have been back in about 1850. I kept remembering women I'd met who were stupid, aggressive, loud, cruel and selfish, the women who lived for shopping and the frippery of fashion. Women who read abysmal gossip rags and bitched about how fat some half-baked celebrity had become. I'd met women who watched appalling television shows about appalling people behaving atrociously and then said such mind-rot was harmless fun. How could those women possibly be superior to some of the men I'd known back in the so called 'dark times'? I'd met incredibly kind, far-sighted men who cared deeply about their children, the earth and the suffering of others; they didn't go around shouting and shooting people because of some God-based nonsense.

I also knew however, that much of what Olumide had told me had a resonance I could not deny. I knew I had felt anger for most of my life, I kept it inside and tried not to express it, anger seemed like such a self-defeating emotion and when I got angry, as I had done with Pete in his store when I confronted him about the fate of the Yuneec, it always seemed to backfire on me and make me feel bad.

As the light faded and the temperature finally started to drop, I looked around the empty courtyard and saw a light coming through a nearby doorway. I stood up and stretched, I stretched for a long time because my legs felt dead. I had been sitting on a cushion on the floor for hours, something I don't think I'd ever done before in my life.

I walked slowly towards the doorway, went inside to find yet another very long corridor. Light was coming from a doorway on the left, I peered in. There was Nkoyo sitting in a chair facing me.

'Hello,' she said. 'How are you feeling?'

I couldn't really speak, I didn't know what to say. I felt I was being observed, tested maybe but I didn't know why.

'We will rest here tonight,' said Nkoyo. 'We have a long day ahead of us tomorrow.'

I followed Nkoyo out of the room and along the cool corridor, up some wide stairs and into large room with a huge bed in the centre. I lay down without further thought and fell asleep.

I awoke early, light just starting to come in through the wide-open window. I lay back and pondered on the nature of the building. No glass in the windows and yet it was cool. The way the window was set back into the building was the first thing that intrigued me, it became clear that the walls of this structure were more than two meters thick, so the window opening was essentially a little like the mouth of a cave.

I wondered about things like mosquitos. It certainly didn't seem like I'd been bitten in the night but I had slept in the tropics in the past and knew those pesky little fellows seemed to love landing on me.

I slid out of the bed and walked toward the window, leant out as far as I could and noticed a breeze blowing across my body. I craned my head around and there was an opening in the structure of the wall, I raised my hand and felt cool air blowing gently from the slit. I assumed this must have something to do with keeping out bugs; my hand tingled slightly as I kept it in the breeze. The window looked down on the empty courtyard I had sat in with Olumide and on seeing it his words returned to my head uninvited: 'The mother is first, the son only follows.'

That notion was so at odds with the world I had grown up in. It sounded a bit spiritual and hippy dippy, things I'd always despised, and yet it didn't feel hippy dippy when Olumide had said it. I wasn't sure I could change and fit in with this new regime. It made me angry, it seemed to deny all the positive things men had done for thousands of years; the blood sacrifice, the effort they had put into technology, medicine, philosophy and building a better world. Surely all that couldn't just be thrown away because these blokes from history had been living under the sexual phallus, it was driving me mad thinking about it, it was doing all the things Olumide Smith had told me I should not do. Be angry, blame other people, shout and fight and smash stuff up.

'Be calm,' said Nkoyo from behind me. I turned and looked at her. She was standing in the entrance to the room looking nothing short of ravishing.

'Oh, morning,' I said. Then I felt a wave of anger flow through me. I couldn't even sit around and mull things over; these bloody people were all over me like a rash.

'Yes, of course you can have private thoughts,' she said calmly as if it should be obvious. 'It's fine Gavin. Live with your questions, they're not wrong.'

The anger left me as completely as a bowel movement. Nkoyo knew what I was feeling, she understood it and the anger was excreted.

'It's going to be hard for you to adjust,' she said.

'I don't want to adjust, I want to go home,' I replied, limply. 'Don't get me wrong, I think this is amazing, your world is amazing but I don't belong here, I shouldn't be here, it's all too...'

I didn't know what it was all too, it was all too something, I knew that. I didn't really like the world I was discovering, there was something more regimented and harsher than the world I had seen in Gardenia.

'We should bathe before we set off,' she said as she walked out of the room. I was wearing a cloth wrapped about my waist but I found my somehow freshly laundered Kanzu neatly folded on a beautiful wooden box by the bed and followed her.

We bathed on separate sides of the pool, my eyes remaining firmly shut when I rinsed off the delightful washing oil foamy stuff and then we left the compound. I saw no one else inside and I have no idea how long we stayed there, how my Kanzu came to be washed or really anything else. It all just happened and I don't think I paid for any of it. I hadn't shaken hands with anyone since I got off the Yin Qui.

The entrance back out onto the jungle street was wide open, as far as I could make out there were no doors. If there are no doors there is no need to keep people out; if there is no need for that then I assumed things like the fear of theft or violence had been removed from this highly developed society.

We walked for about half an hour through the densely shaded pathways. This time there were far more people about, long rows of children walking together towards what I assumed would be schools, many tall African women with wonderful headgear, at one stage a group of laughing men carrying long planks of wood on their shoulders. I noted they were laughing because it looked odd, it seemed they had a task in hand and yet it looked like they were playing a game. One of the men was walking in front of a box that seemed to follow him like a dog, a floating box sliding along behind him. I was staring so intently at this contraption that I momentarily lost sight of Nkoyo, then noticed she had turned down a narrow path to the right and following I found myself in a small café type of a place.

It's hard to describe it as a café; it looked more like an open air jungle kitchen with many African people sitting around peeling fruit with big knives. There was a great deal of intense chatter going on among the diners and I suddenly became aware of music. Really nice African music that seemed somehow familiar, there was actual music coming from speakers somewhere. I couldn't see any sign of them but I could definitely hear music.

'Let's have some breakfast before we get the Nyumbu,' said Nkoyo sitting at an empty space at one of the big tables, an enormous man the other side stood up and gestured to me to sit down. When I say enormous I don't mean fat, I just mean massive, he must have been over two meters tall and he was built like the proverbial brick outhouse, he looked like a larger-than-life, pumped-up rugger player.

I thanked him and took the seat. Nkoyo nodded at the enormous man and then handed me a fairly lethal-looking knife. On the table there was a wonderful array of fresh fruit, bananas, oranges, pineapples, persimmon, pomegranate, papaya, a selection of berries and quite a few odd-shaped fruits I wasn't familiar with. It was just piled up on the table between us. The enormous man put a wooden bowl in front of me, patted me gently on the shoulder with his truly vast hand and said, 'Tuck in, Mr Meckler,' his voice was so deep I felt my body shudder slightly.

He moved away and I couldn't help watching his progress. His stride was almost comical it was so big.

'Blimey,' I muttered, smiling at Nkoyo.

'Impressive isn't he?' she said. 'But he is a nogam.'

'Is that a tribal thing?' I asked. I watched this huge man shoulder a box the size of a compact car and carry it into the building we were sitting next to.

'No,' said Nkoyo with her delightful laugh 'A nogam, it's a slang term I suppose, it means he's sterile.'

This information came as a shock to me. This enormous powerhouse of a man looked so healthy it wasn't funny, and yet he was sterile.

'How d'you know, have you met him before?'

'No,' said Nkoyo flatly. 'It's just his type always are, he's not impotent, he's just sterile, he cannot father a child.'

'But, is he a kind of clone or something, did he come out of a laboratory?'

Nkoyo's smile was delicious, 'No,' she said, 'he came out of his mother, but the seed that started him was from a laboratory. You can see that there is nothing wrong with the seed, he is a very healthy man, he will possibly live even longer than Olumide, all the signs are, barring accidents, that he'll live for about two hundred years.'

Nkoyo handed me some delicious slices of warm mango. I couldn't talk or even think for a moment as I consumed the divine fruits in front of me. I was very clumsy with the knife and relied on Nkoyo to cut up my breakfast.

As we got up to leave I asked Nkoyo about paying for our breakfast. 'I haven't shaken hands with anyone,' I said.

'It's okay, the kidonge system is a lot more sophisticated in Lagos, I paid for your breakfast but it is kind of you to be concerned.'

We walked through the shrubbery back onto the path. 'So what you're saying is in some ways London is a bit behind technologically, Africa is more advanced?'

'You will see,' said Nkoyo enigmatically.

She turned left past an enormous tree and through a dark entrance in a building, I followed her, making my way through a crowd of people coming out.

We descended a wide, brightly lit set of stairs and I knew this was a Nyumbu station. In many ways it was like the car stations in London, only even bigger. On one side of the huge underground atrium was a glass wall, on the other a series of stalls selling coffee, small cakes and many metal containers which I knew contained fruit juices. I felt a strong gust of cool air and noticed on the other side of the glass wall an enormous machine slide into view. A white transportation system, I can't describe it better, yes, a train, but bigger, faster and with no obvious linkage between carriages. It was just one enormously long tube, a massive, seamless subterranean worm. The glass doors which I had hitherto not been able to make out slid open with the speed and silence I'd started to expect, immediately this happened the already crowded station became jammed with people, hundreds of them emerged and made me feel petite and vulnerable. This wasn't because they were aggressive or incautious, they were just enormous, mostly over two meters tall, full of noise and clamour, laughter, shouts, waving, some running, some carrying enormous bags on their backs and of course, mostly but not exclusively women.

I felt Nkoyo's hand grab mine and she worked her way

 through the throng and on-board the giant white worm.

As we stepped on-board I felt the familiar slump in my stomach, not much, just a hint of emptiness.

'This is a Nyumbu,' she said proudly. 'The fastest mass transit system in the world.'

I walked along behind Nkoyo and saw that the interior was fitted with stand-up containment areas a little like the ones I'd been strapped into in the Gardenian pods. Nkoyo guided me into one of them, it wasn't a seat as such; it was a shaped unit that seemed to adjust to my body size as I stood in it.

'Don't be alarmed, the acceleration and deceleration is quite extreme but the seats keep you from harm.'

I was about to say something when my body was encased in a tight kind of bandage. A mechanism gripped my head, it wasn't painful, it was obviously padded in some way, but it restricted what I could see.

Then I felt the machine move, I didn't have any warning, I just felt truly spectacular, fighter jet-level acceleration. There was a low sound of movement. I noticed the odd little creak sound as the acceleration just kept on increasing. There was a couple of minutes when it seemed to die away; there was a tiny sense of movement but almost too subtle to register, then an equally violent and sudden deceleration for about the same time.

Before I could even begin to understand what was going on the restraints came off, my head was freed and the small capsule thing I'd been standing in gently tipped me forward. Nkoyo was standing beside me.

'Wow, that was fairly awesome,' I said. I was about to ask her about it but of course I already knew. We'd got up to 1,700 kph, travelling along an electrically charged maglev track buried 60 meters below the surface of the city. We had travelled in a near vacuum and thereby avoided going through the speed of sound. We had covered a little over 723 kilometres in just a few minutes.

As we made our way through yet more crowds, I sensed a different atmosphere; for a start the crowds around me were almost exclusively women, there were a few enormous African men carrying even more enormous bags on their backs, but women made up ninety per cent of the people around me. I was also more aware of their gaze; everyone within my field of vision was staring at me.

'It's fine, Gavin,' said Nkoyo. 'You are of great interest but there is nothing to be concerned about. We will shortly be in a quiet place for a while.'

I made my way up another wide flight of stairs and emerged into a vast open square dotted with huge trees. The sun was bright and the sky was a crystal clear blue. I was utterly bedazzled by the spectacle, so much colour and vibrancy in the clothing of the women all around me, and then I turned and saw the town hall.

To call a building of this scale a town hall made a nineteenth-century town hall, the like of which once stood proudly in places like Leeds or Manchester, look like a timber outhouse. This place was massive; it was Ridley-Scott-1980s-sci-fi-opening-shot-of-a-blockbuster-movie colossal. Essentially a pyramid, the base of which covered many square miles. It was possibly a mile high. It made me dizzy to look up at it. The best description I can think of is a man-made mountain, I could see there were definitely clouds passing well below the pinnacle of this monster construction.

'This is the Mkutano Mahali, our meeting place,' said Nkoyo. 'It is also sometimes known as the General Assembly, the nearest organisation I can think of from your era would be the Nations United in New York.'

'The United Nations,' I corrected.

'Indeed, just so, so we are here to attend a very important meeting and you, the man from the cloud, are the guest of honour.'

23

Roar of the Weavers

IF THE PRESS CONFERENCE I'D ATTENDED IN the Institute in London was a training session in dealing with mass public exposure it wasn't much use. When I first entered the cavernous hall that housed the Mkutano Mahali I momentarily thought I'd gone outside. This structure was above the scale of mere humans, it was just too big and too elaborate, the very fabric of the place was beyond anything I'd seen in London, so truly high-end in a world where I hadn't seen anything low-end or even vaguely shoddy.

I stood in the entrance to this palatial enclave and my mouth hung open wide. I don't know how many delegates attended this meeting, without doubt many thousands. I don't know where they came from, but judging by the styles of clothing and racial characteristics, I'd guess everywhere on earth. I scanned the many hundreds of faces I could see from my vantage point, a doorway at the rear of the room. Before me were hundreds of rows of spacious chairs, up above the chairs at the far end of the vast hall was a long desk type thing behind which sat maybe twenty women.

I could see some men in the room, quite a few men who seemed mostly old, but they were definitely blokes. However, the vast majority of the delegates were women and they all, so it seemed, were looking at me.

I followed Nkoyo down a long aisle between the endless rows of seats, I noticed that many of the people sitting either side showed a great deal of interest as we made our way toward the front of the hall.

Two very tall women smiled at Nkoyo when we arrived near the front, Nkoyo gestured for me to sit down and I did so. I was staring around all the time I was sat there. This was a fascinating place; there was so much going on, so many people conversing with each other. Every now and then I would notice a huddle of women would turn and look at me before returning to their closed huddle.

'This is amazing,' I said to Nkoyo who had finally taken the seat beside me. The seats were very high so I didn't get the feeling that hundreds of people were staring at the back of my head.

I looked up in front of me and got a nasty shock, they might not have been looking at the back of my head, but they were certainly able to see my face.

There was my mush, must have been eighty feet across on a huge screen above the people sitting behind the raised desks. I tried not to freak out but any tiny reaction on my face was enlarged hundreds of times, it was very disconcerting. I tried to work out where the camera was because I could see no sign of one, this, I soon realised, caused a ripple of laughter in the hall. I must have looked a right nutter, eyes darting this way and that to try and see evidence of a camera.

'Try to ignore it, it's very distracting when you're sitting this close to the front,' said Nkoyo, her thirty foot high profile was clearly visible on the screen as she leant toward me to whisper. She looked pretty stunning though, even at that size.

I somehow knew as I sat next to Nkoyo that I was an attendee at The Congressional Investigative Committee on the Future of the Male. Hefty topic indeed.

This was underlined very reassuringly for me by the screen changing from my face to a blue background with the words '2211 Congressional Investigative Committee on the Future of the Male' in ten meter high letters.

'Delegates, your attention please, the man from the cloud, Gavin Meckler is among us,' said a voice, an African woman's voice speaking English.

This announcement was followed by such an incredible silence it almost hurt my ears. How so many people in such a huge space could remain that quiet is a testament to their incredible discipline.

Again the voice could be heard, 'Gavin Meckler is a man from the dark times, however, he has been thoroughly tested and is of no danger or threat to any delegate.'

I started looking around the room for some source for this voice, it was very loud and clear but I couldn't see anyone talking.

'We have much to learn from this young man, not only about our history but also about the decision we are now facing.'

There was a wave of reaction through the vast gathering, not so much the noise of chatter or agreement, more the impact of recognition, the crisis of the male population was clearly a bit of an issue with these folks.

I raised myself slightly in the chair and looked at the vast rows of seats behind me, many people were still arriving and taking their seats but it was getting close to full. Suddenly a face I'd seen before became apparent to me in the row right behind me, it was Anne Hempstead; the woman I'd met in the Erotic Museum in London. She was staring at me intently, I nodded an acknowledgement to her but she didn't react.

'The Congressional Committee is now in session. Order please,' said the confident voice. The room settled rapidly and I noticed some movement to my right. A very diminutive Asian woman move toward the large table directly in front of the row of raised desks on the sort of stage area.

'We now call on today's first witness, Mayor Nguyen Yen from Phnom Penh.'

The image on the screen changed again, this time to a kind of wide shot of the women sitting behind the desks in front of me. They were near enough to where I was sitting for me to make out their individual features so this screen was clearly for the benefit of the huge crowd behind me.

'Who are they?' I whispered to Nkoyo.

'Relax, and you will understand,' came her familiar reply.

'Good morning your Mayorship,' said a white woman who sat near the centre of the group. 'Thank you for joining us today.'

On the screen above them a small inset box showed a close up of the smiling Mayor sitting before them.

I sat back in my chair and tried to relax as I listened to what was going on.

I knew I was sitting in hall twenty-three at the International Congress. The Congress itself was made up of seven thousand representatives from around the world. They sat in the Hall of Congress which was somewhere in the same building. Somehow, I knew that was situated about twenty floors above the hall I was sitting in.

I knew this committee had been convened to try and discern the mood of the population to the coming crisis and weigh the opposing views of various specialists. The Congress would then create a report which would be sent to the Senate where the topic would be voted on, a law would be passed and the world would continue.

'Your Mayorship, would you care to comment on a recent report?' The woman speaking, this one clearly Chinese, looked down in front of her. 'It's item four thirty-eight in the evidence folder, with the latest criminal statistics.'

After a moment of silence I heard a woman speaking in what I assumed to be Vietnamese, I could see her face on the screen even though she was sitting with her back to me. I started to fidget which I always seem to do when I can't understand something.

'Relax and you will understand,' said Nkoyo softly.

I sat back in my chair and tried to relax again, in a few moments I started to hear English coming from the tiny woman.

'… as you all know, we have reached a crisis point and there is no hiding from it, we have to do something and we have to do it with urgency. The number of men in our world is very low. The number of fertile men is even lower. At current rates, and without intervention, there will be no fertile men on planet earth in sixty years' time. I know some of you think this to be a good thing. We all agree that during the dark times, such a dream was held by many women. There was no question or argument that for thousands of years men were the cause of most of our problems. This, I will argue, is no longer the case. This man we see before us, this man from the end of the dark times is a wonderful example of how the orthodoxy of the Weavers has distorted reality. The man we see before us today, the man from the cloud is not a murderer, he is not a rapist, he will not swim through a river of snot to get to a friendly pussy.'

I don't know if you can really describe eyes as 'popping out of your head' but mine certainly came close. I sat utterly motionless on hearing that last phrase, it was so out of keeping with what this delicate and diminutive woman had been saying, it stopped me breathing. Could I be hearing a glitch in the translation system? I understood that I was hearing a very sophisticated language translation system as opposed to the real voice of the women speaking, but how could you mistranslate such a specific sentence, swimming a river of snot! It was gross.

'It's a famous quote from a political tract from a little before your time,' Nkoyo whispered to me. 'It's from a document called the SCUM manifesto, SCUM short for the Society for Cutting Up Men.'

'Oh my Lord,' I said. 'Sounds a bit heavy duty.'

Nkoyo smiled gently. 'Yes, that is a good term, it was very heavy duty, not unlike some of the women in this room.'

She calmly turned and faced front again, I hardly dared move.

Mayor Nguyen Yen continued: 'It is perfectly true we now live in the most peaceful and prosperous period of all human history. As the report states, last year there were less than one thousand recorded murders on the entire planet of more than eight billion souls. We have had not one report of a rape, not one case of sexual assault against a child and very low property crime. Many women would have us believe that this is entirely due to the low numbers of men among us. However, let me say this, of that one thousand murders, over nine hundred and eighty were committed by women. Four hundred and sixteen of those murders were women killing men of whom they had no knowledge, just a random killing simply because the victim was male. Of the millions of men who have lived out their lives on this planet since the dawn of recorded time, only a very small minority ever committed a crime against women. Only a very small proportion of the male population were killers, violent offenders and perverts. I am not trying to deny their role, there have been many men in history who have proven beyond doubt the darkness in their souls, but a blanket reaction to such statistics will not help us. We are experiencing an imbalance that is bad for us individually, and bad for the health of our society. We must, somehow, breed more men. I ask you, for the good of the human race, let us be a human race, not just a female race.'

The reaction to her final statement was instant and raucous, I could sense the room was divided but at a guess I would claim the majority were on her side. The cheer that sprang up was loud and prolonged, the hissing and booing was intermittent and short.

I was beginning to get a better idea about what was going on. For a start, there really were forces in the world that wanted to eradicate men for good. There were also more balanced voices that wished to facilitate men's continued existence. I started to understand my role in this huge and heated debate; I was a man from the dark times who, the pro-men lobby were suggesting, wasn't all that bad. I think that was the gist of it. It felt like a bit of a responsibility, as if it was down to me to represent my entire gender and all their misdeeds from the year dot. Nice one.

'Thank you, your Mayorship,' said the white woman on the panel.

I watched the diminutive Mayor Nguyen Yen from Phnom Penh stand up behind the table and bow graciously.

The loud African woman's voice came over the public address system.

'The Congressional Investigative Committee on the Future of the Male now calls Professor Ruth Heilman from Boston.'

An impressive figure stood up from a seat further along the row I was on, she walked to the gangway and stepped behind the table recently vacated by the Mayor of Phnom Penh.

Professor Ruth Heilman from Boston was tall, slender with a gaunt expression on an ageless face. I could tell by her hands that she was probably over seventy years old but you would never have guessed from her figure, movement or stature.

'Welcome, Professor,' said the white woman on the panel. 'You will know there are many among us, and indeed many in the Senate who are unsure of the aims of the Weavers. I would ask that we all try and remain calm today, that we stick to the questions and try not to resort to personal attacks.'

'I have no wish to make any personal attacks,' said the Professor. Her voice had an incredible authority, I knew if she told me to do something I'd probably end up doing it even if I didn't want to. She struck me as someone you wouldn't want to mess with.

'Professor, you are well known for your advocacy of terminating the existence of men, would that be a fair assessment?'

'It would,' replied the Professor. I couldn't help reacting a bit. I realised at once that the only thing she'd ever ask me to do was to stop being alive.

'So would you have us exterminate all the men among us now?'

I looked at the Professor's gaunt but handsome face on the screen. She remained very calm.

'I realise there has been much said about us that is, how shall I say, overly dramatic and reactionary. Of course we have no wish to harm any living creature, that is the whole point of our message, for surely it is only men who have ever harmed other living creatures, particularly women. No, we would simply allow them to die out.'

'And how exactly would we allow such a thing to happen?' asked another of the women behind the long desk.

'Sisters,' she said. Somehow the very word sent a chill through me. For a start, she had ignored the small cluster of men who were seated among the delegates, what about them?

'As has been illustrated most informatively by Mayor Nguyen Yen we are indeed at a turning point. We are on the verge of something no woman coming from the same period of history Mister Meckler here could ever possibly have imagined.'

She gestured toward me as she referred to me, but didn't so much as glance in my direction. I was beneath her contempt. Indeed, I actually felt beneath her contempt. Unfortunately, as I was experiencing this particular emotion, my image was projected onto the screen. I froze in terror.

'We are on the cusp of a new epoch in human existence and we are faced with a choice. Do we continue to live with the ever-present danger of men one day turning on us and reclaiming patriarchal power, or do we strive forward and end their influence on our thinking, on our society and laws once and for all.'

There was some very energetic and clearly female cheering from the crowd, but again, I would suggest the majority remained silent. I turned to see the crowd in the area of the hall easily visible from my seat. I then noticed something that surprised me; a man in about the third row was clapping and cheering.

'I am not a fool, sisters, I know there are men among us who are exemplary in their behaviour and attitudes. I want to say here and now that I wish them no harm. I am not suggesting any form of violent or even unfair treatment. I am not suggesting even the most benign curtailment of life privileges for men. It is not necessary and it would undermine what we are trying to achieve. No, what I am saying is let us continue on the course we are now on. As many of you will know, by the end of this century we could be in a position where there are no more men on the planet. I realise that there are many among you who find this prospect to be horrific, it fills you with terror, it fills you with the fear of the loss of the father. Most of the women in this room were raised by their fathers, we have been told since childhood of the importance of the father in our lives, but that importance was chiefly to make us more able to deal with the threat from men in our adult lives. What I am suggesting is this simple understanding. We are trapped by the father, trapped into the age-old patterns of submission and subservience to a weaker, less stable and intellectually deficient other.'

Another small smattering of applause, almost apologetic in its brief existence; however, this limp response didn't seem to curtail the impressive Professor's determination.

'Some women say they would miss the cock. How many women in the world now have ever experienced penetrative sex with a man? According to the latest statistics only about thirty per cent of the world's women. How can you miss something you have never had? We wouldn't miss it, we wouldn't miss men, we would be able to breathe a sigh of relief after forty thousand years of oppression.'

Once again, the eye-popping feeling was upon me, but I kept my head down, I didn't want the delegates to witness my reaction. The Professor's statement was greeted with applause from the crowd so I don't think they were paying much attention to me. I had never heard any woman say she either did or didn't 'miss the cock'. I'd never thought about women's concept of 'the cock' as some kind of entity independent of individual men. I suppose there was a part of me that understood that women wanted to experience penetrative sex with a man, but I had never really thought of it in such graphic terms.

'But remember this, sisters!' Professor Heilman bellowed above the racket in the auditorium, 'it has only been a mere one hundred and fifty years that women have truly been in control of their destiny. It was women who steered this planet away from inevitable destruction caused by the short-sighted stupidity of men. Remember that stupidity, remember that oppression and bullish determination ruled and ruined the lives of women for forty thousand years. It ruled and ruined the lives of animals for forty thousand years, ruled and ruined the stability of the planet for forty thousand years. I do not forget the struggles and sacrifices of my fore-sisters. I do not forget the heartache and pain, the humiliation of rape, the violence, murder and fearful loathing inflicted upon us, generation after generation after generation. To that way of life, to that brutal patriarchy, I say we shall never return!'

It was disturbingly reminiscent of Hitler at Nuremberg. This lady knew how to stir up the crowd, and this time she had a lot more support among the delegates although only one of the men was clapping and cheering, the same chap who had clapped before, only this time he was on his feet nodding at the cheering women around him.

I glanced back at Professor Heilman who sat motionless until she turned to me and smiled and gave me a little wink. This I can tell you, was not what I was expecting.

'Thank you, Professor,' said the white woman at the centre of the panel. The Professor eventually stood up as the clapping and cheering continued. She didn't acknowledge the crowd, she walked serenely back to her seat where she was greeted with enthusiasm by a small coterie of similarly dressed women.

Nkoyo leant toward me. 'Wish me luck.'

The African woman's voice made the next booming announcement causing the crowd to settle down.

'The Congressional Investigative Committee on the Future of the Male calls on Doctor Nkoyo Oshineye from the London Institute of Mental Health.'

Nkoyo stood up and across the floor to the large table. She sat down as her face appeared on the screen above the panel.

The white woman at the centre of the congressional panel, for I now understood that's who they were, an elected group of congress members.

'Thank you for joining us Doctor Oshineye. We would like to learn what you have discovered since the arrival of the man from the dark times.'

Nkoyo looked relaxed and confident as she sat at the big table.

'I would firstly like to thank the Professor for a very stirring speech,' she said calmly. 'I am sure hearing her words was a revelation to our honoured guest today. The man I have been sitting next to is, as you all know, Gavin Meckler, a man born in the twentieth century. You know his story; you know the strange set of events that brought him to us. What you may not know is the nature of the man, if you like, the soul of the man you see before you today. It has been a fascinating experience to meet and get to know him. As some of you may know, he spent yesterday talking with Olumide Smith in this very city and I am happy to report the meeting was a great success. Both men seemed to understand each other on a deep level. I felt it was important to let you know of this meeting, to let you know that the man you see before you is not a demon, a patriarchal zealot or a religious maniac. It is important for all of us to meet Gavin today. He is very unlike what we might have expected from a man of his historical period and many have seen his arrival as some kind of mystical sign. As Olumide correctly pointed out, this is not the case. Gavin's arrival into our world is just a currently inexplicable event due to a unique set of cumulative circumstances. As you may recall, there have been other anomalous arrivals through the same portal in the past few years, never, admittedly as large and challenging as Gavin Meckler.'

I was suddenly aware at that moment that eight years before my arrival a number of swallows appeared in the same square I had arrived in. The swallow had apparently been extinct for over a hundred years and so their sudden arrival was very newsworthy. I assumed they had flown in through the same anomaly that I had, although I didn't realise swallows could fly that high. I'd certainly never noticed any birds above a few hundred meters in my flying experience.

'What Gavin has shown the members of the Institute in London is that we may have a slightly distorted view of our distant past. I am confident Gavin would agree that there were many aspects of the patriarchy that were negative. I'm sure he would agree that the old system kept women oppressed and that whenever patriarchy and religion died in a particular culture, equality, civil order, technological progress, population stabilisation and improved education emerged. It was never, I would argue, individual men who maintained the old system. It was ingrained into the culture for both men and women. Only the tireless struggle of generations of the enlightened gradually changed the way we live together. That is what we are talking about, the ability to live together in harmony, not against each other or within rigid and oppressive social systems as had been the human habit for millennia. We have learned to live together and through doing so, achieved improved mental health.'

The Chinese woman on the panel leant forward at that moment, she spoke carefully and clearly.

'I'm glad you mentioned mental health Doctor, this is certainly a concern among those of us not swept away by Weaver rhetoric. Can you give us the long-term mental health implications of a single gender world?'

'Indeed I can Congresswoman,' said Nkoyo. 'Removing men from the timeline of human history is generally thought among mental health practitioners as not conducive to good mental health. It is a fast track to mental pain and disorder. It is what we deal with day in, day out at the Institute in London. The pain women feel over the loss of men has been overlooked. We need men, not, as the Professor rather crudely expressed it because of "the cock". Not because we need the seed, not because our fathers cared for us, not because we need the companionship of a life partner, no. We need men to maintain the balance within ourselves, the balance of our own male–female personalities. We all understand this, and all the research, all the exhaustive reports from every scientific institution in the world backs this up. Men are part of the human race, without them we will become something else, something unbalanced, something, dare I say it, less than truly human. If there are no men among us, truly no men in the world I suggest that we could be far more susceptible to totalitarianism, to a new form of oppression, not of one gender to another, but from one social grouping to another. The women among us who want to pursue the removal of the male are, I fear, too interested in power and control. I fear they wish to do many of the things we all rightly condemn the old male regime for being obsessed with. We all know in our heart of hearts that it is not men who were or indeed could be the problem. It is us, all of us. It is human beings who, when under pressure, resort to crude means to control the other. If we cannot blame men for all the wrongs of the past because they no longer exist, will we then start to blame each other when we face new problems? Will we start to oppress women who do not fit our worldview? Will we punish women who step out of line? That, sisters – and indeed brothers – is not a world I wish to inhabit. We must live with men, we must know how to live with them, to share our lives with them and accept them as part of ourselves. We need men to grow along with us, to develop more sensitivity and greater understanding of themselves. We cannot do this alone. We need fathers for the balance they bring to our lives, for the richness they can and do impart. A world without men would be barren in more ways than we can imagine. We must turn the situation around, we must let men live.'

Nkoyo stopped there, a silence followed and it was almost

unbearable. Then I heard one person clapping enthusiastically, I craned my neck to see if I could spot who it was and I was once again baffled. It was the same man who had clapped so enthusiastically after the scary Professor Heilman. He was soon joined by other delegates in the auditorium. The reaction was slower and more hesitant but it built and built, more and more people stood up and started cheering and whooping and clapping and shouting. Nkoyo's calm beauty was magnificent. She sat relaxed, arms by her sides, staring around the auditorium in a most regal and yet non-threatening way, a woman whose time had come, a woman who knew she should be where she was. Okay, I was a little bit awestruck but she seemed pretty damn impressive to me at that moment.

When the cheering and applause finally settled, the white woman on the congressional panel leant forward.

'Thank you, Doctor,' she said softly. 'That was very illuminating.'

Nkoyo stood up and the applause started again, she walked back toward me and I have to say I felt rather proud. I did a bit of basking in her reflected glory. It didn't last long.

'Now it's your turn,' she said as she sat next to me. I felt my body spasm with tension. The shock went through me as if I'd heard a gun go off. This was further reinforced by the booming invisible African woman's voice.

'The Congressional Investigative Committee on the Future of the Male calls on Mister Gavin Meckler from 2011.'

I felt a hot flush run over me. It had been bad enough at the press conference in the Institution but this audience was a hundred times bigger. This was an audience of many thousands of people from all over the planet and some incredibly stern-looking ladies who I knew would all be looking at me in the same way the women had done when I arrived in London. Why would they want to hear what I had to say? Then the panic really hit me; I didn't have anything *to* say. Nkoyo was looking at me and smiling, she gestured toward the table. The crowd started clapping again, I knew I had to do it but I didn't know what it was I had to do.

I eventually stood up, bowed a little toward the audience and then for some inexplicable reason I waved. I felt such a fool, why wave? It was pathetic but I was in a blind panic. I eventually found my way to the big table and sat down on the big chair. I felt like a kid, I was a bit short for the huge chair and the table came up to my upper chest. Without warning, the chair rose a little, it was slightly alarming but did mean I didn't look so much like a six-year-old having his tea.

The applause died very quickly, silence descended, I knew thousands of eyes were on me as I glanced up at the screen. There was my pallid-looking face, full of fear. I swallowed.

'Um, hello,' I said. The applause was deafening and for my part very unexpected. I remember thinking that maybe they thought because I came from so long ago I wouldn't be able to talk, just grunt and kill small furry animals which I'd eat raw. Who knows why they clapped?

'Thank you, Mister Meckler,' said the white woman who was now sitting directly in front and much above me. 'It is very kind of you to join us today, we appreciate this may be a little strange for you.'

'You could say that,' I muttered.

'Please be calm, we wish you no harm, you are not in trouble, we are simply trying to get a fuller understanding of the situation.'

There was a short silence. I assumed they were waiting for me to say something, so I did.

'I'm very honoured to be invited here today. Thank you. I'm, um, okay, I'm not used to speaking in public like this. I'm just an engineer.'

Without warning another huge round of applause. If only, I thought, if only some of my nerdy engineering colleagues could see me now. Never has anyone said 'I'm just an engineer' and had that kind of response.

'Well, I should say I was an engineer two hundred years ago. Now I'm just a man who's a bit lost in a world he doesn't really understand.'

This phrase elicited a sound I had heard before, essentially mass empathy on a scale probably rare in history before this era.

'Mister Meckler,' said the Chinese woman on the panel. 'I would like to know what you think of the idea being proposed.'

'What idea is that?' I asked.

'The idea being put forward by the Weavers among others, that we allow the male members of the human race to die out, to gracefully exit the stage, to be no more.'

'Oh that, right, yeah, that's fairly heavy duty,' I said.

'I'm sorry, Mister Meckler, that doesn't translate very clearly,' said the white woman. 'Would you care to explain your reaction using alternative phraseology?'

'I'm sorry, yes. Um, I don't think it's a very good idea.'

Another woman, further along the row in front of me to the left was speaking. I turned to look at her; she looked kind of severe and Northern European, very blonde.

'I don't think we imagined you would find the demise of your gender to be a good idea, but would you care to tell us why, and maybe explain what life was really like back in the dark times?'

I swallowed and tried to speak slowly and clearly. I would much rather have watched from the sidelines, in fact, I'd much rather be doing pretty much anything other than sitting in front of a panel of the most powerful women I'd ever met trying to justify my existence.

'Um, well, yeah, okay, I've been listening today, um, you know, with great interest. I can see now how things have come to this, how it is seen by your time that someone like me, a man, has been the root cause of a great many problems in our history. I'd never thought about it when I was back in my own time. I was just born a man. I didn't know that meant anything. I was raised by my mother as most men were back then. I mean I was raised by a woman, my mum was a woman, like you, she was a lady. Yeah.'

There was no discernible reaction from any of the women, I didn't know what I was saying, words just started to tumble out. I was getting images of my mum and dad when I was a kid, weird flashes of memory, picking raspberries in the garden with my dad on a summers evening, stuff like that.

'I barely knew my father, he didn't talk to me much, he didn't seem to talk to anyone much. He was also an engineer, worked in the nuclear industry, nuclear power, not weapons. So yeah, I can now see how that simple fact affected the way I saw the world and the way I saw women. I definitely can see now that I didn't really take much notice of women, I mean, don't get me wrong, I didn't hate women or anything. Never. I didn't like the way some men talked about women, you know, as objects, that always offended me. It offended a lot of men but, you know, it just was like that.'

I wanted to shut up more than anything. I didn't want to blurt out some of the terrible things I'd heard men say, really horrible they were. I didn't want to say those things, not at that moment. I mean, what could be worse? Then I remembered Olumide, and that made me calm down again.

'Yeah, so talking with Olumide yesterday made me look at myself, re-assess many things I took for granted. I can see that now, here in 2211, things are very different. I'm not certain they are better, but they are different. Very, very different, yeah. But, but actually I don't even want to argue for the continuation of men, I can't, I am one, as far as most of you seem to think I am part of the problem not part of the solution. It's not for me to say, it's your world, I shouldn't even be here much less try and argue that men should be given a fair crack of the whip.'

The white woman leant forward, I don't know how I knew, but I knew I had to shut up and let her ask me something.

'Again Mister Meckler, can you use terms that are translatable, we are getting some very confused images here, I'm sure you didn't mean to say that women should be whipped.'

'No!' I said rather too loudly. 'Oh blimey, fuck.'

My reaction caused a noticeable ripple of distress to surge through the room, I turned and glanced at Nkoyo but she seemed to be above it all, she was just sitting looking calm and serene.

'I'm sorry, I didn't mean to, I meant, look, it's very difficult. All I can say is I think you would be travelling down a dangerous road if you allow men to disappear altogether. Like Nkoyo said, it might lead to a very unbalanced world. I do believe that with all the improvements you've made in the world, in many cases despite my gender, you'd be in a sadder, blander world without a few nice blokes knocking around.'

Again I sensed a murmur of confusion.

'Sorry, is that okay? Do you know what the word "blokes" means? I'm a bloke, a bloke is a word meaning a man, not a nasty, aggressive man, just a regular normal man, a bloke.'

'That is fine, Mister Meckler,' said the white woman.

I glanced back at Nkoyo who was now looking at me and smiling. I decided to use my catch phrase again.

'I thank you for giving me this opportunity to speak, my name is Gavin Meckler. Like all the men on the planet, it seems I really shouldn't be here, but I am here, we are here and we'd like to help.'

The cheer and the roar of thousands of hands clapping made me slightly dizzy, I glanced at Nkoyo who was smiling beautifully, the women on the panel seemed to have lightened up. I think they liked what I said.

24

Lagos to Rio

ONE OF THE THINGS I SEEM TO HAVE DONE A great deal of in 2211 was sleep. When Nkoyo and I had returned to the Yin Qui late that night I felt like I had jet lag. Maybe I had Nyumbu lag, the damn things went much faster than a passenger jet from 2011.

When we emerged from the Nyumbu station at the dockside it was dark, the sky was clear and due to the ingenious nature of the path lighting there was very little light pollution, the stars above us, occasionally visible through the dense canopy of foliage, were breathtakingly intense.

'Is this the same ship we were on before?' I asked as we walked across the open quay side towards the massive vessel. It too had very subtle low lighting all over it giving the massive bulk an ethereal quality as if it were a mere cloud of phosphorescent gas.

'Yes, although it has been across the Atlantic while we've been in Lagos.'

We were joined by a small gaggle of people making their way across the open dock area toward the brightly lit entrance of the ship. Once again we were welcomed on-board by Hamisi before we started the long walk through the endless interior of the behemoth of a ship. This time I didn't have to shake his hand, I guessed I had bought a round trip ticket.

When we finally arrived at our shared cabin I can't really remember getting into the sleeping pod but that's where I found myself the following morning. I stumbled out of bed and saw the temporary wall was up between my pod and Nkoyo's. I made my way along the corridor and into the shower and toilet area. I showered and dressed in my London body suit before heading up to the front restaurant to find some kind of breakfast.

As I paced along the endless corridors I worked out I had slept for over ten hours, something I cannot remember ever doing back in 2011. I'd slept a lot in Gardenia too, maybe it was to do with the pace of life, something in the water, I've no idea. As I passed by a huge viewing window near the front of the ship, I noticed the weather outside looked rather different to anything I'd seen on the first leg of our journey.

For some reason the sea looked lower down but it didn't look calm. There was the most horrendous gale blowing, the waves were gunmetal grey as aggressive rollers approached the ship and disappeared beneath us. I stood still for a moment to see if I could sense any movement. Nothing, not even a mild up-and-down motion. The ship was absurdly stable, while all around us the sea had gone bonkers. I observed the angry ocean for a while and soon understood that the reason the sea looked lower was because the Yin Qui was only in contact with the tops of the huge waves beneath us. I admit that it didn't really make sense and I would have loved to have had access to the outside to see what was going on, but I knew this was pointless, I'd be blown away in seconds.

I entered the front-facing restaurant or eating area, which was already busy with passengers. Somehow I knew where to go and I sat at a large table looking out over the savage seascape outside the long windows. I was sitting with a lot of people I'd never seen before and was immediately aware of many of their names, dates of birth and family connections. I didn't want that much information so I felt myself tighten up, I withdrew in some way and the noise of the information stopped. I picked up a small fruit knife from a container before me and started to peel some fresh fruit conveniently piled up in wooden bowls in the centre of the table.

A moment later a tall North African man poured me a cup of

 coffee, I thanked him and drank with relish. As I put the cup down a name entered my head. Anne Hempstead. I turned to my left and there she was, sitting beside me.

'Oh, Anne,' I said trying to cover my shock. 'How are you?'

'Congratulations on your speech yesterday.'

'Oh, well it wasn't really a speech, I don't enjoy that kind of thing.'

It felt as if she wasn't really interested in anything I had to say, her face stern and she wasn't looking at me.

'You know you turned the vote,' she said, as she too started to cut up fruit. I glanced nervously at the knife in her hand, it was big enough to do some serious slashing.

I shook my head. 'What d'you mean?'

'Yesterday, the vote at the assembly, the proposal was rejected by a majority of one thousand two hundred and fourteen.'

'Wow, is that good?'

'I personally don't think it was good, no, but then what do my opinions mean? You are a man, as long as you're happy that's all that counts isn't it, Gavin?'

I didn't know how to react. Well, I knew that the best possible reaction was to say nothing, which is what I did.

My silence certainly didn't stop Anne Hempstead talking.

'It was neck and neck, there are seventy thousand global delegates with voting rights so a majority of one thousand or so is a close call, but it got through, only a few hundred abstentions.'

'Wow, seventy thousand! I can't imagine how that works.'

'It works very well, oh but wait, of course it can't work well because men don't run the system do they, Gavin?'

Again I said nothing in response to this. It seemed pointless, as it was obvious that women were in total control so what was all this whining about men good for?

'Your presence was seen as decisive,' said Anne after a short period of silence. 'How do you feel about that?'

'I don't know. How should I feel?'

This response clearly baffled the rather hostile woman, there was something about Anne Hempstead that got on my nerves and I couldn't work out why it was. Why should I feel annoyed by this woman? Okay, she was making rash assumptions about me based on my gender, but that said so much more about her than it did about me. I finally decided what annoyed me was her assumption that she could just sit next to me and tell me what I thought while I was having my breakfast. Maybe that's what journalists are like, maybe it was nothing new. I'd never met a journalist back in 2011, I'd never been important enough to warrant their interest.

'I wondered if you felt good about the fact that you have, in effect, helped ensure the continuation of the oppression of women?'

I smiled at her because I knew this was nonsense. I'd done nothing of the kind, I'd just ummed and ahhed in front of thousands of the most powerful people on the planet, who happened to be women and they'd clapped a bit.

'The speech Nkoyo gave was far more impressive than anything I muttered,' I said eventually.

'Are you having sexual relations with Nkoyo Oshineye?' she asked. It's almost pointless to describe the question as blunt. It was like being hit over the head with a brick.

'Blimey, no! But anyway, it's nothing to do with you. Who the hell are you?'

'You know who I am, I'm just trying to get a story.'

'There isn't a story. My name is Gavin Meckler …'

'Yes, I know, you shouldn't be here but you are,' she mimicked rather cruelly. 'Yes, we've all heard that before, but why are you really here? That's what I want to know.'

'Wait a minute,' I said, 'do you really think I'm part of some kind of conspiracy thing? I've been brought through time by some kind of weird unknown technology because I am a man who can father male babies? Is that it?'

'Do you have a better explanation?'

That stumped me because I didn't. Nothing made sense anyway, so the fact that I could be a mere pawn in some massive, time-dilating sub-governmental conspiracy was just as possible as the chances that I'd arrived in Gardenia and the Squares of London by pure time-dilation fluke.

'If the Institute hoped to swing the vote by your presence, then they've been remarkably successful don't you think?'

'Are you asking me or are you positing questions that have the answer within them?' I said, feeling rather clever. That feeling didn't last long.

'Gavin, you are being used as a dupe, you are being wheeled out at big international gatherings as proof that men from the past weren't as bad as we've been told, but you know the truth don't you?'

'Do I?'

'Oh come on,' said Anne. There was something unpleasant about the way this woman looked at me. 'You know that men were far worse than we've been told. You cut off young girls' genitals, you said your male God told you to do it. You threw acid in the faces of young women, you raped women to death and left their mutilated bodies on the street to rot as a way of showing other women what would happen to them if they didn't obey their patriarchal masters. You know that's the truth don't you?'

'Umm, how about no?' I said channelling my annoying brother; that was something he always said when I accused him of taking something of mine when we were kids. 'It wasn't like that.' I said in a droning tone. 'You're making it up. I wasn't like that, no man I ever met was like that, blimey, it was anything but like that.'

My response was pointless, Anne Hempstead knew what she knew and she wasn't going to let me tell her otherwise.

'Now you've landed here and seen that you can't get away with that kind of thing anymore you're playing all innocent and surprised and supportive. You are just what the pro-man lobby groups needed, some kind of proof that men aren't really dangerous. I know you're dangerous, Gavin Meckler, you are a virus that will spread and destroy everything we've built. That's the truth isn't it?'

'I don't think so,' I said, and I suddenly felt Nkoyo's presence.

'Can I help you, Anne?' it was Nkoyo's voice coming from behind me.

'It's a bit late for that isn't it, Nkoyo?' spat Anne. 'I'll leave you with your precious man.' She gave me one last look of unadulterated hatred then got up and walked away, soon lost in the crowds by the entrance.

'You okay?' asked Nkoyo.

'Um, well, I'm still here,' I said. 'I wish I understood what she was on about. Is she one of the mad women who can't find a man?'

'No, Gavin, women like Anne Hempstead don't want to find a man, quite the opposite. She is a prominent worder who supports the Weaver movement, she is very upset about the vote yesterday.'

'Oh right, she's an actual Weaver woman.'

'Oh yes, a very famous one.'

25

A World Built by Women?

FOR THE REST OF THAT LEG OF THE TRIP ONboard the Yin Qui I didn't catch sight of the spiky Anne Hempstead which was a bit of a relief. I worried about her though. I worried about what she'd said and the contempt she held me in purely because of my gender. I admit this was a new experience for me. I'm not trying to claim total ignorance of the rights of women, votes for women, of feminism and all that stuff. I'd heard plenty about it back in 2011 but it never really had much effect on my life. I just did what I did, tried to get along with Beth – okay I failed at that most of the time and ended up baffled, but at least I tried.

I'd heard about moronic and barbaric practices in parts of the world that cruelly affected women but obviously I didn't have anything to do with them personally. If I ever happened to read a story about them in the Sunday papers, which was rare, I'd be as appalled about it as the women in the General Assembly building obviously were. Try as I might, I just couldn't see myself as some big, violent, bullying oppressive patriarch, but maybe I'd been living under an illusion. I'd have assumed that after at least one hundred and fifty years where women ran the joint, all the stuff that men had done in the past would be forgotten.

England had been at war with France a hundred and fifty years before I was born and people weren't still going on about it. Okay, we'd been at war with Germany forty years before I was born and people went on and on about that all the time, and yes, people in Northern Ireland had been killing each other for donkey's years and I never really understood that. They seemed obsessed about some weird battle that took place four hundred years before but that was the exception surely?

The situation in 2211 felt different; to see so many powerful, independent women who weren't oppressed slaves or perpetually pregnant housewives but who were still really angry and anxious about the men around them was really confusing. I kept wanting to say, 'get over it, love,' but something told me this probably wouldn't be constructive.

Where I was maybe having serious problems was in accepting that women had been behind the amazing technological advances I'd seen. Things like the Yin Qui and the Nyumbu trains, the incredible buildings and autonomous transport systems, were they built by women? I admit I kept thinking 'did a woman really design this?' and 'was this really built by a woman?' I was sceptical that they'd be able to do it and that thought alone made me stop and reconsider. Why did I think it unlikely that an African woman could have come up with the design and development of the Nyumbu train? It was one of the most incredible pieces of technology I'd experienced, right up there with the Gardenian pods and yes, according to everything I could understand it was conceived by an African woman who had been educated in an African university and who had never actually left the continent of her birth. I was baffled, humbled and it has to be said, challenged. In my experience blokes made things, blokes designed cars, buildings, trains and bridges. Women, in my experience just weren't interested; well, not many of them. I mean Beth could no more have designed the hydraulic pump system on a heavy earth mover than I could have taught history to a small group of over-privileged children in a private school in Oxfordshire. Could it really be that men had just lost interest in everything they used to be driven to do and had given up and did some gardening and cleaned the kitchen? It just didn't make sense.

I had time to ruminate on these problems because I was on-board a massive ship that was speeding across the tops of the rolling Atlantic waves on route for South America. I had learned from Nkoyo that we were headed for Rio De Janeiro which sounded very glamorous, the only down side was I was yet again going to appear before some vast, braying audience of women.

'It's not like the Mkutano Mahali,' said Nkoyo, 'this is a much smaller affair, only five or six thousand delegates and they are mostly scientists. You'll feel right at home I'm sure.'

'Five or six thousand! For goodness sake, that's huge. Do I have to talk to them?'

'No, you don't have to address an audience, just maybe answer some questions,' said Nkoyo.

'I really need help understanding what I'm supposed to be doing this for,' I said.

I was sitting in my bed pod talking to Nkoyo who was sitting in hers. It was night, I couldn't tell what the sea was like outside and there was certainly no movement in the ship to give any indication of what the weather was doing.

'I understand it must be hard for you. I would only ask for your patience as it will become clearer as the days pass. News of your arrival has spread right around the globe, you are effectively the most famous person on earth at the moment.'

'I really don't enjoy being famous,' I said.

'Don't worry about it, it will pass quickly, some other event will soon take over and you will be forgotten,' said Nkoyo. I knew she meant it kindly but that also felt a bit deflating. It was true I didn't really enjoy the attention but also I didn't particularly want to be forgotten.

'So, I'm just a blip in the news cycle?' I said.

Nkoyo smiled at me, something I always enjoyed experiencing. 'Yes, that is one way of looking at it,' she said, 'but as you can see from the effect you had at the Mkutano Mahali your presence is powerful. The way the world has developed over the last one hundred and fifty years or so has been very different from before as I'm sure you're becoming aware. Your arrival, indeed your body, is of intense scientific interest. If you are amenable, the Rio Institute which is really the centre of medical research in the world, would like to run some more elaborate tests on you than we can do in London.'

I sat in silence for a moment, was I amenable to being tested by a bunch of South American scientists? I wasn't sure.

'What kind of tests?'

'Well, as you will have gathered, due to lobbying prowess of the Weaver women we are having serious problems giving birth to male children.'

'The scary Professor at the Mkutano Mahali didn't look like she'd be that bothered.'

'Professor Heilman, yes, she is a leading voice in the Weavers, she is a very powerful and influential person, she will be in Rio too, in fact she is on-board.'

'What, on the Yin Qui?'

'Yes, she is speaking at the Assembleia Geral but you don't have to attend that, it's more of a political rally,' Nkoyo reassured me. 'You have been invited to help the Rio Institute and I want to say now there is absolutely no pressure for you to do so. You have to do it of your own free will or all the results will be legally invalid. They want to run physical and psychological tests on you to see if there has been any measurable change in the human male since your era. You are the perfect base measure as I may have explained previously.'

'Yes, you have explained, I know I'm just a brutish caveman, that's fine, I'm getting used to it.'

Nkoyo stood up, walked over to me and brushed her hand across my cheek very softly. 'You are neither primitive or brutish, Gavin, I think we both know that.'

She left the room with what I now completely understand to be an enigmatic smile. I remembered looking at the old Mona Lisa in the Louvre gallery when I went to Paris with Beth. I stood looking at that painting for hours trying to understand what all the fuss was about. I knew she had an enigmatic smile because I'd been told that, but when I stared at the picture I saw a painting of a woman, it did nothing to me. The look on Nkoyo's face as she walked out of our cabin left me in no doubt. That was an enigmatic smile. What it meant? I have absolutely no idea. She brushed my cheek, a very gentle and intimate gesture that, coupled with the smile, left me reeling. A smile that said at the same time, 'I want you' and 'I feel sorry for you'. Enchanting.

26

One Second Scan

STEPPING FROM THE COOL TRANQUILLITY OF the interior of the Yin Qui and directly into the hectic, dazzling and utterly overwhelming maelstrom of Rio de Janeiro in 2211 was nothing short of meltdown-inducing overload. It was bloody terrifying.

I would imagine for anyone arriving there for the first time it would be a bit of a shock, but the difference for me was they knew I was coming. When I say 'they' I mean all of them, like the entire population of this ridiculous mega city.

I accept that may not be technically true, but if the crowd outside the exit of the massive ship was anything to go by a sizeable chunk of the population came to see me. The Beatles landing in America was a small village fete in comparison to this. Even the huge crowd and the drummers waiting for me on the quayside in Lagos were pretty paltry compared to this bunch.

'Time to wave again,' said Nkoyo. I did as I was told and this time the cheer actually hurt my ears it was so raucous. It seemed like people were lined up in tiers, the quayside at Rio was right up against substantial mountains and the city appeared to be built into these vertiginous geographic structures. I looked up at dizzying buildings overlooking the sea, they were ridiculously high but they were also built on mountains that were themselves no slouches in the height department.

As far as I could see above me people were waving and cheering. It was hard to make out exactly what I was looking at, I assume a series of paths and steps leading up the mountains between the buildings. It was all on such an enormous scale it was hard to map it out in my mind. Out of this noisy and very colourful throng emerged a very old woman who walked up to me as we made our way towards the shade of a massive quay side structure. As she got closer I could see she was truly ancient-looking and very frail, she was guided by two younger women and a very young boy who held her hand. As she stood before me the huge crowd went much quieter and she started to speak.

'Bem-vindo ao Rio, o homem a partir da nuvem,' she said.

I then heard, 'Welcome to Rio, the man from the cloud.'

I thanked her and said it was a wonderful welcome, there was a small pause until she understood and she smiled a toothless smile. The little lad touched my hand.

'Acolher irmão,' he said. 'Welcome brother.' For some reason I found this very moving, the women on either side of the old lady looked moved too, they were smiling at me and one of them had a tear running down her cheek.

'Many people see you as a saviour,' said Nkoyo as we finally made it into the shade. 'You are very kind to tolerate such attention.'

'I don't know why they'd think that, I don't want them to think that and who was the old lady?'

'Her name is Maria Coradinho, she is the oldest woman in Rio. She is one hundred and forty-eight years old and had asked to be able to greet you.'

'A hundred and forty-eight, wow, that's even older than Olumide.'

'Yes, she is one of our oldest citizens. She has seen many changes in her long life. The young boy, Renaldo, is eight years old and her great, great grandson. He is the first male offspring in two generations so as you can imagine he is very precious.'

I shook my head in amazement as I tried to take all this in. As soon as we walked beneath the giant structure we were faced with a truly spectacular flight of stairs, it climbed up as far as I could see and people thronged up its course to dizzying heights.

'We have a bit of a climb ahead of us, are you feeling strong?'

'I guess so,' I said.

'If you like we can hire some PDPs, some potência da perna,' said Nkoyo who pointed to my left. There was a very smart looking emporium, smoked glass frontage with a very clear graphic image of what Nkoyo was talking about. A pair of legs powering up steps with some kind of leggings attached.

'Wow, how do they work?' I said.

'Try them,' came the response, and we entered the store through the crowd that was watching and calling my name.

Inside I paid a small amount, judging by the barely discernible stomach impact, for what looked to me like a pair of dancer's tights. As I pulled them on over my one piece I could sense there was more to them than was immediately apparent.

'They might take a little getting used to,' said Nkoyo who had stood to one side while I tried on the PDPs.

We left the shop and I was immediately greeted by a great throng of people all waving and smiling. I waved and smiled back and started to climb the steps alongside Nkoyo. Again there is no way I can adequately explain the sensation of having your legs assisted by these weird, semi-transparent leggings. It's not like a Royal Marine is moving your legs for you at yomp speed, or that someone is pushing you from behind with enormous force, but it also is like that. It's as if your legs have ten times the power that you would normally expect but they don't walk for you. It's more like a pedal-assist bike, if you don't pedal, you don't move, but if you do, you move faster than you could alone. However, after about fifty steps which once again were a little bigger than I was used to I was soaked in sweat. The heat in Rio was intense, maybe not quite as chokingly hot as Lagos but still, climbing up shaded steps that just seemed to go on for ever was utterly knackering. After about ten minutes a young woman standing on one of the many short landings handed me a stainless steel bottle, I drank it so fast I'm not sure what was in it, my body just seemed to absorb it like a sheet of blotting paper dropped in a puddle.

'Thank you,' I said, she smiled and touched my arm.

'You will get a lot of that,' said Nkoyo.

'I suppose it's better than if they were chucking rocks at me,' I joked.

'Why would they do that?' asked Nkoyo, she seemed genuinely confused.

'No, it was a joke, I was... never mind.'

The annoying thing about this endless ascent up the endless stairs is that Nkoyo had no such assistance in the leg department and she was also not out of breath. She didn't seem to be sweating and she took the enormous steps with her long legs as if she were walking along a level pavement.

After what seemed like hours but was probably twenty minutes, we emerged onto a very grand square surrounded by three enormous buildings. The square was teeming with people, once again just about every race on earth represented in one way or another and most of them staring at me. I smiled and waved, and they cheered and waved back. I cannot truly say I understood why at the time but I was getting used to my ridiculous celebrity status.

I followed Nkoyo into an impressive building directly in front of us, standing either side of the entrance were two clearly military women, they were holding long poles which they held erect as we entered the doors, they didn't look at me but they were some seriously big ladies. I mean muscular rather than obese, but they were also the fattest people I'd seen since landing in the square.

Inside we were greeted by a much smaller crowd, maybe fifty women clothed in white, head-to-toe white garments; some were body suit type things like I was wearing, some just floor length vaguely Arab-looking tunic things.

'Welcome to the Rio Institute of Advanced Medicine,' said a

woman whose name I instantly knew was Professor Gabriella Estevinho. I took to her at once for one simple reason, she was shorter than me. I'm shallow, so sue me, but after being the shortest person in any city I'd visited and shorter than anyone I'd met who was over about twelve, it was really pleasant to look down a bit to talk to someone.

'We are very excited meet you, Gavin Meckler, I am hoping Doctor Oshineye has explained what we wish to accomplish during your visit with us.'

'She has,' I said, 'but I'm not sure what it entails, I hope you'll understand that I am a little nervous of what may be in store.'

The charming Professor Estevinho led me further into the building, I glanced around to make sure Nkoyo was with us. Thankfully she was, deep in conversation with about half a dozen women who were following us.

'There is absolutely nothing to fear, I think you will find medicine has advanced considerably since the time you were born. However, you are a fascinating specimen for us, forgive me for describing you in such mechanical terms. Obviously you are a human being with a complex mind and a certain human dignity, and I want to assure you this is completely understood by everyone here, but you come from a time before many of the negative influences of our modern world had come into play. You know about the problems we have had with radiation sickness?'

'I saw some mention of it at the museum in London, the history museum,' I said feeling some alarm. 'However, I don't know what effect it may have had.'

'Well, it has had some effect, it is nothing to be concerned about, we have managed to understand the negative effects of radiation on the human body and know how to combat the possible deleterious effects, but the long-term impacts are still being researched. One of them is infertility in both men and women, but mainly, it has to be said, men. From what we understand of your knowledge of yourself, you are not infertile, is that correct Mister Meckler?'

'Yes, a few people have asked me that, I'm afraid I have no definitive proof but as far as I know it all works.' I smiled as I said this, Professor Estevinho smiled back but it wasn't a complicit smile, it was a smile of a very learned person being polite to an idiot.

The Professor opened a door for me, yes, a door, like a large piece of wood type material with hinges on one side that fitted into a similar sized opening. I liked it, it was so simple and easy to maintain although I think my admiration for this simple device confused my host.

The large room I was shown into contained nothing, it was white, bright and entirely empty. The Professor guided me to the centre and stepped away. I think I was expecting some kind of medical equipment to slide out of the walls and floor and a load of people in surgical gowns to enter through an as yet concealed entrance. However, nothing happened. After a moment the diminutive Professor stood beside me again and held my left hand with both of hers. 'Thank you,' she said. 'We have all we need.'

'I'm sorry?'

'Please don't be sorry.'

'No, but, I thought you were going to…'

The Professor gestured around the entirely empty room. 'This is our scanner de corpo, we have all the data we need now, would you like to eat?'

That was it, I had travelled across the Atlantic Ocean from Lagos to Rio De Jainero to undergo some medical tests and I'd already done it. The process took less than a second and it made no sense whatsoever.

'Forgive me, Professor, but if this—' I gestured around the white room, 'this system can scan my entire biological make-up in next to no time, why did I need to travel all this way. It seems you have very sophisticated communications equipment, surely you could have done this while I was in London?'

'Of course we could, we could have got the simple raw data from your body, but we also wanted to meet you in person, we can get so much more from being in the same physical space as you, and we also wanted you to see what we would do with the data, we wanted to be sure you truly understood what was going on, what we intend to do with the material we have gleaned from your body.'

I followed the Professor out of the room where we rejoined Nkoyo and the small group of what I took to be doctors.

'Everything okay?' she asked.

'I think you're asking the wrong person,' I replied, 'I've got no idea what's going on.'

We all entered a room with what can only be described as a breathtaking view over the mountainous city. At a glance I assumed that due to the substantial rise in sea levels much of Rio had been rebuilt on and into the mountains that had at one time been the city's backdrop. I'd never visited back in 2011 so I was going on holiday programmes and tourist videos I'd seen, but the sea fringed the foot of the mountain the building I was in was built on.

The women in white started bringing in food and we all sat down and ate, once again fresh printed beef steaks seemed to be very popular, I chomped my way through a couple.

'Can you tell us,' said a woman sitting opposite me, 'if fresh print beef is comparable with beef from a dead cow?'

I chewed for a bit and swallowed because I didn't want to spray half chewed food across the table, something I had been known to do.

'I'd say it is very comparable, if anything it's better,' I said finally. I then studied the as yet untouched steak on the plate before me. I looked at the others piled up on the serving dish in the centre of the table. I noticed they were all identical, a kind of perfect steak, same size, same weight, same texture.

'They are a bit uniform I suppose, that would be the only possible criticism, in the past no two beef steaks would be identical but that aside, this is pretty amazing stuff.'

This compliment seemed to go down well, everyone looked happy. I was simply waiting to hear what the results of my so-called medical examination would be. The women were all busy talking to each other, passing food and generally having a rather good time.

'I think Gavin is anxious to hear the results of the medical investigation,' said Nkoyo out of the blue. It wasn't as *if* she could read my mind, she was quite simply reading my mind.

'Of course,' said Professor Estevinho, 'we are very pleased with the results, Gavin. Your gonads are in fine condition and you have a very well-balanced sperm count.'

I think my face may have flinched when she said the word 'gonads'. There was something about that word which always sounded like a painful kick in the balls. Testicles is okay, but it's bit of a silly word. Gonads is just an unpleasant word. Even if it was the common term for a flower or tree, the gonad tree, you wouldn't want to sit under it on a hot day.

'That means you have the ability to father male children,' said Nkoyo helpfully.

'Okay, I may be a nerdy engineer from 2011 but I know what she was saying, but what interests me is how this crisis came to be and what on earth my role is in rectifying it.'

Professor Estevinho took a deep breath, her face was delightful, smooth and calm. She smiled a very gracious smile in my direction. 'Gavin,' she said, 'do not be concerned, we are not going to expect you to mate with thousands of women, we are not going to milk you of sperm in some inhuman, mechanical way.'

Again I feared my face may have given me away, I admit there was a background fear that I would be used in some sort of agricultural-style breeding program and, I will further admit, that the prospect of such a weird notion wasn't entirely disagreeable; however, I was also genuinely relieved.

'We have scanned your biological system in minute detail and have your entire genome stored in our system. As you may know we have genomes data stored from your era but the sophistication of the technology used at the time was not adequate for the work we do. I have no wish to be rude about your achievements back then, but it was rather crude.'

'I'm sure you're right,' I said. 'It was all still fairly experimental from what I knew of it, which wasn't much.' I glanced at Nkoyo who was staring at me intently. 'I was an engineer, working on heavy machinery, not a biologist.'

'We know that, Gavin, we understand,' said the Professor kindly. 'So, what I am explaining is that we can use the information we have gleaned today to create a new seed bank if you like, we can create a fresh selection of viable spermatozoa with the required chromosome make-up which will allow us to successfully fertilise women who wish to bear male offspring. Up to now we have only had such information from our current stock of males and due to many genetic factors I don't want to bore you with, we have been dealing with a serious problem.'

I glanced at Nkoyo again to try and ascertain how delicate the discussion should be, I had no idea of the ramifications of my questions, of who these women were and what their opinions of men were like. They could all have been Weaver women who had simply used their medical technology to extinguish any chance I had of procreating, for all I knew I was about to become a eunuch.

27

Rest Before the Storm

I WALKED WITH NKOYO FROM THE MEDICAL centre and down a series of winding, shady streets and long flights of steps.

I was deep in thought, this place really made me think about things I'd truly never considered for a second in my previous life.

Some people were still able to create male babies like the young lad I'd met on the steps when I arrived in Rio. They were able to procreate naturally and have sons, but not that many. I was starting to understand the problem, if women could tell which particular man was most likely to create female children and generation after generation had chosen those men to breed with, you would rapidly end up with an imbalance. I recalled that at about the time I left Kingham in 2011, the number of women graduating from college had overtaken the number of men. I didn't know much about it back then, I couldn't sense the beginning of such a massive cultural shift but it was apparently taking place. I had landed in this world at a time where this imbalance had reached a crisis point and everyone was not surprisingly getting a bit het up about it. I remembered a family that lived near us when I was a kid, they had four daughters. Of course, back then it was the mum who wanted a son. I can't remember hearing about what the dad wanted, but my mum used to feel sorry for her. My mum had two sons and even though we tore the house up fairly effectively, Giles by running into things and breaking them and me by taking stuff to bits and leaving it lying around, she was obviously very proud of us.

I can remember as an adolescent looking at the dad with the

four daughters, I think he was called Peter, and I distinctly remember thinking he was a bit weird. This was because I'd done enough biology at school by then to harbour the suspicion that his sperm only carried the X chromosomes, and not the really butch Y ones like my dad. The other thing I remembered about those four girls is they were really weird, all of them horribly academic and introverted. They would physically flinch when I walked near them as if they were terrified I might attack. That reaction would be understandable if my brother Giles ran past them, as he was very likely to barge into them in true rugger-bugger style and claim it was 'just for a laugh'. But I was far more timid and quite evidently constituted no danger.

That memory resonated with me. There was something familiar going on. I was starting to make connections that led to a greater understanding not only of myself but the way others perceived me. It was something along the lines of being seen as a potentially violent man, being grouped together with 'all men' when my own personal history was one of utter non-violence. I'm talking physical violence, I've never hit anyone, man or woman, never been in a fight, never experienced violence on a physical level. I can understand that some people – okay, Beth – might accuse me of a sort of emotional violence in that I wouldn't engage and wouldn't respond when she got shouty. I can see how that kind of passivity can be very annoying and damaging, but I certainly never got shouty back or in the least bit violent.

We passed many people on the steps as we made our way down the side of the mountainous city, most of them greeted us and shouted my name, well, my public name, 'man from the cloud'.

Having these distractions while I was also trying to take in the incredible architecture in Rio was a recipe for a memorable and intense journey. My vague impression of this city from back in 2011 was that it was divided into a small enclave for the ultra rich along the beach, surrounded by millions of ultra poor up on the steep mountains. If that was the case back then, it was a very different city I was walking through that evening.

We eventually turned off what seemed like an endless flight of steps down the side of the mountain and into a delightful little courtyard surrounded by a series of low buildings.

'This is a Senate guest house,' said Nkoyo as we arrived in front of a rather old-looking building, it was bathed in the soft sun of late in the evening. 'We have been given two rooms here for the duration.'

'That's very nice of them,' I said as we entered the refreshingly cool interior, although it was late in the day the temperature outside was still stiflingly hot.

Nkoyo seemed to know her way around the little house so I just followed her down a dimly lit corridor and into a very charming sitting room with a view onto a small garden.

'Wow, this is a beautiful place,' I said. I flopped down on a low chair overlooking the garden and let my head rest back. I knew at once that the house had been built in 2083 as part of the original Senate construction. It was designed by an architect called Martha Rodriguez who had studied in London and was very determined to introduce zero energy homes into Rio. The house I was in was part of a complex which used many breakthrough technologies as they were seen at the time, graphene solar absorbing paint, geothermal heating and cooling and inbuilt water capture and storage. It all sounded very clever to me.

The resulting building was very much on a human scale, not some massive, overpowering edifice but a gentle, softly shaped and homely residence. The furnishings were comfortable and gentle on the eye, the whole place had a restful quality to it.

Although the cities I'd seen up to that point, London and Lagos, were both built on grids around large squares, Rio was very different. I suppose due to the mountains it was built on, it had a far more dramatic aspect; huge towers on top of huge mountains, terraced banks of buildings on either side of the mountain range and many long shady streets joining them together. It was a very exciting place to be, there seemed to be music everywhere, something that I hadn't really considered when I was in London; music and very, very bright colours. It made London look a bit dowdy and dull. Rio was spectacular in every sense. Therefore the arrival in the Senate guest house came as something of a relief, it was quiet, dark and very peaceful. I took a deep breath and relaxed. I may even have nodded off for a while, I'm not sure, but when I came around I looked over to Nkoyo who was standing by the door to the garden.

'So, the Senate? What's that?' I asked.

'The Senate,' said Nkoyo, she turned and looked at me. 'We're in Rio.'

'I know we're in Rio, it's pretty obvious even to a cave man from the dark times but that doesn't explain much.'

Nkoyo's normally perfect brow furrowed. 'I'm sorry, I assumed you would have accessed the information when we were on-board the Yin Qui.'

'What information?' I asked pleading like a teenager confronted with a huge pile of homework. 'What have I got to access now?'

'The political structure and institutions of the world, small topic,' said Nkoyo with a refreshing attempt at humour.

'Oh right, but I thought the place where I got questioned in Lagos was the parliament type of thing.'

'That is the Congress.'

'The one that moves about?'

'Correct,' said Nkoyo as she passed me a metal water container. I took a few gulps.

'So the Senate is in Rio,' I said. Nkoyo nodded. 'And does that move about too?'

'No, this is, effectively the seat of government.'

'For the whole world?'

'Well,' she hesitated for a moment. 'Everywhere except Pyongyang, what you would have known as North Korea.'

'What! North Korea is still a pariah state?'

'Well, they have nothing to do with the rest of the world, no. The ruler of Pyongyang is still a man, it's the only place in the world where that is the case.'

I couldn't help laughing when she told me that.

'That is amazing. I mean you have to take your hat off to them. They were bang out of order two hundred years ago, how on earth have they managed to stay the same? Impressive.'

'It's a great tragedy for the people there. We have to deal with refugees from Pyongyang all the time, all women. From what we can tell the population there is about eighty per cent male, quite the opposite to the rest of the world.'

'It's all so difficult to take in,' I said. 'When I was in Gardenia, the other world that does or does not exist, I went to New York and learned there was a wall around an area they called "Midwest" and no one seemed to know what went on inside, they didn't want to know and it all sounded rather unpleasant.'

This time, Nkoyo looked intrigued. 'That is fascinating,' she said eventually. 'Thankfully that's not the case here, the area you would have known as North America is now a very important part of the global organisation of City States.'

'And all run by women?'

'Yes,' said Nkoyo, she sat opposite me. 'Tomorrow you will see the Senate in action and don't worry.' She held her hand up to emphasise your point. 'You won't be asked to speak.'

'So what's going on tomorrow?'

'There is a very important bill up for a vote. It's essentially a bill supported by an affiliation of radical groups, the most prominent being the Weavers.'

'This is a bill to let them kill all the men, I take it.'

'No, it's not quite like that,' said Nkoyo calmly. 'It's designed to allow the male half of the species to die out naturally.

We don't kill people any more, that's what used to happen.'

'You mean that's what used to happen when men were the dominant rulers in the world?'

Nkoyo just smiled. 'Nothing is ever quite that simple.'

'Okay so you don't kill people, you just don't let them be born if they might have a willy.'

'A willy?'

'A penis,' I said.

'Ahh, I'm not familiar with that term,' she said with a gentle smile. 'It makes it sound very harmless.'

I drank some more water while staring at Nkoyo and wondering if there was subtext to what she was saying. If the word 'willy' made the penis sound harmless, did she really mean that it was in reality harmful, like a gun, in the sense that if you call a gun a peacekeeper that makes it sound more reasonable? I don't know, I couldn't tell, I wasn't proficient enough with my kidonge to be able to read her thoughts. I know I wanted to continue that conversation, I wanted to understand the difference between the Weaver women and, well, the rest of the world. I couldn't judge the difference, it really did seem like all the women of the world were very happy with the status quo that existed. I hadn't met any men who seemed to violently disagree with it, although there had been a hint of disquiet from Judd, the Tudor costume-loving student I met in the Museum of Human History. However, I didn't get the chance to find out anything as that's when the guards came in.

They didn't smash the doors down and fire a tear gas grenade into the room, they weren't covered in protective suits with masks on, but they did look a little threatening.

I didn't understand what was being said, it was all very sudden and I couldn't relax enough to allow me to access the Portuguese to English translation system. Nkoyo had no trouble speaking Portuguese but she didn't look happy. She turned to me in alarm.

'Is this true?'

'Is what true?' I asked, now completely baffled. One of the guards stood behind me and put a powerful hand on my shoulder.

'The recording of what you said to Anne Hempstead?'

'A recording? What recording?'

28

The Recording

'I CAME HERE FROM 2011, I PLANNED IT, TIME travel is possible. I'm a man, I believe in patriarchy, it's my right to rape women, I want to crush women back to the dark times, I want to be the dominant master race, I think women are second class citizens who should live their lives barefoot and pregnant at the kitchen sink.'

There was no question, it was me saying it. It was my voice and it was incredibly clear, not like a hissing cassette tape or a compressed MP3, it sounded like I was in the room saying these dreadful things to myself.

'It's been changed!' I pleaded. It was glaringly obvious to me, not quite so obvious to Officer Velasquez who was looking at me across the big table.

The big table was in a huge room in a vast building. I'm not sure exactly where the building was as we left the peaceful confines of the Senate guest house and used another subterranean transport system, not cars or buses, this was more like a train.

We travelled, I assume, from one part of the city to another although it only took about three minutes.

Nkoyo travelled with us but I was clearly in the control of a handful of very muscular women, the leader of whom I knew to be Officer Velasquez. Martha Velasquez was thirty-seven but looked to be about eighteen, startlingly beautiful and on the surface at least, fairly friendly.

Once we arrived at our destination, I emerged into a large underground area where I saw many more women dressed in a similar way to the guards I was being escorted by.

I didn't have much time, or indeed desire, to study the intricacies of the transportation system I'd just used, it was very long, dark grey and went very fast along some kind of imperceptibly smooth surface inside some kind of smooth bore tunnel.

We ascended in a room-sized lift with seats around the edge, it was almost full of women and I felt increasingly out of place. That many women all together in a confined space was nothing other than properly spooky, I realised that I'd never actually thought what a world exclusively inhabited by women would be like until that moment. I'll say now without hesitation, it didn't strike me as a good idea.

I was escorted into the big room and one of the guard type women gestured toward me and indicated a seat at the table. I sat down and Nkoyo stood by one wall with a couple of the guards, she looked properly worried.

That was when Officer Velasquez played the recording, well, she didn't press a button or anything, she sat down next to me, said something in Portuguese and the recording played instantly.

It was chilling to the extent that it felt like a death sentence. It was chilling in the fact that I could hear it so clearly and there was no doubt it was my voice. It didn't sound edited, it sounded like me saying it, there weren't any barely audible clicks and pops or words that didn't quite finish correctly. The human ear is very tuned to the human voice, little adjustments to a recording like that jump out. We're so used to hearing natural speech that we can pick up on slight discrepancies. There were no discrepancies, slight or otherwise.

'So you claim you did not say this,' said Officer Velasquez in English after the third time of playing the recording. Listening to myself saying such outrageous and offensive things in a room full of some of the toughest, hard-assed women I've ever seen did not make for comfortable listening.

I stared at Officer Velasquez as the recording played for the third time. She had her eyes shut as she listened, I couldn't read a reaction on her perfect face. When the recording stopped playing she opened her eyes and looked at me, her stare was so intense I felt a shock go through me. She was nothing other than magazine model stunning. Dark hair swept back and tied neatly in a bun, long neck, unbelievable lips and incredible dark eyes. It wasn't like being questioned by some overweight, out of condition, chain-smoking cop with thinning hair, Officer Velasquez's outrageous, un-enhanced beauty made living through this whole experience much harder for me.

'I do claim that,' I said as calmly as I could. 'If I remember correctly this was part of a conversation I had with a woman called—'

'—Anne Hempstead,' interrupted Nkoyo. 'A Weaver worder.'

Officer Velasquez nodded her understanding without glancing at Nkoyo saying. 'And where did this conversation take place?'

'In a library, at a place in London called the Erotic Museum.'

Even as I was describing the venue my heart began to sink. The Erotic Museum sounded so seedy, like I'd gone there out of some uncontrollable kinky need.

'The Erotic Museum,' repeated Officer Velasquez. The way she said it made it sound incredibly appealing rather than seedy, I could have listened to her saying 'Erotic Museum' all day, it was her soft S, it was the way she said erotic, it sounded like 'errodhick' and the way her lips moved as she spoke. I was finding it very difficult to concentrate.

'Yes, she called me in the car, you know, the phone thing in the car,' I glanced up at Nkoyo who gave me a barely perceptible nod. 'It was just after I'd spoken to Nkoyo about my plane, and suddenly I got a call from this woman Anne Hempstead, I'd never met her, I didn't know who she was but I was, well, she told me to meet her at the Erotic Museum so I did.'

I realised as I was saying this that I got the call from this vile woman when I was in a particularly bad mood, when I'd just discovered my plane was hanging up in the damn Museum of Human History. Something told me not to divulge too much, not to explain I was really angry as that might lead them to think I had a reason to say such vile things. I glanced back to Nkoyo who still looked very anxious, I shrugged, I didn't know how else to react.

Officer Velasquez removed a small sheet of material from her belt pocket and put it on the table. She moved her hands over the surface of the sheet as soon as it had settled and studied the complex graphics that I couldn't quite make out as they were upside down to me.

'Was this on the fourth of last month?'

I tried to work it out. My grasp of time since I'd landed in London was more than a little hazy. 'I would think so,' I said.

Nkoyo moved in toward the table. 'Yes, the day he's referring to was the fourth,' she confirmed.

'So tell me what happened, Mister Meckler. You went to the Erotic Museum, you met this woman Anne Hempstead, then what?'

'She led me upstairs, I mean I followed her up a few flights of stairs, she wasn't forcing me or dragging me, I don't mean that. I also want to point out that I didn't follow her because, well, because I found her attractive in any way. She had a very odd manner and I didn't find her in the least attractive. Not that I'm saying this has any bearing on the matter.'

I could hear myself babbling on. I knew it was because I was nervous, they would be more than capable of seeing that but they might misinterpret why I was nervous. I took a deep breath.

'Anyway, I followed her up the stairs and into what I assumed was a library. She then asked me to sit down and pretend to read a book in case anyone came in, she also said she was using a blocker, a small black case,' I gestured the size with my hands. 'I don't know if that was what it really was, I don't know what a blocker might be, it may have been a voice recorder.'

Officer Velasquez pushed the sheet across the table toward Nkoyo.

'Break in the timeline at fifteen twenty-five on the fourth. She was using a blocker.'

I was looking at Officer Velasquez's mouth all the time she was speaking, I'd never seen a mouth like it. There was something about this woman that was utterly captivating, I closed my eyes tightly and rubbed my face.

'Are you okay Mister Meckler?' she asked.

'I'm fine, just utterly confused about this, why would she go to all this trouble?'

'That is what we intend to find out,' said Officer Velasquez. 'In the meantime, would you like to explain to me what you were saying, would you like to explain what you think you did say at this time. I am assuming you accept that this recording is your own voice?'

'Yes, it's my voice.'

'So you must have said something a little similar to this?'

'Yes, well, no. I mean I said exactly the opposite. She started accusing me of being a rapist and a man from the dark times sent here to reinstate patriarchy or something, I didn't even understand half of what she was on about. She's a very angry person, she was quite aggressive. I was trying to point out that men from my time, most men from my time were not like that, I said I'm not a rapist, I don't think women are second class citizens, I don't think all the things the recording sounds like I do think.'

The room went quiet, it was clear the women didn't quite know what to do. Nkoyo stood at the other side of the table, both her hands to her face. She looked as if she was thinking a lot of thoughts. There was no chance of me being able to listen, guess or even entertain the notion of understanding what she might be thinking. I was so tense there was no way I could access any kind of information. It would have been useful if I could, I would like to have known about the people in the room with me, what their position was, if they were police or some kind of security force, if they had the death penalty for being a sexist idiot in Rio, any tiny bit of information about my position would have been useful. I could sense nothing.

'It is important we protect you at the present time,' said Officer Velasquez. Again, those lips, I barely heard what she said. 'This recording is in the public domain. Already many millions of people will have heard it. There is even greater interest in you now, Mister Meckler.' She stopped and smiled the most enchanting smile, this observation has to be balanced with what she actually said. 'Not all of this interest has your good health as a primary objective.'

I nodded my vague understanding. Officer Velasquez stood up and clapped her hands together. 'So, we will protect you here until we can find out exactly what it going on.'

She then turned to Nkoyo and spoke in Portuguese.

One of the very impressively large guards motioned for me to stand. Not once had I been touched or manhandled in any way. All instructions were communicated to me by gesture alone.

'They have arranged to talk to Anne Hempstead,' said Nkoyo as I started to leave. 'She's staying at the Weaver building here in Rio.'

I was shown into a perfectly pleasant room with a large window looking out over the city, the billions of lights spreading out in a square pattern as far as I could see. I was very high up. I'd had no idea where I was until that point. The guard left the room and a very substantial door closed behind her. Clearly, I wasn't going anywhere for a while.

29

Inappropriate Image

WHEN I WOKE UP THE FOLLOWING DAY, I initially had no idea where I was or more importantly, why I was where I was. I stared around at the strange room I found myself in. It wasn't that big but it wasn't like a prison cell as it had a window and plenty of furnishings. It was more like a mid-range hotel room, although there were plenty of clues I wasn't in some obscure hotel outside Derby in 2011. It was the structure of the walls that gave a clue. They weren't constructed out of flat sheet material by blokes wearing tool belts. There were no corners, no edges to the walls, floor or ceiling. Like most of the buildings I'd been in around the world in 2211 they looked like they'd been moulded out of one piece of material although I had no clear idea how. I pondered on the possible construction methods, a habit I'd been criticised for in the past by Beth. The room's shape did seem somehow familiar, maybe something I'd seen in Beijing in the other 2211 I'd visited.

Something was going beep beside me, I rolled over and looked, it sounded like it was coming from a small grey square thing resting on the shelf beside the bed. I sat up and it beeped again so I picked it up. It was completely blank, a flat, blank grey square thing going beep. No markings, no buttons, no wires, nothing.

'Gavin, you're awake.'

It was Nkoyo's voice, I momentarily looked around the room to see where she was. I was alone, I glanced back down at the square grey thing in my hand.

'What, sorry?' I mumbled.

'Turn it over,' she said. Again there was a beat as I had no idea what she was talking about, I finally twigged and turned the square blank thing over and there was Nkoyo's face, crystal clear and looking magnificent as usual. She had her eyes tightly shut.

'Oh blimey, I had it upside down,' I said with a chuckle.

'Thank you, now I've seen your penis,' she said flatly. 'Have you turned it over?'

'What! Yes, oh my God!'

She opened her eyes and looked at me.

'It is fitted with what you would know as a camera,' she said. I glanced down, I was naked and I immediately realised what I'd done. The flat grey thing was a kind of phone and I had the camera pointing at my nethers, I pulled a bit of bedcover over myself quickly.

'Sorry, sorry.'

'It's fine, don't worry. I'm just glad Officer Velasquez wasn't with me when I called you, things are bad enough already.'

'Oh, right, I see. Except I don't see,' I said. 'I have no idea what's happening. What on earth is going on?' The previous day's events were flooding back to me in a nauseating wave of horror.

'You certainly know how to make an impact, Gavin. This makes crashing your drone into a children's play area in London look like a non-story. It seems everyone is talking about the secret patriarchy reinstatement agent-provocateur from the future.'

'What. People think I've come from the future!'

'It seems so, yes, the recording we heard yesterday, well, everyone on earth seems to have heard it now, everyone is talking about it. Of course today is the day the Senate are going to vote on the Weaver proposal so it's obviously double newsworthy.'

I scratched my head for a while as I started to take in what was going on. I'd been used as a pawn in some weird political struggle I didn't fully understand.

'So people are believing that dreadful woman? She spins some cock and bull story to me about being a journalist, a worder or what ever, recorded me saying I wasn't a rapist, edited the recording and released it the day before the Senate vote in the hope of steering events and ensuring the end of the male half of the species?'

There was a short pause before Nkoyo replied. 'That would seem to be the case, although the reference to cocks and balls seems a bit unnecessary.'

'No, cock as in cockerel!' I protested. 'A cockerel, a boy hen and bull, bull, as in male cow, as in a bull with horns. Blimey, it's just an old saying meaning utter nonsense or lies or elaborate fabrications. Cock and bull, a cock and bull story is nothing to do with human genitalia. You lot are obsessed for goodness sake!'

I realised I was shouting, which with the technology I was using probably wasn't necessary but it seemed everything I'd said was being deliberately misinterpreted. I glanced back at the screen and saw Nkoyo laughing.

'What's so funny? I'm up shit creek, no one is going to believe me, every woman on earth is going to hear that recording and think I'm scum.'

'You have a funny face when you get angry, it makes me laugh.'

I shook my head in disbelief. 'Well I'm happy for you.'

'Listen, this will pass. It seems the Senate security people, that's who turned up at the house last night, it seems they are pretty certain it's a doctored recording.'

'They are?'

'Well, they're sceptical, they were recording your voice patterns when you were being questioned last night, there are certain subtle anomalies in the Hempstead recording which they are investigating. They are currently talking to Anne Hempstead and a large group of Weaver women who are all, as you would no doubt expect, full of righteous indignation.'

'Of course they are. Fuck they're a nasty bunch of…' I

 checked myself. I was going to say something sexist like cows or bitches or worse. I swallowed, 'I don't like them, is that okay to say that?'

'Perfectly understandable.'

'But she's not going to admit she fiddled around with the recording is she?'

'Doubtful.'

'So how hard is that to do now? I know it would have been very possible in my era, I would have been able to download software that could edit a sound file.'

'It is very easy to do now,' said Nkoyo. 'It is also very easy to make it impossible to tell if it has been doctored in any way. What would really help is if you could remember what you actually said.'

I rubbed my face with my free hand. 'Blimey, can you remember word for word what you said three months ago?'

'Yes.'

Her answer was so flat, just a simple statement of fact.

'How?'

'It's easy, unless someone has used a blocker.'

'So that's what she really had. It blocks the signal from your kidonge?

'Yes, this is essentially the hole in their plan. Officer Velasquez has checked Hempstead's timeline too. She clearly has some very sophisticated technology at her disposal as at first glance there is no break in her timeline.'

'What?'

'No, her timeline indicates she was at the same location at the same time as you, but there appears to be no break in her timeline.'

'What? Sorry, you've totally lost me.'

'She made a tiny mistake, Gavin, that's what it means. I've been in touch with London and they have checked their system, they are fairly certain there's been some tampering. It's a very complex and secure system, only someone with very high-level access could even attempt such a thing and there are so many safeguards and back-up systems it is effectively impossible to totally change your history. It's caused quite a stir in London.'

'So you're saying there's someone in a high-ranking position in London who has helped the horrible Hempstead woman?'

'It's beginning to look that way, there are not many illegal devices like the blocker in circulation, the device you describe sounds like something that is banned throughout the world, they have been for years. The only reason anyone would want one is to do something underhand. I've never seen one but we can tell from your timeline that something happened at the time you were in the Erotic Museum.'

I didn't like the way Nkoyo said 'Erotic Museum', there was a scolding wife type of tone inherent in her delivery. A downtrodden wife who's had to put up with her husband's shenanigans for years and doesn't like directly referring to the offending article.

'Explain the timeline thing to me,' I said, deciding to try and change the subject. 'I couldn't make out what you were looking at yesterday, it was all upside down.'

'Security services like Senate Security or the Mayor's security detail in London have unlimited access to anyone's time line. It's essentially a recording of everywhere an individual has been, what they said, who they connected with, everything.'

'You are kidding,' I said, my mouth hanging open.

'I'm not sure what your reaction is meant to imply, it sounds like you are questioning the veracity of my previous statement. If so, then I want to assure you I am explaining exactly what happens.'

'But, but . . .' I was rendered temporarily speechless by the true horror of what she'd just told me. It was appalling. This supposedly benign, gentle, war free, technologically sustainable world I was living in was an Orwellian nightmare of intimate surveillance.

'That's so far beyond an invasion or privacy, that's a pogrom of individual freedom. It's a total nightmare.'

'That was the original idea, yes.'

'So that's okay? Do you really think that's okay? I mean, even this conversation we're having now, someone could listen to it?'

'Yes, of course, anyone who knows you or has repeated contact with you has access to it. Everyone does, everyone, everywhere all the time.'

Again the flat response like it should have been obvious.

'But isn't that a bit, I don't know, doesn't that mean that you have to watch what you say all the time?'

'No.'

'Well, it makes me nervous,' I said. 'I don't want people hearing everything I say.'

'Why not?'

'Well, it might be private. I don't mind you hearing me if I'm talking to you. I know you, you understand the context in which I'm saying things, but as I've just experienced in a very horrible way if something you've said is taken out of context, adapted, changed, twisted, then for fuck's sake, everything turns into a nightmare!'

Again Nkoyo was silent for a moment, I was wondering if there was some kind of delay on the line, she looked like she was thinking.

'I think your current situation is an anomaly. The fact that we can't go back and listen to exactly what you've said has caused the problems we're having now.'

'Listen, I don't know much about information technology but we learned many years ago that however super secure and egalitarian any complex system is there's always a way to mess it up. There's always a workaround and the Hempstead woman found one. She messed the system up, which means the system is flawed.'

'Indeed,' said Nkoyo, calm as ever. 'It certainly raises some very difficult questions. The systems we use are so embedded it would be next to impossible to remove them. This is why I was very anxious when I first heard what it sounded like you said.'

She paused for a moment. 'If what you are telling me is true, if indeed you never said those dreadful things, then the Weavers have taken an enormous risk in fabricating this. If the truth comes out, if the recording is proven to be fake then in effect that is the end of the Weavers influence and no doubt the end of the movement itself.'

We sat in silence for a moment, the flat grey thing was resting on my lap which I eventually realised was probably giving Nkoyo a view up my nose. I held it up in front of me.

'I can't believe this is happening,' I said eventually. 'There's plenty of things I've seen since I arrived that I don't understand, but this whole lack of privacy thing? Jesus wept, what is supposed to be a ubiquitous and totally secure system is in fact riddled with security holes which means people can destroy each other's lives on a whim.'

'That's why this is far more serious than the things you are supposed to have said. At present I think you should consider yourself lucky, Gavin,' said Nkoyo with a serious look on her face. 'Your isolation is probably the best thing at the moment. We've never had to deal with this kind of situation before. Indeed, as you say, it does throw the whole system into a new dimension. There are already reports that the Mayor of London has been detained for questioning, the Senate house is a seething mass of people, everyone is very anxious. I have a hell of a day ahead of me and all you have to do is stay there and keep quiet.'

'I don't even know where I am!' I whined.

'It's not important, you are in a very secure location, I know where you are, that's all that matters. I won't leave you there, don't worry. I will talk to you later on today after the vote. Wish me luck.'

That was it. The incredibly high definition image of Nkoyo's face disappeared and was replaced with the most nondescript flat grey surface. I dropped the phone thing on the bed and crawled under the covers.

30

Officer Velasquez

THE VIEW OUT OF MY WINDOW WAS BREATH-taking. I was perched high above the city of Rio de Janeiro with a view to the West. I'm assuming this was the case because of the shadows; the sun was rising from behind me. I don't know how far I could see, maybe fifty or sixty kilometres and there was no sign of the edge of the city. Unlike London, although it was built around large squares stretching to the horizon, they had also built this city on rolling hills. The centre of the squares looked like jungle, thick green vegetation abounded. I recalled looking out of the window the night before and seeing lights stretching off into the distance, in the morning the view looked different, I felt I could see much further.

About an hour after I spoke with Nkoyo, the door opened. Even to me, the door looked a little archaic, a door with hinges just seemed a little dated. The person who opened the door filled me with equal measures of delight and dread.

'Good morning, Mister Meckler,' said Officer Velasquez. 'I hope that you slept okay.'

'I slept a bit,' I said. 'I've been very worried though.'

'You should have come and seen me,' she said. 'My office is just down the hall.'

'But I thought I was . . . '

'You thought what?' her stare was absurdly captivating.

'Well, I thought I was a prisoner, I thought I was locked in.'

She smiled at me which just made things worse. 'That is very charming,' she said. 'I have read history, we don't do that any more,' she gestured to the door. 'See, no locks.'

I felt like such a fool. She was right, there was a simple sprung ball catch on the door, the sort of thing you'd get on a kitchen cupboard. I could have left at any time. I hadn't even tried to open the door.

'You are free to move around as much as you want. The reason you are here is for your own protection, not from murder or physical harm as may have been the case in the dark times, it is more that you are protected from the rather heated attention you may receive on this day.'

'I'm sorry, there are many things I don't understand, the fact that I'm not a prisoner is just one of them.'

'Have you had some breakfast?'

'Nothing, I've just had a drink of water.'

Officer Velasquez looked genuinely surprised and concerned. 'That is terrible, you poor man, come with me and we will get you something to eat.'

Thankfully by the time Velasquez had arrived I'd already donned my one piece so I was respectable, I followed her out of the room and into a huge area I had no memory of.

'Wow, did we come through here last night?' I asked as I scanned the vast hall we'd entered.

'No, we moved you last night, your room is like a pod that can slide about on the outside of the building. We're twenty floors higher up here.'

That explained why I was confused by the view from my window, it was a different view. 'Wow, I didn't feel the room move,' I said.

'It moves very slowly,' she explained as she gestured toward a table set up in the middle of a hall, 'Here, have some coffee and chipå. I will cut you some fruit.'

She extracted a rather savage looking knife from her belt and picked up a papaya. 'You like?'

'Yes,' I nodded nervously and poured some coffee from a very recognisable coffee pot. The coffee was stunning, the papaya was delicious, the chipå, a kind of cake with some kind of cheese in the middle, well, I'll stick with describing the fruit. Officer Velasquez seemed to delight in cutting fruit for me, she did it with expert hands and great skill, and guess what, I was transfixed.

We weren't alone in this large room, there were many women standing around talking, some it would appear were talking to each other in the classic old style of communication; i.e. they stood close to each other face to face and did talking. Most were alone and also talking although not to any obvious device, they were seated around large tables covered in piles of lightweight material, that's the best description I can give. I think these were communication or information devices of some sort but how they operated or what their purpose was I cannot verify.

'It is all very interesting is it not,' said Officer Velasquez as she sat opposite me on a small table. 'We are very busy at the moment keeping order in the squares around the Senate building. It is a very busy day for us as you can see.'

Velasquez rolled out a sheet of material on the table between us and an incredibly detailed picture emerged, a view of a truly massive crowd outside an even more massive building. The view was, I assume, from somewhere above the square holding the huge crowd of people.

'You are in this building here,' said Velasquez pointing to a building to the left of what I assumed was the main Senate building. 'So you can see, wandering outside could be, how should I say, very exciting.'

'I'd rather not find out,' I said. 'I assume all these people believe I said those dreadful things.'

'Many of them, yes,' she said without emotion. 'We thought we may have found what we need to prove what your claim is correct. The heat sensors in the Library at the Erotic Museum.'

'The heat sensors?'

'Yes, all buildings constructed in the last one hundred years

are intelligent. I think that is how you would describe them.
They are aware of the presence of a human body inside the building and they react accordingly, with temperature and lighting. In order to do that they sense the heat your body gives off, your heat signature.'

'Okay, I can understand that, the theory anyway,' I said.

'Well, the building keeps a record of this data, it stores all data no matter what it is. This isn't for us, I mean humans. It's the way the system works, it learns and adapts to new situations. No one is interested in it normally, but as we know, these events are not normal.'

'Right, so this heat data, what does it say?'

Officer Velasquez smiled. 'It doesn't say anything, the buildings aren't magic, they don't talk to us like in a fairy tale.'

'Yeah, okay, I get that,' I said, feeling for the first time, mildly tetchy at Officer Velasquez.

'One of my officers managed to construct a recording from the sensors. They operate with a different protocol to general communication and data systems so it appears Anne Hempstead didn't affect this data.'

'The blocker thing?'

'Correct, so she appears to have made a small error. We have a recording of the heat signals your body gave out, the breaths you released while you were talking. There is a clear discrepancy between the heat recordings and the words we can hear. Do you understand?'

'Probably not, I may understand more if I see whatever it is you're talking about. Is it possible to see this heat recording?'

Officer Velasquez nodded and brushed her delightful brown hand across the cloth-like screen between us. It transformed into a truly incomprehensible mass of data that meant absolutely nothing to me. She pointed to a stream of binary code running down a small text box to the left.

'If I run the data through a sequence, like so,' she did something delicate with the tips of her fingers. I knew I should have been looking at the image but I was looking at her fingers.

Once she removed her hands the image became a kind of heat map, I could just about understand what I was seeing, a very dark picture with two vaguely human shaped figures, as I watched every now and then a small cloud would emerge from the head of one of the figures.

'That is your breath as you speak,' said Officer Velasquez. 'As you can see this image is open to interpretation but it suggests what you say in the audio recording from Anne Hempstead doesn't match the heat sensor image we are looking at here.'

'Doesn't it? I mean, I want to believe you, but I can't tell.'

'We believe it does not match but it is not enough to convince the Senate.' She tapped her fingers on the soft material on which the weird shapes were still moving. 'This evidence could still be argued over. The original audio recording is a very reliable and convincing piece of evidence. Trying to find the methods used in its construction and distortion has to be equally reliable and convincing, you understand?'

I nodded. I didn't want to stop her talking; essentially I didn't want to stop her talking ever. I wanted to sit opposite Officer Velasquez and listen to her explain things way above my head for the rest of my life.

'So just this morning while you were sleeping we got a lucky break. We have just been sent some new data.'

'New data?'

'Yes, although we are keeping this information to ourselves at the moment.' She gave me a little knowing smile.

'I didn't think you could keep anything to yourself. I thought everyone knew everything about everyone else all the time.'

"I know you will find it a little difficult to understand,' she said after a brief pause. 'It is a very unusual day, there is much at stake as I think you can understand.'

'The end of men,' I said.

'Precisely. This piece of data I am talking about has been extracted by a man you see.'

'A man?'

'Yes.'

'And that's a problem is it?'

'Not normally, but today it could be used as an argument.'

'Because it came from a man, as the old saying goes, "he would, wouldn't he?"'

Officer Velasquez nodded. 'It is very difficult today,' she repeated. 'Not only the fact that he is a man is a problem, he is also someone you know.'

'Someone I know, I don't know anyone except Nkoyo.'

'His name is Peter Branson, you would maybe know him as Pete.'

She brushed her hand over the material on the table between us. Pete's big grinning face appeared as if he was looking at me through a window.

'Oh my God, Pete!' I gasped. 'What did he do? What a dude, what did he do?'

'Your friend Pete managed to extract what you would call a recording from the building frame.'

'What? What?' by now I was utterly bamboozled.

'Pete wanted me to tell you that he has fixed many things at the Erotic Museum, he said you'd understand. So what he managed to extract is essentially the vibration data coming from your vocal chords. Because you are a man and your voice vibrates at a fairly low level and because Pete is very experienced in building maintenance, he managed to extract vibration history from the time you were in the library in the Erotic Museum and send us the raw data. We have been working all night to clean up that complex information, clean it up enough to finally know exactly what you really said.'

She brushed the sheet again and some rather rubbish quality sound emerged, about the quality of a much-used audio cassette circa 1993. It was my voice, very obviously my voice. I sat motionless as I heard myself say.

'I don't know what you're on about, all I know is I came here from 2011, there's no way I could have planned it, as far as I'm concerned time travel is impossible, well, as far as I knew before I arrived here. I'm just a man who arrived here due to some kind of freak, meta-physics, I'm an ordinary man, I don't believe in patriarchy or believe it's my right to rape women, I don't want to crush women back to the dark times, I don't want to be the dominant master race, I don't think women are second class citizens who should live their lives barefoot and pregnant at the kitchen sink. I'm just a bloke from two hundred years ago who wants to go home.'

I sat in stunned silence when the sound of my voice stopped. All the way through there were weird rumblings and creaks, some of the time you could barely make out what I was saying, the background noise levels would cover moments of speech, what was very clear however was the truth, what I had actually said in that wretched library. As soon as I heard it I remembered it very clearly.

'I am very pleased,' said Officer Velasquez when the sound of my voice receded. 'I am very happy.'

'I'm very happy too,' I said. 'I'm also very impressed, Pete did that? I thought he just fixed doors and toilets and mended my plane.'

'Well, to be fair to my officers, he didn't do it but he understood how a building interacts with its occupants. He knew the sensitivity of the building's structure and how it records everything that takes place inside its walls. It was just a case of extracting that data from the correct period. We had access to some very sophisticated machines that ran through the vibration time line data until we found the moment you spoke those lines.'

'This is fantastic!' I said. 'I knew I didn't say those things and now it makes sense. Can you please tell everyone I'm not a rapist from the dark times or a patriarchal warrior from the future?'

Officer Velasquez pulled the sheet of material we'd been looking at toward her and screwed it into a tiny ball. She stared at her clasped hands for a moment.

'Well, it is complicated,' she said slowly. 'Just before I came into your room this morning I had a conversation with the Senate office. I wanted to do just as you suggest and release this information immediately. I wanted people to know that this statement you are accused of making is not true. However, the Senate are very concerned about the situation. If we release data supplied by a man, they believe it will play into the hands of the Weaver lobby. It could strengthen the Weaver position, releasing this today, before the vote could cause a very dangerous reaction.'

'Like a conspiracy between two men who want to take over the entire female population of several billion women and just reinstate the patriarchy,' I said. Finally, the rather unpleasant picture was falling into place in my mind.

'Very accurate,' said Officer Velasquez, 'we will of course release all the information after the vote and your name will be cleared. But for the time being, we can do nothing.'

'And when is this vote taking place?' The knowledge of the Senate timetable came to me as if I'd known it all my life.

'Oh, right now.'

31

The Vote

I RETURNED TO MY MOVABLE ROOM AFTER Officer Velasquez left, along with many of the other officers. She explained to me that she had to make sure the crowds surrounding the Senate were safe and she rather touchingly assured me they didn't police or oppress the crowds, they merely acted in an advisory capacity and were on hand to deal with people who found the hundreds of thousands of people packed in the squares overwhelming.

I watched her leave the room. I couldn't seem to take my eyes off her as she walked away from me, there's no point denying it, I was a little infatuated.

I didn't have to go back to my movable room, no one made me go, no one locked the door. However, as I sat alone in the huge room with all the empty tables stretching into the distance I felt a little bit lonely, really for the first time since I'd arrived in the Squares. Plus I couldn't see out of the windows, they were placed too high up alongside the cavernous ceiling and walking into my little room felt comforting and familiar.

I sat on the bed and surprised myself by deciding to think about women and gender and men and oppression and all the things I'd learned since I'd arrived. This is not something I'd done before, if I ever did sit and think about things it would normally have been about how high-pressure hoses need to be fitted around compression pumps in confined spaces; important if that's the field you work in, not really earth shattering or anything to do with changes in society.

This time I actually decided to consciously think about the

impact men had made on the history of the human race. It was uncomfortable at first, it felt like some kind of half-baked mental exercise and I was sure I'd be bored in a few moments. However, the thoughts tumbled over one another, the conversations, the arguments filled my head with noise as I sat in the silent little room.

From my point of view, the impact of boys and men was fairly finely balanced; I truly believe men had done amazing things in our history, they'd made incredible discoveries, built machines and systems that had clearly helped the human race to develop. They had dreamed amazing dreams that had sometimes come to fruition. I found I truly believed most men had done their best to curb their baser instincts, they had tried to live well, help others, sometimes sacrificed themselves to protect the weak and all that stuff. But they had also murdered, raped, belittled and crushed the spirits of women for thousands of years.

That much I could understand, while at the same time hearing the wails of men who felt hard done by, whose mothers and fathers had let them down; I felt the cry of men who had been brutalised by war and poverty, struggle and hunger; men who had been cheated by women and teased and belittled by their greater emotional strength. None of it was cut and dried but there were so many examples of truly appalling traditions, absurd rulings and brutality carried out by men, sanctioned by men, enforced by men on women, that the balance started to tip in my mind.

It seemed that the women of 2211 could easily reproduce without need of men, they had the technology to do so and I could see their point. I didn't think it was a good idea, don't get me wrong, but I could see their point.

'Hey, it's the man from the cloud,' said a voice behind me. I turned and saw a young man standing in the doorway next to one of the officers who had escorted me from the Senate house the night before.

'I would like to shake your hand señor,' he said. I stood up and walked toward him, he had a wonderful dark complexion and a thick mop of black hair and I noticed, even with his smoothly fitting once piece that he was very powerfully built. We shook hands and I felt a rush of reassuring pleasure flow through me. This man, who I instantly knew was Tadeu Bolus, had just handed me a serious dollop of bits.

'Wow, thank you very much, Tadeu,' I said. 'I don't quite know what I've done to deserve this.'

Tadeu turned to the officer standing behind him.

'How is it he doesn't know?' he asked, although I'm pretty sure he said it in Portuguese as his lips didn't quite match what I was hearing. This also informed me that I must have been more relaxed. When I had been not-quite-arrested the night before, I was so terrified I couldn't comprehend a word anyone was saying.

'We have been a little busy making sure the crowds are safe,' said the officer, this time I knew for sure that I was hearing a translation as I caught a bit of Portuguese before her words were translated, and I could tell by her manner that there was a lot more sarcasm in her delivery than the translation gave credit for.

The beaming Tadeu turned to me. 'The Senate has rejected the proposal, it was close but the vote has been won,' he said, he then embraced me in a powerful hug. I can tell you I felt very awkward and English as this happened.

'The Weavers are furious!' he said with a big grin after he released me. 'They are claiming that some of the Senators have been threatened by you. It has all become very silly. Anyway, forget about them, I have been around all my friends and we made a collection for you just to say thank you.'

I only had the vaguest notion of what he was on about, clearly the vote to permanently remove men from the planet had been rejected and for some reason that meant who ever Tadeu's friends were, they'd chipped in somehow and given me some bits.

'That's, well, that's very kind and really unnecessary,' I said. 'I wish I knew what was going on, what about the recording? Does anyone know I didn't really say those dreadful things?'

'Yes, we all know,' said Tadeu, 'the truth is spreading like a fire through dry grass. You are a hero for many people, you are a hero for me señor, you are a hero for all men.'

I sat back down on my seat. I didn't really know what to make of any of it. I didn't feel comfortable with the whole hero thing. I think it's because I don't like upsetting people, and even though the two examples of the Weaver women I'd met hadn't exactly been pleasant, I could see their point.

Tadeu stood looking at me as if he was expecting me to say something. The problem was, I didn't have anything to say. I was therefore very grateful when I saw Nkoyo and Officer Velasquez run into the big room behind him, they too had grins on their faces.

'I got here as soon as I could,' said Nkoyo who ran up to me and also gave me a hug. It was quite uncomfortable, she was a good bit taller than me and she had very strong arms.

'Oh thanks,' I said, my head squished sideways into Nkoyo's shoulder. 'So, it's all okay then?'

'It's more than okay, it's fantastic news, Gavin!' She released me from her crushing hug and held my shoulders at arm's-length, which, considering she had such long arms meant that I was quite far away. 'The build-up to this vote over the last three years has been very disruptive but the result is incontrovertible, the Weaver proposals have been rejected by a big enough majority for them to be forever marginalised.'

Officer Velasquez stood beside Nkoyo, her smile was of course, fairly enchanting. 'We are all very happy,' she said. 'Although I don't have a man in my life, I would be very sad if there were no men on the world.'

I felt my face give me away, I was trying not even to think that

I was wanting to say if she needed a man in her life she could always give me a call. I glanced at Nkoyo who had clearly picked up on this rather embarrassing train of thought.

'Let's have a drink to celebrate!' she said, just slightly too loudly. 'I think we all deserve it.'

'Good idea, we can have a drink on the top terrace so we can see the crowds in the squares,' said Officer Velasquez. As a large crowd of officers entered the room there was a sudden rise in noise levels as shouting and laughing filled the air. There were quite a few men in the large crowd, there was a lot of hugging going on and the scene was so hectic and fast-paced I lost all trace of who was saying what to whom.

I followed the crowd across the big room, more officers were arriving all the time, they all seemed to be in very good spirits and I got a lot of hugs and powerful pats on the back. I got an enormous hug from the woman who had stood right next to me in the Senate house the previous night. At that time she looked Terminator-scary, now she had a big smile across her huge face.

'I always thought you were too little to be a serious problem,' she said with a big laugh. I laughed back. I didn't want to upset her again.

Tadeu walked along with Nkoyo and I, Nkoyo seemed very at ease conversing with Officers in high speed Portuguese. I didn't know why Tadeu was there or if he knew the officers, or even if he was one himself. He wasn't wearing a similar outfit but no one seemed to mind his presence.

'Tadeu is a Senator,' said Nkoyo discreetly. As always, she knew what I was thinking, I wasn't even surprised, it was normal.

'He's a Senator! He only looks about fifteen years old.'

'He's forty-seven,' she said flatly. 'I thought you'd know. Anyway, he's one of the five.'

'The five?'

'There are five male Senators who sit in the house, as you can imagine, he has had a very busy day. His speech was nothing short of inspiring.'

‘Wow. I’ve met a Senator.’

‘Yes, you have,’ said Nkoyo as we entered one of the room-sized elevators with everyone else. The noise in the elevator was deafening, what now seemed like hundreds of officers and a fair-sized crowd of men were laughing and joking with one another as we ascended.

When the large lift doors opened Officer Velasquez stood to one side and said, ‘Welcome to our terrace, Gavin. I hope you don’t suffer from vertigo.’

I walked forward onto a wide terrace with a purely glass balustrade running around the edge. The distance I could see from right by the door gave the clue that on this side of the building it was a very long way down to ground level. As I approached the glass wall at the edge of the terrace I admit my heart leapt into my mouth for a moment. As the building was constructed on the ridge of a fairly big mountain the drop was stomach-churningly far.

‘Wow, what an amazing view,’ I said, Officer Velasquez standing close beside me.

‘Look down there,’ she said pointing down and to the left.

At first all I could see was a patch of intense colour among the other incredible buildings of this mega city. I soon realised I was looking at what could have been a hundred thousand people gathered outside the Senate house. I could tell there was a lot of noise coming from the crowd but it was so far below us it was barely audible. The scale of the city was so far removed from anything I’d seen, the square was of epic proportions but it was dwarfed by the scale of the building surrounding it. I spent a long time looking out at the vast arena of structures, realising too late that Officer Velasquez had long since departed to join her mates. I turned to see one of the really enormous officers carry a large steel box to the centre of the group gathering on the terrace. She dropped it down, opened the sealed lid which made a slight hiss as the seal broke.

‘You want a beer, English?’ she asked with a big grin, offering me a large bottle with a reusable cap, it was just the same design as had been used on bottles three hundred years earlier.

I took a beer, chinked it with various members of the Senate security forces surrounding me and took a swig. It was cold and delicious. It was the first beer I had drunk in months. I then tried to join in. Well, I suppose I did join in a little, I chinked my bottle with so many of these enormous, powerful, confident women I cannot begin to remember them all. I felt like a wallflower though, the men and women on that incredible roof terrace had so much to say to each other, I couldn't really join in. Nkoyo was right in the middle of it clearly lapping up the attention. It wasn't so much I was left out; I just felt this wasn't my battle even though many had implied that I was in some ways the focus of it.

I couldn't quite work out why I felt uncomfortable about the whole thing. Something about being the man who saved the entire male race didn't fit with me. I didn't want to be part of it. I think the fact that the Senate, and, I suppose, the people of the planet had decided to allow men to survive was a good thing but the whole notion struck me as barking mad. The Weaver women were clearly a couple of picnics short of a nice day out but the feeling I couldn't shake was that maybe they had a point. I stood by the glass balustrade looking over the vast city as the light slowly faded, this city was built by women, this world was run by women and for all the failings and upheaval I had to admit it was better than the world I'd left in 2011. I think that fact alone made me unable to sing along with the boisterous crowd of Senate security officers and their boyfriends.

I somehow knew at that moment that what ever deeply buried interest I'd had in Officer Velasquez would remain unrequited. She was standing with a large crowd of people at the far end of the terrace, one of them was a young man and she had her hand on his back as they talked and laughed, then she leant toward him and kissed him tenderly on the neck.

I don't think it was only jealousy I felt. It was an incredible feeling of loneliness. I was utterly alone in a strange world. It was absurd because at any time that evening I could have struck up a conversation with anyone, they were all incredibly friendly but I knew it was pointless, I didn't belong, I really was an anomaly.

32

Voyage Home

I HAD MY OWN CABIN ON THE YIN QUI ON the way back to South London. I say cabin, it was more like a luxury Russian oligarch nouveau riche apartment in a high-end development in Miami or Cape Town. It was too big, too brash and too ostentatious for my already fragile state of mind.

I had been hated one moment, lauded the next and it felt like I didn't do anything either time. The cabin windows looking out over the bow of the ship were so huge I felt dwarfed by their technological magnificence. How a sheet of glass could withstand the pressure of being pushed along at hundreds of kilometres an hour was finally causing me to give up interest. They were sloped at a steep angle and auto tinted depending on the position of the sun. I stood under this huge expanse of glass staring out at the sea. The whole arrangement was far too grand for my modest taste.

As was so often the case during my stay in 2211, it took me a while to understand what was going on. Everything just happened, there was no itinerary, no printed docket or boarding pass, no e-mail string advising me of travel arrangements. I simply walked down the hundreds of steps with Nkoyo the following morning until we reached the dock. During this long hot descent I was mobbed with people who, it seemed, just wanted to look at me. They lined the steps as we made our way down the mountainous passageway. They cheered and clapped as we passed them. Nkoyo was lapping it up while I was feeling distinctly awkward.

It was therefore a relief to finally find myself alone in the huge cabin at the front of the Yin Qui. The peace engulfed me instantly; I sat down on a rather ugly chair as I watched the rolling waves of the South Atlantic slide beneath the vast bulk of the ship, again feeling no movement.

I was drained. I had lost the will to understand what was going on, I'd lost my interest in finding out how things worked. It was too complex, too different, something had happened to my brain, something I'd never experienced before. I was full up. I couldn't take in any more information.

I started to wonder if I really wanted to do anything, there wasn't much I could do in this place. There were no worn-down hydrogen-powered earth movers that needed fixing, I couldn't understand how a coffee pot or a door worked, far less a seven million ton ocean craft with no moving parts in its propulsion system. I imagined Nkoyo finding me dead in my enormous cabin, maybe it would be better to just die. That was an alarming moment. I'd never thought that before, but if I didn't die, then I'd have to live somewhere and surely I'd have to do something.

I wandered around my massive cabin; what I was experiencing in the world of 2211 was nothing short of extraordinary and yet I felt flat and bored. It was ridiculous, I jumped up and down a few times to try and shake off the feeling, I tried to find a positive spin on the whole thing, I was living in an amazing world and I had loads of money.

That stopped me dead. I had loads of money in theory. I didn't know how much, I'd never thought about it before. I wanted to know how much money I had left. As these thoughts raced through my head I suddenly knew I had three million, seven hundred and twenty-two thousand, four hundred and eleven Kwo. I wanted to know what a Kwo was, and of course I immediately understood that Kwo was the global currency, not based and backed by gold or some arbitrary algorithm produced by a national bank, it was based on kilowatt hours. Kwo, commonly described as bits, just like bucks for dollars and quid for pounds, was a currency based on energy. It was simple, standardised throughout the world, not based on shortages, hoarding, theft, war or pointless greed. It was based on energy and the cost of producing and transmitting this power. It was stable and fully understood by everyone.

Jumping up and down to try and energise myself and understanding Kwo was the first time I knew anything about my wealth. I merely had to wonder how much money I had and I knew. How I had never accessed that information before was a total mystery but I suppose I'd never really had the thought. I wanted to know how much it had cost me to travel on the Yin Qui. One hundred and eighty thousand. I knew instantly, but what I didn't know was how that related to any currency I might know about. Nothing. I couldn't seem to access that kind of information.

The door slid down and there was Nkoyo.

'You don't look happy,' she said at once as she walked into my hanger-sized cabin.

'I'm knackered.'

'Is that good?'

I shook my head. Nkoyo sat on a chair facing the bed. She was still a long way away from me because the cabin was so enormous.

'You've been through a lot,' she said. 'We'll be back in London tomorrow evening but you don't have to do anything. No one is going to ask you to speak or visit anything. You can have a rest at the Institute and gather your thoughts. There's no rush.'

'But I have no idea what to do,' I said flopping back on the enormous bed. 'I don't really want to stay here. I thought I didn't want to stay in Gardenia but after a while I sort of got used to it. Gardenia was very simple, this world, your world, it's really complicated. There's so much I don't understand but there's quite a lot I don't want to understand. I don't think it's because women are running everything, I think it's a world that's just got too complex. Not on the surface, underneath. I find the hidden aspect of this world really disturbing.'

Nkoyo sat looking at me for a while, she looked mildly concerned. 'I don't know what to suggest other than you take your time to try and adjust. There's no precedent, Gavin, no human being in history has had to deal with what you're dealing with. There is no manual.'

33

Talking Cure

IN ALL THE TIME I'D BEEN LIVING AT THE Institute of Mental Health in London I had no idea they had their own entrance to the transportation system that ran beneath the buildings, squares and pathways of the enormous city.

My return to the strangely familiar surroundings was entirely discreet, also not a complete surprise. Nkoyo had explained everything when we were still on-board the Yin Qui. She informed me there was now increased public interest in my activities and the historic events that had taken place in Rio; the recording, the revelation of what actually happened, and the backlash that had apparently resulted in unanimous global condemnation of the Weaver women. As if that wasn't enough, London had been through its own political drama while I'd been away.

The Mayor of London, Hilda Mickleton, who was publicly sympathetic to the Weaver cause had, it turned out, been involved in the cover-up surrounding my doctored recording. She was in a position to alter my timeline and that of Anne Hempstead.

I learned that she was no longer the Mayor of London. She was living in isolation on the coast. I've no idea what that meant but there was due to be a sudden and unexpected election and campaigning for the position of Mayor was already underway.

I remembered Hilda Mickleton vividly from my first day in the Squares, an old and slightly stout woman with a big chain around her shoulders who seemed genuinely offended at everything I said.

I'm sure some white men from back in my day have experienced this kind of reaction from a woman although I don't think I ever had done before. I imagine it's what many black and Asian people have experienced from white people. I think it's called prejudice; not only is it annoying it really is soul destroying. The Mayor didn't know me, she didn't know anything about what I was really like. She had been reacting in a negative way just because I was a man. She was reacting to a generalised grouping, just as white people have done with black and Asian people and, I had to reflect, I had sometimes done with homosexual men.

Nkoyo ushered me back into the Institute very quietly via a private underground entrance, I followed her through the building and up a few flights of stairs until we entered a large room I'd never been in before, my vague understanding of the enormous building told me I was a few floors above the main entrance lobby.

Nkoyo stood to one side of a ceiling-height window and asked me to join her and take a look. I was a little shocked by what I saw, beneath us in the entrance garden and all along the path outside a large crowd of men had gathered. By large group I mean huge, like the audience at an open-air rock festival, the only difference being they were very quiet. They just stood around chatting with one another, some would occasionally glance up at the building but mainly they just seemed to be waiting.

'Probably best not to let them see you just now, if you want a bit of peace,' said Nkoyo. 'Don't worry, they can't see through the window, it's reflective, it looks like a mirror from the outside.'

I nodded my understanding. I knew the window was essentially a transparent energy gathering laminate of silicon and graphene, the single pane I was standing in front of produced seventy kilowatt hours of electricity a day and the building had 900 windows exactly the same. I knew all this and I also knew the information was pointless. There was no role for me in this knowledge. However, the view outside the window indicated that there was a role for me with the large gathering of men, the problem was, I had no idea what that role was.

'What am I supposed to do?' I asked.

'You don't have to do anything,' said Nkoyo.

'But what do they want?'

'They want to thank you.'

'But you and I know I haven't done anything.'

'Well, I think you have to accept you represent something to these people, they've been here since the vote in Rio last week.'

I turned to look at Nkoyo who was staring out of the window. 'What, all the time?'

Nkoyo nodded.

'Thats insane! What on earth can I say? I'm not a rock star, I can't go out and sing them a song.'

Nkoyo turned to face me. 'You don't have to do anything, Gavin, they will leave eventually, it's going to take a while for things to settle down. Eventually you'll be left alone but we do have to start thinking about what you're going to do. Where you might want to work, where you might want to live, if you're going to start a family. I know you have some Kwo left but that isn't going to last your whole life, you have to remember you could easily live another hundred years, maybe a bit less considering what you've been exposed to before you arrived.'

'A hundred years!' That suggestion hit me like a punch in the belly. 'A hundred fucking years, that's...' I sighed deeply. 'That's a really long time.'

As we'd been talking, I noticed the crowd outside the Institute had grown even larger, it was all very civilised, they were just standing around chatting with each other. A number of the men had small children with them. It wasn't like a demonstration or political rally, rather a huge crowd of men standing around waiting for something. In any other circumstances I might have wanted to join them and have a party, but they were waiting for me.

After a long time staring out of the window feeling more and more trapped and hopeless, Nkoyo showed me to a new room on the same floor. Thankfully it was overlooking the gardens at the rear of the building. This was a much bigger room than the one I'd originally stayed in at the Institute, just a large empty room with a pile of what looked like cushions in the corner.

'These are gifts from some of the men outside,' said Nkoyo. 'Don't worry, we've scanned them all, they're perfectly harmless.'

'Cushions! They've given me cushions! Can I just say men have changed quite a bit since my day.'

'Not just cushions,' said Nkoyo. 'Also furnishings and fabrics to make you feel a little more homely.'

I looked down at offerings, just a pile of small mustard brown cushions piled up against one wall. Nkoyo stared at me and smiled. 'Of course, you haven't seen this before have you? It's a bit like clothes only bigger.' She bent down and picked up one of the cushions, tossed it back on the pile and found another.

'Your bed,' she said and handed the object to me. There was a tiny tag hanging out of the side, Nkoyo pointed to it with her exquisite long finger. I pulled the tab and the cushion flopped open and expanded so quickly it pushed me against the wall causing Nkoyo to laugh discreetly.

'Quite a big bed,' she said as I watched in amazement, the peculiar material slowly and methodically formed itself into a bed frame, I touched the corner to discover it was a soft loose-formed foam material, hardly ideal for a solid piece of furniture.

'It takes a few seconds to harden, in a day it will absorb moisture and gain weight,' said Nkoyo who handed me another cushion. 'An armchair.'

After about ten minutes my room was fully furnished, one of

 the smallest cushions became a very soft deep red patterned Tuareg rug. It looked incredibly familiar and homely and for some reason I cheered up a bit. That didn't last long.

Nkoyo and I sat facing each other in two recently formed armchairs. It's not like we were exhausted or anything, furnishing a room has never been less stressful. However, we sat in silence; I didn't have anything to say, after the sudden activity I found I was feeling just as bereft as before we'd started. Eventually Nkoyo shifted in the armchair and said, 'In the meantime…'

'Doctor Markham wants to listen to me blabber about my inner mother problems,' I said quickly and I felt my heart rate increase again. I said this before I could consciously grasp the incredible fact that I'd somehow known this is what Nkoyo was going to suggest.

Nkoyo's eyebrows raised and she smiled. 'You're getting the hang of it.'

'Do I really have to? I don't think I can deal with the criticism.'

'You feel Doctor Markham is critical of you?'

I nodded.

'I see. I can only say I don't think this is the case. It's true she is concerned about you, concerned for your mental well-being. The strain you have been under, the problems we had in Rio, we have to accept these sort of experiences have an effect on us.'

'You're not kidding,' I said.

'No, I'm not kidding,' Nkoyo answered flatly. 'If you don't wish to spend time with her, that is entirely up to you. However, I would like you to understand that Doctor Markham has enormous pressures on her time and yet she truly wishes to discuss things with you because of who you are, because you are such a special case, a man raised by a woman. There are very few examples of such people in the world now. You are pretty much unique.'

Why did I go? I was annoyed with myself, but to be fair I didn't have anything else going on, all I could do was sit on my own and ruminate pointlessly, or go and see some tall, apparently non-judgemental woman who looked like Vanessa Redgrave and talk about my blasted childhood. So, an hour later I was sitting on another chair in the big downstairs room where I'd previously been head-shrunk by the freakishly silent Doctor. I felt as if I'd already spent years of my life in that peaceful, oh-so-calm room. Doctor Markham was sitting opposite me so perfectly still anyone not used to her demeanour would consider her to be a fairly realistic statue.

Something drew me there, I don't know if it was subtle intervention on the part of my kidonge, I don't know if in fact there was some kind of mood or decision control elements in it's make-up. I only knew I wanted to try and work out why I felt so deflated.

Of course for the first ten minutes or so nothing happened, nothing as in she didn't ask 'and how do you feel about things, Gavin?' She just sat completely motionless and in total silence. The annoying thing is, if this was an exercise designed to encourage me to start talking, it worked.

'I want to go home,' I said after a long time sitting quietly. 'I can't go home but that's what I want to do. I think it's great that the world is now run by women, really I do. I think it's much better than it was back in my day, back in the dark times, but I want to go back to the dark times where I know what's going on. I am perpetually baffled by everything here.'

Still no response.

'So, if I've gone a little bit batty it's not really surprising is it?'

She replied after pause long enough to make me very twitchy. 'Are you asking me?' she said.

I decided to leave an equally long pause before I responded. I counted to one thousand really slowly, then said. 'Yes, I'm asking you.'

Her answer was delivered immediately, softly and with a carefully modulated tone and calculated rhythm. 'I don't think you are mentally unbalanced if that's what you mean by "a little bit batty". I think you have experienced a trauma, a mass rejection, an experience of mass dislike which may have exposed long-buried emotional scars from your upbringing.'

'Oh, of course, stupid of me, it's all because of the way my mother breastfed me isn't it?' I snapped, I was feeling snarky and I was also aware that my heart rate had increased.

'The idea seems to make you a little upset, could that be a signal that there are some unresolved problems you haven't faced?'

'Yeah, maybe, but so what? There's bugger all I can do about my childhood now isn't there? My childhood was two hundred and thirty years ago.'

Another long silence. My mind was racing, coming up with all sorts of arguments against my mother's behaviour in the early 1980s.

'Can I suggest,' I said eventually, 'that there were very real reasons to be upset about what took place in Rio, very tangible reasons for me to think everything here is a bit fucked up?'

There was another long silence which, damn it, made me reflect on what I'd just said. There were real reasons and although I hadn't quite said the things I'd been accused of, I had used strong language and kind of disturbing images which came out of me, came from somewhere I didn't know existed. I had to admit they came from somewhere angry. Was I justified in being angry about what that dreadful woman said to me? That was the question I couldn't really answer.

Eventually Doctor Markham said. 'I'm suggesting you may be feeling upset but again I am suggesting it might not be to do with your current predicament which is very real, but maybe the physical reactions you are experiencing, the raised heart rate, the mental turmoil you are experiencing are in fact connected with events in your childhood.'

I shook my head in disgust.

'I grant you,' said Doctor Markham calmly, 'there is nothing you can do about your childhood, nothing any of us can do, but the parenting you received would now be considered cruel and brutal, almost as if it was designed to cause distress later in life.'

This time I merely snorted in disagreement. I felt very strong images of my childhood bubble up, completely at odds with what the annoying Doctor was suggesting. How could she possibly know anything about the way my mum and dad treated me?

I easily recalled the photographs in my mum's slightly tatty album, those early colour polaroids. My dad loved his polaroid camera, which he thought was cutting edge technology. In all the family pictures we looked happy, well, fairly happy. Then I could suddenly see myself in a cot, I always remembered this particular moment from my very early days. I was alone in my room in High Wycombe and it must have been an early evening in summer, I have very strong memories of the light coming through the thin cotton curtains hanging over the little dormer window. I could only remember the house from faded photographs but I did remember the room. I could remember standing in my cot and picking at the flowery wallpaper on the wall beside me. I was crying, I don't know why I was crying but I remember being uncomfortable, I can remember my face feeling hot and the cries coming from deep within me. I was watching my little fingers try to peel the wallpaper off the wall, I can't remember anything else about that moment, nothing that may have happened before or after, just this moment. Picking at the flowery bedroom wallpaper and crying.

'Do you think you needed your mother or father at that moment?'

I would suggest that anyone who wasn't used to the ability this annoying woman had in reading your thoughts would find such an intrusion frightening but by then, for me it was no surprise.

'Yes,' I said although I had no idea why.

'D'you think you may have learned to be a little withdrawn and distant, emotionally distant because of the cold way your parents treated you?'

This time I know I sat still for a long time, I was reflecting on what she said, rushing through a thousand memories of my mum; I could somehow only conjure up what she looked like from behind, she was always busy. Standing on the black and white tiled floor of the kitchen in High Wycombe looking up at my mum's back.

As an adult I completely understood why she was busy, she would be cooking or washing clothes, she would be sweeping the kitchen floor or using the knackered old vacuum cleaner in the hallway. It made sense now, I didn't have any conscious or intellectual criticism of my mother, but I couldn't recall her holding me, reading to me, talking to me.

The stupid thing is, I know for a fact that she did all those things. It was a common experience to hear her speak of our early childhood when my family were gathered together on various occasions. All the old pictures we had depicted what looks like the classic 1980's nuclear family. Slightly balding and tired dad with droopy moustache and huge collars on his shirt, mum looking like a character out of *Blake's 7* with her nightmarish haircut, my bother looking like an overgrown street thug and me, sitting on the floor, a bag of bones in shorts and a Transformers T-shirt.

'Yes, that's possible,' I said eventually.

'Might you fear rejection, you've told me of the complications you had with your wife, Beth.'

I nodded.

'Is it possible if you took the chance, if you really had connected with her, opened your heart and made yourself vulnerable to her she could also turn her back on you, reject you. Might that be too painful to bear?'

I know my face creased up with pain at the point. Not the pain of realising the Doctor Markham was right. She may well have been right, it was more the pain of the crassness of the analysis. It just seemed plodding, like a subheading above an article in a garish woman's magazine, like kindergarten psychology: 'He Found Rejection Too Painful to Bear' above a black and white picture of a male model with his head in his hands.

Although I could understand what she was telling me, I was worried it was only 'an' answer rather than 'the answer'. I could come up with numerous other solutions as to why Beth and I didn't really get on; we had a different outlook, we either believed in or accepted different realities. I'd come to understand that since I'd left my time.

'What if, okay, you may be right in what you say but what if Beth and I were quite simply incompatible.' I was simply allowing my train of thought to become vocalised.

'Incompatible. That is an unusual word.'

'What, are you telling me you don't have people who are incompatible any more?'

'No,' came the now familiar flat, emotionless response from the hollow-eyed Doctor.

'Oh come on,' I said. 'You mean to tell me that with enough of this process, me talking to you, if I spent enough time with you talking about my mum and dad, you know, coming to terms with being a badly-treated baby, I could eventually get on with everyone regardless of their outlook or behaviour.'

'Yes,' again, that flat delivery I was finding increasingly annoying.

I sat looking at my hands, they were resting motionless on my legs, they weren't twitching around or writhing together as normal, I was feeling quite calm.

'Gavin, I see it like this, you seem very able to cope with the very extreme changes you have experienced since your arrival from the cloud, but you are occasionally held back by something very strong and powerful.'

My hands were instantly twitching again and I blurted 'Yes,

 it's called being a bloke, being a man and having to deal with a load of bossy women who always assume they know better. Women who look at you in the way you're doing now, like you fully understand what's going on, the look which says you know me better than I do myself and it's just a matter of time until I, a cave man from the fucking dark times, work it out.'

'So the notion that someone might understand things you don't makes you angry.'

'Yes! Of course! It pisses me off because you haven't got a fucking clue what's really going on in here.' I jabbed the side of my head with my finger as I said this, which hurt both my finger and my head. 'I don't accept your talking cure, I don't accept that you know better, that's just like religion, I am expected to believe you! I am expected to believe that your understanding of the workings of the human soul is perfected! Don't make me fucking laugh!'

Another long silence, I could feel my heart pounding in my chest, I was upset but I could always see very obvious, almost mechanical reasons to feel that. I'd been torn out of the world I knew, entered another time, been wonderfully cared for and learned a great deal, then torn again into another world which on the surface seemed very benign and caring, but was actually a little bit frightening. That all made sense to me; trying to understand my upbringing, my childhood, the way I was treated by my mum and dad, that was all hazy and misty and totally reliant on vaguely held memories. I could not envisage how I could learn anything useful from trolling through my distant past.

'If your mother was as emotionally distant as you've often said your father was, if they kept themselves a little further away from you than you needed when you were a very small child, that experience will set up behaviour which will affect you in later life. The fact that you are annoyed at women who may comprehend something greater than you can comprehend is a very clear indication that you are still deeply affected by your close and dependent relationship with your mother.'

I sat staring at Doctor Markham as she spoke, I felt the anger wane, I felt myself relax and become calm again. For all my misgivings, and they were many and solid, the way my body reacted to what she said underlined the truth behind it. I wasn't defeated, I didn't feel less of a person, I wasn't proved wrong, I wasn't living in a world where women had succeeded because they were better, I was living in a world where women had succeeded because men had resolutely failed. Their struggle to control the chaos they so feared with guns, bombs, machines of death and domination, their industries and corporations, their hierarchies and political structures had all been proven weak, hopelessly short-sighted, greedy and ultimately doomed.

Men had learned to let go, to flow with time and to accept their fate with dignity and it seemed on the surface at least, they were happier and healthier for it.

34

Pete's Plan

I SPENT THE NEXT FOUR DAYS AT THE INSTI-tute essentially sleeping, eating and digging earth in the morning, then talking to Doctor Markham in the afternoon. I didn't have to do any of these things, I could do as I liked, but strangely for this period of time, this was what I actually wanted to do. It was the first time I'd ever done gardening. I didn't really enjoy it but I got some physical exercise and slept like a log each night.

At the far end of garden was a large bed that needed digging over, I was given simple tools by the silent man I'd seen working in the garden that strange first day. His name was Hector, he was sixty-three years old and he didn't speak but he was very good at showing me what to do. He'd dig a row of earth over very expertly and then hand me the shovel. You didn't have to be a horticulturalist to know what he wanted me to do. When I'd dug over the whole bed – it took me three days – he walked up to me, his odd face cracked into a subtle smile and he patted me on the back very gently, took the shovel and walked off.

On the morning of the fifth day, I was sitting in the canteen room having some fruit and porridge for breakfast when Nkoyo joined me. This was unusual, I normally saw her briefly in the evening so as soon as I saw her I sensed my normal routine was about to be interrupted.

The odd thing is I was really enjoying the mental relaxation of having a humdrum daily routine, I didn't need to think about anything, I had a few very simple tasks to do and I had become very relaxed. My eyes couldn't help but follow Nkoyo as she walked up to a food door as it opened, she extracted a steel canister of coffee before sitting opposite me on one of the long tables.

I knew by this stage that the food that appeared inside the small boxes was prepared by people in a kitchen the other side of the rows of folding doors. The people who worked in the kitchens were under constant supervision and were kept in complete isolation from the world and everyone else in the Institute except, I suppose, for trained staff.

'Are they dangerous?' I asked Nkoyo.

'No, not necessarily, some of them have committed grave crimes but mostly they are a danger to themselves. They are kept there for their own protection, a little bit like you only with a little more security. As you understand, we don't have any jurisdiction over you, you can leave at any time. They, however, cannot.'

'So it's sort of like a prison,' I said.

'Well, only in the fact that they've had their freedom curtailed until they are cured. They have their kidonges neutralised so they are unable to communicate or access data, so they are the exception rather than the rule.'

'Wow, they're kidonge free. That is serious isn't it? How do they know anything?'

'Interestingly the human brain has the capacity to store an enormous amount of information without the benefit of the kidonge,' she said, as if I didn't know this already. I nodded and felt a big grin on my face. She smiled back, almost showing signs of embarrassment.

'They don't suffer in any way other than they have the inability to communicate outside the walls of the Institute.'

'So they are the really mad people who are seen as a threat to society?' I said as I chewed through a delicious apple.

'Yes.'

'And yet we eat the food they've prepared,' I was smiling as I said this. Nkoyo looked at me blankly. 'Meaning they could poison it, or put broken glass in my porridge, or piss in your coffee.'

Nkoyo started laughing. 'You can take the man out of the dark times, but you–'

'–can't take the dark times out of the man,' I said, grinning too. 'You are an amazing woman Nkoyo. Is it okay if I say that?'

Nkoyo brushed her hand over her shortly cropped hair and smiled coyly.

'Why thank you, Mister Meckler.'

'No, I mean it. I could not have coped with being here if it wasn't for you. If I'd been born here, if I'd grown up here and wanted to meet someone I could love and have children with, I'd be hard pushed to find a woman better than you to do that with.'

'That is a very kind thing to say. Thank you.'

Nkoyo sat looking at me with no fear, no anxiety that I was making some kind of subtle move with sexual intent. It didn't feel sexual because it wasn't. I don't know why, all I knew was she understood me perfectly and that was incredibly reassuring. A woman understood me. I didn't feel any different; I wasn't putting on an act in the hope that it would chime with her. I told her what I felt, I knew the feelings were real and she responded accordingly. It was revelatory.

'Well, on that note, how would you like to become more independent, move out of the Institute, make the first step into becoming a normal member of society?'

'Seriously?'

'Yes. Seriously. I have been talking to Pete Branson, you remember him?'

'I do remember him. I've been hoping to see him because I really want to thank him. He sorted out the recording nightmare when we were in Rio.'

'Indeed. But let me explain a little bit about Pete. You see he spent a long time living here a few years ago. He was a very troubled man. Did he ever tell you about his mother?'

'No, he never told me about his life, just that he can fix things.'

'Yes, that is true, he is extraordinarily gifted at maintenance. Many see this skill, limited though it is, as being inherited from his mother. She was a very influential engineering scientist who sadly died when Pete was a very young boy. Obviously his father raised him but this man was so distraught at the loss of his partner I fear much damage was done in Pete's early life.'

I nodded knowingly at this information. I still had a couple of cynical sinews left deeply embedded and took comfort in them. My impression of Pete was that he was a bit thick, clearly hadn't inherited much of his mother's intelligence. I then realised that was a very cruel and judgemental thing to think, Pete had shown enormous intelligence and foresight to get the recording from the Erotic Museum's infrastructure data.

'We treated Pete here for many years, he was prone to bouts of depression and self-harm but he is very much better now, he lives in a kind of half-way house in Carson Square, on the opposite side to the Erotic Museum.'

'I remember now,' I said. 'When I first met him he told me he lived in a house with a blue door with an eight painted on the front.'

'Yes, eight Carson Square, that is the address of the safe house.'

'It's a safe house, what, like top secret, used by MI5 and stuff?'

'I don't know what you're talking about,' said Nkoyo flatly.

'No, sorry, no, I mean the term safe house, it was used back in the dark times, where secret agents hid people under threat of assassination and stuff.'

'I still don't know what you're talking about, so let me explain,' said Nkoyo with just a hint of impatience. 'There is a room available at the house. It's up to you, you could live there if you wanted. You'd have to support yourself, pay a ground charge and share in the house tasks. Do you think you might like to do that for a bit?'

'Yeah. If that's what's on offer, as I think you know I don't have many alternatives,' I said feeling very non-committal about the whole thing. Much as I was grateful to Pete for what he did for me when I was in Rio, the idea of living with him was a bit of a big ask.

'It's not just Pete in the house, there are forty rooms so there are thirty-nine other people there. Mostly women but there are five men including Pete.'

'Oh I see,' I said again realising just too late that Nkoyo had heard my thoughts and responded accordingly.

'Have a think about it. Pete is coming around this morning, you could talk to him about it if you want.'

'Okay,' I said. 'And how are you?'

'I'm sorry?' said Nkoyo, she looked mildly concerned.

'I just, well, I was just asking how are you, you know. Just a friendly question,' I said nervously. It didn't sound like a rude thing to say but I still seemed to get things wrong all the time in London.

'You know how I am,' she said, then smiled. 'Well, you could know how I am.'

'If I relaxed and listened.'

Nkoyo nodded, then stood up. 'I'm actually rather busy, we've had a lot of new patients lately, mostly Weaver women who've been causing a bit of difficulty since the vote.'

'Oh, what kind of difficulty?' I wanted to know what these nut bags were up to.

'It's nothing to worry about, just some civil disorder, fairly inconsequential.'

'Like riots?'

Nkoyo put her coffee container back in the box it came from, the door melted closed and she turned and smiled at me.

'No, not riots, just a bit of shouting and crying.'

Nkoyo walked out of the canteen room, and a moment or two later Hector walked in looking like a Dickensian ghost of gardeners past. He was holding a small tool in front of him which I instantly knew meant he wanted me to follow him out into the garden.

It was brutally hot outside as I walked across the garden to one of the long beds by the far wall. Hector bent down and used the tool, it was a three pronged fork similar to the thing my grandma used to toast crumpets on the fire in her old cottage in the Forest of Dean. Hector touched a sprout of chickweed with the end of this tool and it immediately burst into a puff of green powder. It wasn't a violent event, the fork thing made the weed disappear with a vaguely audible pop. He ran his fingers along a row of some kind of vegetable seedlings that were planted in the bed, I knew he meant that I shouldn't use the tool on them. It was just for the weeds. He held prongs of the tool near his hand, turned his sad old face toward mine and slowly shook his head. Simple to understand, don't touch yourself with the prongs. Hector stood up and handed me the tool, patted me on the back and went away.

So, for the next two hours I was bent over in the baking sun touching weeds with a weird fork and watched them pop into oblivion. Of course, I was tempted to touch one of the prongs on my hand just to see how painful it would be but thought better of it. I didn't fancy seeing my hand make a gentle pop sound and turn to pink mist.

'Hey, Gavin my man, look at you, a genuine son of the soil!' said Pete. I hadn't heard him enter the garden but then I was very lost in removing a patch of dense weeds in the far corner of the vegetable bed I was working on.

We greeted each other with a hug, it was a little like hugging a king-sized mattress, Pete was truly enormous.

'Thank you so much, Pete,' I said as we finally disengaged. 'The Weaver women thing, the recording.'

'Hey, don't worry about that, it was fun. I said to my house-mates, I said, hey, I can fix that and I did. I went over the old

 Erotic Museum and got into the sub-basement, all the data collection points are there. Not many people would know where to look, but I know. So it was fun, and it showed up those Weaver ladies. I'm not going to pretend and be all benign like the big girls say I should, I don't like the Weaver ladies and I never did. There, I've said it.'

'Good for you, matey,' I said. 'I'm not too keen on them either. And yes, Nkoyo did talk about me coming to live in your house.'

Pete's enormous face broke into a massive grin, he pointed at me and nodded excitedly.

'Hey, look at you, all tuned into your kidonge, you know what's happening now, Gavin matey, you know what I'm thinking. You are so clever, took me years before I could do anything with mine.'

I received another massive pat on the back which nearly sent me flying into a nearby bush.

'Let's walk up here,' said Pete. 'I've got something to tell you.'

35

Fractal Fireworks

I WALKED OUT OF THE INSTITUTE'S FRONT door very early the following morning with a sack of furniture cushions in a large bag on my back. I had chosen to go early in the hope that there wouldn't be many people about. It was mid-September, the air was hot, the sun was high and paths were busy. I was immediately engulfed in a large crowd of men, a sea of eager, happy faces surrounded me. Suddenly I saw one I recognised. It was Tudor boy, it was Judd, the student I'd walked around the Museum of Human History with.

'Mister Meckler, please allow me to carry your bag, it would be a great honour,' he said.

'Oh, there's really no need it's not—' but the bag was lifted from my shoulder and this rather frail looking young man started to walk ahead of me.

'Thank you, Gavin,' said a very tall, rather gaunt looking man who walked beside me. 'Thank you for all you've done.'

I smiled at him. I had no idea what to say. Someone else patted me on the back, the crowd increased in size and I quickly realised that it was a very bad idea to leave the Institute through the front door carrying a large bag first thing in the morning. Of course everyone was awake, it was the obvious time to do things, six in the morning was before the temperature got really high, as it seemed to be every day in London 2211.

'Are you going to live with Pete?' asked a man who was walking on the other side of me.

'Yes,' I said, I couldn't think of any reason to say 'none of your business mate.'

 'I was only going to suggest you are very welcome to live in my apartment, I have a spare room.'

I looked at the man, he seemed perfectly normal but why would he ask a stranger to move in with him? It sounded dodgy, but then I realised that this was me projecting. Then I pondered if it was because I was some kind of celebrity and these people all wanted some kind of reflected glory thing, I don't know what it was but it felt strange and slightly unnerving.

'I'm just staying with Pete for a while,' I said through the jostling throng, ''til I can find something to do.'

'You can come and work with me, I repair cars, I've got a workshop at my place,' someone shouted.

'Come and talk to the kids at my school,' shouted someone else.

'Tell us about war!' said another voice. It was getting a little heated. I kept my eye on Judd the Tudor boy and pressed forward. I knew I just needed to get to the transit entrance, get down the stairs and get into a car. They couldn't all get in with me.

'I'm really sorry,' I shouted. 'I've got nothing to say at the moment. I kind of need to be left alone, you know, just a bit.'

I was trying not to be rude, I didn't hate these men but I had no idea what I could do for them.

'Were you a soldier?' one asked, a very tall man walking behind me, he had his hand on my shoulder, it wasn't aggressive, he wasn't threatening me but it was a bit of an intrusion. I saw another man gently remove his hand.

'Let Gavin be,' said the intervening man. 'He just needs some time alone. Let's leave him alone.'

'Yes, leave Gavin alone,' shouted another man.

Over the next few meters the crush around me receded and I continued on my way. Soon it was just me and Judd trudging along the path, a few women were walking toward us, they stopped and stared as I walked past but thankfully they didn't say anything.

When we got to the corner where the transit entrance was Judd turned to me and handed me the large bag.

'There you go, Mister Meckler. Thank you for letting me help you.'

'I think I should thank you, Judd,' I said as I swung the bag over my shoulder. 'Maybe you can explain to me what all those men wanted?'

'What they wanted?'

'Yes, with me, what they expected me to do, or to say to them. I really don't understand.'

'You are a hero, they admire you as I do,' said Judd with a look of surprise on his pristine young face. 'Do you not understand that?'

'To be perfectly honest, no I don't understand.'

Judd looked positively dumbstruck.

'Look, I haven't done anything,' I said. 'I didn't change the Senate vote, I was being kept in a moving room on the side of the Senate security building in Rio when the vote took place.'

'But you showed the powerful that all the stories of the dark times are not true. You showed that men weren't always bad, not all men.'

'Is that really what you've been told?' I asked. I'd never quite got to the bottom of how the dark times were perceived.

'Yes, we learn, and there is plenty of historical documentation to back this up, that up to a hundred and fifty years ago men were almost fanatical in their desire to destroy, to dominate and control. Men thought of women as their possessions.'

'You obviously haven't met my wife.'

'Men forced themselves on women whenever they wanted.'

'You obviously haven't met my wife.'

'They used the earth as a possession, they stripped resources without a second thought, they wasted those resources, wasted their own lives in wars, wasted everything they had been blessed with. You showed us this wasn't completely true.'

'Did I?'

'Yes!' shouted Judd. He started jumping up and down as he spoke. 'You showed the world that a man, okay, only one, but a man from the dark times didn't want to do all these things. Thought it was wrong for a man to kill and rape. You showed that men are not the only culprits of the crimes of the dark times.'

I stood looking at Judd for a moment. I admit that I felt guilty about the slightly homophobic thoughts I'd had about this young man. I had reacted to him in a fairly negative way when I'd first discovered he liked to dress up in Tudor clothes. Now he'd just explained something very clearly, something that had been worrying me since my arrival in the Squares.

'Thank you, Judd,' I said and I gave him a hug, just like that. I gave him a hug as if it was the most natural thing in the world. Of course I'd been hugged my numerous men since I'd arrived in the confusing city but I'd never, in my life, given a man a hug, especially one who might be a gay Tudor re-enactor.

'I understand, and I'm very pleased I was able to help even though it doesn't feel like I did anything.'

Judd was smiling as I left him and descended the stairs into the transit hall. I had to wait about a minute for a free car to arrive. I hopped in and was quickly joining the incredibly high-speed traffic silently rushing through the tunnels. After another two or three minutes the car came to a neck straining halt and I exited on Carson Square. It was the first time I'd been back since my fateful visit to the Erotic Museum and I realised how much I'd changed since that day. I felt very different as I emerged into the hot sun. I glanced up at the sign and made a mental note to find time to read 'The Silent Spring' as soon as I got the chance.

I turned in the opposite direction to the Erotic Museum and before I'd even had time to register where Pete's house might be, a huge gathering of people further up the path gave me a painfully obvious location point. Outside the blue door with an eight painted on it was another massive crowd of people. I could see there were women among the men, but they were in the minority for once. As I approached I could see some people pointing at me, a huge cheer went up and suddenly the most extraordinary fireworks shot into the sky. I don't have any other way to describe them, I knew immediately they were not in the least firework like, I'm sure no gunpowder, strontium, calcium, barium or copper chloride was used to create what were essentially light patterns that shot skyward at eye-defying speed. They opened into massive, ornate and multicoloured displays before dispersing into a trillion fragments of bright light. I suppose virtual fireworks would be a better description, fractal fireworks maybe. They were amazing, and I know I was stumbling toward this crowd with my mouth open as I observed the spectacle of intense light, even against the bright blue sky they were clearly visible.

As I got closer four rocket type things fired at once, they didn't make any sound but a rocket is the best way I have of describing the sudden burst of light that emerged from the middle of the gathering. High above them the words 'Welcome Home Gavin Meckler' appeared in perfect Avenir Book font. I stopped walking and watched as the letters glowed in the sky, slowly dispersing and melting away like showers of sparks.

'Bloody hell,' I muttered as I was engulfed in a seething crowd of well-wishers. My assumption that they were well-wishers was based on their smiles, cheers and friendly back slaps.

'Well done, Mister Meckler!' I head someone shout.

'Good job, Gavin!' another voice from the throng.

I was swept along by this happy gaggle and suddenly noticed an oversized face grinning at me. It was Pete standing in the open doorway of number eight, Carson Square. He nodded to his left and I knew at once what he was gesturing at, I managed to crane my neck and see, through the jumping and shouting crowd around me a long row of figures dressed in black standing slightly away from the seething mass around me. It was a row of what I assumed were women, Weaver women, their heads covered, dressed in shapeless, floor-length black gowns looking exactly like women from Muslim countries during my era.

 Above them, only not as high up and using a rather ugly font, I think it was Tahoma, the words 'forever oppressed by the male gaze' were hovering. The women weren't chanting or shouting, they were just looking at the crowd with emotionless faces. Okay, there was some emotion in their expressions. That of judgemental anger I suppose, disgust maybe. I could now see this was a street riot 2211 style. The men around me were making more fuss than they possibly might just to show how much they disliked the Weaver women's philosophy. They were rubbing it in, I suppose and this made me feel distinctly uncomfortable. I didn't want to be a target for these angry women, the whole thing was ridiculous.

I slowly made my way up the wide steps to Pete's front door and was hugged and lifted off my feet by the human backhoe digger that was Pete Branson.

'Welcome home, Gavin my friend,' he said when he finally let me go. He lifted the huge bag of furniture off my shoulder and stood to one side to allow me into the house.

There was something immediately reassuringly familiar about number eight Carson Square, it reminded me of my student digs at Leeds University when I was studying engineering there. It was the chaotic mess, the piles of components, half-built machines, tatty furniture, sheets of material leaning up against the walls and a pervasive smell of burnt food.

I stood in the front room and my spirits dropped a little. It was full of eager looking young men. I had left the Institution thinking I would get some space to myself, thinking I would be left alone, but now, in the scruffy dump that was to be my home was yet another crowd of annoyingly eager well-wishers.

They didn't speak, they didn't jump up and hug me or slap my back heartily, they just sat looking at me.

'So, Gavin Meckler, we have a plan,' said Pete. 'And I think you're going to like it.'

36

Weather

FORECASTING WEATHER IN 2011 HAD CERtainly moved on from some grass-stalk-chewing peasant standing on a hill looking at clouds and knowing when the Hawthorne should start to blossom.

However, in London 2211, weather was a hundred per cent predictable for the coming ten days, down to the most minute fluctuations in temperature and even the shapes, heights and density of clouds.

I learned this on my first full day at number eight Carson Square, from a young man called Whitchitt. He had studied meteorology at primary school and it clearly held a fascination for him. He had specialised in the subject before he had children. He told me that when his children were older he hoped to go back to studying it and maybe get work in some research area.

He explained how global temperatures had increased by eight degrees since 2011 and how this had affected sea levels, the fact that the earth had only one polar ice cap in the Antarctic and that well-established agricultural communities had been thriving on the coasts of Greenland for over eighty years.

He unrolled a sheet of material on the large table in the kitchen of number eight. I found it hard to concentrate on what he was saying as the whole house seemed to be a hive of activity. True, most of the occupants were women but they were very different to the women I'd met at the Institute. They were younger and seemed to be talking very loudly about who was at what party and who did or didn't have sex.

Sitting at the table in the kitchen that morning was not a

 relaxing experience. For a start, I felt old; the noisy banter, laughs and screams of excitement were very distracting and as a new face on the scene I received rather more attention than I desired. However, at this point I kept my head down and tried to concentrate on what Whitchitt was telling me.

'Next Thursday morning, 7:08 A.M. for approximately seven minutes the same cloud anomaly you arrived through is going to be generated again. This is down to solar activity predictions, the projected power draw at that time and the ambient temperature and prevailing wind.'

He looked up at me. I nodded, I understood what he was saying and I certainly wanted to witness this bizarre event but beyond that it didn't mean much.

'The same cloud event that brought you here is being repeated,' he said, this time emphasising the word 'same'.

'I understand,' I said.

'Hey, Gavin, there's a party tonight on the other side of the Square!' shouted a rather scarily crazed-looking woman on the far side of the table. 'At the Erotic Museum, you've been to the Erotic Museum right? You know about it don't you, the Erotic Museum?'

This woman's repeated use of the term Erotic Museum caused much raucous laughter from the other women in the room. I noticed Whitchitt making a big effort to ignore them.

'It's going to be marathon mentalist, there's no way we can get in, it's only for poshos, but you're famous, they'd let you in. We could be your special bodyguard!'

'Not really my thing,' I said, smiling weakly.

'But you're a hero, you're famous, everyone wants to fuck you, I mean meet you,' said the woman. Again this clearly intentional slip of the tongue caused another gale of laughing and cackling from her sisters.

'Still not really my thing,' I said. I'd never experienced anything quite like this interaction before, it was almost as if these women were a bunch of football hooligans, a bit pissed on a Saturday afternoon and they suddenly had the attention of a young woman. They were behaving like idiots. I'm sure individually they'd be perfectly charming, but in a big group like this they were positively threatening.

'Oooh, we're not good enough for you are we?' said the woman, getting to her feet and looking rather aggressive. 'Mr big-hero, I-saved-all-the-men-from-the-fucking-Weaver-bitches.'

'Ignore her, she's kurva blazen,' said Whitchitt under his breath. I immediately understood the term to be Czech street slang for 'fucking crazy'.

The woman who'd invited me to the marathon mentalist party leant right across the table and grabbed Whitchitt's face in her impressively large hand. 'You sulking because you're not pozvany?' she said. I knew this meant 'invited' but I was getting concerned for Whitchitt's well-being. I was considering physical intervention when Pete entered the kitchen looking like he'd just got out of bed, which of course he had. The whole atmosphere reminded me of student life, the chaos of freedom after years living with your parents, except this crowd didn't seem young enough, certainly not student age as I would have understood it.

'Please, Wendy,' said Pete to the woman. I may already have known her name was Wendy but hearing Pete say Wendy was a surprise. She didn't look like a Wendy, she looked like a mad woman. Which, I was soon to learn, she was. Interestingly Wendy's rather violent grip of Whitchitt's face instantly relaxed and she stroked his cheek quite tenderly.

'Sorry, Whitchitt, I'm a total bastard, ignore me,' she said and slid back across the table and sat quietly.

'I'm sorry I was rude, Wendy, ignore me more,' said Whitchitt, and from then on they ignored each other. Baffling.

'Has Whitchitt told you about the cloud in Franklin Square on Thursday morning?' said Pete as he sat down next to me and started eating a mango. No question, a bowl of fruit on a table was a common sight everywhere I'd been in 2211. It just seemed the natural thing to eat.

'He has, it's fascinating. Can we go and see it?' I asked.

'Oh yes, we'll see it okay,' said Pete with a big grin. Pete's grin was big enough for me to get my shoe into, sideways. 'I got Whitchitt to check because he really knows about the wetter.'

I blinked a couple of times, not fully understanding what Pete meant. Did they called weather wetter because of rain, or did only Pete call it that because he was a bit messed up in the head? All these possibilities raced through my thoughts until I suddenly knew it was simply German for weather.

Pete grinned at me and we sat in silence for a moment. The noise level in the room started to rise again as some other women arrived, there was a lot of screaming, shouting and gesticulating going on.

'While they're making all this noise, I'll tell you what we plan to do,' said Pete, leaning close to my ear. 'All this noise means our signals should go unnoticed, if you don't want to do the plan, just say and I'll never mention it again.'

'Depends what it is you're planning,' I said, speaking directly into Pete's oversized ear.

'Oh, I think you'll like it drone man. I think you'll like it very much.'

37

Fly Away Home

IT WAS A RIDICULOUS PLAN, IN ANY OTHER circumstances I wouldn't want anything to do with it, but the feeling I had in London 2211 was always as follows; I have nothing to lose, nothing to live for and most importantly nothing to do. So the chance of getting caught as I followed the small group into the museum in the dead of night and doing something profoundly wrong held less terror than I would normally have felt.

I'm absurdly law abiding, I hadn't even considered exactly how law abiding until that night. I've never murdered anyone, raped anyone, cheated on my tax return, I've never had a speeding ticket, never been interviewed by the police and never taken anything that wasn't mine.

Now I was hiding inside the Shard building with fourteen men, wearing skin-tight black body suits with a very uncomfortable black band of some unknown material wrapped tightly around my left shin.

We had gone to the Museum of Human History in the mid-afternoon. I travelled with Pete, the rest of the group arrived in small groups or pairs. We viewed the exhibits along with the crowds which, unfortunately for us were a little less numerous than on my first visit. At a pre-arranged time we entered the front door of the Shard building which contained exhibits about the history of corporations from the turn of the nineteenth century until 2070.

Behind one of the large exhibit stands was a doorway, by the time Pete and I arrived it had been opened so quite how that was accomplished I never knew. We knew the door was there, we waited, looking as interested as we could at a description of the demise of corporate governance in late 2050, then Pete tapped my arm and we quickly moved around exhibit and slipped through the door.

The interior of the rest of the building was clearly not quite the same as when it had originally been constructed at the start of the twenty-first century. The entire building was hollow, held in place by a mesh of organically grown concrete branches emanating from a central pillar.

We walked though this labyrinth of strangely shaped stonework until Pete spotted a man called Vull. I'd met Vull briefly at number eight, he was even taller than Pete and originally, I would guess, of South Eastern European extraction. He looked like a giant Serb, big thick eyebrows and almost black eyes, a huge nose and a small mouth to which he held his finger as we approached and gestured that we should get down behind the bizarre outcrop at the far end of the space.

It's hard to describe the interior of this building. I'd never been inside when it first opened in London although I had met one of the architectural engineers who worked on it. The building wasn't complete when I left Enstone airfield so I have no idea what was originally there. As I squatted next to Pete, Vull and a small gang of other young men I stared up through the curling branches of solid, nanobotically shaped concrete above my head. Whatever the interior of the shard was like in 2012, it wasn't like this. I tried to picture the many floors, steel trusses, lift shafts, service shafts, wiring systems and air conditioning, all the old paraphernalia of old-fashioned buildings that would once have been so proudly installed.

We waited a long time in that little hideaway. I became thirsty after about an hour and took a sip out of the fluid pack I had in my belt. It was very tasty fruit juice which contained something that really gave you a kick in the pants.

'Don't waste that,' said Pete. 'You'll need it later, here, have a suck on my viz.'

I remained motionless as I waited to understand what viz was. It took enough time for the other men to be amused. It was water, the Hungarian word for water, I suddenly knew and then realised that Pete had been using odd terms all the time and I'd known what they were without hesitation. However, due to the kidonge blocker strapped around my left shin there was a delay of quite a few seconds before the information made itself available to me.

'Thanks,' I said, and accepted the oddly pink-coloured tube coming from Pete's sleeve. My mouth filled with cold water and I gulped away which again caused some mirth in the hushed assembly.

'That looks sikilmis bizarre,' said Vull. Again a slight delay until the translation arrived. Fucking. Sikilmis was Azerbaijani for fucking. The image of me sucking Pete's pink tube looked fucking bizarre, I couldn't disagree with that.

After another long silence during which time I could tell the museum outside the Shard was getting darker, Vull motioned for us to gather around.

'Okay, we have about an hour at best, the authorities will be aware that there's an anomaly in numbers, a discrepancy between the entry and exit figure.' I had the impression this was being explained for my benefit. 'The only advantage we should have is the trans-bands and the heat suits. Everybody has their bands on, yeah?'

One by one people showed the various limbs their kidonges were located in. We had discovered this the night before when another man, I believe his name was Kevin although I only met him very briefly, used a small scanning device to locate where our particular kidonges were lodged. Mine was discovered in my left shin bone hence the rather uncomfortable band around my leg. A lot of the men had their kidonges in their fingers and merely wore a kind of black bandage around the digit in question. I learned that fingers or toes are the most common location for people who are fed their kidonge when they are babies.

The black bandages were transmitters, they didn't block the signal, that was illegal and could result in long periods in talking therapy which, I was amused to note, none of the men in this small company was keen to embark on. The bandages sent the kidonge signal to a remote location, in my case number eight, Carson Square. If anyone ever checked in future, it would appear that 'on the night in question' I was sleeping in the house. Not that, theoretically at least, there was any need for me to be concerned one way of the other. I was, however, concerned for the others.

While we were in the museum, the authorities, and I still had no idea who they might be, but the authorities would not be able to locate us. The reason we struggled as quietly as we could into our one-piece black body suits was to eliminate our heat signal from any sensors there might be in the building.

I heard a small beep which I assumed came from a device someone was carrying.

'We climb,' said Vull. He stood up to his fairly impressive height, I'd guess around two and a half meters tall at the very least and moved silently to the central nanobotically grown concrete trunk of the support tree that had been grown inside the shard.

I'm a pilot, I don't get vertigo. At least, that's the theory. I started to climb up the small inset footholes that I assume had been grown into the original Shard support structure so for the first fifty meters or so the climb was relatively easy. The oddly organic-looking concrete structure initially formed a gentle slope but before long it became truly vertical. The footholes and handgrips were secure and plentiful; anyone who'd ever done any rock climbing would find it easy. I'd never done any rock climbing and my heart was pounding like a bass drum in a Led Zeppelin drum solo.

Only once did I make the fatal error of looking down, I could see the ten or so black-clad figures climbing up below me but the angles and terrifying distance to the ground made my head spin. I pushed my head against the inert mass of the concrete tree and tried to regain my composure.

'You're okay,' said Pete who was right behind me. 'I'll catch you if you ucmaq.'

I was too stressed out to receive a translation but it was fairly obvious what he meant. If there was ever a human being who could catch a full-grown man as he fell off a nanobotically-grown concrete support structure inside a twenty-first-century office tower, it was Pete.

I concentrated on making sure I always had three contact points as Vull had instructed me, and climbed for what felt like hours. As both my arms and legs were shaking with exertion I heard a deep voice above me say softly, 'I've got you.'

I felt myself lifted up as Vull, who looked like a fairly strong bloke, took my entire weight with one hand gripping the webbing safety harness I was wearing and hauled me onto a wide flat area very near the top of the building. I could understand where we were by the narrow structure above my head. I was literally standing in the pointy bit of this extraordinary building.

'Thanks,' I whispered to Vull, I couldn't see his face as with all of us, it was covered in heat restraining material. We all looked like weird 'Black Theatre of Prague' mime artists crossed with extreme mountaineers.

I sat down with my back against a massive outcrop of concrete and waited until normal breathing returned. I had to wait a while and in that time the entire group assembled around me. Annoyingly they all seemed fairly relaxed and happy as they clambered up over the edge of the concrete platform.

Pete then clambered up the concrete plinth I was leaning against and reached above his head before very slowly and quietly removing a metal panel from the structure of the original building. Through that you could see a spar of the massive roof that covered the museum so far below.

Vull squatted down beside me and put his hand on my shoulder. 'That was the easy bit, now it gets a little risky,' he whispered.

When I got to my feet and looked up, Pete was already outside the structure standing on the bottom edge of the opening. He pulled something from his belt and attached it to the beam of the roof above him. I couldn't make out what he'd put there until it was my turn to clamber up, Pete had by this time moved away somewhere, I couldn't see him. Vull pulled a small clip from my harness and clipped it to what looked like a piece of cotton thread attached to the beam.

'Don't make any sound,' said Vull and suddenly the world went very scary. I was 308 meters or, in old money, 1,010 feet above the floor of the museum, hanging by a thread so fine I could barely see it and a clip that looked like it would have trouble restraining a lazy Chihuahua. I could now see everything and that really didn't help. Far in front of me, Pete was hanging from a beam by one arm, over a thousand feet above the floor. He was attaching the far end of the thread to something. I looked up, the massive I beam above me had a lip that you could hold on to but only an idiot with a death wish would try.

'Let go,' whispered Vull right into my ear. I did and then immediately I wished I hadn't. I suddenly really wanted to be where my kidonge said I was, in my expanded foam bed on the third floor of number eight Carson Square. Instead I was a thousand feet above a museum floor sliding along a thread I couldn't really see towards a man who was just a black shape in the darkness.

I think I may have gone measurably mad at that point. This insanity increased momentarily when I stopped sliding down the thread. The monstrous expanse of the museum roof sloped down very gradually from the tip of the Shard to where Pete was hanging on another thread, but not steeply enough for me to continue. I had to reach up and use the beams above my head for leverage to continue my precarious journey. I felt my hands shaking uncontrollably as they came into contact with the structure above me, I couldn't look up, I definitely didn't want to look down, I just stared at Pete as I slowly edged my way forward.

'You're doing good Gavin,' Pete whispered as I got closer to him. He suddenly put his finger in front of the black mask covering his face and pointed down. I shouldn't have looked because I almost lost control and screamed. I did glance down momentarily, just visible a thousand feet below me was a figure walking along through the museum exhibits. Pete and I froze, I think I may have held my breath and I felt sweat stinging my eyes.

A tap on my shoulder indicated that all was clear. I'd been hanging by a thread with my eyes tightly shut. I felt Pete's enormous arm around my waist as he supported my entire weight and quickly unclipped me from one thread and onto the next.

I don't know what the climber's term is for what we were doing, Pete had strung up a series of cables across the ceiling of the massive museum. Of course the cable was so thin that thread is a more accurate description; it would have been invisible from the ground but we would not.

The next length of supporting thread, the thing I was entrusting my life to, went down at a much steeper angle. Pete showed me how to grip the thread with my gloved hand.

'Don't let yourself go too fast, I'll be right behind you,' he whispered then pushed me away. At first I just sort of bobbed along the thread, the little clip making a faint sound as the wind started to rush past my cloth covered ears. My right hand was above me gripping the thread. I had to twist my arm to increase the friction on my glove. Although it protected my hand from being sliced in two I could still feel intense heat the friction generated as I tried to control my speed. At the far end of the thread I could see my goal, a metal framework, under which hung a very familiar object.

The Yuneec.

 When I finally reached the complex grid of metallic pipework that formed a kind of twisting sculpture from which the Yuneec was hanging, I breathed a sigh of relief. It took me a moment to regain my composure and move out of the way of the next black-clad figure serenely sliding down the thread toward me. Beyond him I could just make out Pete helping people move from the first length of thread to the next, and beyond that, the dark shape of the Shard in the distance. It was a baffling spectacle, but as I was now standing on a large metal structure and holding on with both hands, I could take a moment to look around, and down. About a hundred meters below me I could make out the shape of the Yuneec hanging from a thread that I couldn't see. This was our goal. This was what we had gone through this secretive nightmare journey for.

'All good,' said Vull as he joined me on the increasingly crowded structure. The last person to arrive was Pete. He slid down the thread at great speed, slowing down with apparent ease and very little sound.

'Okay, I'll go down and dismantle the drone,' said Pete. 'You all know what to do.'

For the first time that night I did know what to do. I had a tool on my belt that Vull had shown me how to operate. I slowly made my way up the complex tubular framework from which the Yuneec was hanging.

Once I reached the level of the museum roof I located a small nodule in the skin of one of the struts and placed the point of the hand tool onto it. The nodule instantly disappeared leaving a neat hole, no noise, no smoke, no sparks. This was the coolest hand tool I'd ever used. With a little supporting assistance from one of the black-clad figures in our group, I managed to reach every nodule supporting the massive sheet of transparent material. I can't call it glass, it wasn't glass. The reason I know this is that when I'd managed to remove the last fixing, Vull reached past me and pushed it upwards. I am happy to acknowledge this giant of a man possessed impressive upper body strength but he managed to move the large sheet with the tips of his fingers.

He slid it gently to one side and then with a clearly well-trained agility, hauled himself up through the hole. Within moments his arm reached down, I grabbed it and was pulled up as if by a machine, emerging onto the vast expanse of the museum roof. I knelt on all fours by Vull's feet as he pulled up other members of the silent group. After a minute at most, the full team was on the roof in a neat pattern around the opening. This hole in the roof was about four meters across, and they all stood around it as if they were standing around a puddle on flat ground. I was laying spreadeagled on the floor, peering over the edge where I could just make out Pete's black form moving around the now gently swaying Yuneec.

Vull knelt down beside me.

'We have a couple of minutes at most,' he said without lowering his voice. 'The removal of the pane will cause a pressure change in the upper part of the museum.' I understood as I could feel warmer air rushing up through the hole we'd made. 'We have to act fast,' Vull added in a very serious tone.

I nodded my understanding then noticed movement behind Vull and saw one of the black-clad figures feverishly hauling on a fine thread that had been lowered through the hole. I glanced down through the hole and saw the right wing of the Yuneec being hauled towards us, with a small scrabble of manhandling it was placed neatly on the vast expanse of Museum roof around us. This was quickly followed by the left wing, and finally, with everyone hauling on seven separate threads, the fuselage and Pete. This took some serious heaving, even I got involved, although I was a shaking jelly by this time so I don't know how much I actually assisted.

'This is just brilliant,' said Pete as we finally settled the Yuneec into a position where we could attach the wings. Pete gave me a massive pat on the back which nearly knocked me over. 'I got your bloody plane back,' he said, even through the feature-obscuring black face cover I could tell he was grinning.

'Pete, you are a bloody genius,' I said and gave him a hug as best I could. It was a bit like trying to hug a cart-horse, but I could tell he appreciated it because I felt his body start to shake with sobs. I patted his enormous back. 'Cry it out, Pete, that's right, cry it out mate.'

Vull broke up the bromance by grabbing my arm and walking toward the cockpit door. 'You need to start the drone,' he said. 'We have one minute.'

At that moment the ground beneath us lit up, someone had switched on the lighting in the museum. The authorities knew we were there, the alarms had gone off, stuff was happening.

I clambered into the cockpit and went through the start-up procedure with Pete's enormous head poking through the passenger window.

'Toggle switch under the safety cover, up for on,' he said. This was about the only part of the Yuneec controls that was familiar. I flipped the switch and the control panels came to life in an instant. Wonderful screens lit up before me, the central one giving an exact location in a plan view scrolling map.

The whole plane shuddered as the team attached the first wing, the one sided weight started to tip the machine over but this was rapidly rectified by Pete who put one arm up to steady it.

'Green button above the toggle, wait!' said Pete as my finger hovered above the green button. The plane shuddered again as the opposite wing was inserted, I heard the familiar clunk of the locking bolt system. Vull appeared by the pilot window. 'Good to go,' he said.

'Stand back, drone prop spinning up, hold the tail!' shouted Pete.

I glanced around, no one was standing near the front of the plane and just about everyone who'd been on this crazy venture was standing around the tail.

'Wait!' I shouted. I jumped out of the cockpit. 'Wait, I have something to do.'

'No time,' said Vull.

I held out my hand toward him.

'No need,' he said, he clearly understood what I was thinking.

'There's no need for me to keep it. Quick,' I said. I shook his hand and felt the body blow to my belly.

'Thank you,' he said. I moved along the row of black-clad figures, shaking their hands one by one and feeling the intense shock to my solar plexus each time. Finally I reached Pete.

'Mate, I saved the last for you,' I said, braced myself and took the blow as we shook hands. I could tell Pete was crying but I had to let go and return to the plane. I had just shed a little over three million Kwo to this incredible team of nutters.

I checked the time, 6:03 A.M., we were three minutes late but it was fine, I had plenty of time to reach the Singh power-field. I pushed the green button and silently the limp propeller started to spin, a fabric propeller seemed so ridiculous, it was as if a violently shaken tablecloth was flapping around the nose of the Yuneec, but it soon became rigid as the revolutions increased. I eased the throttle control forward and said 'Shit, Oh Lord.' As I felt the instant power the rebuilt Yuneec had been given.

I undid the strap around my leg which was a huge relief, then pulled the black cloth off my face. I rubbed my face vigorously with both hands. I really needed to be awake for what was coming next.

I put my head out of the window and smiled at the black-clad team behind me. Between them they were going to have to do many thousands of hours of talking therapy for taking part in this caper. In fact it was quite likely that for the rest of their lives they would be encouraged to analyse what drove them to undertake this dangerous prank.

I gave them the thumbs up sign and I saw Pete momentarily take one hand off the tail to return the gesture. Then, as I'd been instructed, I pushed the throttle control to maximum and the plane immediately lifted vertically. I can barely remember what happened because of the sheer terror of the experience, the plane was spinning but also climbing at great speed, I was trying to turn against the spin but having little success, after a few seconds, again as I was advised, I eased off the throttle and the spinning decreased until I could sense the controls having more effect. I managed to level out and fly straight but the experience of flying the Yuneec was utterly transformed. What had essentially been an experimental light aircraft was now a very sophisticated and fast aerobatic plane. The power of the motor was staggering and when I opened the throttle I could see by the shadow they created the individual propellor blades became longer, therefor giving even more forward thrust.

I circled high and wide around the museum, the true scale and and awe-inspiring beauty of the building was suddenly apparent to me for the first time. Already the tiny black-clad figures were mere ants on a vast triangular patterned carpet. I was flying at 2,500 meters and yet I it seemed like was still only just above the roof. As I flew over what must have been the front entrance I had arrived at with Professor Etheridge months before, I saw more figures appear on the roof from a conventional exit, they were making their way slowly toward the group I had just left.

I turned hard and tight, finding the G force quite a strain to deal with, the old Yuneec would never have managed the speed, let alone the turn.

I came in low and fast over the roof as I knew the guys would have wanted to see this. I passed no more than fifteen meters over their heads travelling at close to 400 kph. Fast and low, just as they'd asked.

I climbed up with such speed I was almost in need of oxygen by the time I levelled out, although the plane had been upgraded to an amazing degree the cockpit wasn't pressurised and I needed to be aware of that. It really wouldn't do to lose consciousness at 10,000 meters over a city where flying a drone was strictly against the rules.

The sun was up by this point and the vast array of the squares below me was exactly what I'd seen when I came out of the cloud. However, now it all made sense, I knew the layout of the dozen or so Squares I'd seen from the ground. Now I could see them stretching away into the distance, mile after mile of squares all the way to the horizon, some hugging the sides of distant hills. In all the time I'd been in London I'd seen but a fraction of this mega city.

I banked around slowly and descended toward the museum again, it was very easy to spot even from this distance. It essentially had the same footprint as one of the squares.

As I got closer I could see the black-clad figures had now removed their face coverings and were huddled in a group surrounded by many other people, clearly women from the museum security section. It wasn't a riot or a fracas, it looked more like a rooftop garden party, no one was running around trying to escape, Pete had explained to me that for them there was no escape, once I'd taken off they would be detained for a while as their cases were assessed.

I did another, much slower fly-by, waving as I swept past them, some of the women who'd joined them waved as well. I climbed again and scanned the horizon as I flew in a wide circle above the museum. Off to the east was a perfectly clear sky, the sun now quite high, but in the distance, maybe fifteen or twenty kilometres away, forming in a long tunnel of misty cloud was the anomaly, just as Whitchitt had predicted. I quickly checked the time, 6:58 A.M., only another ten minutes until the cloud was predicted to be at its most intense.

I levelled out and pointed the nose to the ever-increasing bulk at the centre of the cloud. I was feeling fairly relaxed at this point, I knew that if nothing happened, if I just flew through the cloud and came out the other side, still above London in 2211, I would head to Northern France where Pete had advised me there was far more open space to make landing a lot less dangerous.

I also didn't experience the same emotional wrench I had felt as I took off from the Bow Field in Gardenia, seeing Grace standing there with the people from Goldacre Hall. I wasn't leaving anything behind that I thought I would miss; maybe Nkoyo, she'd been so kind to me but always rather distant. I was relieved I hadn't completely fallen in love with her.

As I continued to approach the distant and already much larger cloud I noticed a building to the left, I don't know why it caught my eye but I knew at once it was the Institute, maybe my kidonge was working and alerted me to the fact. I checked the time and the distance to the cloud, I could do it. I turned and dived gently, I didn't want to alarm anyone on the ground so I kept at a reasonable height and circled around the long building. I could see people standing outside the front entrance and my curiosity got the better of me, I reduced my altitude further until I was just safely above roof level. I could now see clearly that there was quite a large group of people standing around the main entrance looking up at me, without question I made out Nkoyo, she was waving frantically. As I circled around again I slowed down to what would have been the normal speed the original Yuneec could have managed, I pushed open the passenger window and waved as I banked over the building.

I knew at once that I would miss seeing Nkoyo, not anyone else from the Institute, although even Doctor Markham had grown on me a little.

I opened the throttle again and climbed back up to about 3,000 meters and turned to the cloud. Even in that short time it had increased in size and darkened in colour, now a large, tubular grey cloud which reached to the heavens way above me and stopped about a thousand meters above the square below. Other than this one peculiar cloud, I could see nothing else in the perfectly blue sky.

I levelled out and was impressed to discover at about half throttle the plane was perfectly balanced, it essentially flew itself,

I let go of the controls, adjusted my four point harness and aimed the Yuneec for the very centre of the cloud. My heart rate increased. Once again, I had no notion of what might be on the other side of the cloud.

Subscribers

UNBOUND IS A NEW KIND OF PUBLISHING HOUSE house. Our books are funded directly by readers. This was a very popular idea during the late eighteenth and early nineteenth centuries. Now we have revived it for the internet age. It allows authors to write the books they really want to write and readers to support the writing they would most like to see published.

The names listed below are of readers who pledged their support and made this book happen. If you'd like to join them, visit: www.unbound.co.uk

John Abraham
Geoff Adams
Eric Aitala
Richard Allen
Fran Anderson
Steve Angell
Richard Angus
Brian Appel
Paul Arman
Helen Armfield
Robin Armitage
Marc Armsby
Fred Armstrong
Simon Arthur
Darren Ashby
Donna Askew
Lucent Askew
Matthew Atkins
Michael Atkins
Nick Baber
Kevin Bachus
Mitchell Bacon
Karen Baines
Ken Baker
John Baldwin
Graham Ball
Arthur Banks
Chris Bannister
Dave Barfoot
Stuart Barkworth
Tom Barnard
Kate Barnett
Fiona Barres
Simon Barry
Michelle Bartholomew
Cat Barton
Matthew Baxter-Reynolds
Daniel Bayliss
Emma Bayliss
Julian Bayliss
Matthew Beale
Gerald Beattie
Pete Beck
Mak 'maqist' Beech
Andrew Bell
David Bennett
Amanda Benson
Calum Benson
Tim Biller
Rachel Blackman
Alan Blackmore
Neil Blakely
Philip Blom
Nathan Bloomfield
Christof Bojanowski
Phil Boot
Duncan Booth
David Boston
Karl Bovenizer
Douglas Bowers
Alison Bowles
Darren Bowles
Nicci & Simon Bradley

Julian Bradshaw
Roger Braithwaite
Donal Brannigan
Christian Bray
Jon Brazelton
Vicky Breading
Jon Breen
Jon Breen
Mark Broadbent
Daniel Brook
Derek Brown
Oliver Brown
Scott, Sophie & Finlay Brown
PJ Bryant
Paul Bucknell
Peter Buckoke
Geoff Bullock
Ali & Tony Burns
Hannah Butcher
Marcus Butcher
David Callander
David Callier
Clare Cambridge
Paul Carlyle
Caroline-Isabelle Caron
Alexis Carpenter
Barry Carpenter
Susan Casey
Naomi Castley
Tony Castley
Dominic Cave
Chris Chadwick
Rohan Chadwick
Darren Chandler
Martin Chapman
Phil Chapman
Mark Chatterley
Benjamin Chiad
Chippy Chin
Joel Chippindale
John-F. Chmiel for my son Finnian
Paul Churchley
Ross Clark
Greg Clarke
Stephen Clay
John Clayton
Robert Clements
Garrett Coakley
Mark Cockshoot
Nicholas Cohn
Sean Colbath
Daniel, Marie, Ruby, Laura & Sophie Cole
David Coles
Stevyn Colgan
Matthew Collins
Timothy Collinson
Dave Compton
Mark Constable
Ryan Conway
Rodger Cooley
Laura Cowen
Luke Cresswell
James Cridland
Mark Crump
Anne-Marie Curran
Jane & Richard Dallaway
Peter Dalling
Gerald Daniels
Josephine Daniels
Glyn Davies
Ian Davis
Jonathan Davison
Paul Davison
Tony Dawber
Darren Dawson
Bev Dean
Matt Dean
Paul de Greef
Ryan Dehmer
Jamie De Rycke
Andy Devanney
Michelle de Villiers
Gavin Dietz
Rebecca Donaldson
Stephen Donnelly
Roger Downing
Lawrence T Doyle
Simon Drinkwater
Will Dron
Jonathan Dubrule
Andy Dudley
Christopher Dudman
Lee Duffy
Keith Dunbar
Dave Duncalf
Justin Dykes
Cariad Eccleston
Gordon Edwards
Joe Oliver Edwards
Roger Edwards
Stuart Edwards
Christophe Egret
Thor-Dale Elsson
Charlotte Endersby
Jamas Enright
Derek Erb
Bill Evetts
Per Fagrell
Di Farence
Emma Fearnley
Greg Fenby Taylor
Matt Fiddes
Anna Figueroa
Paul Fisher
Liam 2X4B Fitzpatrick
Bård Fjukstad
Sharon Forman
James Fowkes
Ilana Fox
Rachael Fox
Isobel Frankish
Laura Franks
Adam Fransella
Alan Freeman
John Frewin
Anthony Froissant
Graeme Fullerton
Stephen Gage
Hilary Gallo
Ina Gallo
Gareth Gamble
Chris Garnham
Colin Garrett
Saman Gerami
Meredith Gertz
Andy Godden
James Godfrey
Neil Godfrey

Paul Golder
Richard Goldsmith
Leslie Goode
Mark Goody
Nikki Gordon-Bloomfield
Amanda Graham
Jean Graham
Neil Graham
Kerrie "Caflas" Gray
Janine Gredig
Arthur Green
Simon Greenaway
Mike Gregory
Paul Gregory
Darren Griffin
Mike Griffiths
Kevin Groombridge
Anna Hackett
Simon Hackett
Lance Haig
Nell Haig
Thomas Haley
Andy Hall
Rachael Halliwell
Alex Hansford
Marie Hanson
Pete Harbord
Peter Harrigan
Paul Harris
Rob Harris
Vron Harris
Bryan Harrison
Kris James Harrison
Richard Harrison
Stacy Harrison
Caitlin Harvey
Bastian Hauptstein
Dave Hawkins
Darren Hawkshaw
Michael Helm
Elizabeth Henwood
Richard Herschy
Paul Hickford
Steve Hickman
E O Higgins
Stuart & Katherine Higgins
Adam Highway
Adam Hinton
Paul Holmes
Karen Holtorp
Mark Honeyborne
Christine Hopkins
Richard Horsley
Rod Howitt
Brian Hughes
Jack Hughes
Owen Hughes
Jordan A Hulme
Luci Humphreys
John & Natalie Hunt
Andrew Hunter
Peter Hunter
Ian & Tracy
Deb Ikin
Antony Ingram
Martyn Ingram
Thomas Ingram
Tom Ingram
Richard Isherwood
Lee Israel
Glyn Jackson
Steve Jalim
Chris James
Fiona James
Karolien Jaspers
Michael Jenkin
Rob Jennings
Adam Johnson
Dan Johnson
Dean Johnson
Ian Johnson
Olivia Johnson
Gail Jones
John-Paul Jones
Peter Jones
Stephen Jones
Deborah Jones-Davis
Ola Jonsson
Richard Judd
Juho Juopperi
Jasmine Kaul
Andrew Kavanagh
Mike Keal
Andrew Kelly
Martin Kelly
Scott Kennedy
John Kent
Mark Keogan
Phil Kernick
Alex Kerridge
Philip Kerridge
M Keys
Matthew Kidd
Martyn Kiely
Dan Kieran
Andy Kiernan
Michael Kilshaw
Steve Kirtley
Peter Knight
Alexis Kokolski
Jan Kristensen
Karim Kronfli
Stephen Landry
Karen Langley
Mats Larsen
Zoe Laughlin
Tracy Laurence
Andrew Lawes
Gareth Layzell
Jimmy Leach
Holly Leeds
Rutger Leunen
Russ Levett
Andy Lewis
Ian Lewis
Monika Lewis
Wendy Lewis
Tor Olav Lien
John Lindsay
Mark Lis
Jonathan Littlewood
John & Christine Lomax
Andre Louis
Lars Lunøe
Deirdra Mc Allister
Rod McDonald
Shane McEwan
Kass McGann &
Robert P Davis
Beth McGeachy-Blay
Tracy McGill

Stuart McKears
Ben McKenzie
Gavin McKeown
Alistair Mackie
Nicola Mckissick
Matthew Maclellan
Ewan Mac Mahon
John Macmenemey
Simon Macneall
Cait MacPhee
Iain McSpuddles
Ian McWilliam
Kevin Mahy
Mark Mangano
Sarah Markall
Charlie Marriott
Gary Marriott
Karen Marshall
Tim Martin
Karen Masson
Joseph Mathews
Richard Matthias
Neil Melville-Kenney
Deborah Metters
Tamsin Middleton
Miggi
Daryl Millar
Richard Miller
Nick Milligan
Richard & Tracy Mills
Michael Mitchell
Scott Mitchell
Deena Mobbs
Danny Molyneux
Tom Moody-Stuart
David Morgan
Dave Morriss
Michael Mortensen
Nik Mortimer
Timothy Mortlock
David Morton
David Moss
Liane Mount
Robert Naylor
Christopher David Neale
John New & Deborah Lough
Paula Newens
Alex Newsome
Simon Newson
John Nichol
Stephen Nichols
Al Nicholson
Colin Nicholson
Chris Nicolson
Martin Nooteboom
Bethany, Grace & Morgan Norcutt
Paul Michael Harries Norman
Stuart O'Connor
Brigitte Ogilvie
Neasan ONeill
Erwin Oosterhoorn
Lesley Orrell
Antony O'Sullivan
Danyal Outten
Stuart Owen
Lawrence Owens
Louise Paddock
Sal Page
Michael Palmer
Yianni Papas
Kevin Parker
Mark Parkinson
David Parry
Chris Parsons
Rob Parsons
Kevin Pascoe
James Craig Paterson
Mark Paterson
Seb Patrick
Andrew Paul
Shaun Payne
Neil Pearce
Lisa Pearce Collins
Dave Pearson
Bella Pender
Abigail Perrow
Dan Peters
Mark Phelan
Chris (furrie) Phillips
Eric Phillipson
Steve Pike
Laura Pinborough
Brian Pitkethley
Kevin Pitkin
Laura Polaco
Justin Pollard
Edward Pollitt
Dominic E. Potts
David Powell
Jon Prendergast
Christopher Pridham
James Pritchard
Maya Pryjomko
Fiona Pugh
Andy Pullan
Adam J Purcell
Huan Quayle
Anne Raison
Dawn Raison
Idham Ramadi
Mark Randall
Hans Rasmussen
Baldev Rayat
Colette Reap
Ian Reeves
James Reid
Craig Reilly
Paul Renold
Andy Rice
Kathryn Richards
Christopher Richardson
Andrew Riddell
Ian Roberts
Andy Robinson
Anne Rock
Petre Rodan
Mike Roest
Gareth Rogers
Harry Rose
Lorna Ross
Ian Roughley
Lynn Rowlands
Chloe Rowley-Morris
Claire Rudkins
Allan Russell
Paul Sadler
Adam Salmon
Adrian Samm
Jonathan Sartin
Steven Saunderson

Neil Sayer
Carol Sayles
John Scally
Hugh Scantlebury
Alex Scott
Claire Scott
Keelan Taylor Scott
Stephen Scott
Tony Scott
Chris Scutcher
Pat "Samhain" Seery
Chris Senior
Katherine Setchell
@setithing
Jonathan Sharpe
Samantha and James Shelley
Darran Shepherd
Karl Sherratt
Jennifer Shipp
Andrew Shugg
Jon Shute
Sam Sibbert
Darren Sillett
Aleasha Simpson
James Sinclair
Vicki Sivess
Wendy Skinner
Rohan Slaughter
Alison Smith
Brendon Smith
Lauren & James Smith
Mathew Smith
Matt Smith
Steven Smith
Trevor Smith
Little Smudger
Nat Snell
Nicholas Soucek
Mark Sourbutts
Chris Spath
Lorelei Spencer
Mark Spencer
Rich Spencer
Andrew Spokes
Mat Stace
Andy Stanford-Clark
Ed Stenson
Adrian Stewart
Alan Stirling
Jack T Stonell
Dave Stowell
Peter Strapp
Charlie Styr
Mark Sundaram
Lindsay Swann
Robin Swindell
Trina Talma
Kay & Andrew Taylor
Mark Taylor
Jayne Thomas
Jo Thomas
Luke Thomas
Mark Thomas
Ralph Thomas
Andrew Thompson
Scott Thomson
Mark Thorpe
Barry Tipper
James Tombs
Craig Tonks
Matthew Towlson
Ole Traumüller
David Tubby
Ben Tumney
Pete Tyler
@unclewilco from
readersheds.co.uk
Rav Vadgama
Sarah Van der Veken
Hank van der Wijngaart
Mark Vent
Robert Vincent
Steve Wadsworth
Yasuhiro Waki
Nathan Walker
Robert Walker
Steve Walker
Stewart Walker
Antony Wallace
Bobby Wallace
Nick Walpole
Katherine Walton-Elliott
Emma Ward
Rachel Ward
John Warren
Paul Warren
Paul Alexander Warren
Emma Watkins
James Watts
Paul Wayper
Glenn Wehmeyer
Carl Weller
Karen Wells
Tom West
Alan White
Devlin Hugh Francis
Whitfield-Martin
Matthew Whittaker
Carol Whitton
Jason Wickham
Rob Widdowson
Tom Wilkinson
Craig Williams
Andy Willy
Matt Wilmshurst
Donna Wilshere
Keeley Wilson
Martin Wink
Graham Wise
W. Mark,
Dr. Les Witherspoon ND.,
Aryeh, Amber, Chaya,
Yitzi & Eli
Ian Wolf
Chris Wood
Rupert Wood
Steven Wooding
Rachel Wookey
Alan Wright
Chris Wright
Colin Wright
David Wright
John Wright
John R Wright
Rachel Wright
Simon Wright
Tim Wright
Paul Wyatt
Ian Yates
Kym Yeap
Jennifer Young

A note about the type

THE BODY TEXT OF THIS BOOK IS SET IN LTC Cloister, designed by Morris Fuller Benton (1872–1948). Benton was chief designer at the American Type Foundry from 1900–1937 and was America's most prolific modern type designer, responsible for Century Schoolbook, Franklin Gothic and the revivals of Bodoni and Garamond. Cloister is a roman face based on the work of the 15th century French engraver and type designer Nicholas Jenson (1420–1480), who was based in Venice and had been a pupil of Gutenberg. Jenson is credited as the inventor of roman type. Previously, books had been set in the gothic 'blackletter' style. Jenson's elegant type was much admired by William Morris (1834–1896), the founder of the arts and crafts movement. Chapter headings are set in Morris Troy, an adaptation of William Morris's semi-Gothic Troy type designed for use in his Kelmscott Press books. The Kelmscott Press's great project was the production of a hand printed edition of Chaucer's *Canterbury Tales*, which contained eighty-seven illustrations by Edward Burne-Jones. A masterpiece of book design, it is the embodiment of Morris's theory that work should be collaborative and the results both beautiful and useful. Burne-Jones called it 'a pocket cathedral'. The ornamented initial letters are also adapted from Morris's designs for his Kelmscott Press editions.